I0775657

# PRIZE PLAY

**THE ADVENTURES OF ELSABETH SOESTEN**

NO GOOD DEED...

BAIT AND SWITCH

PRIZE PLAY

GONNES OF NAVARRE

**FORTHCOMING**

THE CONFESSION AT GODRA

THE ADVENTURES OF ELSABETH SOESTEN

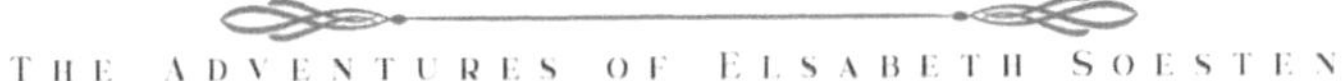

# PRIZE PLAY

## D. E. WYATT

Wyrmfyr Press
St. Louis, Missouri
2023

This is a work of fiction. Some characters, settings, and events have been inspired by historical record, but any direct depiction of historical events and individuals both living and dead is unintentional.

The Adventures of Elsabeth Soesten: Prize Play

Copyright © 2023 by D. E. Wyatt

All rights reserved. No parts of this publication may be reproduced in any form without the express written consent of the author, barring excerpts intended for critical review.

Copyediting by Debbie Manber Kupfer
Cover Art by Rebecca Frank, Bewitching Book Covers, LLC
(bewitchingbookcovers.com)
Heraldry image resources sourced from HeraldicArt.org

ISBN-13: 979-8-9853905-4-4

Many thanks to Rainy, for all your help trying to get me pointed in the right direction.

A NOTE FROM THE AUTHOR


A number of terms contained within this work may be unfamiliar to you, the reader. As such, I have provided a glossary at the end of the book for your convenience, along with a quick guide on how to read the blazons for the coats of arms described herein.

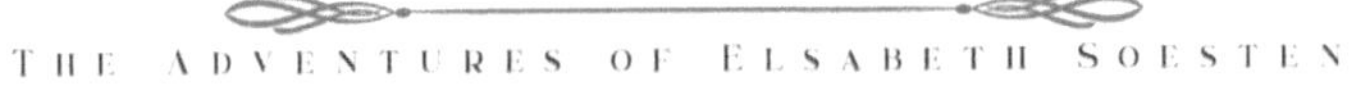


# PRIZE PLAY

# 1

IS FIST CONNECTED WITH HER GUT, AND all the air rushed from her lungs with a sickening grunt. Elsabeth felt herself falling and watched the ground come up to meet her, but she did not quite reach it. Rough hands grabbed her under the armpits and hauled her, with no particular gentleness, back to her feet again before she could collapse. She gasped in desperation for a breath, but another blow to the belly just beneath her ribs cheated her of the effort. She might have regretted misplacing her doublet and enjoyed the satisfaction of her tormentor's bare hand smashing against the concealed metal scales, but all her attention for the moment was focused on gasping for big gulps of sweet, lovely air, while stars danced around her eyes

Elsabeth slumped in the hands grasping her bloodied shirt. Her hands were bound behind her, and her legs threatened to collapse beneath her. Blood from an open cut above one eyebrow dripped into her eye, and when she finally managed a random, hacking breath her mind turned itself to more practical matters, like outrage over the thought she might be left with a scar. She was not given long to gather her thoughts before the back of his hand flew and landed across the corner of her jaw.

"Quim!" Caspar von Bech snarled, his Boehman spoken with a cultured and generally superior accent, wholly at odds with the vulgarity of the curse.

Elsabeth spat blood from her mouth and smiled up at him. "Oh Caspar, whatever is the matter today?" she said.

Caspar seized her roughly by the chin and wrenched her head around to face him. Eyes blue as ice bored into hers, and his lips twisted into a scowl beneath his well-manicured mustache. His hair was the color of straw, silky, and neatly groomed. She might ordinarily have found him a quite handsome man from across a tavern, but unfortunately for him she also knew him far too well already to be fooled by such appearances.

"You know 'whatever is the matter,'" he snapped. "I want it!"

"Well if that is the way you ask for it, then 'tis no wonder every woman from here to Köln has refused your bed."

The words were no sooner out of her mouth than his hand flew again. He delivered a powerful cuff to her temple that snapped her head around and momentarily blinded her with a flash of light across her eyes. Only the firm grip of Caspar's men kept the impact from driving her into the dirt. Elsabeth shook her head to clear away the ringing in her ears, decided his reaction had been worth it, and grinned up at him again.

"Where is it?"

"I don't know, maybe you should ask that idiot Vorfechter of yours," she said.

That earned her another solid punch to the stomach, and again Elsabeth gasped for breath. Caspar seized her roughly by the hair and pulled her head back. "Take a good look around," he hissed between his teeth. His ordinarily fair-skinned face turned bright red as his temper got the better of him.

They were in a small clearing of widely spaced trees, grass, and wildflowers. It was a beautiful autumn evening, aside from the company, with a wide and clear sky set on fire as the sun slipped down into the west, while a cool breeze wound between the trees and set their branches in motion. The area was also conspicuously absent of any sign of human life. There was no road or trail, no sound of voices or other activity, no abandoned carts, garbage, or anything else associated with people having passed this way any time recently.

"If you wished for time alone with me you could always have asked," she said, when she managed to regain her breath. The last blow left her belly tying itself in knots, and her last meal threatened to claw back up her throat.

Caspar seized her by the throat and squeezed. Elsabeth felt the blood flowing through the veins in her neck strain against his grip, and she had difficulty drawing a breath. "You are alone, whore! The Master is no longer here to take care of you. I could crush your throat here and now and leave you for the wolves, and no one would ever find your miserable carcass."

He released her with a violent shove. Elsabeth's neck throbbed in protest at the manhandling, but she refused him the satisfaction of reacting to the pain.

"Tch. Ever the jealous sort, Caspar. How many times need I tell you Paulus did not share your sort of affection?"

Another crack echoed across the wood as he rounded on her again. Elsabeth spat out more blood, and ran her tongue over the gash torn in her lower lip. Caspar grabbed her by the chin and put his face in hers. The veins in his neck and temple were bulging. "Don't you dare insult me like this!"

"Well, you always were envious of my closeness to him, and you certainly never made a move on me, though you had plenty of opportunity. Not that I ever would have accepted, of course. Even then you were a disgusting pig, and you certainly have not improved in our years apart. But it does make one wonder."

This time when his hand flew, it was not the back of his hand to the side of her face or a fist to the gut. Instead, he balled his hand and delivered a vicious hook to her temple, and once again Elsabeth saw stars. Such was the force of the blow that the men holding her lost their grip, and she spun face-first into the dirt.

Her ears rang, her vision swirled about her, and Elsabeth was only vaguely aware of the hands seizing her and dragging her to her knees while Caspar stepped around in front of her. Had she the mind, she might have considered delivering a solid head-butt to his groin, for which she found herself at the convenient height. But, dazed as she was, Elsabeth could not even remain upright, much less formulate any particular strategy to avenge the battering. So instead, she just hung suspended from the men gripping her arms, spat the blood out of her mouth and fought back the rising urge to vomit while the world spun about her.

Caspar crouched in front of her, seized a fistful of her hair, and wrenched her head around, forcing her to look at him once more. There were now two of him spinning in circles about each other, and the idle thought of *two* Caspars in the world made her suddenly desperate for him to go on and kill her, even if it did mean his countenances would likely be the last thing she would see.

"I tell you one last time: Return it, now!"

Elsabeth winced against the strain the awkward turn of her head put on her neck. "And I am telling you one last time I have no idea where it is!"

He released her with a rough shove and nodded to the men behind her. They yanked her back to her feet and dragged her towards a large oak tree with several branches of convenient height. She made an effort to break free, but her captors were too many, too strong, and with her hands bound she was left with only her feet as weapons. Elsabeth kicked at whatever shin, knee or groin presented itself as a target, and tried to smash the back of her head against anyone standing behind her. But her struggling quickly proved futile, and any fight she had left in her was ended by yet another solid blow to her belly that drove the air from her lungs and left her gasping for breath and on the verge of vomiting.

A length of rope was thrown over one of the branches perhaps twice her height above the ground, and one end was knotted into a noose. Elsabeth fought down the surge of panic as the full realization of Caspar's intent settled over her. "Oh, really, Caspar?" she said when she managed to draw enough breath again to talk. She made her best effort to keep her voice level and her anxiety out of it. "Is this really supposed to convince me to tell you something I have already told you I know nothing about?"

"You had your chance, bitch," he snarled. "You are a thief and a liar, and 'tis long past time someone treated you as such."

*Perhaps I am, but damned if I die like this.*

"And I tell you I dispute your charge," she said. "Give me a sword and let us argue the point like civilized folk, so I can cut your head off rather than listen to your slander any longer."

He glowered at her. "Do you take me for a fool? I know what will happen if I put a sword in your hands, and I shan't let you slip away again."

"Oh, so you are still a coward, then. You would not dare fight me as a student, and you daren't fight me now. It defies belief the Brotherhood ever made you Master in Soest."

He snapped his fingers, and the noose was unceremoniously lowered over her head and tightened. Three of Caspar's men took hold of the other end and tested it and the branch, and Elsabeth felt the rope tug against her throat. Desperation to delay what was to come so she might find a means of escape overrode her revulsion of what she now considered.

Elsabeth made a pout and gave him a quick bat of her eyelashes.

"Come now, Caspar, I am sure there must be something you and I could work out together ..."

She trailed off suggestively, but grimaced inwardly. *I think I may be ill...*

However, Caspar just gave her a vicious and humorless smile. "Oh no, you don't cry, kiss, or fuck your way out this time. Your charms are wasted on me. Hang her!"

The next thing Elsabeth felt was the rope pulling taut, and she was hauled roughly off her feet by the neck. Her body thrashed and kicked in a desperate attempt to find some sort of purchase to lift the pressure off her throat as the noose tightened around it, but the effort was in vain. She gasped in anguish, and her blood surged against the rope cutting off the flow to her head. Pressure built in her head and face, and her tongue swelled and tried its best to force its way out of her mouth. Her last conscious thought as darkness intruded on her vision was how grey and lifeless everything around her now seemed.

Then all she knew was black.

*One week earlier...*

HE CITY OF AIN STOOD BESIDE THE RIVER whence came its name, at its confluence with the Rot flowing out of Boehm to the east. The river's rolling, meandering waters then flowed north along the border between Navarre and Boehm. It was a grand place of white stone walls enclosing a somewhat ovoid cluster of buildings atop a low rise overlooking the western bank, with gates in each of the four cardinal directions. The East Gate led to the great fortified stone bridge spanning the waters of the Ain, while the North, West, and South Gates opened to roads passing through the fields of the Comte D'Ain. He governed the river and its environs from Castle Ain, a towering stone edifice built on a hilltop a mile southeast of the city at the very edge of the river. Ain, therefore, served as a major crossroads for traffic and trade moving between Boehm and Navarre.

As Elsabeth and Hieronymus passed through the West Gate on their way into the City, they found its narrow cobbled streets a churning and crowded sea of people, horses, carts, and wagons, with only the most basic of organization to the chaos. The fragrance of cooking food — freshly-baked bread, meats, fruits, and exotic spices — mingled with the stench of too many people and horses crowded into too small a space. A tumultuous roar of voices and traffic echoed along the streets, punctuated here and there by the lighter sounds of laughter, the sharp clacking of hooves on cobblestones, and the ringing of a smith's hammer in some corner of the City.

Elsabeth sat astride Felis, her sword hanging from her saddle, and wrapped in her long, brown leather coat against the autumn chill. She adjusted the rakish angle of her broad-brimmed, black felt hat, its brim pinned up on the right side, to shield herself from the morning sun as it crested the horizon in the east. It spread its golden light across the open fields and glittered on the river as it rolled past the City. Hieronymus rode at her side on his old bay Hackney, Josephus, with a well-stained cloak about his shoulders and a new staff in hand to replace the one he had shattered during their adventure in Auch.

"Well, Tetty," he was grumbling as they passed through the gate with only a cursory inspection by the guards, and made their way up the street. Upon sight of the press of bodies crowding around them he carefully moved his coin purse to a more secure place on his belt, and wrinkled his nose at the pervasive odor of so many human and animal bodies pressed together into such small confines. "Here we are. Now do you mind explaining to me what in the name of the Lord of All has dragged us all the way back within spitting distance of Boehm?"

Elsabeth swept her green eyes across the shops lining the streets on either side; tailors, cobblers, taverns, inns, and other businesses aimed at travelers newly arrived within the walls dominated the commerce in this part of the City. Those nearest the gates catered to the more destitute of travelers. With a decent bit of coin still in their pockets, Elsabeth sought more reputable accommodations, so pressed on into the City. "We are here because you agreed after the disaster of our last adventure it was my turn to choose our next bit of work," she said. "After the excitement of our last few jobs I thought we could stand for something a tad more relaxing."

He grunted indignantly. "I still don't see what it is you have to complain about, that business with the boy paid well enough."

"And it might have gotten us both hanged, something I could rather use some time to wind down from."

Hieronymus glanced sidelong at her from his horse. "That was weeks ago, and you have had more than enough time to find us a suitable job since then. Yet here we are with nothing to show for it, and ever since we passed through Laon you could talk of nothing but reaching Ain. So out with it!"

Elsabeth scowled at him. "After all the times I have asked you where we were headed or what mad scheme was bouncing around your demented mind, and I had to endure all manner of permutations of, 'Patience is a great virtue to the Lord of All, my dear Tetty,' I would have hoped you could exercise some of the Lord's bounty of it yourself."

He harrumphed. "And yet I had to endure all manner of pestering and badgering because of your lack of it! The turnabout, my dear, is by all means fair play."

She smirked across the space between them as she swayed in the saddle. "Yes, it is," she said.

Hieronymus rolled the eyes skyward. "Lord, I do indeed beg of you for patience, lest I take your daughter across my knee!"

"And 'tis only in your prayers I will find myself anywhere near your knee, love. Now, seeing as we are here, if you must know I was checking the bulletins posted at the inn at Laon, and saw a notice that the Master of the Longsword of Ain was summoning all practitioners to a testing of his students, and a general contest of arms. There will be swordsmen from across Navarre, and surely Boehm as well, and perhaps even a few from the Free City-States."

Hieronymus groaned loudly once he pieced together her intentions. "God in Heaven, girl! You and I both well know this will end with you piss drunk in the nearest tavern, trolling for minstrels for the most undignified debaucheries in your misery that no man would dare to permit you to enter your name in the lists. Much less deign to fight you even if you could!"

"I do not need a reminder of the shortcomings the Lord of All placed betwixt my thighs, thank you. And I should say that you have no place to lecture me on miserable and undignified debauchery! I am not here to enlist in the fights myself."

"Then let us be on for greener pastures, as with so much competition to be had among the hired swords who will assuredly be in attendance, you and I shall find little fare."

She hooked a stray copper lock behind one ear. "This is my turn! And I never said I do not intend to fight at all."

Hieronymus eyed her suspiciously. "Then what do you have in mind?"

"As much as his stories and plans were built on lies — something with which you are yourself quite familiar — Maerten suggested something to me when he was trying to entice us into following him on his little quest that had a ring of truth to it. What I need is to find a patron; some rich fellow of standing and influence."

"I fail to see what climbing into such a fellow's bed will do for you, beyond sate your urges for a time before moving on. Not to mention how I would profit in this."

"What I need is support, love," she said with an indignant scowl. "I could thrash any sword-arm in Navarre and Boehm in a tournament — especially those bloody fool followers of da Lucca and Russdorffer — and you know it."

"Aye, Tetty, I do, and more is the pity because I would quite enjoy seeing many of those so-called 'masters' knocked down a peg. But I fail to see how this will let you connive your way around what the Lord of All placed between your legs."

"This is not Boehm, and the Schwertbrüder do not hold monopoly over the sword in Navarre. There, yes, I suspect things would be rather hopeless for me, but here if I could draw the attention of some influential — and preferably bored — fellow who might find it amusing to see a woman fight, he could use his influence to gain me a place on the lists."

"And how do you intend to convince him? While you have been blessed with several particular charms, I am not sure it shall be your proficiency with the sword he will be thinking about."

"That is how you will help," she said.

Hieronymus frowned at her. "Oh, is it now? And here I thought I was only coming along to extract you from whatever trouble you inevitably find yourself in with your intended patron's wife."

Elsabeth quirked a mischievous grin. "You and I are about to become entertainers."

As they talked, they steadily made their way closer to the heart of Ain where, in the main square, a great scaffold with a rectangular platform had been erected. There was a narrow stair on each short end, with boxes for seating on the long northern side. At the center was a luxurious box beneath a canopy, with a banner displaying the Comte D'Ain's personal arms — *Quarterly 1st and 4th Gules, a bear rampant Or Quarterly 2nd and 3rd Or, three swords proper in fess* — doubtless whence he would be viewing the bouts. The sound of hammers and saws and the shouting of many voices filled the square while workmen hurried to finish construction of the scaffold, while the crowd watched with fascination.

Elsabeth turned aside and down a narrow street lined with market stalls, and ignored the calls of the vendors as she led Hieronymus to another open square in the Northwest Quarter. Jugglers, jesters, and musicians performed for the crowd, and more merchants lined the cobbled streets in front of the more affluent shops encircling the square. The mingled scents of spices, cooked meat, and sweet pastries filled the air, and the stalls of the vendors competed with their destination ahead.

At the far end was a large timber building on a lawn of green grass. It was almost a small complex all to its own, surrounded by a low stone wall that came about to her waist, and a stable in the yard behind it. A boy of about ten summers leaned against the broad entrance, and immediately straightened when they approached. She and Hieronymus dismounted and led their horses by the bridles to the gate.

"Can I take your horses, Brother?" the boy said with a respectful bow to Hieronymus. His Navarrese was lightly touched by a hint of Boehman, and this close to the border, Elsabeth suspected he might have near kin from the other side of the river. "Only a *denier* and I'll put them up for you. 'Tis five *deniers* each to stable them for the week."

Hieronymus planted the end of his staff on the ground. "Thank you, my son!" he said. "Do pay the lad, will you, Tetty?"

Elsabeth rolled her eyes as she retrieved her sword and hung it at her hip. The boy eyed her warily, but any suspicion was wiped away when she thumbed a silver *pfennig* from her purse and flipped it to him. He bowed graciously. "Thank you, Madame!" he said pleasantly. "You want to speak to my father inside if you wish to arrange board, and I shall bring your packs to your rooms."

"Thank you again, my boy, we shall certainly do so," Hieronymus said. "May the Lord of All bless your day."

Elsabeth gave her old brown-and-white pinto Lizarran jennet a gentle pat on the flank before the boy led the animals away. She leaned on her sword at her hip and surveyed the square with a smile.

"I think this will do wonderfully," she said. "We are near the square where the bouts are to be held, and this seems a fine enough neighborhood there ought to be plenty of men of means about on business."

"Hm. And I see there are already fools out shilling to the masses, so what difference two more?"

Elsabeth rolled her eyes. "Oh shush. I have done far more degrading things at your request than this. We make a little coin demonstrating for the folk here, and with luck catch the eye of some bored princeling or another."

"And what do you do if it is your more obvious charms that catch his eye rather than your sword-arm? Do you intend to buy a place in the lists from your back?"

Elsabeth folded her arms across her chest and glowered down at him. "I'll manage that as I come to it."

Hieronymus sighed and pinched the bridge of his nose. "And this is why I have thus far made all our plans. I am sure by the time the week is out I will once again be saving you from yourself."

"Oh please. Just who needed saving from that mob in Wald who insisted on using you for archery practice?"

"I told you before, I had everything under control!" he protested at the reminder.

"They were chasing you with actual pitchforks! They would have skewered you like a suckling pig had I not been there, though I am to this day amazed at just how swiftly you can run."

Hieronymus straightened indignantly. "The proper motivation can do wonders for making one fleet of foot. Now if you don't mind, Tetty, I would rather like to see about arranging a place to stay for the night, and if we are to debase ourselves for this mad scheme of yours, I would like to get it over with swiftly so we might be on our way to finding real work again."

"Oh, very well. And do be a dear and help me scrounge up a few good wasters; there ought to be some market stall or other doing such business."

Elsabeth then sketched a mocking bow and waved him towards the door. Hieronymus waddled past grumbling under his breath, and she fell into step behind him with a smirk and an exaggerated swaying of her hips.

# 3

T WAS NOT YET NOON WHEN CASPAR VON Bech entered Ain. The road south out of Boehm was choked with people on foot and horse, driving wagons, or pulling hand carts, and he sniffed disdainfully from atop his great black courser as he and his company were ushered into the lines of common folk queued to pass through the North Gate. Here and there he caught the gleam of sunlight on steel betraying those among the procession who had come for the bouts, but most were farmers bringing goods to market: laborers, craftsmen, pilgrims come to visit the City's cathedral, or the occasional minstrel. The collective roar of many voices all talking over one another filled the air, and the wind rolling along the river carried with it the stink of the refuse and human waste clogging its swirling waters. A thin layer of dust from the road coated his fine green doublet and the longsword hung from his saddle, (and for that matter, much of everything else) and Caspar desired nothing more than to be done with the ride and relaxing with a good drink.

"You would think all of Boehm and Navarre had come to Ain," came a voice in Boehman from beside him. Merklin Adler sat astride his brown palfrey, and regarded the crowd with practiced condescension. Caspar's Vorfechter was a plain-featured youth of some seventeen summers, with short-cropped dark brown hair and eyes to match, and though he was only of average height, he was nonetheless quite strongly built. The remainder of his retinue was made up of the eldest students of his schola.

Caspar grunted at Merklin's observation. "The Graf D'Ain could have better managed the flow of traffic," he said, and cared little whether his voice was heard by the crowd. "I have no desire to spend all afternoon wading through rabble before I leave the road behind me."

"Have they all come for the fights, do you think?"

"Some of them, it seems. The Grand Master will be here; it was he who insisted upon our presence. I for one would rather have spent this time more productively than wasting it observing the state of Navarese swordsmanship."

"With your permission, Master, I do wish to enlist in the bouts. If this is to be a gathering of the flower of Navarese swordsmen, I am eager to measure myself against them."

Caspar nodded, and a trace of amusement at the enthusiasm in his pupil's voice tugged the corners of his mouth into a faint smile. "I expect that you do, and have little doubt that you will do myself, the schola, and the Brotherhood proud." He twisted his lip. "But first we must clear this damnable road!"

In truth, his impatience notwithstanding, it took them little time to enter into the City proper. They were met upon passing the gates by an aide to the Grand Master — a mousy little man with the crossed longswords of the Guild's coat of arms embroidered over his heart — who guided them southward through the maze of narrow streets. Tightly clustered blocks of shops and homes loomed up on either side, and everywhere there were people: Vendors plied their wares to the pedestrian traffic, while guards patrolled the streets for cutpurses and to settle arguments. There were Izmiri traders and black-skinned foreigners from the sun-blasted south beyond even those distant borders, and the glowing olive complexions of the Free City-States. He heard his native Boehman intermingled with the local dialect of Navarese, the rare bit of Coventrish, and here and there some Lizarran.

They passed men with swords at their sides boasting of past victories and making bold claims of ones yet to come, and even if not all the visitors to Ain had come for the contest of arms, there was little else on their lips.

Caspar and his company — all of his students neatly and uniformly dressed in red doublets with the Guild's arms embroidered over their hearts, and with only Merklin's blue garters setting apart his rank in the school — drew a fair amount of attention from the throng as they passed, and they were chased down the street by curious and laughing children. Vendors in the many market stalls held out morsels of food, jewelry, knives, and other odds and sundries for their perusal. Some of the younger students were distracted by the displays and soon found themselves surrounded and overwhelmed by an army of merchants. Caspar left them behind to enjoy themselves in whatever manner suited them, and soon he and Merklin found themselves riding alone with only the Grand Master's guide to keep them company.

Their course veered somewhat southwesterly and away from the main square nearest the heart of the city, where the scaffold for the bouts had been erected, and pressed on towards the richer and more affluent neighborhoods at the edges of the mercantile and administrative buildings at the city center. As they drew nearer their destination, Caspar's attention was drawn by a commotion from one of the smaller market squares up ahead and along the streets leading towards the West Gate. It was accompanied by a marked increase in traffic, and soon the way ahead was mired in a sea of bodies crowding towards the square.

"What in the name of the Dark One is this?" Caspar groused in exasperation. "Clear the road!"

When his demands fell on deaf ears, he spit his guide with a withering glare. "What is this?"

The mousy little man flinched at the sharpness of his tone. "I don't know, Master," he said. "The road was clear when the Grand Master sent me to meet you."

Caspar stood up in his stirrups to peer over the heads of the crowd, but he could see nothing beyond, nor hear anything but the pervasive murmur of hundreds of voices all talking at once. He glanced at Merklin. "Come on," he said, and without sparing an apology started his horse into the crowd and used its body to force a path to the end of the street.

After a few minutes he and Merklin finally reached a point where they could hear and see what manner of disturbance had so congested the city streets. They found themselves approaching a square in one of the more affluent districts of Ain, from behind the inn that occupied much of the northeastern side. People crowded around an open space in front to watch a demonstration taking place in its shadow.

A short and quite fat older man with wild silvering hair and an unkempt beard, dressed in the black habit of an Olivian friar, gesticulated wildly with his staff in one hand, and a wooden waster in the other. A wooden bowl filled with a few coins lay at his feet, with a tankard of ale nearby. His voice carried across the crowd with the practiced oratory of his profession, but, much to Caspar's surprise, it was not a sermon he delivered that day.

"Yes! Come closer, my children!" he cried to the crowd, his Navarrese strongly colored by Boehman. "I present to you a most marvelous spectacle! For a pittance given to a most worthy charity, I present to you a remarkable wonder; a student of the great Paulus von Soest himself!"

That piqued Caspar's curiosity, and more than a little indignant ire.

"Master?" Merklin murmured in his ear. "Who is this fellow, and why does he speak of Master von Soest?"

"Hush! Let me hear!" he hissed. As he listened to the friar's exhibition, he self-consciously twisted a golden ring on his left hand.

The friar reverently laid aside his staff, and then swept his free hand to direct the crowd's gaze towards someone emerging from the inn. Caspar craned his neck to try and catch a glimpse of him around the wall of the structure, but could see nothing. The crowd fell into uncertain silence somewhere between confusion, awe, and amusement, and that only fueled Caspar's desire to learn the identity of this man impersonating a student of Master von Soest even further.

"Is she not a marvel, my children?" the friar continued. Caspar blinked, unsure whether or not he heard the man rightly, and dark suspicion settled over him.

*She?*

"I can see the doubt in your eyes, but I assure you this lovely creature is indeed the one and only woman ever trained by the Schwertbrüder. Perhaps a demonstration is in order if you are still in doubt?"

Caspar blanched, and his eyed widened. "Lord of All, it cannot be ..."

"Master?" Merklin said, evidently aware of his distress. "Master, what is it?"

But Caspar paid him no heed, and forced his way through the crowd to a place where he could see her. In the end he need not move very far; the friar took up his waster and stepped towards the center of the space given to him by the crowd, and Caspar watched as *she* emerged from around the corner, waster in hand, and a black wrath settled over him as he laid eyes once more upon Elsabeth Hereford.

"A woman?" Merklin said, dumbfounded.

Elsabeth and her companion took up their places, and she inclined her head to him and touched her brow with the flat of her waster. Caspar gritted his teeth at the display. She was two years his junior, and was as striking a beauty as when last he saw her. But, unlike the rest of the fools in the crowd ogling her, (in her disdain for propriety and place, she had donned a pair of hose that left little of the shape of her legs and backside to the imagination) there was no room for lust in his heart.

"That Coventrish bitch!" he snarled, caring little whether anyone heard him. However only Merklin paid him any heed; the rest of the crowd focused intently on the bizarre display shaping up before them.

"Master, you know this woman?" Merklin asked.

Elsabeth exploded towards her opponent as she began her display. It was insult enough to drag down Master von Soest's name with her continued association, but to so exploit him for a few *pfennig* like a common street performer? Caspar had half a mind to charge through the crowd and run her down, but the press of bodies between them cheated him of the pleasure, and he could only watch the deft maneuvering of her waster when she quickly upended her rotund companion to the great enjoyment of the crowd.

"Master?" Merklin pressed when Caspar did not answer.

He gritted his teeth and tightened his hands around the reins. "I know her," he acknowledged with a hiss. "A whore out of Coventry that Master von Soest took on as a private student."

"The Master trained a woman?"

He scowled at the old memories of having to share the hall with that abominable girl surfacing from the deepest, darkest corners of his mind whence he buried them. The crowd, at least those who were not themselves practitioners, greatly enjoyed the spectacle as time and again she fought through her companion's best efforts to defend against her, and the old, cold envy gnawed at him as he watched her. The handful of others who studied the sword arts all saw as Caspar did — this was no charlatan whoring for coin in the streets, but a master of her craft. And that it was a *woman* indulging in their art was a thought they could little abide.

Caspar tore his eyes away from her and he gave Merklin a significant look. "She is the one responsible for his death."

Merklin's jaw dropped in astonishment. "She is the one? I thought that was only drunken rumor."

"Every word of the story is true. Soest was slain, and she fled into the night with his sword never to be seen again. I would have run her down and cut off her head myself but by the time anyone knew what had transpired she had murdered three men in a tavern and was gone." Caspar's cheek twitched, and he turned his eyes back onto Elsabeth and her partner in this mockery of their art. Most of their fellow practitioners shook their heads and forced their way back through the crowd, while the peons watched her enraptured.

He glanced back at Merklin, whose own expression was torn between awe, disgust, and lustful thoughts. "That woman is a succubus, boy," he said sharply, and Merklin tore his eyes away from her in chagrin at the rebuke. "She beguiled the Master, and that led to his downfall. Remember that. She is nothing more than a demon in fair guise, and should long ago have been put in her place."

"Then why do we not now, while she is here?" Merklin said. "Surely, she is no match for you."

Caspar felt a queasy churning in his belly, and he quickly looked away from his pupil. "Not now," he said. "Her time will come soon enough, but we are here as guests, and we will conduct ourselves as such. No doubt the Grand Master will desire to know that she is here, as well."

Merklin looked between him and Elsabeth. Caspar kept his gaze fixed on the woman and buried the churning in his belly behind a disgusted scowl, but he could not tell if Merklin saw through him or not.

The crowd around them was aroused to fevered delight by the display, and every time she scored a blow against her sparring partner a cheer broke out. The friar was no novice with a sword himself, but she clearly had him overmatched. Finally, he called a hold to catch his breath, and murmured something in the woman's ear. Soon they moved on from wasters, and with the rasp of steel on wood she returned to the square with Master von Soest's longsword, while the friar brought out a sword and buckler, and fell into one of Leonardus's wards.

Caspar growled through gritted teeth at the sight of that blade in her slender hands. The clash of steel rang out across the square as the pair began sparring with live blades. Finally, he could bear no more, and spun his horse around. "We have tarried here long enough and are now overdue."

Without another word he forced his way back through the crowd and returned to the side of their guide.

S IR STEMHAM CROSSEBY STOOD ATOP the scaffold erected in the main square of the City, with the laborers assigned to the task of preparing both the platforms and the boxes for the attendees. The sounds of hammers, saws, and shouted instructions filled the air, which smelled strongly of sweat and sawdust. Crosseby paced the platform and shouted orders in Navarese, touched only lightly by a hint of his native Coventrish, and lent a hand at times to hold a plank being cut or hammered into place, haul up equipment or supplies on the winches surrounding the construction site, or discuss the progress with the master builder.

"How much longer do you think before the platform itself is finished?" he asked during a brief pause in the work, and mopped his brow on the back of one sleeve. The top of the platform was currently a mess of planks and beams, toolboxes, and workbenches. There were barrels and crates of supplies, and the ring of a smith's hammer forging the heavy iron nails holding the entire construct together echoed across the square.

"It ought to be done by midday tomorrow, Monsieur," the master builder said. He was a short and squat fellow getting well on in age, and dressed in a fine doublet better suited for sitting behind a desk than for the active work of construction, a fact to which his portly build attested. His silvering hair fell to his rounded jaw, his blue eyes were small and round, and he had a habit of squinting which suggested to Crosseby he seldom left whatever dark corner he secluded himself in to work while his apprentices did all the real labor. By contrast, Crosseby's tall and powerful frame was dressed only in a sweat-stained linen shirt and a pair of hose, ready for the good hard work of preparing the scaffold.

He nodded. "Good, very good! See to it that 'tis ready, as I would like to have some of my students test its suitability for the playing."

The master builder eyed him with amusement. "And I thought you intended to finish raising it single-handed."

Crosseby chuckled and clapped the builder on one shoulder. He ignored the distressed expression that flitted across the man's features as he hastily brushed away dust left by Crosseby's hand. "I am afraid I have a great deal of other work before me, so will be unable to help you more today. So, I'll leave the rest of the construction in your capable hands!"

"Very good, Monsieur," the builder said, visibly appalled at the dirty handprint on his shoulder.

Crosseby ignored the builder's fussing with his doublet, and instead put an arm around his shoulder and led him across the unfinished platform. "Do be sure the ring is laid out properly," he said with a sweep of his arm across the construction site. "You do have the measurements I gave you, yes?"

"Of course, Monsieur! Have no fear. Everything will be done to your specifications."

"Excellent! I wish to have the actual ring for the combats roped off," he added, and sidestepped a coil of rope and a stack of wooden planks cluttering the center of the platform, all the while leading the hapless builder with him as he made his way towards the flight of steps leading down at the western end of the scaffolding. "Do make sure to leave enough of a walkway that the audience has room enough to reach their seats without intruding on the ring."

"Yes, Monsieur, though I must remind you I have taken all your requirements into consideration in planning the scaffold," the builder said. A touch of irritation at the questioning of his abilities colored his voice. "I assure you everything will be as you desired."

Crosseby again ignored the man's display of exasperation, and just turned and patted his cheek. "Wonderful! Then I have nothing to fear! Monsieur le Chevalier recommended you quite highly for this task, so I'll be sure to pass along to him just how superbly you have carried out this noble endeavor."

Unsure what to make of Crosseby's remark, the builder merely bowed politely. "Thank you, Monsieur," he said.

Crosseby chuckled and gave him another hearty slap on the shoulder. "Good man! Good man! Now if you will pardon me, I shall leave you to it!" He grabbed his blue woolen doublet from where he had left it hanging on a post, and threaded his arms through its close-fitting sleeves as he made his way down the stairs to the cobbled streets below. He was met at the foot of the stairs by a rather nondescript-looking fellow in a plain brown doublet, and whose most distinguishing characteristic was his neatly-groomed beard. "Ah, Richard, there you are," Crosseby said in Coventrish, and busied himself fastening the buttons of his doublet. "Have you learned anything of who has responded to my invitations?"

"Yes, Sire," Richard replied in the same tongue.

"Who do we have, then?"

"Grand Master von Aich of the Schwertbrüder has arrived," Richard said. He waited patiently while Crosseby finished with his doublet, then held out the scabbard containing Crosseby's longsword once he finished. The guard and wheel pommel of his sword were cast from bronze, with fittings on the scabbard to match, while the upper half of the waisted grip and scabbard were both covered in blue leather. The rest of the grip to the pommel was wrapped in copper wire. "And I have heard that Caspar von Bech of that guild was seen entering the North Gate with a small retinue, as well. Morelet and Gaston d'Aubigny both arrived late yesterday afternoon, as did Oudart Gaude, Simon de Craon, and Loys Oger. All have brought their students with them."

Crosseby accepted his sword from Richard and hung it from his belt. He took a moment to adjust it at his hip before starting off up the street, with Richard falling into step behind him. "So, two parties from Boehm and five from elsewhere in Navarre. Something less of a turnout than I had hoped."

"There was correspondence from several others, Sire," Richard offered as they walked. "So some may yet be on their way. And I believe Oudart Gaude mentioned passing Bartolomé Ruiz and several of his students while on the road east, apparently taking quite the liberty of the local tavern."

Crosseby considered that with some amusement. "Ruiz has come all the way from Lizarra, then? What about that fellow ..." He snapped his fingers for a moment when the name, hanging on the tip of his tongue, refused to come. "Oh, you know, he commands the guard at Carcassonne."

"Robin de ..." Richard began

"Robin de Sens," Crosseby said with him as soon as the name left his companion's lips.

"I have not heard any word of him, but the Count of Carcassonne does keep him rather busy on some affair or another."

"Well, I shall take it, then, that Sir Robin shall not be attending."

"I would assume that would be the safe bet, Sire."

He shrugged. "A pity, as I had greatly looked forward to sparring with him again. But no matter, at the very least I have a few of those arrogant Schwertbrüder to play against."

"You intend to fight in the contest of arms then, Sire?" Richard asked.

Crosseby nodded. "Of course! What sort of master of arms would I be if I did not set the example to my students of bouting at every opportunity that presented itself?

Especially if it means putting a few of those Boehman bastards in their place. Now then, what is left for today?"

"Tanguy has finished the rebated arms for the playing this morning and inquired as to whether you wished to inspect them before taking delivery."

"Oh, that I am sure is unnecessary," he said, and waved the matter off. "I have complete faith in Tanguy's work."

"Should I tell him?"

Crosseby considered a moment as they continued along the street. The narrow avenue was crowded by men going about their business, women with their children, and merchants working their elaborate displays to entice the pedestrians to a closer look at their wares. He paused at a cart operated by a striking and exotic young girl out of Izmir with dark hair and eyes, and dressed in the brightly-colored robes of her homeland. She bowed her head when he approached the cart and murmured something in her native tongue Crosseby could not understand. She tended a chip pan filled with hot oil, and the air around her cart was heavy with the scent of honey and cinnamon. Crosseby's mouth watered.

"Lokmas, five for a *denier*," she said in broken Navarrese when she noticed him looking over her wares.

Crosseby fished into his purse and offered her a silver coin, which she accepted with a gracious bow of her head before handing him a cloth bundle of the fried balls of dough fresh from the pan. He inclined his head in thanks and resumed his walk down the street.

"Sire?" Richard pressed from his side when he did not immediately respond.

Crosseby casually popped one of the lokmas in his mouth, and immediately yelped and hissed in a breath to cool his burned tongue. As the sensation passed, he was left with the lingering aftertaste of the sweet honey blended with the hot and aromatic pungency of the cinnamon. "No, that shan't be necessary," he said with an effort around the scorching mouthful. "As we are already heading that way, I may as well have a look, if only to offer my compliments on his work in person."

They did not get very much further along the street before the flow of traffic ahead ceased almost entirely. The narrow path through the city was packed with bodies all trying to crowd into one of the market squares up ahead. "What the devil is this about?" Crosseby asked, and glanced sidelong at Richard.

"I know not, Sire," he said with a helpless and bewildered shrug.

Crosseby tossed another lokma into his mouth and licked the syrupy honey coating from his fingers. He craned his neck this way and that in an effort to see around the wall of bodies in front of him. Finding no way through to investigate the source of the traffic jam, he turned and started briskly down an alleyway with Richard scrambling to keep up. Refuse and waste was strewn about the narrow and cramped passage, and Crosseby was grateful for his pattens to keep him out of the muck. A muffled curse from behind told him Richard had not been so fortunate, and he glanced back to watch his man scraping something particularly disgusting from the bottom of his shoe.

The alley opened out again onto another narrow street that, because of its dark confines, was not regularly traveled by pedestrians. Crosseby threaded past the few people within and chewed on a lokma as he hurried along. In this manner of moving from alley to alley he eventually reached one that opened out onto the market square that had drawn so much attention from the population.

He arrived at the far end across from the inn. Carts and stalls lined the fronts of the other buildings overlooking the square, and there were a few musicians, jugglers, and other street-performers taking advantage of whatever had drawn such an unusually dense crowd to this particular market. Most of the audience paid them little mind, however, and were instead focused on something happening out front of the inn itself. Crosseby popped the last lokma into his mouth and wiped his hands off on his thighs, but could still not see past the bodies pressing in towards the square.

Richard, red-faced from the brisk walk and still vainly kicking the mess on the bottom of his shoe on the cobblestones and walls of the buildings on either side of the alley, finally caught up with him. "Do you see anything, Sire?" he asked.

Crosseby frowned. "No. Half a moment ..."

And with that, he pushed into the crowd, with a few polite but insistent "pardon mes," and "stand asides." Nonetheless, the closer he pressed towards the front of the crowd, the denser and tighter the wall of bodies ahead of him became, and eventually he could no longer make a hole. There was certainly a great commotion from the square, and he heard the distinct clack of wasters, a few chortles and cheers, and an indignant yelp that drew another round of laughter from the front rows of the audience.

*Damn if I miss whatever the excitement is.*

Crosseby looked about on either side of him, and found that he was not too far from one of the merchant stalls ringing the square. He pushed his way in that direction, ignoring a few curses as here and there he stepped on a foot or jostled another of the spectators. Upon reaching the stall he quickly clambered up despite the protests of the vendor when the wooden structure swayed and creaked under his weight, and rattled the copper pots, cast-iron pans, and cutlery hung from pegs on the frame. From his new vantage he had a clear view over the heads of the crowd, and noted Caspar von Bech on the far side astride his great black courser investigating the disturbance as well.

But his eyes were quickly drawn to the street in front of the inn, and his breath caught in his throat in amazement at what he saw.

A tall figure of slender athleticism was locked in mock combat with a short and heavy-set fellow in the habit of an Olivian friar, wielding a waster with the skill and poise of a master. But what astonished him most of all was that the friar's opponent was a woman, dressed in men's fashion. Crosseby distantly felt a smile tug at his features while he watched her lithely dart around her partner's attacks and defenses, and he knew at once this was no mere show-fighter; her attacks were direct and efficient, and her defenses were quick and clean. Yet she married the power of her handling of the sword with a distinctly feminine grace of movement. Every step, every cut, was fluid and sinuous.

Her long fall of hair, the color of burnished copper, floated behind her like a banner caught in the afternoon breeze. Her athleticism did nothing to spoil her feminine shape, and Crosseby's face heated at the way her hose hugged the shapely contour of her bottom and legs, and left little need for his imagination to fill in her figure.

For some time he watched her enraptured, the friar's words during their infrequent breaks lost among the rumble of their audience, and Crosseby was deaf to the merchant below yelling at him in the Tranian dialect of the Free City-States to climb down from his perch atop the stall.

# 5

ELSABETH CLOSED HER EYES AND RAISED the large wooden tankard to her lips, tossed back her head, and drank. Music from a small band tucked away in one corner filled the inn, men pounded their fists on the oaken tables, and raucous cheers goaded her on. She drank and drank without pausing. Ale sloshed past her mouth, trickled coldly down her neck, throat, and chest. It soaked the front of her shirt, and that only enflamed the cries of encouragement. On she drank, in big gulping swallows and without stopping for a breath; one pint, two pints, three pints. The longer she drank the further she leaned back until she bent herself nearly double backwards. Finally with a flourish she downed the last pint, and slammed her now-empty tankard down on the table to a roar of approval from the men crowded around her. Elsabeth laughed heartily as she felled her opponent, a handsome blacksmith named Tanguy, with a clean-shaven head, broad chest, and arms that might have been as big around as her thighs.

The clinking of money changing hands pierced through the background hum of the tavern. Some men cursed, others groaned, and almost all called for another round. Vanquished, Tanguy started away with an astonished shake of his head, but Elsabeth quickly caught him by the arm and spun him back to face her again.

"Oh, don't take it so hard, love," she said, and flashed him a mischievous smile. "It takes more than a mere few pints to choke me." That remark drew a howl of approval from the crowd. "But let me offer you some consolation for your valiant effort!"

And with that, she took his face in her hands, and pulled him into a deep, passionate kiss that tasted strongly of the ale lingering on his breath. Tanguy's massive arms encircled her waist as he kissed her back, and Elsabeth might have collapsed utterly when he leaned over her, had he not pulled away before he bent her backwards onto one of the tables. The revelers incited him to take her right then and there in the common room, but propriety prevailed, and Tanguy stood away from her with a satisfied grin on his face. Elsabeth was left breathless, and leaned against the table for support until she regained the strength in her legs.

"You are a dangerous woman," the big smith said. "If word of this were to reach my wife, she would skin me alive."

"If you are still thinking of your wife just now, then I have clearly lost my touch!" she said, to the riotous amusement of the spectators.

"I have no wife!" a voice interjected from the back of the crowd. "What would it cost me for your companionship for the night?"

Elsabeth snatched a fresh tankard from one of the men clustered around the table (who gave it up with not so much as a token growl of disapproval, so entranced was he with thoughts of what she might do next) and drained it with one long gulp before slamming it down on the table. "Monsieur, I think you have mistaken me for a common bawd. There is nothing at all common about me, and in fact I am not here to offer my companionship at all. Quite the contrary, I am seeking some for myself!"

"And what are you looking for in a companion?" another voice called out.

"For starters," she said, and picked up the empty tankard for emphasis, "Someone who can do something about this!"

The common room exploded into motion as men scrambled over one another to have her tankard refilled, and Elsabeth laughed and dove into the mayhem with relish. The roar of the crowd and music shook the inn to its foundations, and more and more of the passersby who stopped to witness her demonstration in the market, or those come to investigate the uproar at the inn, crowded within its walls until the common room was all but bursting at its seams, with only the heavy timber beams and columns supporting the ceiling holding it together. The plates sitting on the decorative shelves lining the walls rattled and threatened to topple over, the lamps hanging from the beams and ceiling swayed to and fro, and the tables bounced to the rhythmic drumming of hands and mugs on their tops, and the stomping of feet on the hardwood floor.

Elsabeth danced through the maelstrom, a tempest of spinning limbs and flying hair as she spun and stomped, stealing drinks from her eager audience, slipping deftly around some groping hands, and cozying up for a kiss and a pet with others. The musicians struck up a swift and raucous local folk dance. She soon lost herself in the sound of pipes, harps, fiddles, drums, and lutes, and the common room spun around her in a dazzling and dizzying swirl of light and color. She passed from man to man. Course hands encircled her waist as she drew them into the chaos of her dancing, and laughed off the occasional stolen pinch of her bottom or grab for her breast.

Ale flowed freely from the inn's kegs. Elsabeth drank heartily, and soon put even the largest and stoutest of her fellow revelers to shame. The wood-plank floor was soon slick with it, and the sour odor filled the air, mingling with the herbs and spices of the night's meal and the sweat of so many bodies pressed so closely into so confined a space. Her chaotic weaving soon found her mounting the tables and dancing with wild abandon from tabletop to tabletop. And then she found herself among the musicians, hopping from lap to lap as they played, so full of drink she sang along loudly and heedlessly of her lack of ability, but all the more to the delight of the crowd at her bawdy turns of phrase.

She pressed herself suggestively against a piper standing in the corner and drew him into a deep and lingering kiss. Then she spun away from him, dropped into the lap of a lutenist, and appropriated his instrument and plucked clumsily at the strings, while he unflinchingly shifted his hands from gliding skillfully along the neck of his lute, to sliding with equal deftness along her body. Elsabeth squirmed and broke out into a fresh bout of laughter when he found a ticklish spot before filling his hands with her breasts, then she slipped his grasp and returned the gesture with a grope between his legs before she relinquished his lute, all with nary a missed beat.

There were more drinks to be had, more laps to sit upon, and more mouths to kiss. She was the eye of the storm of merriment, and allowed herself to be swept away by the chaos, throwing herself heedlessly wherever it led her and all to the delight of the patrons of the inn who plied her with more and more drink, until finally the world around her blurred and then vanished into warm and inviting darkness.

IERONYMUS SAT AT HIS TABLE IN A FAR CORNER with three other men, and watched Elsabeth make a scandal of herself dancing aimlessly from man to man in a most unseemly manner at the other end of the common room. The inn was filled to all but overflowing that night, the crowd lured in by their curiosity over the day's demonstration, and the hopes that one of them might be lucky enough to find their way into his companion's bed. He took a long draught from his ale and wiped his mouth on the shoulder of his habit, and turned his wavering eyes from Elsabeth's dizzy revelry and back to the two dice — or was it four? They seemed to have multiplied as the night wore on — spinning on the table in front of him.

"'Tis your cast, Father," one of his companions said. He was a rough-featured and shaggy-haired man of portly build not unlike his own, and his voice was barely audible over the roar of the crowd as Elsabeth's antics whipped them into a frenzy. The shouts and laughter, the stomp of boots on the hardwood floors, the sharp clapping of hands, and the dull thud of fists and tankards beating the tables filled the common room, and over all of it the musicians played, their tune building to a dizzying tempo and deafening volume.

"I am quite capable of keeping track of the turns, my good man!" Hieronymus growled indignantly over the bedlam inside the inn. "I am merely considering my wager!"

"You have been considering a good while now," said the second, a rail-thin fellow with a wiry yellow beard.

"Patience is the Lord's counsel in all matters of time, my son. I shall make my roll when God deems it time, and not a moment earlier." He took another drink, set his tankard down, and then added a few *deniers* for his wager. His opponents added their stakes to match, then he took up his dice and rolled. He grunted in satisfaction at the result of a three and a four. "The Main will be seven, then," he said, and cast his dice again. They skittered across the table, bounced with the rhythmic pounding on the floor, and finally came to a rest showing two fives.

"The Chance is ten," his third companion, the master of the house, said. "Two-to-one payout, the lucky bastard!" He was a man of average height and stout build, with dark hair showing streaks of silver, and keen blue eyes. Alone of the four he had not partaken of the ale, and Hieronymus therefore watched him with a suspicious eye.

"There is no fortune in this world whether good or ill, my son, but only the will of the Lord," Hieronymus said, and ignored the master of the house's oath when he picked up the dice again. "I wager another five *deniers* I hit my Chance before the Main."

Hieronymus gave the dice a good shake, and rolled again; a three and a two. He rolled twice more; a two and a one, and on the second he smiled broadly when the dice landed on a four and a six. "Blessed be the Lord, who has seen fit to grant me good fortune this night!" he said, and made a grab for his winnings.

Yellow Beard groaned and slumped back in his chair. "May He have mercy upon me; that is four victorious throws in a row!"

Hieronymus chuckled, and took a celebratory drink. "Remember well that lesson, my son: The Lord of All watches over those who serve Him faithfully, and He shall provide to them in their need!"

Shaggy took a long drink of his own beer to mask his growing frustration at Hieronymus's good turn with the dice. "Clearly I should have joined a monastery myself; if only for the better fortune with the dice."

"'Tis God's will, and nothing more."

"Oh, I am certain. Just as it was His will that finds you traveling with that lovely creature." He jerked his thumb towards Elsabeth, who had paused in her revelry to take on yet another challenger, and was bent backwards nearly double draining the great tankard without pause for breath. And like the mighty smith before him her adversary fell. Before she could give him a kiss for his trouble, Elsabeth let out a squeak when, emboldened by the quantity of ale he had already imbibed, he instead seized her and trailed a series of sloppy kisses down her neck and chest to sample the spilled drink from her fair skin.

"My dear Tetty is indeed quite the picture of virtue, is she not?" Hieronymus said, and watched the display with equal measures of condemnation and envy. Elsabeth managed to free herself from the embrace and delivered the fellow a bemused swat on the cheek, then gave him a proper kiss before sending him on his way with a playful kick to his backside. With no further challengers to her remarkable capacity for engorging herself on such vast quantities of ale, she turned once more to stealing drinks from whatever man presented himself, and dancing and carrying on in a most undignified manner while the music continued to play. She swayed on her feet and stumbled from suitor to suitor, oblivious to the enticing vulgarity of her gyrations when she danced.

"Surely you have had an opportunity to sample her charms for yourself in your travels," Yellow Beard said. He gawked slack-jawed at the display.

"I am a servant of the Wheel!" Hieronymus said indignantly around another mouthful of ale — one too small for his tastes, as he found his tankard distressingly empty. "My good man, I seem to have come up empty, another if you will!" he said in an aside to the master of the house, before turning to address Yellow Beard once more. One of the girls quickly came round with a pitcher to refresh Hieronymus's tankard. "I have not laid so much as a finger on the Lord's magnificent work with that dear girl."

"And I am sure it makes your vows all the harder to follow, eh, Brother?" the master of the house said with an amused twinkle in his eye.

"Indeed, indeed," he said absently, and trailed off to admire the shape of the serving girl's figure beneath her cotehardie. The master of the house narrowed his eyes in silent warning, and Hieronymus reluctantly tore his eyes away from, what he guessed from her age, was the man's daughter. "'Tis quite the challenge to reconcile those most holy vows of chastity when the Lord of All creates a thing of such magnificent beauty. After all, He does nothing without a purpose, and why would He see fit to grace her with such an abundance of charm if not for it to be enjoyed by the eye, hand, and other parts of one's anatomy. Though I lament that my entreaties have gone unanswered."

Her task finished and Hieronymus's tankard filled, the serving girl inclined her head politely to him and scuttled off through the crowd to make her rounds with her pitcher of ale. She dodged with practiced ease past the grasping and groping crowd whipped into a frenzy by Elsabeth's shameless display, and was soon lost among the sea of bodies.

"I would consider it myself," Shaggy said, "but alas I have a wife awaiting me at home and can afford no mistress."

"Do not count yourself out of the competition so rashly, then," Hieronymus said around a mouthful of beer. "Many are the arguments between man and wife that began betwixt that dear girl's thighs. And I have seen her toss her dignity aside for nothing more than the cost of a few good pints, or as little as a well-sung tune."

As if to emphasize his point, the rollicking folk dance finally came to an end with Elsabeth stomping and spinning merrily atop one of the tables with a tankard in each hand. She drained both in quick succession to the delight of her suitors, swayed unsteadily, and laughed uproariously as she lost her balance and toppled over entirely. Only the waiting arms of her erstwhile dancing partners kept her from falling all the way to the floor. The lutenist then plucked a clear, high note on his instrument and, as if to calm the gathering before Elsabeth could whip them into an outright riot, began a slow and melodious ballad.

A hush fell over the crowd as he began to sing, accompanied only by his own hands dancing along the fretboard. It was not a song Hieronymus recognized, and was in a tongue with which he was unfamiliar, but the crowd stood transfixed by the lustful sensuousness of his countertenor voice. Elsabeth broke free of the hands that saved her from a split skull on the hardwood floor, and took a seat at the table nearest the musicians' corner. She watched enthralled with widening eyes, and her head supported in her hands. The common room fell into total silence while he sang. Soon his voice was echoing in the rafters, and the sweet strains of his lute wove through and around the lyrics, both entwined like lovers writhing together in harmony.

Even from across the room the effect on his companion was plain for all to see; her breast heaved, and she alternately nibbled and licked her lower lip. Her eyes closed and she began to sway in rhythm to the music. Hieronymus took a long draught of his beer and watched the display with disapproval. Her response to the song was not lost on the lutenist, who never took his eyes from her.

And then, like a lover's final exultant release, his song ended, and both voice and lute rang as he held out the final note. The gathering burst into applause, and Elsabeth leapt atop the table in her enthusiasm to lend her voice to the ovations. The lutenist stood from his chair and swept his arm to the side in an exaggerated bow, with a wink and a smile in Elsabeth's direction. With no further need of encouragement, she vaulted from the table. She all but leapt into his arms and pulled him into a kiss, again to the delight of a crowd expecting the resumption of her vivacious antics.

Instead, upon pulling away from his lips she whispered something in his ear that made the lutenist's face flush (no doubt helped by one of her hands straying down the front of his thigh). She seized him by the hand and dragged him, lute and all, towards the flight of stairs leading up to the private rooms on the level above. They did not quite make it all the way up before a yelp and a giggle echoed down the stairwell, but soon Hieronymus heard the slamming of a door above, and they were gone.

The unfortunate fellows who had until now been filled with hope that they might find themselves invited up to Elsabeth's room fell momentarily into dejected silence. But then the musicians left behind struck up another rousing dance number. The reappearance of serving girls with fresh rounds of drink lifted their spirits again, and the inn was filled once more with the sounds of merrymaking.

Hieronymus just chuckled softly into his tankard and regarded the stunned looks on his companions' faces. "Well then," he said around a mouthful of ale. "I do believe we have seen the last of my dear Tetty tonight, though I suppose we shall find the rest of the evening a good deal quieter for her absence." He picked up his dice again, and threw a few *deniers* into the middle of the table. "Now then, shall we continue?"

Yellow Beard, Shaggy, and the master of the house just groaned in irritation as they contributed their share to the pot, and Hieronymus rolled for his Main.

<br>

HOUGH OUTWARDLY Castle Ain was a formidable presence overlooking the Ain River and the City it commanded, the interior of the great hall was a grandly-furnished and magnificent living space.

Crosseby entered through the screens passage beneath the minstrels' gallery situated at the western end of the hall. He swept his eyes across the cavernous chamber of cream-colored plastered walls between decorative spiral columns of dark timber, and a floor of brown and gold marble in a checkerboard pattern. The plinth of each column was engraved with the arms of the D'Ain, the capital was carved into the form of the spreading boughs of a tree, and molding decorated with elaborate scrollwork of the same dark wood ran the perimeter of the chamber just beneath a vaulted ceiling. Tapestries depicting scenes of hunting, court, and warfare adorned the walls, and here and there were trophies taken by D'Ain throughout his lifetime: swords, the head of a boar, a rack of antlers of remarkable span, and several complete suits of armor.

He strode purposefully down the length of the hall, past guards in ceremonial dress bearing tall halberds, along the long tables set out to seat D'Ain's guests for supper, and exchanged pleasantries with the other guests invited to dine that evening. Men in their finest doublets talked and laughed merrily amongst themselves or admired the rich décor of the hall. Most were strangers to him — some functionary, or chevalier, or member of a lesser noble house come hoping to ingratiate himself with D'Ain — but here and there he caught sight of men he knew, either personally or by reputation, and who had come to Ain in acceptance of his invitation for the playings.

Morelet, Simon de Craon, and Oudart Gaude gathered in a small knot next to a large oriel window in the middle of the long wall on his right. The window looked out onto the inner bailey where, beyond the glass in its decorative gilded frame, lay the neatly manicured lawn and gardens of the bailey. The windows stood open for the evening to allow fresh air in, and the scent of the autumn breeze lent the hall an invigorating aroma. Though further east the sky was darkening to night, the sun had not yet slipped beneath the horizon to the west, and so cast a dying golden light onto the bailey.

The three men conversed quietly with two fellows out of the Free City-States: Giacomo del Brun and Antonio Guarin. Of del Brun Crosseby knew little. Guarin, however, Crosseby knew well, and rolled his eyes at the sight of the strutting peacock in his gaudily-colored dress. He suspected the man was more concerned with the shine of his armor than the practical use of it, and even more to his detriment, he was a disciple of that flailing clown da Lucca.

Directly opposite the window was the hall's great fireplace. The firebox, hearth, and filler panels were of white stone, the rest, of the same dark wood as the columns and molding supporting the ceiling. Its legs, header, and crown were carved with elaborate scrollwork, and a large shield bearing the arms of D'Ain hung on the overmantle. A fire blazed in the hearth to warm the hall and fill it with a fresh and fragrant scent, which mingled with the aroma of cooking food wafting into the hall from the nearby kitchens.

Bartolomé Ruiz, who had finally tired of sampling the local ale, was engaged in a lively debate near the fire with the Navarrese Nicolas d'Orgremont, and Lucha da Pavia out of the City States. The animatedness of their deliberation was grounded as much in Ruiz barely speaking a word of Navarrese that bore repeating in polite company, and da Pavia's lack of mastery of Lizarran, as it was in the actual subject of their discourse. As he passed them by on his way to the dais it became apparent to Crosseby that the argument chiefly lay between Ruiz and da Pavia, with the hapless d'Orgremont trapped between them to serve as translator.

Crosseby carefully evaded entangling himself in the various debates as he hurried the rest of the way across the floor to his destination: the foot of the dais at the far eastern end. This was mounted by five broad steps, where the high seat of D'Ain gazed down upon the main floor. Large double doors in each corner led through richly decorated archways to the private living areas beyond, and banners and tapestries hung from the back wall. The high table, draped with an embroidered cloth for the evening, stood at the edge of the dais. The hall was brightly-lit that evening by the dying sun shining through the windows, and the lamps hung from the columns and set out on the tables. The polished marble floor reflected the light, and the whole of the chamber seemed to glow of its own radiance.

As Crosseby approached the dais he noted D'Ain with Caspar von Bech and Stefan von Aich, the Grand Master of the Schwertbrüder.

Monsieur le Chevalier Raoul Alexandre, Comte D'Ain, was some fifteen years Crosseby's elder. He was still tall and hale, but thickening round his middle as the years crept up on him, and his dark hair was beginning to thin and was shot through with streaks of gray. He kept his plain face clean-shaven, and his hair fell to his shoulders in a manner that artfully framed his features. He wore a doublet of fine blue velvet, but the most overt signs of his wealth and prestige were the rings he wore on his fingers. Bech was dressed rather plainly that night, with only the glint of lamplight on his golden Master's ring catching the eye. He wore his straw-colored hair pulled back from his face, and a neatly groomed and waxed mustache.

It was the Grand Master, however, that commanded one's attention as they drew nearer the dais. Though nearing his seventieth year, if Crosseby remembered rightly, Aich's body had lost none of the imposing formidability of his youth; he was tall and strong, with no softness of age or indication he had grown sedentary in his position. His face was lean with a prominent nose, and he wore his white hair and beard long in the manner of a wizened old sage. Aich's dark eyes were clear and penetrating, and his voice was still a strong and deep baritone that shook the hall when he spoke. He dressed in the white ceremonial vestments of his guild and station, with the arms of the Brotherhood embroidered on a crimson stole draped around his shoulders, and the golden chain of his rank around his neck.

Each of the three held a crystal glass filled with wine, and drank at their ease while they conversed quietly among themselves. Upon noticing Crosseby's arrival, D'Ain signed for Aich to pause in his discourse, and raised his glass in greeting. The Grand Master skillfully disguised his annoyance at the interruption by making a show of pausing to take a sip of his wine, and Crosseby could not help but feel as if Aich's dark eyes searched him down to his very soul upon his approach.

"Ah! Monsieur Crosseby!" D'Ain said in warm greeting, and in Coventrish colored by an accent that was a peculiar blend of Navarrese and Boehman. "You are here! Now we may begin properly!"

Crosseby returned his patron's greeting with a deep bow ending with an exaggerated sweep of his arm. "I apologize for my tardiness, Monseigneur," Crosseby said in Navarrese. "I was unavoidably delayed seeing to a few preparations for the playings."

D'Ain brusquely waved off the apology, and stepped forward to take him by the arm and personally lead him the rest of the way to where the two Schwertbrüder awaited him. "No matter, no matter, my friend. Come! I would like to introduce you to these two good fellows. And where is that dreadful boy with the wine!" D'Ain swept his eyes across the hall. "Wine!" he called out, when he caught sight of the servant refreshing Gaston d'Aubigny's glass while he admired one of the tapestries in the corner. "Come, boy! Fetch a glass at once!"

The boy hastily finished his task with d'Aubigny, and rushed to carry out D'Ain's command. Moments later Crosseby's hand was no longer empty, and he held a glass of a fine, strong red wine from the southwest of Navarre near its border with Lizarra.

"Now then, my friend," D'Ain continued once Crosseby had been tended to his satisfaction, "I would like to introduce to you Stefan von Aich, Grand Master of the Brotherhood of the Sword, and Caspar von Bech, Master of the Longsword in Soest. Masters, I am pleased to present to you my good friend le Chevalier Stemham Crosseby de Coventry, Master of the Longsword in Ain, and the host of the playings to which you have been invited."

Crosseby bowed respectfully to the pair. Aich gave him a subtle nod of greeting — as much as he expected from a man of the Grand Master's prestige — while Bech returned his courtesy in equal measure.

"Masters, welcome to Ain," Crosseby said. "I am pleased that you saw fit to accept my invitation."

"I admit I am quite intrigued to learn more of these 'playings,' as you call them," Aich said. "This is a practice particular to the Coventrish schools of defense, if I am not mistaken."

"You are indeed correct, Master. I find it quite beneficial for the students to have an opportunity to test themselves against all manner of masters and fencers from beyond just the local school."

"And you have certainly managed quite the turnout," Bech said. He swirled his wine about his goblet as he swept his icy gaze across the hall and took in the gathering. "There are quite a few masters of some esteem who have come. Oh, and there is Guarin, also."

Crosseby chuckled softly. "Well, perhaps he will at least provide some amusement for the crowd between the more serious bouts, and without need for the additional expense of hiring a professional fool."

"I thought the followers of da Lucca were professional fools."

He quirked a grin at the remark and took a drink. It was an earthy vintage with hints of black cherry and licorice, and quite potent. "Indeed, if one were to enjoy such tedious spectacle."

"So tell me, Master," Aich asked after a swallow of his wine, "how does a Coventrish knight come to be a Master of the Longsword in Navarre?"

"That is something of a long story," Crosseby said, and his face heated a little at the question. However, before Aich could press him further, D'Ain clapped him heartily on the shoulder and laughed.

"As it should happen, I was quite displeased with the previous Master here; I learned by chance that Monsieur Crosseby was seeking employment and, knowing his quality after a personal favor he rendered to me some years ago, I turned the old fellow out and insisted Stemham come to me here in Ain."

Aich raised an eyebrow. "Surely the Navarrese guild of defense had issue with such an appointment. Particularly that of a knight of Coventry."

"Yes, yes they did," D'Ain said, then smiled around a sip of his wine. "But I am lord here in Ain and insisted. So I quieted their dissension."

"With respects, Monseigneur, I cannot imagine the guild would be so amenable to such meddling in their affairs."

If D'Ain took offense from Aich's comment he did not show it, and merely waved it off. "Bah, a generous donation convinced them otherwise."

Crosseby rolled his eyes at his patron's shameless admission of inducement, and tipped his head back to finish the rest of his wine before signing for a refill. "For my part," he said, "I care little for such politics. I would rather a scholar be free to wander and learn from whomever he may, than be beholden by charters."

"But surely you must agree that it is the guilds that ensure the consistency and quality of instruction," Bech said, taken aback.

The servant returned with the wine, and Crosseby held out his glass. "Yes, but by whose measure? What is more, I find the utter monopoly of the Schwertbrüder of the art in the Empire to be troubling. That a man such as myself cannot enter into Boehm or Žatec or Krems and teach without incurring the wrath of the Brotherhood, even in towns where they have no actual presence. Unless, of course, I were to forswear any other affiliation and petition to be admitted into the guild ..." Crosseby trailed off as a servant finished refilling his wine, and paused for a drink.

Aich scowled behind his thick beard in aversion to the criticism. "Our charter was granted to us in order to protect the art we teach within the bounds of the Empire."

"What I see it protecting is the pay of a few soldiers of the Empire, or am I mistaken that those conferred the rank of Master of the Longsword receive double the pay of those without such a title in their military service? Which, I am sure, benefits the guild greatly."

The Grand Master straightened his shoulders in indignation, and Bech's own face turned crimson at the accusation. "My foremost concern, Monsieur, is the integrity of our art. If the Empire were to allow just any man to hang out his shingle within its borders and without the approval of the guild, we would be inviting all manner of inept and unqualified instructors, and charlatans and swindlers of the worst sort to prey upon the uninformed."

"Oh, I am not arguing that the guilds do not serve their purpose, Master. But with your sole control over teaching of the sword within the Empire what you are doing is secreting knowledge away and worrying over it like a mother hen, and doling it out only to those whom you alone deem worthy, as would a petty God bestowing favors upon his lowly faithful. For where else may a man go in Boehm but to the Brotherhood for instruction in this noble art? And who, then, acts as check on the guild itself, and ensures their own competency?"

"As fascinating as I find this debate on the merits of such institutions," D'Ain said with a warning glare between the three of them when he noticed Aich's building anger, "do remember you are in my house, and I have no desire to see such a merry gathering spoiled by bickering the likes of this."

Crosseby inclined his head in contrition. "Forgive me, Monseigneur," he said, and offered another small nod to

Aich. For his part the Grand Master returned the gesture, though neither he nor Bech relaxed from their defensive posture. "Perhaps, Master, we may continue this debate another time when we might hear from all the masters on the subject. After all, 'tis not for the purposes of the playing alone that I extended my invitations, but so that we might have a dialogue among all the guilds to discuss our craft."

Aich drained the last of his wine and summoned for the boy to refill it. "Perhaps, if my time here allows it. At the very least I will be certain that Master von Bech attends on my behalf if I must decline."

Bech glanced between the two of them, though what he thought of being volunteered for such a conference he kept to himself. Crosseby, however, had little doubt that Aich would see to it that he would be called away. *The damned tyrant simply cannot abide the thought of sharing his little kingdom.*

"Well, Master, may I say that you would be most welcome to attend if that is the case," Crosseby said instead, with a polite nod to Bech, which the latter received and returned with some thinly veiled disdain.

"Of course. If my Master so commands it."

"Wonderful!" D'Ain exclaimed. "We are all friends again. I must say, Monsieur Crosseby, that I am quite looking forward to seeing how your students fare. As the esteemed Grand Master pointed out, you have certainly collected quite the gathering."

Crosseby smiled. "I am certain they will acquit themselves quite well."

"So how is it that these playings shall work, if I may ask?" Bech inquired.

"Of course, Master, and in fact I expected you would. I suppose 'twill not be all too dissimilar with the manner in which the Schwertbrüder test their students. The masters you see gathered here," he said, and swept his wineglass about in an arc to take in the gathering of fencers and masters, "will be testing and evaluating my students. Ordinarily it would be masters of the school who would judge their performance, but as I have only recently established myself in Ain I have yet to fully staff it, and for the purposes of the playings I have made an arrangement with them to assist me.

"The students must fight two bouts each against ten senior fencers, and each bout will be played to five hits. They will not fight in harness, and must test with a variety of weapons. They need not win their bouts, however, as the entire purpose of the playings is but to test their progress. If the masters deem they have demonstrated sufficient expertise they win their prize and secure promotion within the school."

Aich considered this while his wine was refreshed. "'Tis indeed not too dissimilar from the public testing our students undergo, and in fact sounds quite demanding."

"Quite so," Crosseby said with a wistful smile. "In fact, by the end of playing for my Master's prize I could barely stand, much less lift my sword. To say nothing of partaking in the celebration that followed!"

As they spoke a servant wove through the gathering and approached D'Ain to whisper something in his ear. D'Ain nodded and tossed back his wine with one great swallow. "Pardon the interruption," he said, when Crosseby finished and left him a brief opening to interject, "but I have a small matter to attend to before supper begins. As much as I have enjoyed this discussion, I must leave you now."

The three bowed deeply to him, then he departed and for a moment left them alone. However, before they could resume, a fresh voice behind Crosseby remarked, "I do hope Monsieur le Chevalier is seeing to traffic through the West Gate. The situation is deplorable!"

Crosseby turned to find himself looking over the auburn head of Loys Oger.

Oger was a man of about his age, though a half a head shorter (thus the ease by which Crosseby looked past him when he turned) and stockier in build. He kept his hair short and matched it with a neatly trimmed beard. However, his most distinctive feature was the streak of white through the hairs tracing the line of an old scar slashing his left cheek. His grey eyes quickly appraised the three of them, and he inclined his head respectfully to Aich upon recognizing his chain of rank.

"What is the matter with the West Gate?" the Grand Master asked with a curious frown. "I myself had little trouble crossing the Ain and entering from the east."

"There is some circus or other at an inn in the Northwest Quarter not too far from the main square, that is slowing traffic all the way to the Gate," Oger said, and Crosseby could not help but notice Bech's countenance darken considerably. In spite of himself, Crosseby felt his own heart skip a beat at the reminder, and he recalled the sight of the woman dancing with grace and skill through the square. "I myself could not get close enough to see what the fuss was about, but 'tis making that quarter a veritable quagmire to negotiate! It took me near to an hour to meet some friends who were arriving this afternoon."

Aich took notice of his subordinate's reaction to Oger's remarks, and eyed him closely. Bech turned to him with a scowl and said, "She is here."

The Grand Master stood back on his heels as if he were struck at Bech's remark, and his eyes darkened considerably. "You are sure of this?"

"I saw her with my own two eyes, Master," he said.

Crosseby blinked, and his breath caught in his throat in astonishment that here beneath the very roof of his patron were two men who knew of the vision he had spied in the market. He peered intently at Bech while the latter swirled his glass, and an expression of consternation, which he tried vainly to mask with a long drink of his wine, tugged at his features. "Pardon me, Monsieur," Crosseby said, and Bech met his gaze. "But you know of this woman?"

Oger frowned and looked between the three of them. "What woman? Monsieur Crosseby, do you know something of what is happening?"

"Yes, I know her," Bech said with a catch in his voice, and ignoring Oger's inquiry. He tore his eyes away from Crosseby and looked to Aich again. "She is giving demonstrations in the market, advertising to all she was a student of Soest."

Aich tightened his fingers around the stem of his glass until his knuckles turned white, and Crosseby thought it might shatter under his grip. "Why did you not tell me of this?"

Bech's face paled at the wrath in the Grand Master's voice, and even Crosseby was startled when his voice trembled with barely-restrained rage. Oger, discomfited by the display, fell back a pace and glanced at Crosseby as if seeking an answer to his question but was afraid to ask it again. Crosseby merely shrugged in confusion.

"Forgive me, Master," Bech said, "I intended to address the matter with you earlier, but the streets were so crowded that by the time I reached the lodgings you had already departed for the castle. I then thought to address you privately after supper, as I felt it best not to trouble you with it here."

"Well, now I am troubled with it!" he snapped, and a hush slowly spread across the crowd in response to the outburst. "And you tell me now that she is here, and prancing before the churls in the streets like a common wag?"

"Forgive me, Master," Oger said, "but what woman is this?"

Aich rounded on him and his dark eyes flared dangerously, but before he could utter another word a bell sounded to summon the gathering to their seats. The two Schwertbrüder turned and headed for their table without giving Oger an answer, and he stared after them in bewilderment. For a moment he and Oger remained where they stood and watched them go, while the rest of the crowd slowly filed around them to find their seats.

"Now that was peculiar," Oger murmured, and rubbed the back of his head.

"Indeed! Our good visitors from Boehm seemed quite put out about that curious creature in the square."

"Which brings me back to my question, Monsieur: What damned woman are you talking about?"

Crosseby chuckled, clapped a hand on Oger's shoulder, and guided him after the rest of the crowd to find their assigned places at D'Ain's table. "Quite a remarkable one, though I saw her only for a moment. Let me tell you what I know ..."

Crosseby glanced towards Bech on his way to the table. He could not put the thought of that brief vision of her from his mind.

ROSSEBY FOUND HIMSELF UTTERLY INCAPABLE OF focusing his attention on supper that night. He was invited to sit at the high table in accordance with his role in the proceedings to follow over the next week. Though he talked and laughed politely with the guests, and answered questions from those whom, like the Schwertbrüder, were unfamiliar with the practice of the playings, Crosseby's thoughts ever returned to the woman from the market. As much of the night was spent in banal discourse on swordcraft — the usual disagreements upon the best attacks and counters, questions on the meanings of a manuscript written by a master a century dead, bickering over how long a sword ought to be, or the delineating of territory between the guilds — Crosseby found his thoughts drifting more and more as the night wore on.

The Schwertbrüder conversed mostly in hushed tones between themselves, though at times some angry word or other from Aich rattled the hall and made his subordinate flinch. There were stretches in which they paused in their private discourse to join the flow of the conversation around them, though they politely refrained from sharing the guild's perspectives on the various debates on their shared art. Otherwise they remained content to speak on their own business.

Supper stretched on, though Crosseby paid little heed and could scarce recall the minutiae of what was discussed that night until, as the hour grew late, the guests of D'Ain slowly broke up and departed for their own lodgings. Aich retired early, leaving Bech alone to represent him for much of supper. Crosseby watched him brusquely deflect attempts by Ruiz and Guarin to engage him in conversation for some time, though neither man appeared to think much of his reticence, and soon moved on to pestering Oger to settle whatever debate they were holding.

Finally, Bech drained the last of his wine and politely excused himself, and headed for the screens passage. With his own responsibilities for the evening's entertainment concluded, Crosseby begged his own leave and, dodging a few attempts to draw him into some private debate or other among the knots of people still loitering in the hall, hastily set off in pursuit of Bech.

"Master!" he called when Bech reached the screens passage and turned for the door leading out into the bailey. "Pardon me, Master von Bech!"

Bech had just reached the doors when he realized that it was he Crosseby addressed, and paused with strained politeness for him to catch up. "I am sorry to depart in such a hurry, Master Crosseby," Bech said with a contrite bow. "But the hour is late and the road was long today."

"If you please, Master," Crosseby said, "I wished to speak with you privately a moment."

From the look Bech gave him Crosseby thought he might well have sprouted a second head upon his shoulders, but after half a moment of deliberation he inclined his head and motioned for the door. The guards standing sentinel opened it wide, and together they stepped out into the night.

Castle Ain was a massive concentric castle of two curtain walls enclosing its inner and outer baileys. The inner enceinte rose twice the height of the outer, and both were further defended by fortified towers. Most space within the inner bailey was given over to storehouses, barracks, and guest houses, with a large lawn of grass surrounding the great hall itself. During daylight it would be a marvel of white stone rising from the green grass of the bailey, but now its walls were no more than a black void against the deep indigo of the night sky, rising from a silver sea rippling in a gentle breeze under the starlight.

It was a cool autumn evening, with a fresh breeze out of the fields and woodlands to the southwest. They stepped together down the short flight of steps from the entrance to the hall, and onto a broad cobbled path which led towards the castle gates. The fresh scent of turf mingled with the crispness of autumn, and provided a welcome respite from the confines of the great hall. The bailey was lit only by the light of the stars and a few torches set in iron brackets along the walls, leaving much of it blanketed in deep shadow.

They walked in silence for some moments while Crosseby ordered his thoughts.

"Is there something you needed of me, Master Crosseby?" Bech finally asked in a voice colored by mild annoyance. Though Crosseby could see little of his features, shadowed as they were in the dim light of the bailey, he could nonetheless feel a sense of haughty disdain for the delay as they walked.

"There was something I wished to ask of you, if 'tis no trouble," Crosseby said.

"'Twould depend on the nature of the question, and though I may regret the asking; What may I do for you?"

Crosseby regarded Bech with displeasure over the rudeness of his response, but said nothing of it. "I assure you, Master, 'tis no great matter. But as I understand it you have some familiarity with the woman who was performing in the streets this afternoon. I myself only saw her from something of a distance, but I am nonetheless intrigued and had hoped you might tell me more about her."

Bech nearly missed a step. "I would suggest you not inquire too closely," he growled. "I know not what your intentions are, but I warn you against meddling with the Brotherhood's private matters."

"You see, that is one thing I find curious; you say she calls herself a student of Soest, whom I can only assume means Master Paulus von Soest."

The other sighed heavily. His shoulders slumped, and he pinched the bridge of his nose in aggravation. "That woman is a troublemaker, Master, and I suggest you stay clear of her."

Crosseby chuckled and folded his hands at the small of his back. "Indeed? For her to so trouble the Schwertbrüder I must confess only piques my curiosity."

Bech glared at him, but, mindful of the guards patrolling the grounds, restrained himself from harsh words he might regret, and fell into silence as they drew nearer to their destination.

Against the inside of the inner wall of the castle, and nearest its heavily fortified gatehouse, stood a stable for the keeping of horses for the castle's couriers, and here the freshness of the night air was replaced by the fouler odor of manure and the moldering straw scattered about the floor. A figure emerged from the shadow of the stables to meet them upon their approach, and Crosseby greeted him with a raised hand.

"Have my and Master von Bech's horses brought out, we shall be returning to the City," he said to the stablehand.

"At once, Monsieur!" the boy said upon recognizing him, and bowed deeply before scurrying off to see to his task.

Crosseby leaned casually against the wall of the stable and folded his arms across his chest while he studied Bech. The other man visibly chafed with impatience to be away from the castle, and for this conversation to be done with.

"So, who is she, then?" Crosseby pressed, when Bech gave no indication of continuing his tale.

Bech sighed in resignation. "Her name is Elsabeth. She is one of your countrywomen, from Hereford if I recall rightly."

"She is quite a ways from home then."

"As are you, Master," Bech said.

Crosseby chuckled again. "Indeed. So how does she come to be demonstrating in a market in Ain?"

"How she came here I cannot say, nor do I care, except to find with some regret that she is still alive after last I saw her. Her father was a knight of Coventry, though what his name might be I could not tell you, nor do I care much to know of him, either. All I do know is that he made some arrangement with Master von Soest to teach his daughter the sword, and so he took her on as a private student."

"She is not a part of the guild, then?"

Bech bristled at that suggestion. "Of course not! She trained in his school, and as Vorfechter under the Master I was at times required to instruct her in his stead when he was unavailable, but the arrangement was always a private one. Elsewise I imagine the Grand Master would never have allowed it. If only that were the case."

Crosseby regarded Bech with a raised eyebrow and a frown. "And why is that?"

"That woman was never more than a disruption, and in the end the Master forfeited his life on her account."

He blinked in surprise, astounded by the bitterness in Bech's voice, but also at the unexpected answer to the oft asked question of the final fate of Paulus von Soest. Crosseby, of course, had heard the rumors, but nothing more than what he had dismissed as the fancies of minstrels. However, any further musing on that part of the tale was ended when the stablehand returned leading two fine coursers by the bridle. Bech's animal was tall and black, and stood with its head raised with much the same sort of arrogance as his master. Crosseby's own horse was of no less stature, but his coat was a rich bay.

"Now if you are finished pestering me with such vexing gossip, Master, I shall take my leave of you," Bech continued as he took hold of his horse and led him away from the stables towards the open gate. He paused and turned back momentarily, and from his rigid posture Crosseby could imagine the glare on his shadowed features. "I'll leave you at least with this word of advice, as clearly you have some foolishness in mind: Forget that woman even exists. I cannot imagine why she is here in Ain to begin with, but I would even suggest you have Monsieur D'Ain expel her. Now good night!"

And with that, Bech swung himself into the saddle and started off into the night. Crosseby shook off his surprise at the contempt dripping from the man's voice throughout their conversation, and wistfully repeated the woman's name over and over again in his mind as he walked his horse out through the inner gates and into the outer bailey.

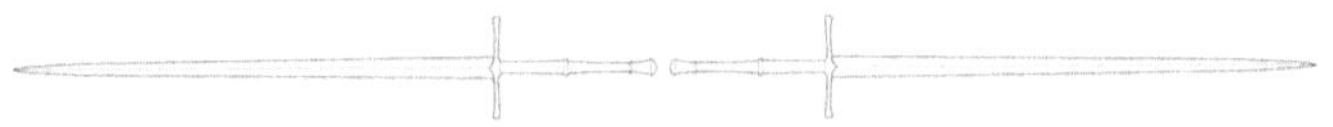

CROSSEBY MADE HIS HOME IN A COMPLEX IN the Northeast Quarter of Ain not far from the main square. A large building housing his school stood on the eastern end of the complex, with his living space — itself a veritable palace — occupying much of the western side. Both structures dominated this part of Ain. They rose in multiple stories above the street, with towers lending the whole of the complex a martial quality that he found most suitable for the purpose of the building. A modest stable with room enough for several horses was tucked away in the southeast corner, and this was connected to a small carriage house with an entrance opening out onto the street. Open-air arcades linked all the buildings together and encircled a large garden courtyard at the heart of the complex. Rows upon rows of windows gazed out onto the street and gardens.

By the time he returned from the castle it was well past midnight, and the streets of the sleeping city were silent and empty. Lamps created isolated islands of golden light in a sea of darkness, and aided the night watch while they made their rounds to discourage thieves and other troublemakers still abroad. Or at least confine them to the poorer neighborhoods where some more disreputable business was still being done.

Crosseby guided his horse through one of the large archways in the arcaded walkway along the southern side of the complex and entered the courtyard. He was met there by the night guard, who bowed deeply upon recognizing him, and called for a stablehand. A bleary-eyed youth stifled a yawn as he emerged from the stables, but snapped suddenly to alertness when he became aware the master of the house had returned. The boy took hold of Crosseby's horse after he dismounted, then led the animal inside to put up the harness and secure him for the night. Crosseby then turned up the arcade for a side door of the house and made his way inside, closing out the night behind him.

It was dark inside the foyer, though a few lamps elsewhere provided just enough light for him to see by. Most of the staff by this hour would be asleep, but one he knew was likely still awake. Sure enough, he heard the treading of feet on the hardwood floors almost as soon as he stepped inside, and Richard's familiar figure emerged from the hall, silhouetted by the light of the lamps flickering dimly behind him.

"Is that you, Sire?" he asked.

"Ah! Good evening, Richard," Crosseby said, and started for the hall beyond him. Richard fell into step at his shoulder and accompanied him into the screens passage, and then the dimly-lit great hall beyond. "The staff did not get up to any mischief while I was out, did they?"

"No, Sire, it was in fact rather quiet tonight, considering the excitement in the rest of the city."

"I imagine. I am sure the inns are full to bursting with all the visitors come for the playings."

"May I ask how supper with his Lordship went?"

"Quite enlightening, actually. And in fact, I was hoping you would still be up and lurking about awaiting my return. I have a task for you tomorrow."

"Yes, Sire?"

"Come with me, please."

Whatever curiosity Richard had as to the nature of the task he did not ask, and merely followed Crosseby through the great hall in obedient silence, up the dais at the northern end, and through the doors leading to his private living areas. He paused only long enough for Richard to fetch a lamp and light the way into the darkened study beyond.

There was little to see in the darkness of the study. The windows of the triforium and clerestory along the outer wall on his right allowed in a pale silver light, but the ribbed arches of the ceiling were lost in the shadows above. The colors of the chamber were washed out in shades of grey, except for where the circle of golden light from Richard's lamp rolled back the night clinging thickly to the interior space. Polished parquet flooring glowed beneath the lamplight, and the bookshelves lining the walls stood out as vague shadows against the surrounding gloom. Crosseby made his way to a secluded corner of the chamber where his ornately carved oaken desk stood beneath a large arcade window looking out onto the courtyard.

Crosseby slipped around the desk and settled himself in the padded leather chair between the desk and the window. He rummaged through the stack of papers on his desk until he found a blank sheet of parchment, took a quill pen in hand, and scratched out a short note. He signed it with a flourish, and neatly folded it once the ink dried. Crosseby then lit a sealing wax candle on the flame from the lamp and sealed his letter.

"The woman we saw at the inn this afternoon goes by the name of Elsabeth Hereford. Tomorrow morning take her this letter with my compliments. See to it that 'tis delivered directly into her hands, or, if necessary, read it to her." Crosseby handed Richard the letter, and his servant tucked it securely away inside his doublet.

"If she has already moved on from the inn?"

"If she is still in Ain, find her. I cannot imagine that would be a difficult task considering the spectacle she made of herself. If she has already left the City ..." Crosseby sighed and leaned his head on his fist. That she might have only come to Ain long enough to earn a few *deniers* giving demonstrations in the street before departing again was a thought that had not occurred to him. "If she has, then I think I shall feel as a man lost in the desert allowed only a distant glimpse of water."

"Is there anything else you need of me tonight, Sire?"

Crosseby waved him off. "No. No, go on and get some sleep, there is nothing more I require of you tonight. But do see that I am awoken at first light. I have much yet to do to finish the preparations for the playings and will need an early start."

Richard inclined his head, then turned and retreated from the study, leaving Crosseby alone in the light of the lamp. His imagination ran wild with thoughts of the strange woman dancing in the streets.

HE AWOKE TO THE SENSATION OF something tickling the back of her neck.

Elsabeth moaned softly, and as her eyes slowly fluttered open she found herself lying naked on her stomach, with her face buried in a pillow. A dense fog clung tenaciously to her senses, and her head throbbed fiercely in a steady rhythm. How precisely she got here and in this state of undress she could not recall. In fact, nothing from the moment she and Hieronymus retreated to the common room after the afternoon spent demonstrating for the crowds until now could claw its way back from the dark, ale-drowned recesses of her memory.

The tickling continued. As she slowly shook off the haze of her drunken stupor, she was conscious of an arm wrapped around her waist, and a weight settling across her back. Lips slowly glided down the side of her neck towards the ball of her shoulder, and half dreading the sight that awaited her, Elsabeth rolled herself onto her back. The handsome face looking down on her came as some relief, as it was far from the worst sight she had awoken to.

"Good morning," the man said, in what sounded to her befuddled mind as Navarrese.

Elsabeth murmured something that might have been a response to the greeting, and threw an arm across her face to shield herself from the sunlight streaming through the shutters covering the window. It may as well have been the light of the Lord of All himself beaming straight into her eyes. In fact, she was not quite sure it was not God gazing down on her in disapproval, as if the pounding in her temples and the queasy churning in her belly were not punishment enough for the past evening's raucousness. Her erstwhile bedmate seemed to pay no mind to her current state, and lowered himself over her to resume nibbling at her neck, while taking a handful of her breast. Elsabeth rolled away from him so she could gather the twisted and half-discarded blankets to recover her modesty, and slowly sat upright.

She instantly regretted the change in posture when a fresh spike of concentrated agony lanced through her skull. It worked its way up the back of her neck, and around to the space between her eyes. Her stomach danced like a fool turning somersaults within her belly, and whatever she had to eat and drink — almost certainly mostly the latter — the night before threatened to claw its way back up her throat again.

"This is not my room," she slurred. The blade spearing through her brains slowly withdrew, but twisted a bit as it went to ensure her a few more moments of anguish. The fog tenaciously clinging to the nooks and crannies of her consciousness slowly evaporated along with it.

"Nor is it mine," he said, not the least bit troubled at the thought. "Someone must be rather put out, as there was no one else with us last night."

She groaned and pinched the bridge of her nose. "That comes as small comfort, love."

The man chuckled and lifted the hair away from the back of her neck to kiss her again. Elsabeth twisted away from him, and that drew a frown to his features. "Is something the matter?"

"Only that I cannot remember a moment of last night, and not at all who you are."

"You wound me," he said, with a pout. "And after what pleasures you and I shared last night!" He stretched himself out on the bed next to her, and Elsabeth colored a little when she saw that, whatever they had gotten up to the night before, he was clearly anticipating a continuation of their escapades.

"Do not take it so closely to the heart, love. This is hardly the first time I have awoken in such circumstances." Elsabeth gave him a small grin and took advantage of his posture to appraise him better now that her initial embarrassment had passed. His figure was as handsome as his face; about her height, hale, and he had much to take pride in. "Though I have certainly awoken to worse."

"I particularly enjoyed our little game of me playing the lute while you played my shawm."

Elsabeth's face heated a little more.

"And who was the winner?"

He sat up, still shameless in his state of undress, and leaned in close to steal a kiss. "You, of course. I did not even make it through the first chorus before I missed a note on your account."

"I do have my special talents," Elsabeth said, and leaned back into him to draw him into a slow, lingering kiss. She let the blanket clutched to her chest fall, and he ran his hand from the side of her face and down her neck, until once more he gently took her breast in his hand.

"Indeed, and I shall even compose an ode to your prowess," he breathed when their lips parted, then began to kiss his way down her neck to her chest.

Elsabeth gasped softly, and the throbbing between her temples was momentarily forgotten at the touch of his lips on more sensitive areas. "I seem to collect more and more of those at every inn I visit ..."

He was just beginning to roll her beneath him when the sound of something hard striking the door shattered the moment and skewered her head on red-hot pokers. Four sharp raps echoed across the room, and Elsabeth moaned in agony and clutched the sides of her head.

"Bugger," she mewled softly.

When neither of them answered, the door was flung wide open, and Hieronymus strolled in with his staff in hand.

"I beg your pardon, Brother!" her bedmate snarled in indignation at the intrusion. He immediately clambered out of bed and stepped around to shield her from view, unashamed at his own nakedness in front of the friar.

Hieronymus showed no indication of embarrassment at the sight, and merely peered around him to address her.

"Ah! There you are, Tetty!" he said, much too loudly for her liking, and his voice twisted the pokers jabbing her in the brain. "For God's sake, girl, 'tis nigh on midmorning and here you are still lying about engaged in the Lord of All knows what manner of debauchery!"

Elsabeth hastily snatched up the blankets to cover her breast and raised herself up on her elbows. "What are you doing in here?" she snapped, and instantly regretted her raised voice. She squeezed her eyes shut against the pain in her head.

"I could ask the same of you, my dear, but, seeing as this is the nearest unoccupied lodging to the common room, I think I can piece together the entire sordid tale on my own." He eyed her bedmate — who thanks to the interruption was clearly no longer up to resuming the tryst — with equal measures of disgust and what was doubtlessly envy. "Clearly in your eagerness to debase yourself with this villain you could not wait to get him back to your own room, so dragged him into the first empty one you could find."

The man bristled, and his face turned red at the insult. "I am not one to strike a man of the Wheel, Brother, but you are sorely testing my patience!"

Hieronymus disregarded him with a wave of his hand. "Do not trouble me with idle threats, my son, particularly when your shortcomings are so clearly on display. I am twice and then some the man you are."

Elsabeth glared at him. "Get out!"

He turned his attention back to her and impatiently thumped his staff on the wooden floor. She felt each dull *thud* beginning somewhere in her teeth before it wound its way around her neck again. "Now, now, my dear, this entire scheme we have in Ain was your idea! I am merely trying to keep your mind to the task at hand!"

She scowled and raised one hand towards the door. "Out!"

Hieronymus met her eyes and Elsabeth glared back. Finally, he muttered an oath under his breath, made the sign of the Wheel, then spun around and stormed from the room. He slammed the door shut behind him, and Elsabeth's skull threatened to explode along with it. She mopped her face and let out a moan of exasperation. The bed shifted as her companion seated himself beside her.

"Please forgive him," she murmured, "he knows not what he does."

"I had half a mind to teach him some manners," he said.

"In all honesty, had you done so I would have been left to carry you back to your room unconscious; though he may not look it he is not a man to be trifled with."

He scooped up her hand and gave it a kiss. "Whyever do you travel with that lout?"

"That, love, is a question I ask myself every day. Sometimes more than once." She heaved a sigh. "Unfortunately, I must confess he is also right; as much as I would love to sleep the rest of last night off, among engaging in other more enjoyable distractions that have come to mind, I have work to do today. But I plan to be at the inn a few days more ..."

"Alas I was due to move on this morning," he said. "It seems that this is where we must part."

Elsabeth made a show of slumping her shoulders in disappointment. "A pity, as I would have rather enjoyed another round, particularly now that my head has cleared enough that I would remember it."

He quirked a grin and gave her a final kiss on the lips before he left the bed to gather up his discarded clothes. "Then I shall have to remember it for both of us, and perhaps we will meet again on the road someday."

"As much as I would like otherwise, I learned long ago not to hold out hope on such agreements."

AS BAD AS ELSABETH FOUND THE THIN SHAFTS OF light through the shutters of the room, the lamplight out in the hall was all but blinding, and she shielded her eyes and lay a steadying hand to the wall as she made her way down the stairs to the common room.

It was well into the morning and the room was largely deserted. This came as some relief since it meant the ambience was subdued, though it was even brighter there than the hallway. Hieronymus sat alone at a table in the far corner, gorging himself on a breakfast of buttered bread and eggs, with a mug of small beer at his elbow. His staff was propped against the table beside him, and Elsabeth felt an overwhelming urge to smash it over his head.

Instead, she quietly stumbled across the common room, half-blinded by the light of the Lord of All himself seeking to sear the morning onto her brain, and dropped heavily into a chair across from him with her back against the wall. A sudden churning in her belly accompanied her swimming head, and she promptly folded her arms on the table in front of her and buried her face in the crook of her elbow.

"Well, I am pleased you decided to join me, Tetty," Hieronymus said around a mouthful of eggs, a little too loudly for her liking. "You certainly seemed to enjoy yourself in abundance last night."

"Oh shut up," she murmured into her elbow.

Hieronymus chuckled softly. "This, my dear, is why God preaches temperance and moderation. Here I am, having restrained myself from such shameless overindulgence, bright and ready to face the day. A lesson you could do well to learn."

Elsabeth raised her head from her arms. She instantly regretted the shifting of her position, but there was no other means by which she might spit him with the glare she had worked up.

"And just how many times have I had to drag Your Immensity to his room for the night — fending off, I might add, all manner of assaults upon my intimate places because you cannot keep your bloody hands to yourself — after I have found you lying unconscious on a tavern floor after a night of 'temperance?' I swear that on your dying day, if you were to arrive at the gates of Heaven and find that there was not a drop of ale to be had, you would gladly bid your farewells to the Lord of All and march your fat arse right down to the Underworld!"

He responded with an indignant grunt and a scowl. "My word but you are testy this morning!"

"Love, the only reason I don't break that staff in twain over your fat head and insert both pieces sideways somewhere so uncomfortable you will never be able to mount a stool at any tavern ever again is because 'tis all I can manage to not leave last night's supper all over the table!"

Elsabeth moaned at the fresh stab of pain in her head from the outburst and mopped her face with one hand. "God. The master of the house does not know where I might find a couple eels and some almonds, does he?"

Hieronymus twisted his lip in disgust. "Why in God's name would you ask for such a thing?"

"'Tis something my father always asked for the morning after a long night of carousing, of which there were many. Chopped eel garnished with bitter almond."

"Bah! My dear girl, that is nothing but folk tales and nonsense," Hieronymus said, and sniffed contemptuously.

Elsabeth narrowed her eyes. "If you have a suggestion, love, I am listening. Otherwise, I am in no mood for your blathering."

"Well, then we shall have to do something about that, shan't we?"

Hieronymus called loudly for the serving girl — a young lass of about fifteen summers whom she recalled was the master of the house's niece — and the sudden piercing sound of his whistle sent a fresh spike of pain racing from her sinuses back down her spine. Elsabeth squeezed her eyes shut tight, pressed her palms to her temples in a desperate effort to keep the demon bashing against the inside of her skull contained, and let out a soft moan of agony.

The girl hastened to their side and inclined her head politely upon reaching the table. "Is there something more you needed of me, Brother?" she asked, in passable Boehman.

"Yes, my dear," he said. "If you would be so kind as to bring my companion here a tankard with two eggs — not beaten as the yolks must remain hole — added to a mixture of one part broth made from boiled cabbage — the older the better — one part the brine having been used to pickle herring — and in fact, a plate of rollmops to go with it — and one part bacon grease."

Elsabeth's stomach threatened to turn itself inside out as he rattled off the ingredients, and the serving girl's face likewise turned a peculiar shade of green. But nonetheless she inclined her head and hurried off to carry out the request.

"What in God's name are you intending to poison me with?"

"Poison?" Hieronymus barked in indignation, and the sharpness of the rebuke made her head spin. "My dear girl, you are about to benefit from a secret handed down by the most learned of my Order, devised for those times when we have tested the fruits of our brewing with an excess of enthusiasm. I guarantee 'twill relieve you of your surfeit."

She mopped her face. "Oh, I am sure your Order has devised any number of illicit concoctions, but this sounds absolutely vile!"

He harrumphed, crossed his arms across his chest, and slumped in his chair with a pout. "My dear Tetty, have I ever once led you astray?"

"I hope you don't expect a serious answer to that question."

"Impossible girl!" he snapped, and Elsabeth winced as his pique attempted to drive the spike drilling down to unleash the demon pent up inside her head even deeper into the skull. "I am sharing with you one of the most closely-guarded secrets of my Order — the result of generations of labor and experimentation — and there you sit profaning my sincere offer with doubt, and no small measure of derision!"

"All right! All right!" Elsabeth interjected, loudly enough to instantly regret it. She hung her head in her hands and sighed heavily. "If you swear 'twill help, then fine! I will try your remedy."

Hieronymus quickly made the sign of the wheel. "I swear on my own solemn vows, drink this and the fog will be lifted from your mind."

She eyed him from beneath her fingers while she massaged her temples with her thumbs. "You are not exactly filling me with confidence."

Any retort died on his lips when the serving girl returned with a platter of rollmops, and a tankard filled near to the brim with as horrid-looking a draught as the most unspeakable sort of witches' brew sung of in minstrels' tales.

The two egg yolks floating on the murky surface stared at her like the eyes of some beast lurking beneath, and the whole thing smelled as fetid as a privy shaft. Their server's face was nearly the same shade of green as the lethal mélange, and she hastily bolted from the table as soon as she placed both platter and tankard in front of her. Elsabeth's stomach lurched at the sight and smell of the rollmops and Hieronymus's remedy, and she felt her bile threatening to rise up in her throat.

Elsabeth pressed one hand to her belly and the other to her mouth. "Oh dear Lord of All. I am beginning to have second thoughts."

"Go on, my dear, drink! And last night's misadventure will be forgotten!"

She eyed him carefully, looking for the hidden smirk of amusement that would warn her this was all some cruel jest at her expense, but Hieronymus was wearing his minister's face, and she was unable to conclude whether or not he was sincere. Elsabeth sighed and lifted the tankard. She moaned in disgust at the stench of its contents.

"Oh, and one more word, Tetty; it must be drunk all in one swallow lest it lose its potency."

"Of course it must."

Elsabeth hesitated a moment, then tipped her head back and swallowed. The egg yolks slid down whole in a briny, syrupy mass, but the concoction never made it all the way down; no sooner did it pass the back of her throat then she gagged and her stomach heaved in disgust. She scrambled to her feet and bolted for the door, but made it no more than a few steps before she collapsed to her knees and Hieronymus's remedy worked its way back up whence it came and splattered wetly onto the floor (the eggs by some strange miracle still intact). Her belly churned and rumbled, and everything she imbibed the day before quickly followed as her stomach voided its contents in protest of the loathsome potion she attempted to slip down her gullet.

She hacked and coughed, and her body heaved dryly for some moments more, though there was no longer anything in her stomach to expel. Elsabeth heard the thudding of boots on the wooden floors as their server and her uncle rushed into the common room at the sound of her retching, and she felt Hieronymus at her side pulling her hair back from her face to keep it out of the slowly expanding slimy puddle.

"Easy, girl, easy," he said, his voice lowered to his most soothing priestly drone. "Good, get it all out."

Elsabeth gagged and coughed again. "Oh you bastard ..."

"There now, feeling better?"

"You should be running right now."

Hieronymus just chuckled, and gently patted her between the shoulder blades. Elsabeth took little comfort in his declining to take advantage of the undignified posture in which she found herself. "Come now, Tetty, at least now you can worry about something other than a little headache!"

Elsabeth just spat the last bit of bile from her mouth, and wiped her face off on her sleeve.

ASPAR RODE AT THE GRAND MASTER'S side as they wove through the streets of Ain. Aich eschewed his formal robes of office in favor of a nondescript doublet and hose, with his longsword hung from his saddle. They made their way towards the Northwest Quarter of the City, and the inn where he had witnessed Elsabeth playing to the crowds the day before.

Rumor of the exhibition had spread like fire through dry grass across the City. By morning every inn and tavern in Ain was filled with curious travelers begging for news from those who professed to have seen her the day before, until it nearly rivaled the talk of the playings set to begin within the next few days. Aich received the tales with his lips twisted into a scowl, and demanded he be taken to where Elsabeth was practicing her craft. He spotted several of the other masters who had responded to Crosseby's invitation also picking their way through the crowd, either on horse or by foot, in the same general direction. Clearly they, too, were driven by curiosity to see the truth of these rumors for themselves.

The morning was warm and the sun was bright, but the pleasantness of the weather did little to lift Caspar's mood as he and Aich slipped through the crowds of merchants, tradesmen, and other common refuse drawn to Ain for work or the market. Here and there were fencers of diverse ages and quality of cloth and equipment, and Caspar twisted his lip disdainfully at what were little better than common thugs and street brawlers of no formal discipline, come to witness or even participate in the playings. Most were sorts that the Brotherhood would have turned out on their ears had they come knocking on the doors of one of the Guild's halls, but here they sought the chance to enroll for formal study. Caspar could only sneer at such audacity.

*This is truly a failing of this Coventrish tradition; to encourage such rabble to beg at their Masters' doors.*

As on the day before, the flow of traffic soon slowed to a crawl when he and the Grand Master neared the place where Elsabeth set herself up to play before the crowd. The mob pressed forward; most were unaware of what was holding up their progress and were eager to be on their way, while still others sought to find their way to the front of the pack to observe the demonstration. Those on horseback — himself and Aich among them — found forcing their way through the wall of pedestrians ahead of them a much simpler task, and soon carved a path through those making their way by foot.

The sharp rapping of wasters punctuated the low background drone of the crowd as Caspar and Aich forced their way nearer to the market at the end of the street. They passed merchant stalls and storefronts, and knots of locals gathered at corners to idly chat and watch the flow of foreign traffic making its way through the City streets. Soon they drew near enough to the front ranks of curious onlookers to see the spectacle for themselves.

The pair had set up in front of the inn once more, and Elsabeth leaned casually on one of the wasters while her squat companion gesticulated towards the crowd, the black mantle of the Olivian order he wore starkly at odds with the busker's flamboyance with which he addressed the crowd. The woman herself was dressed in men's fashion: a red velvet doublet and woolen hose in a pale golden color hugging the shape of her legs in a most obscene manner, with a broad-brimmed hat of black felt pinned up on one side perched atop her head at a rakish angle. Caspar scowled in disgust at the sight of her, and Aich's own lip twisted. It was the first time the Grand Master had himself laid eyes upon the woman, and his displeasure was evident on his features.

"That is her?" he asked?

"Yes, Master," Caspar said.

Aich's dark eyes studied her closely, and his frown of disapproval deepened. "What can you tell me of her companion?"

"Nothing, I am afraid," Caspar admitted. "The man is unknown to me, though as you can see he wears the garb of an Olivian friar. 'Tis more than six years since she fled Soest. She might have taken up with him at any time since then."

Aich sat silently astride his horse for some moments and watched the friar's gesticulations towards the crowd. Caspar thought he heard his voice rising among the babble, but he could make no sense of it.

"What is he saying?" Aich asked.

"I cannot hear from this distance," Caspar said, "but I suspect 'tis much the same as yesterday."

"Come, let us move closer, then. I want to hear what is being said for myself."

And with that, Aich pressed forward once more, his great horse pushing aside the people in front of him. Caspar followed in the opening left in his wake. After a good deal more shoving and cajoling, they finally neared the front of the audience gathered in the market square, and came close enough to hear the friar's words for themselves.

"...yes, my children," the friar was saying, "this lovely creature standing before you is indeed a student of the great Paulus von Soest, and the only woman in creation formally trained in the deadly arts of the Brotherhood of the Sword! Who among you would test yourself against her?"

Aich's eyes narrowed upon hearing the challenge, and Caspar's mouth fell open in disbelief. "What madness is this?"

Caspar glanced aside to the Grand Master, and his belly knotted itself at the silent and angry consternation twisting his features. "Master, I assure you I—"

"Be silent!" Aich snapped, and raised a warning hand.

Caspar turned his attention back to the demonstration. No one dared step forward to answer the challenge. No matter whether their audience believed the friar's assertions, no man among them was willing to risk the emasculation that would follow should he be bested by a woman, even during a sparring match at wasters.

"Surely there is some man among you with the courage to accept the challenge, and this rare opportunity!" the friar continued, and hefted one of the wasters in his hand. This time Caspar heard the sound of voices from one end of the square, and he and Aich craned their necks to follow the commotion to its source. A small knot of men — among them several students of Simon de Craon and Loys Oger — squabbled among themselves. From his vantage at this distance, Caspar could not hear what was said, but when one of their number was thrust forward into the square — his youthful features twisted up in vexation while gesturing angrily at his companion — he concluded the lad had been pressured and shamed by his comrades into accepting the challenge.

The crowd rumbled in amusement as the youth strolled towards the pair with an exaggerated swagger, and made a show of depositing a coin in the bowl at the friar's feet.

"My children, we have a challenger!" he pronounced to the delight of the crowd, and handed over the waster in his hand. "The play shall be to the touch. Do you wish to make a wager on the outcome, my brave son? For each successful touch you make you shall win double your stake!"

His audience answered for him, their voices rising in laughing encouragement and all but demanding the youth accept the terms. Loudest of all were the comrades who had cajoled him into coming forward to begin with. They hooted and taunted him until, with his face turning a brilliant shade of crimson, he turned to the friar. "I wager five *deniers* for every touch she makes," he said. "And I think that generous, for I intend to prove your claims are false!"

Caspar's lip twisted into a scowl. "So that is what the quarrel was about: The fool did not believe the tale and his comrades insisted he make good his accusations," he mused under his breath. Aich regarded him solemnly for a moment before returning his attention to the square without a word.

Elsabeth and her opponent stepped away from the inn and into the open space prepared for them in the market square. A hush fell over the crowd as they took their positions.

"Lay on!" the friar cried, and the clack of wasters split the air as Elsabeth laid in to her opponent. The first bout lasted no more than two strokes before she landed a solid touch against her opponent's shoulder — as much because her adversary was so certain of the demonstrations being a sham he did not commit himself fully to the bout as to her skill — and the assembly howled its delight.

"That was no hit!" the youth protested over the roar of the crowd, and he drew a few jeers from the front row who had clearly seen it for themselves.

Elsabeth did not say a word. She merely took up her position again in *pflug*, and awaited the sign of her accomplice in this farce to begin again. Her opponent acquitted himself much better this time, but Caspar knew too well he was still overmatched. Nonetheless he made it to four strokes before she slipped the point of her waster under his guard and struck him beneath the wrist. Again the audience bayed, and again the youth insisted that she had not landed a blow.

This time her annoyance was evident on her features while she reset, and more of the crowd murmured their displeasure; most of the churls pressing inwards like sheep to fill the market cared little for the intricacies of the art, and watched only for the rare spectacle of seeing a woman fight.

Her adversary casting fair play aside spoiled the sport of the event. The practitioners, however, watched with concern, (aside from the companions of Elsabeth's hapless opponent, who delighted in seeing him so emasculated) and Caspar frowned as well. He knew how this would play out.

The third time the youth attacked even before the friar could finish signaling for them to begin, and launched into an aggressive series of blows that Elsabeth effortlessly defended. But she changed her strategy, now, and rather than pressing into him she darted around his attacks, not in the exaggerated manner of Russdorfer or da Lucca intended for just such an audience as this, but every cut was clean, short, and quick, just enough to cheat her adversary of a blow, and opening him up for a counter which never came. Her purpose this time was not just to land a touch against his body, but to strike at his esteem.

Caspar took his eyes away from the spectacle to search the crowd. He spied Morelet and Gaude in one corner of the market astride their horses, with a small group of their students arrayed around them. Del Brun stood with d'Aubigny, da Pavia, and d'Orgremont, and Ruiz watched alone while nibbling on a pastry from a nearby vendor. All saw what he already knew: she was toying with her opponent in retaliation for his behavior, and her skill likely matched their own. But the crowd digested the performance with glee, and as the exchange drew on their excitement whipped into a frenzy. Caspar heard wagers being shouted back and forth, and voices rose in encouragement. The sharp *rap* of the wasters kissing with each blow pierced through the deeper roar of the crowd, punctuated every now and again by the grunts of the combatants.

Elsabeth was almost casual in her defense setting aside blow after blow, every step and movement effortless, and that only agitated her adversary more. His attacks soon became wild and sloppy as he hammered against her waster. Finally, when she wearied of her sport, Elsabeth made her move to decide the action.

The youth overextended on a powerful downward strike at her left shoulder, and Elsabeth met him in a bind. He tried to muscle through her defense, so she turned her waster in her hand and dropped her point. His blade slipped harmlessly off to the side, while his momentum carried him forward and right into her waiting pommel. She allowed him to do all her work for her as she drove her pommel into his teeth, and a shark crack split the air, followed by an audible and distressed groan from the crowd at the blood arcing from the youth's mouth. The impact lifted him from his feet and into the air, and he landed hard on his back with a solid *whump*. He lay dazed and unmoving. The peasants exploded into frenzied applause at the sight.

Elsabeth followed through her blow with almost casual indifference and turned on her heel. She dropped into *alber*, with her point leveled at her opponent's face. He regained enough mastery of his faculties to raise his hands in surrender, and his companions were called forward to take him away (but not before the friar ensured he was relieved of the fifteen *deniers* he rightfully owed them).

Most of the masters shook their heads and departed the market, having seen enough for themselves, though d'Aubigny and Ruiz remained to watch the aftermath. The majority of the practitioners come for the playings stormed away with them, though here and there were small knots animatedly discussing what they just witnessed. Money changed hands with an audible clink, and the audience stirred impatiently while they awaited the next challenger bold enough to step forward.

"I always knew the Schwertbrüder were naught but a bunch of women cloistering themselves away in a convent," came a voice from Caspar's side, and his face flushed in anger when he looked down upon Antonio Guarin, who watched the aftermath with an amused smirk. He juggled a small stack of coin in his hand, having clearly profited from the bout. "At least this one actually looks the part. She may actually make your guild meetings worth attending."

"That quim has no place within the guild!" Caspar snapped.

"A pity, Master von Bech, as she assuredly is much prettier than you. And if the last time I saw you bout is any indication, she may actually wield her blade in a more manly way."

"If you desire a demonstration that can be arranged, Guarin. I shan't sit here and idly take such insults from the likes of you!" Caspar made a move to climb down from his saddle.

"Caspar!" Aich rumbled, and Caspar froze and gritted his teeth at the rebuke. "Though you have clearly forgotten Monsieur le Chevalier's ban on dueling while we are his guests, I have not. I have seen enough of this charade. Take me back to my quarters."

"Yes, Master," Caspar said, and forcibly swallowed his pride.

"A wise decision, Master von Aich," Guarin said, the smirk still plastered across his smug face. "The

Brotherhood could ill-afford another embarrassment like this while they are in Ain."

"As for you, Master Guarin," Aich said, and his deep voice turned icy as he stared down the strutting peacock. Guarin, for his part, flinched back under the Grand Master's glare, and his smile faltered a bit. "I hold to courtesy only so long as we are guests of Monsieur le Chevalier, and that courtesy does not extend to the road home from Ain. The Brotherhood forswears any association with that woman; she operates under neither our protection nor our charter, and we take seriously any unlawful use of our name on her account. This is a Guild matter. I advise you to stay out of it!"

And with that, the Grand Master spun his horse around. He ignored the cries of protest from the peasants he all but trampled as he did so, and started back the way they had come. Caspar followed and left the market and the cries of the friar behind him.

ELSABETH MOPPED HER BROW ON THE BACK of her sleeve. She took a long drink from her pitcher of small beer, then leaned over the table and wearily rubbed her temples. Though Hieronymus's remedy had, after a fashion, relieved her of the queasiness she had felt all morning, her head continued to pound, and the warmth of the day and steady rumble of the crowd did her no favors.

"So are you going to make it through the rest of the day, my dear? Or should we call an end to it here and now?"

Hieronymus asked between sips from his tankard while he counted out the pile of coin heaped on the table in front of him. It was near the noon hour, and the common room was filled with people relaxing over the midday meal. The sound of so many voices echoing in the rafters had her head ready to split in two.

Elsabeth looked up at him from beneath the hand across her brow. "Love, I have been fighting bouts all day while all you need do is stand about listening to yourself talk. I think I am doing rather well, all things considered."

"Well, you certainly have them eating from your hand, though I imagine more than a few would rather be eating from other places. Perhaps you ought to have joined a minstrel troupe a long time ago."

"And deprive myself of your company while you drag me into all manner of unseemly escapades?"

Hieronymus took another drink, and wiped his mouth dry on the sleeve of his habit. "My dear Tetty, 'unseemly' follows in your wake like a wayward puppy! And, in fact, 'tis my presence alone that manages to get you out of the trouble you make for yourself."

"Oh, please. Just who was it who nearly got himself strung up by the balls after cheating those fellows in Tusnitz over dice? At least this time we won't need to turn over our earnings to placate the locals." Elsabeth paused for a long draught before continuing. "And I may as well ask, how are we doing in that regard?"

"Not too bad, I must say," Hieronymus said as he slid the coin between piles and tallied their earnings thus far. "We certainly ought to have tried this scheme years ago."

"Well, that certainly makes me forget this bloody headache," she said, and smiled into her tankard. "If only you would place the same trust in me that you demand every time some mad adventure takes your fancy."

Hieronymus harrumphed and paused in his work long enough to take a drink. "There is no madness in what I do! And on the rare occasion things go astray ..."

"... 'tis only the will of the Lord of All testing us," she finished for him around a swallow of beer. "Love, I find it rather distressing that God seems to take such a profound interest in screwing up our plans day in and day out. One would think He would have matters of greater import than meddling in ours on a whim."

"My dear, we are but humble players in His designs, and who can say what He intends in the end. Ours is just to carry on as we would, and place faith that He shall see us through as is meant to be."

"Well, I pray he deigns to send along some good upstanding fellow of means before the bouts get underway," she said. "'Tis all well and good to thrash a few challengers in the streets for a small bit of coin, but I am eyeing larger stakes, here."

Hieronymus considered a small sliver of lead slipped into their earnings with a scowl and tossed it aside. "I still think that you would fare better in that regard as a courtesan, than this convoluted scheme. The sort of attention you are inclined to draw in this manner is either likely to end with us both run out of town, or at the very least would be of a most disreputable—"

The sound of someone clearing their throat interrupted the friar's ranting, and they both looked away from their drinks to find a man standing patiently at the table beside them. Aside from his neatly groomed beard he was an otherwise ordinary-looking fellow with brown hair and eyes, dressed in a neat but plain woolen doublet.

"Yes, my son?" Hieronymus said, and leaned out over the table in such a way as to encircle their earnings within his arms, like the wall of a castle round its bailey. "Is there something that troubles you?"

"I beg your pardon for the interruption," he said in passable Navarrese, and bowed his head apologetically before fixing his attention on her, "but may I ask if you are Mademoiselle Elsabeth de Hereford?"

"I am, though I have not gone by that name for some time," she said. "If you have come for the demonstrations we expect to resume within the hour."

The man reached into his doublet and withdrew a folded piece of paper sealed in wax. "My Master bid me deliver this message into your hands, or read it to you, if need be, and await your response."

Elsabeth accepted the message, and he folded his hands behind his back and waited silently as she broke the seal and unfolded the paper. The message itself was in Coventrish, written in an elegant and firm hand, and one eyebrow peaked in curiosity when she read it:

*Dear Mistress Hereford,*

*I humbly request your presence at my estate
for supper this evening if you would be agreeable. I
am most intrigued at making your acquaintance.*


*Your servant,*


*Sir Stemham Crosseby*

*Master of the Longsword to his Lordship the
Count D'Ain*


*P.S. If you should see fit to accept my invitation, I
insist that you dress in your usual fashion, and
bring with you your sword.*


A smile came to Elsabeth's lips as she read the letter
once, and then twice. Hieronymus's blue eyes narrowed in
suspicion when he took note of her response, but she
ignored him, and neatly folded the letter and tucked it away
inside her doublet.

"Tell your Master I would be delighted to accept his
invitation," she said, and the man inclined his head in a stiff,
formal bow.

"A summons will be sent when it is time for supper.
Until then I bid Mademoiselle a good day."

And with that, the messenger spun about smartly on
his heel and departed, and Elsabeth smiled broadly and took
a swig from her tankard. Hieronymus eyed her with his best
disapproving scowl.

"What?" she said after a few moments, when the stare became unbearable.

"And just what was that about?" he asked, and his eyes never looked away from her.

"I should say 'twas the Lord of All providing, as you are so fond of saying. It seems the Master of the Longsword to D'Ain himself has taken an interest in me and invited me to supper."

Hieronymus scoffed. "Oh, I am sure he has, my dear Tetty. You are not seriously considering accepting, are you?"

Elsabeth swirled her small beer around her tankard — it was now a bit empty for her liking — and downed the rest with one swallow. "Well, if you were actually listening you would know I already had."

He rolled his eyes and heaved a sigh. "Oh, good Lord."

She gave him her best innocent shrug, but the gesture was lost on the friar, who sat glowering in disapproval at her from across the table. "What? I told you I was hoping to draw the attention of some man of means who might be able to get me into the bouting. I cannot say I expected to catch the eye of the Master of the Longsword himself, but nor can I imagine a better eye to have caught."

"And I have thought from the start this was a bad idea."

"Oh, please. After following you into one ill-advised misadventure after another, 'twould be a welcome change for you to support my venture."

Hieronymus grunted and took a draught from his own tankard. "Ill-advised is precisely what I call this."

Elsabeth rolled her eyes. "I am only going to make a new friend."

"Yes, and I know how you tend to make new friends, or need I remind you about your escapades with Cuncz?"

She narrowed her eyes to slits and spit him with a glare. "No, you do not. But need I remind you that the entire reason I was there to begin with was because you dragged me into that whole adventure?"

"Ha! While I take full responsibility for the affair with that stolen reliquary, hopping into his bed was entirely your plan!"

"It worked, did it not?"

"Oh, yes, it worked. But only because the bastard let you think it was working." He wagged his finger at her. "And I suspect that even should you have known then what we know now from the start, you would have nonetheless leapt at the chance to spend an undignified evening bobbing on his scepter."

Elsabeth's cheeks flushed. "I assure you, love, you need not let your jealousies get the better of your judgment tonight. I am merely going to supper. And as he wishes for me to bring my sword along, I suspect he desires to meet with me swordsman to swordsman."

Hieronymus harrumphed and tossed back the last of his small beer. "Well, I am willing to wager thirty *pfennigs* that ere the night is over the good Master will have you spit upon his blade, one way or another."

She rolled her eyes. "Oh let us just go back to work, and pray I don't break out my steel on you for our next bout."

Hieronymus finished counting out their earnings and swept them back into his purse, less the coin to pay for their meal. He then scooped up his staff and waddled towards the door. Elsabeth followed behind him, a smile returning to her lips as she recited the letter over and over again in her mind on the way back out to the market. Hieronymus was worrying over nothing; she was but an evening entertaining the local Master of the Longsword from her goal.

The Lord of All was indeed smiling on her, after all.

HE SUMMONS CAME LATE IN THE afternoon, just as the sun began its slow descent into the west, and the sky was lit like a fire burning on the horizon. Elsabeth, dressed in her finest shirt and hose, adjusted the angle of her hat. She decided to forgo her armored doublet for the night, and instead chose one of green velvet with gilt buttons fastened from waist to neck. Her boots and pattens were cleaned of the dirt and mud from the road. She hung her freshly oiled and polished sword low at her hip, and she swept the tail of her long leather coat behind her and leaned on her scabbard.

She made her way from the inn in the company of the plain-looking messenger who visited her earlier in the day — who finally introduced himself as Richard when he came to fetch her. Here and there they passed knots of men walking the streets or loitering at corners with swords at their waists. From their speech she ventured they came from not only elsewhere in Navarre, but also Boehm and the Free City-States, and the bouts were foremost on their lips. Most of them ignored her after a cursory looking-over missed the particulars of her anatomy that betrayed her gender, but those who looked more closely and recognized her as a woman stopped and stared. Some sneered. There were disapproving shakes of the head, and crude remarks muttered just loudly enough by design that she would hear them. Not one of them approached her or addressed her, and any who might have, quickly thought otherwise at the sight of her guide through the city.

They reached the house of Richard's master without incident, and for a time she just stood and gazed on its stone façade, lofty towers, and peaked roofs. Though the arcaded walkways granting access to the gardened courtyard within were open, the complex nonetheless possessed a martial quality not too dissimilar from Castle Ain. The school of defense itself was a large, rectangular building occupying much of the eastern side of the complex, and she felt a deep pang in her belly upon realizing that, despite the differences in architecture and building materials, it reminded her much of Paulus's schola in Soest.

That, however, was not her destination, and she followed her guide to the house itself. Though occupying less of the grounds than the school, the house stood twice its height, with many towers raising its height above the street even further. Lights in the windows gazing out onto the street and garden beckoned for her to enter, and smoke rose from the chimney. A few of the Master's students loitered around the complex long after the day's lessons concluded, and discussed their craft or the playings. For their part they regarded her with more curiosity than scorn, and, like the other practitioners she met on her way through the city, they passed without attempting to interrupt her progress.

Richard led her to the main entrance off the street. They passed through the large iron-bound timber doors and into a grand entry foyer, lit by lamps bathing the room in golden light in such a way the elaborately carved wooden trim, columns, and parquet flooring seemed to glow. A servant met Elsabeth upon entering and took her pattens, hat, and jacket, and Richard then directed her into a short hallway past a side door leading in from one of the arcaded walkways outside. She let her eyes wander the interior as they made the short walk towards the screens passage. Ribbed arches supported the tall ceiling. Windows in the clerestory and triforium allowed in light from above, while those at ground level looked out onto the gardens on her right. Tapestries depicting scenes of hunt and battle — some of which she recognized as events of the wars between Coventry and Navarre — decorated the walls on her left.

Richard turned down the screens passage, and from there into the great hall itself. This was a tall, cavernous chamber with a ceiling twice the height of the passage through which she entered, and it occupied much of the ground floor. More rows of windows in carved wooden frames looked out onto the garden, and a bronze chandelier hung from the ceiling. Trestle tables ran the lengths of the walls on either side of the central aisle, and a large stone fireplace with two crossed ceremonial swords behind a shield — *Or, on a bend Azure between two dragons segreant Sable, three crosses Argent* — hanging on the overmantle occupied much of the wall on the left. A fire crackled in the hearth, and the scented wood lent the entire chamber a rich, spicy perfume.

The rest of the hall was rather plain in its decoration, except for the large tapestry of a battle scene dominating the wall behind the dais. One armored figure scaled a castle wall bearing a shield matching the blazon of the one staring down from above the fireplace, while archers on the battlements loosed arrows on the warriors below. Two doors on either side of the dais led to the private living quarters beyond, and the high table had been set for two in front of the tapestry.

And awaiting her at the foot of the dais was her host.

He was a tall and handsome man perhaps a dozen years her senior, with short tawny hair and keen grey eyes, clad in a fine blue doublet with silver buttons, and pale woolen hose that fit him snugly without being scandalous. His tall and powerfully built figure stood perhaps half a head taller than her. Elsabeth was at once reminded of her first meeting with Cuncz so many months ago, but there were differences: where Cuncz met her with cool composure and an easy smile, her host this night was possessed of a surplus of nervous energy. He rocked from one foot to another, and before she even crossed half the expanse of the hall, he left his place at the stairs and closed the remaining distance between them to meet her.

"Welcome! Welcome!" he said in Coventrish, and he scooped up her hand and kissed it gently on the back of her knuckles. "I am Sir Stemham Crosseby, and I am delighted you chose to accept my invitation!"

Elsabeth quirked a grin at the infectiousness of his excitability, and gave him a short, formal bow. "The pleasure is mine, Sire," she said.

Crosseby at once waved her off. "Come now, I have little taste for such ceremony, my dear. Please, call me Stemham."

Her smile broadened. "Very well, Stemham. It seems I have no need to introduce myself, as you apparently know me already."

Stemham favored her with a smile of his own, and Elsabeth's heart fluttered a bit in spite of herself. "Yes, well I must confess to having inquired after you when I saw your demonstration yesterday." He stepped back from her slightly and looked her over from her boots to the top of her head. Elsabeth blushed a little at the scrutiny, not least because she realized she did not exactly find it unwelcome. "Simply marvelous! And wonderful, you brought your sword! The moment I saw you I knew I simply had to meet you. If you would forgive my impertinence, I have to say the fleeting glimpse I caught of you practicing your craft hardly does justice to seeing you standing before me."

Elsabeth colored again, but if he noticed he did not show it. Instead, he took her by the hand, and, with the other lightly on the small of her back, guided her towards the dais. "But come, I did not invite you here to lavish you in flattery."

"I won't be put off to hear a little more, actually," she said. "In fact, I find it quite a refreshing change."

"You certainly have caused quite a stir among some of my other guests since your arrival."

Elsabeth quirked an eyebrow. "Will others be joining us tonight, then?"

"Oh, no. In fact, they have lodgings of their own in the City, and are not so much my guests as they have merely accepted my invitations to the playings."

They started up the stairs together, and Richard followed behind them to pull Elsabeth's seat away from the table. She favored him with a smile, and a slight flutter of her lashes. "Wonderful, I can be rather loath to share." Elsabeth unhooked her sword from her belt and leaned it against the table as she took her seat. Stemham shooed Richard away so he could scoot her chair beneath her himself, then took his own seat beside her.

"Richard, do see if the cook is ready, and have the wine brought out."

Richard inclined his head. "Yes, Sire," he said, and hurried off to see to the request.

Stemham returned his attention to her. "As I understand it you were trained by Master Paulus von Soest?"

Elsabeth nodded, and tried her best to ignore the stab of pain in her gut at mention of his name. "I was, yes."

"Do forgive my curiosity, but I am given to understand that the Schwertbrüder have never admitted a woman to their guild."

"Nor have they yet. I was no member of the Brotherhood. The arrangement to teach me was a private one."

Stemham nodded. "Yes, so I heard. How, if I may ask, did that come to pass?"

"I make no great secret of it," she said. Richard returned with a silver tray bearing a bottle of red wine and two goblets. He set down the tray, placed and filled one for each of them, then retreated to an out-of-the-way corner and waited to be called on. Elsabeth picked up her goblet, swirled it around, and took a deep sniff; it was a light red wine from central Navarre, and smelled of raspberries and violets. She took a small drink and found it was also quite potent. "My father was dispatched on an embassy in Köln when I was ..." Elsabeth paused for another drink, and to recall the date. "Oh, I suppose I was not quite in my sixth summer, yet. My mother accompanied him, but she daren't leave me behind, so they bundled me up and off I went."

"May I ask your father's name?" Stemham asked, and thoughtfully swirled his own goblet.

"Sir Thomas Hawke."

He stilled his glass and regarded her with some amazement. "You are a daughter of Hawke?" he asked.

Elsabeth blinked in surprise at the recognition on his features. "You know my father?" she said, no less taken aback than he that she might meet someone so far from home who knew her family.

"By reputation only; I regret that we have never had the honor of meeting either in court or in tournament, even when I still had the favor of the King. But I have heard it told he was in his youth one of the greatest sword-arms in all of Coventry."

Elsabeth gave him a wistful smile. "I would wager he could argue he is still among them even today. 'Twas he who first taught me to fence."

Stemham sampled his wine and leaned on his elbow while he listened to her story with rapt attention. One eyebrow perked up. "Truly?"

"Yes. In fact, he insisted that all of his children learn to handle the sword. My brothers, of course, were expected to follow him in the King's service, but he demanded it even of my sister and me, as he felt it important that we all be able to defend ourselves at need." Elsabeth took another drink and chuckled softly at hazy memories of watching her sister from her mother's lap. "My sister, of course, despised it, and my mother sympathized; she was always the proper lady who insisted her daughters focus on making themselves suitable matches for a suitable husband. But my father insisted, and so until the day she married she spent nearly as much time in the training yard as learning to keep a household. 'Twas not until we arrived in Köln that I was old enough to lift a blade myself.

"Much to my mother's dismay, once I picked one up, she could not pry it from my fingers, and I was a terror to the boys of the household. Father, of course, would remind me that one day I would need to lay aside my sword and learn to become the lady of a household, but he and I were more alike than he was even to my brothers, and I suppose he quietly enjoyed the time we spent in the yard."

"How then did you come under the tutelage of Soest?" he asked around a mouthful of his wine.

Elsabeth hid a sigh behind her goblet and tried her best to wash away the sorrow threatening to well up at the memories the question dredged up from the back of her mind with a long drink. "In our third year in Köln there was a tournament, and swordsmen from all across Boehm came to participate. Paulus was one of them, and he was lodged by the family with whom we were staying. My father took me to watch the bouts, and I was entranced watching him fight. My father was a master, certainly, but I have never seen the like of Paulus. I suppose he took some amusement in seeing my father giving me lessons, as he watched us during his stay, and he offered some advice of his own whenever I approached him."

She sighed again and gazed into her wine glass. "Upon the conclusion of the tournament, I found myself dreading the day that he would depart to return to his schola. So I went to my father and begged — and I do believe I even threw myself on my knees before him — that he allow me to go to Soest to study. Well, my mother of course little liked the idea, but my father ..." Elsabeth took a drink, and considered that moment as her father lay a hand on her shoulder and looked her deep in the eye when she made her plea. "He went right to Paulus that very moment and asked that he take me on as a student. He, I am sure, was quite taken aback by the request. But in the end, the day the caravan returning to Soest departed I found myself riding at his side." Elsabeth smiled. "As hard as it was to say my farewells to my mother and father, that was nonetheless one of the happiest days of my life."

Stemham smiled broadly. "Simply remarkable!" he said, and Elsabeth smiled back. A small flutter worked its way through her belly at the warmth and wonder in his expression. "I do wonder that the Guild did not object. My experience is that the Schwertbrüder are quite discriminating in their selection of students, and are zealous in the protection of their monopoly."

Elsabeth shrugged. "As the arrangement was between Paulus and my father, I think that forestalled any objection on their part. Even the Grand Master of the Schwertbrüder daren't refuse Thomas Hawke."

Their conversation was interrupted when the door from the kitchens was thrown open, and the sewers of the household entered bearing trays of food for the first course, which they set out on the table. The fare of Stemham's table was not to the excess which she expected from a man of his clear prestige in Ain, but there were custardes stuffed with veal and spices; a soup dish of chicken, cinnamon, and ground almonds; almond pudding; and a few other dishes filling the hall with the rich aroma of spices.

"The Brotherhood certainly takes a dim view of you," Stemham said around a mouthful of custarde.

"I think it owes much to the fact that though the Lord of All saw fit to make me a woman, I could best many of them." She quirked a grin and helped herself to a modest sampling of the offered sundries. "And there are some who had other designs on me who walked away with only a few bruises for their trouble."

Stemham chuckled softly. "'Twould seem, then, your father possessed a great deal of foresight. Surely you must be overwhelmed with such attention."

"'Tis not always unwelcome, I confess, though at times there are those who cannot accept my disinterest. My first duel, in fact, was fought in response to one such fellow who could not keep his hands to himself."

He quirked an eyebrow, and paused in the middle of another custarde. "That sounds like a tale worth telling."

Elsabeth's face heated a bit at the memory. "'Tis actually a quite hard-learned lesson, and I must admit to feeling a touch of shame at my part in it."

"My dear Elsabeth, now you have my interest fully piqued."

She let out a rueful chuckle and swirled her wine in her glass. "If you must know, I was not yet sixteen and I made the rather foolish mistake of venturing unescorted into a tavern, with no consideration for what a man would think of a woman under her own devices in such circumstances. Well, one drunken lech chose to make his thoughts on the matter clear, and when I refused him, he sought to lay hands on me without my invitation." Elsabeth paused and emptied the last of her wine. Almost immediately Richard appeared at her side with the bottle, and she did not continue for a few moments.

Stemham leaned in beside her, eager for her to resume her story. "What, then, did you do?"

"I smashed a tankard over his head," she said. "He, of course, grew angry and struck me in turn, and soon the magistrate was called. None of the witnesses would come forward with the truth of what happened, so the next morning we fought it out."

He clicked his tongue. "Such cowardice that no one would bear witness to the truth."

Elsabeth took another drink and let the wine slosh around her mouth for a bit, before returning her attention to her supper. "That was one of many lessons about life I learned that day," she said over her soup. "I could not sleep a wink that night, and in the morning when I was led to the field I thought I would be sick ere the fight began. But I am sitting here with you today, and he is keeping company with God, I suppose."

"Well, then I must be sure to give my thanks to the Lord of All that you still grace this earth to share my table tonight."

She giggled softly around a mouthful of soup. "So tell me, why is it that you have really invited me to your home tonight? I cannot believe 'tis only to hear stories of my wild youth."

Stemham leaned his head on his hand and regarded her intently. "In fact, my dear, I have found you quite intriguing from the moment I saw you in the market."

"Ah, so I am a curiosity to you, then?"

"Yes, of a sort," he said. "You are quite the uncommon creature."

"I have been called many different things by as many different men, love, and that is certainly one of the more original." Elsabeth flashed him a mischievous smile. "So if you are making insinuations you ought to know I can be quite a lot of trouble."

"Nothing, I am sure, I can't handle. More than anything, I am impressed with the way you handle your blade. I have known many a master in my day, but dare to say you put many of them to shame. And you certainly present a more pleasing sight to the eye."

Elsabeth's cheeks heated a bit at that, though as she considered the wine sloshing about her glass it occurred to her it might also be the drink. "The regard you hold for my skill is much appreciated, as 'tis much more than I am accustomed to. Had I been born with something other than what the Lord of All saw fit to put twixt my thighs I might long ago have been well on my way towards being made Master of the Longsword myself. I have accepted that this is the way of the world, though 'tis a harsh lesson nonetheless."

"So why do you not return home, then?"

"It may be the way of the world, but I still desire to find my own place in it, not one that others would make for me, however difficult it may be. I would love nothing more than to participate in the bouts here in Ain, but am content to play to the crowds in the market if I must. There are worse ways for me to earn a bit of coin."

He seemed to consider that for a moment as he stared at his wine, then drained his glass and held it out for Richard to refill. "If 'tis not presumptuous, when I spied you in the market yesterday it was from a great distance. Perhaps after supper you might be agreeable to a friendly bout in the yard?"

She blinked in surprise, and for a moment could not find her voice to respond as she studied the open earnestness of his face. Stemham frowned at her hesitation when she did not answer.

"Is something the matter?" he asked.

Elsabeth shook off her disbelief and took a long drink of her wine. "No, nothing. I beg your pardon, but I must confess you are not what I was expecting," she said when she found her voice again, and trailed off into an embarrassed laugh.

"What were you expecting, if I may ask?"

She laughed again and sought for her wine to still the giggles. "Honestly?"

Stemham made a show of considering that for a moment. "If you like, but I for one prefer to build my relationships on truth."

"Then honestly, in no small part thanks to the nervous twittering of a certain meddlesome friar I know, I half expected that all of this curiosity was but a pretense."

He twitched one corner of his mouth into a wry smile. On other faces it might have come across as a predatory leer, but there was an earnest playfulness in his eyes she found quite disarming. "Let me assure you that my curiosity is indeed genuine. Oh, I will not deny that your loveliness is a part of what piques my interest, but I, for one, am no drunken lech who would lay hands where they are unwelcome and uninvited."

"Well, it certainly gives you a lead over most of those looking to make my acquaintance."

"Good, as I always have preferred to strike from a position of advantage."

Elsabeth hid another giggle behind her hand, and it was becoming harder to lay blame for the fits on her wine. "Take care you don't strike rashly," she said, "lest your blow fall wild."

"But too much patience and the opening may pass before one can put their advantage to use."

"True enough, though sometimes it may be but a feint to lure one into opening themselves for a counter-stroke."

"In which case 'tis worth throwing the strike nonetheless as part of a longer play to seek a true opening."

"And should you find it?"

"Strike directly and with assurance."

Elsabeth hid a smile behind her hand. "You certainly understand the language of the play."

"I take that as high praise, but I ought to point out you have yet to give an answer to my request."

"I have not, have I? Then let me say I would be delighted to cross swords with you."

Stemham smiled broadly and raised his glass to his lips for another drink. "Wonderful! After supper we shall go to the yard and measure ourselves against one another. I only pray you don't find me lacking as an adversary." The last he added with a wink from behind his goblet.

Elsabeth giggled softly and took another drink herself.

**11**

LSABETH FOLLOWED HIM OUT INTO THE courtyard, a pair of light leather gauntlets clutched in one hand. Stars sparkled overhead in a clear autumn sky, and the golden light of lamps cast long shadows among the stone benches and rosebushes neatly bordering the lawn of grass. A white marble fountain, graven with elaborate scrollwork and ringed by a matching bench, stood at its heart, and the sound of water falling into its basin filled the night air. The school and house towered overhead on either side, and lights in the many windows beckoned invitingly for them to return. The breeze was cool and crisp with the subtle bite of autumn, and beyond the arcaded walks enclosing the courtyard Elsabeth heard the distant sounds of laughter as the denizens of Ain enjoyed their evening.

Stemham led her to the fountain and directed her to take a seat on the bench, while he lowered himself next to her. He poured them each another glass of wine from a fresh bottle he had pilfered on his way out the door, and Elsabeth giggled headily after a long drink. She ignored the fuzziness in her head while they waited and listened to the tinkling of water falling into the basin. Richard soon emerged from the shadow of the school with a pair of *Federn* leaning against his shoulder. Stemham made a show of hiding his wine glass behind his back and shushing her, and Elsabeth giggled into her hand again.

"Ah! There you are Richard! Thank you, you may go," he said, and waved him away.

Richard leaned the training swords against the bench and inclined his head. "Yes, Sire. Will there be anything else you require of me tonight?"

"I suspect I shan't need you for a time, but please see to it that my guest and I are not disturbed."

"Yes, Sire. Goodnight, Sire." Richard bowed stiffly, then turned on his heel and made his way for the house.

Elsabeth took another sip of her wine and watched him go. "He seems a touch stuffy, don't you think?" she asked.

Stemham chuckled softly and drained his goblet with one long swallow. "I have known Richard almost from the day I was knighted, and he has followed me ever since," he said. "Oh, he is certainly a rather joyless fellow, but loyal to a fault, and utterly indispensable in running my school."

She turned back to face him, and let her hair fall across her face before she hooked it behind her ear again. "You are quite fond of him."

"Richard has earned my trust many times over," he said. "I don't give it lightly, and I hold those worthy of it in high esteem."

Stemham gave her a small smile, then slapped his thighs. "Now then! You and I have some business, to attend!"

Elsabeth smiled and drained the last of her wine. "Indeed we do!"

Stemham pushed himself off the bench and extended a hand to help her to her feet. Elsabeth accepted the offer and fell into another giggling fit, then slipped on her gloves and armed herself. The *Feder* was somewhat shorter than and not quite so well-balanced as her own sword, but nonetheless felt good and natural in her hands. Stemham led her to a clear space in the grassy swath at the heart of his compound, well away from the obstruction of the fountain, and the bushes and benches laid out around it. Upon reaching their positions, Stemham raised his hilts to her and bowed in a salute, and Elsabeth responded by touching the flat of her blade to her brow. Then they took their wards; Elsabeth raising her *Feder* overhead into *vom tag*, and Stemham dropping low into a Coventrish ward she recognized as the Dragon's Tail.

They circled each other, each shifting from guard to guard as they gauged one another and sought for an opening to their liking. Elsabeth found hers first, and she lunged at him in a falling blow from her left shoulder. Stemham met her with an aggressive cut mirroring her strike, which she quickly offset by shifting her hilts to her right hip and dropping into *pflug*, then countered him with a thrust to his face. He snapped his hilts above his left shoulder into *ochs* to guide her point safely past him, and counter-thrust at her shoulder. Elsabeth stepped into his thrust and put her sword between her and his blade to deflect his point, then lunged to her left and whipped her point around and under his guard, and delivered a level slash from her right that caught him across his left hip.

Stemham yelped as her blade struck him a solid blow right on the bone, and he hopped away from her and shook out his leg.

"Ow, I would call that a touch," he said, and gently nursed what was assuredly going to become a bruise the next morning. "That will cost you."

Elsabeth said nothing and merely favored him with a victorious smile when he withdrew from her. Stemham regarded her with his features twisted into an expression holding the middle ground somewhere between impressed and chagrined as he undid the buttons of his doublet, and tossed it aside to strip down to the shirt beneath. She did the same, and then they returned to their positions again for another round.

They circled one another as before, and then Stemham lunged towards her. Their blades kissed, and he drove aggressively towards her seeking to press against her body and tie up her hands. Elsabeth slipped around him when he drew nearer, and their blades glided against one another as he wound his *Feder* around hers, and sought to thrust for her opening. She deftly twisted away from him, and for some time they danced; Stemham pressing her with aggressive strength, Elsabeth yielding to pass his strokes harmlessly by and keep him at a distance. Try as she might, this time she could not regain the initiative, and found herself inexorably driven into the defensive.

Their blades met and caressed, and Stemham's *Feder* spun deftly through his strong hands, deflecting each counter as he pressed her closer and closer. Elsabeth's heart raced and her breath came in heaving gasps as he darted in and out, putting her off balance, his face a mask of concentration while sweat beaded on his brow from his exertion. She moved with him, and every time he pressed to close, she stepped round him to keep her distance.

She defended a cut to the shoulder, and Stemham stepped in, pressed against her body, and used his elbow to turn her so he could cut at the back of her head. Elsabeth hung her blade behind her head to defend the stroke, spun away and extended her point in a thrust to force him back, but now that he was inside her he did not give ground. Stemham casually guided her point past him and lunged towards her. He seized her about the waist, pulled her against his hip, and pinned her weapon against her.

Thus locked together, they wrestled against one another for a time. Elsabeth sought a means of escape, but while Stemham held fast, he could not gain an advantage to take her to the ground. This close she could feel his breath on her neck, and she grunted and fought against his hold on her. He hooked one foot behind hers to trip her, and she quickly replaced her feet to keep him from unbalancing her. Stemham's face hovered not more than an inch from hers, his grey eyes peering deep into hers, and his lips turned upwards in a slight smirk. Her breath came in ragged gasps at the effort of fighting him, and her heart hammered against her breastbone. She abandoned her *Feder* and turned her focus on grappling him, and it landed in the grass at her feet with a dull *thud*. Elsabeth was aware of the full length of his body pressed tightly against hers, and her face flushed from the effort of fighting against him as he slowly used his leverage and strength to bend her backwards.

Finally, she could resist no more, and Stemham took one leg out from beneath her and down she went. He came down to his knees atop her and straddled her thigh. He gripped his weapon half-sword and pinned her to the ground with the point at her throat. She did not move, but gazed up at him looming over her from her back with her hands raised in surrender. They both panted from their exertion, and sweat trickled from their faces at the intensity of the exchange. For a moment they stayed as they were in the aftermath of the bout, their eyes locked on one another.

And then Stemham withdrew his point from her neck and leaned down and kissed her.

She cupped his face and feverishly kissed him back, and the spice of his breath mingled with the raspberry overtones of the wine she could still taste on his lips. One of his hands brushed her cheek, then wandered down until it came to rest on her breast. She hung her arms around his shoulders as he pulled his lips from hers and kissed the side of her neck.

As she gave herself to him right there in the garden, Elsabeth was never more content in her life to lose a bet.

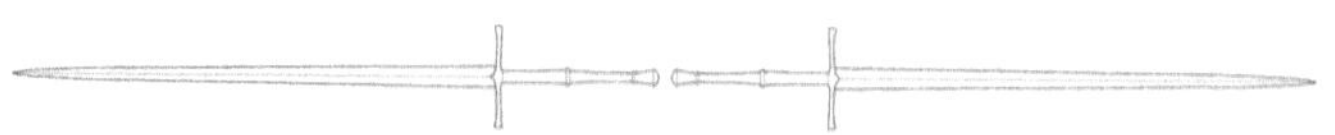

CROSSEBY GENTLY KISSED THE CURVE OF HER shoulder. She giggled softly at the touch of his lips and reclined into his arms, the length of her naked back pressed against him.

They lay in his bed with his arms around her and the covers flung aside in disarray. A thin sliver of moonlight found its way through the open windows. The moonlight turned Elsabeth's fair skin silver and cast long shadows across the room. A fire crackled in the fireplace occupying the center of the south wall. It cast a flickering rosy light that mingled with the moon's silver radiance, and filled the chamber with a fragrant aroma. This mingling with the crispness of the evening breeze invigorated him, something Crosseby found most beneficial given the evening's exertions.

Elsabeth sighed contentedly while he traced a slow line of kisses from the ball of her shoulder to the base of her neck, before nuzzling the back of her head and burying his face in her long, disheveled copper tresses. Crosseby breathed deeply of her scent and let his hand wander her body. His fingers glided along her taut abdomen and prompted a quiet and throaty laugh at the sensation of his touch tracing the muscle beneath her skin, past the point it met the sinew at the base of her thigh, and turning inward to the space between her legs. Her giggle was cut off by a ragged moan when his fingers probed her crevice, still warm and slick from their earlier exertions, and in anticipation of the resumption of their nocturnal bout.

But he only lightly teased the fringe of flesh on either side for a moment, before his hand retraced a path back along her thigh and up her belly, until he filled it with a breast as round, full, and firm as a ripe peach. He gently kneaded and stroked her, and pinched her upright nipple between his thumb and finger.

"I must confess this was not the sort of bouting I expected us to be doing this evening," she breathed at his touch.

"I think much of what we have done tonight would put us afoul of the Bishop should he find out," he said, and gently sucked her earlobe into his mouth.

Elsabeth gasped softly in response. "I promise I can hold on to a secret if you can."

"'Tis agreed, then: We shan't say a thing. I for one daren't tear his Excellency away from his concubines at such a late hour."

She shifted her body against his and moaned appreciatively at his attentions. "Good, as that would mean stopping what you are doing and calling for Richard to take the—" Elsabeth's words were interrupted by a delighted squeak when his hand found a particularly sensitive spot on her breast. "To take the message," she finished when she regained control of herself. "And I must imagine if the Lord of All found what we are doing distasteful He would surely have made His displeasure clear by now."

"The night watchman certainly did."

"I think that bit of disturbing the peace had as much to do with the clash of steel as the way we were carrying on."

Crosseby chuckled and kissed the ball of her shoulder again. "If I may say so, I find your skill at handling a blade remarkable."

"The night is young, love, and I have yet to truly get started."

He smiled at her back. "That was not precisely to what I was referring, though I'll not dispute you, either."

"Very wise of you."

"I have my moments. If I may ask, have you studied further since your time as a student to Soest?"

Elsabeth's shoulder heaved in a heavy sigh, and she removed his hand from her breast and twined her fingers around his. "No, much to my regret. Oh, Hieronymus is no easy mark as a sparring partner, but even when I first knew him there was nothing more he could teach me."

"He is the Olivian, yes?"

Crosseby felt her nod. "Though he came to his calling late in life," she said, "and I am not entirely convinced there was not some ulterior motive in taking the cloth. Especially as I have not known him to be averse to overlooking his vows at need.

"But I find there are all too few men willing to swallow their pride and take me on as a student, now that I no longer have my father to make such arrangements."

Crosseby considered that, and leaned his chin against her shoulder. "Well, I am quite impressed by what you have accomplished despite want of further formal study."

"I have had much practice by necessity. It seems there is always someone wishing to separate my head from my shoulders—"

He gave her neck a kiss and a nuzzle. "What a tragic loss that would be."

"—and I would rather like to keep it there."

"Clearly you have done a marvelous job of it, much to my delight, otherwise we mayn't be sharing this evening now."

"'Tis certainly one of the many benefits of keeping my innards internal. But I know there is so much more to learn: for one I am not nearly so strong at polearm as I am with the sword."

"I would never have guessed," he said, "given the skill by which you worked my staff tonight."

She giggled and leaned back deeper into his arms so she could twist her head about and kiss him on the mouth. The full length of her body was pressed against him now, and it took much of his willpower to not roll her beneath him again right then and there.

"Well, love," she said when their lips parted again. "There is working, and there is wielding. At working I would venture to say I am without peer."

"An assertion I shan't dispute."

"At wielding, however, I am sorely lacking."

"If you would be willing, I would not be indisposed to offering you my knowledge while you are visiting Ain. And not just at polearm, but there is much about the sword you might benefit from, as well."

Elsabeth turned to face him and raised herself up on one elbow. Crosseby laid his hand on her hip, and slowly ran it along her shapely thigh. Her skin was smooth and supple, but taut over the firm muscle beneath. A fact he discovered of the rest of her body during his exploration of every curve and contour of her figure which, for all its athleticism, was no less womanly. And he had explored every cranny by hand, lips, and tongue. He lifted himself up on his own elbow to look her in the eye as she gazed at him in a mix of disbelief and elation. "You would truly do that?"

He took his hand away from her leg to hook a stray copper lock falling across her face back into place behind her ear. "'Twould be a pleasure. As I said earlier, you fascinate me." Crosseby twitched one corner of his mouth into a smile. He gently ran his finger along her jaw, and playfully tipped her chin. "And I do confess I take no small pleasure in the thought of the consternation 'twould cause the Schwertbrüder should they learn of it."

"Oh, I am certain the Grand Master would be livid." Elsabeth then lowered her chin to look up at him through her lashes and made a playful pout. "'Tis all that I would be, though?"

"Not at all," he said. "'Tis not your sword-arm alone I find so intriguing, and in fact I would be honored should you deign to remain as my personal guest here for the duration of your stay."

Elsabeth smiled broadly, and her face lit up brighter than the stars winking from their fine silver net in the darkness outside. "I would like that very much," she said.

Crosseby shifted a bit on the bed to pull her nearer until he felt the full length of her body against his once more, and Elsabeth leaned over him and cupped his cheek in one of her strong but slender hands. She kissed him deeply on the mouth, now nibbling gently on his lower lip, now their tongues briefly meeting and twining together. Her breath still tasted of the wine, and Crosseby felt himself stir again as her kiss and her touch reinvigorated him. He gently stroked her back with his free hand — the other still holding himself partly upright — then slowly caressed the curve of her bottom and pulled her hips tightly against his.

Elsabeth swung her leg over him to straddle his hips and reached behind her, gently seizing his manhood by the shaft and guiding him into her. Her breath escaped in a pleasured gasp when he pierced the folds of her purse once more, and gingerly lowered herself until he filled her completely. Crosseby moaned at the velvet warmth of her enveloping the length of him.

And for the rest of the night, all he knew was her scent, her taste, and her warmth, and all other thoughts vanished from his mind.

**12**

THE MINGLED ODORS OF ALE, FRAGRANT spices, pungent herbs, cooking food, and too many bodies packed into too small of a space greeted Merklin upon setting foot inside the common room. A fire crackled in the hearth and filled the room with a rosy and welcoming glow, and the lamps and candles throughout the timbered hall provided plentiful light to see by. Musicians played a jaunty dance tune in the corner, though the men gathered within focused on their meals and their drinks. Servers moved among them bearing trays and platters, or made the rounds with pitchers to refresh the ale flowing from the inn's casks. The mood was quiet but merry, with coarse and raucous laughter at times drowning out the music and the sound of many voices in quiet conversation.

Merklin Adler picked up bits of gossip over the local news, or here and there a discussion on a matter of business, while a few practitioners of the sword arts come for the playings boasted and traded good-natured barbs and wagers.

He sniffed and raised his nose at them; none of them belonged to any formal school he knew of, and he quickly dismissed them as common tavern brawlers at best. He ignored them and let them drown themselves in the cheap piss foisted upon them by the master of the house, and turned his attention to the business which led him to the establishment that night.

One of the serving girls hurried past him with a tray laden with empty plates and bowls balanced carefully in one hand, and Merklin stopped her on her way to the kitchens.

"I would have words with your Master," he said, in heavily accented Navarrese. "Go and fetch him at once."

The girl inclined her head — an impressive feat of dexterity to do so without so much as disturbing a plate — and disappeared. Merklin casually leaned on the sword hung at his hip while he waited, and quietly surveyed the room. A few eyes took note of him upon entering, most focused on the arms of the Brotherhood embroidered on his doublet, or the garters of his rank worn over his hose. They whispered quietly among each other, but no one dared call out to him or approach him. Much of the crowd, however, was lost in the shadows along the edges of the common room, lit only by lamps and candles, with little of the cheery glow of the fire reaching them.

A few moments later the master of the house emerged and folded his arms across his broad chest. "My niece says you wanted a word with me?" he said, and his blue eyes studied Merklin closely. "What can I do for you, Monsieur?"

Merklin clasped his hands at the small of his back. "I seek the Coventrish woman, Mademoiselle de Hereford. I understand she is staying in your inn, and I have a message I was bidden to deliver."

"I don't know a Mademoiselle de Hereford, but if you mean the lass that was demonstrating in the market yonder this morning and yesterday," he said, and nodded casually towards the door leading back out into the square, "you missed her by some hours. I can't decide whether that be a good or bad thing; the inn is a might bit quieter without her jumping on my tables, but she certainly drew a good crowd."

He frowned at this bit of news. "Do you expect her to return?"

"Possibly. I think she had some business in the City tonight, but I can't tell you when she might be back. That Olivian she works with out in the courtyard is certainly still here, drinking up all my best ale." He waved vaguely off towards one corner, lost in the shadows clinging to the edges of the common room. "You can leave your message with him, if you like."

Merklin peered in the direction the master indicated, then turned his attention back to him once more. "Very well, thank you." He fished into his purse for a silver *pfennig* and flipped it to the master for his trouble. The fellow caught and pocketed it in one smooth motion.

"If you need anything else give me a holler, and I'll have one of my girls around with supper for you in a moment."

"That won't be necessary, Monsieur," Merklin sniffed. "I shan't be eating."

"Suit yourself. Oh, and mind yourself with the dice," he added as he started away, almost as an afterthought. "The good Brother has had a remarkable run of luck."

He inclined his head stiffly. "I will take that under consideration. Good evening to you."

The master returned the gesture and returned to his work, and Merklin was left to see to his business.

He made his way across the common room, and deftly picked a path past the wandering servers and tables. Most of the patrons ignored him, seeing just another traveler come to relax and share the news of the day, but those few who took note of the crossed swords of the Schwertbrüder on his breast watched him with intense curiosity. More than a few of the tables he passed spiritedly discussed the woman's demonstration in the market that morning, many taking amusement in regaling anyone who missed her with stories of their red-faced companions coming forward to challenge her only to be soundly beaten.

"A pity she is not here tonight!" another said. "You should have been here yesterday evening, she even outdrank Tanguy!" He chuckled and puffed out his chest. "And I tell you, lads, her kiss will take your legs out from beneath you! Aye, 'tis a pity she is not here tonight, as I would love the chance to take her for a ride. She must be quite the spirited mount, 'tis no exaggeration."

Merklin curled his lip in disgust at such plebian vulgarity, and brushed past them without a word.

He found the friar seated at a table in a corner, with a tankard of ale at his elbow, and a portion of the evening's meal — a meat pie of pork, minced raisins, and ground almonds spiced with cinnamon and cloves — on the table in front of him. He was a slovenly character wrapped in a travel- and ale-stained black woolen habit of the Olivian Order over what may have once been a white gown, and his prodigious belly hung over the woven cord straining to contain the bulk of his waist. Wild and unruly silver hair framed his portly round face, and he wore an unkempt and scraggly beard with a few black streaks at his lips betraying the color of his youth.

The friar took a long draught from his tankard, belched, and wiped his mouth on the sleeve of his habit, before returning his attention to his supper. After a few bites he licked his fingers, took a drink, and repeated the whole process again. Merklin let out a groan of disgust at the uncouth display, but continued forward until he stood across the table from him, and waited patiently with his hands clasped at the small of his back.

At first Hereford's companion seemed to take no notice of him, and just continued to gorge himself. However, before Merklin could make a move to get his attention, the friar spoke.

"Yes, my son?" he asked, without even looking away from his pie.

"You are the Olivian who travels with Mademoiselle Elsabeth de Hereford, is this true?" Merklin asked.

"'Tis true, 'tis true." He scowled in disgust at the scarcity of his last swallow of ale, and thumped the tankard on the table impatiently to summon one of the serving girls. "What may I do for you?"

"I come with a message."

"Bah! Everyone has a message for that aggravating woman!" he slurred. "And yet off she goes to make a disgrace of herself with who-knows-who at who-knows-where, and here she leaves me to be her noticeboard!" One of the girls quickly responded to the insistent thumping and attempted to refill it from her pitcher. However, the friar began to gesticulate as he ranted, and with a moving target to hit nearly as much ale found its way to the table or floor as reached the inside of his tankard. "The Lord grants me patience, but ever she finds the means to drive me to wits' end, despite all I do for that ungrateful girl!"

Merklin shifted uncomfortably while the friar vented his drunken frustrations over his companion.

"Ah! But Lord of All forgive me, where are my manners? Sit, my son, and share in this repast with me," the friar continued. He motioned to an empty chair across from him, and pushed his half-finished supper towards him. The server finished her task and hurried away. He took another draught and issued a long, deep belch that shook the common room to its foundations.

Merklin fought to keep his disgust from his features. "With respects, Brother, I am a messenger only."

The friar waved him off with an annoyed growl. "As am I, my son! But you don't see me neglecting the Lord's bounty this evening. I say sit!"

There was a note of command in the friar's voice, and Merklin pulled the chair from beneath the table and sat across from him with a heavy sigh. The man chuckled merrily.

"There we are, my lad! Now where is that dear girl with the ale?" he said, and made a show of sweeping his wavering blue eyes across the common room before finally settling on her while she tended to a nearby table and flirted lightly with the men gathered around it.

"With respects, Brother, I am—"

"I never trust a man who would not share a drink with me. Love! Where are you? My man's hand is empty of God's great gift of drink. Hurry now!"

The server muttered an exasperated oath beneath her breath, tore herself away from the other table, and hurried to carry out the request. Merklin suspected as much out of a desire to placate the friar as any concern over whether his hand was, in fact, empty. His face colored in embarrassment at the eyes watching his unwanted companion's antics with amusement. With swift and practiced grace, the girl retrieved an empty tankard and promptly returned, set it before him, and filled it to the brim. Once finished she scurried off again with a wary eye at the friar's hand.

The friar ignored her and let out a satisfied chuckle, then raised his tankard. "There now! Now we may speak."

Merklin heaved another sigh and rolled his eyes, but out of forced politeness returned the gesture and took a drink. Much to his chagrin, he was forced to admit that the quality of the inn's ale was, in fact, quite excellent, and he took a long draught which seemed to please the friar greatly.

"Tell me, my son, do you play Hazard?"

Merklin mopped his face in frustration. "Forgive me, Brother, but the reason I am here—"

"Yes, yes, you have a message for my dear Tetty. I may be growing old but my faculties I assure you are quite intact. And whether you give it to me now or after a few rounds of dice makes little difference, as I have already wagered a tidy sum I shan't see that vexing girl 'till she stumbles back to the inn on the morrow. So you and I have plenty of time for business. Besides, I have not had a good game all night because these cowards lack the fortitude to roll with me!"

The last he added with a deliberate raising of his voice at the rest of the crowd, but no one offered so much as a dirty look in response. He grumbled in indignation and took a pull of his ale. "'Tis disgraceful, I say. What does a man come to an inn for but for the drink, the food, and the dice?"

"Brother—"

"Bah! Now, then, do you know the game?"

Yet again Merklin sighed, and leaned his elbow on the table and rubbed his forehead in exasperation. "No, Brother, I confess 'tis one I am unfamiliar with."

"Wonderful!" the friar said, and chuckled eagerly as he fumbled about somewhere around his middle with one hand. He quickly produced two leather pouches; one was his purse, which he set aside to the jingle of the coin within, the other a small dice bag. He thumbed open the drawstring and shook five dice out into his palm. "'Tis a Coventrish game Tetty taught me once. The girl is a sore loser, let me tell you; she never played me again after that night! Now then, we play with two dice. Hm, I think these two will do." He slapped a pair of dice down on the table and stuffed the other three in his pouch. "And as generosity is one of the Lord's great virtues, you may be the first caster."

"Most gracious of you, Brother," Merklin grumbled, and accepted the dice the friar slid to him.

"Now then, what shall be your wager?"

"Would you care to explain the rules to me first?"

The friar waved him off. "'Twould be easier to show you as we go, as I imagine you would rather not sit and listen to me talk. So come on, man, place your bet!"

Merklin reluctantly freed his purse from his belt, laid it on the table, and thumbed it open. The glint of lamplight on the silver within caught the friar's eye, and he regarded the contents closely until Merklin warned him off with a glare. He thumbed out a *pfennig* and made a show of slapping it on the table. "There, I have made my wager."

The friar harrumphed at the trifling sum. "That is it?"

"I have no desire to fatten your purse tonight, Brother, but if this is the only means by which I can deliver my message, then I shall play this farce out to its conclusion."

He merely shrugged and took a drink. "Fine, fine, suit yourself. The first thing you must do is roll to set your Main."

Merklin scooped up the dice, shook them in his hand, then rolled them across the table. They landed showing a two and a three. "Now, as I was saying, I have a message—"

"Hm, a five," the friar said, and cut him off. "Now you know your Main. You cast the dice again, and if the dice should show another five, you win equal to your stake."

He sighed in aggravation and palmed the dice once more. The friar studied him closely as he shook them, and just as he was about to roll, spoke again.

"You are one of the Schwertbrüder, are you not?" he asked.

Merklin threw the dice; a six and a four. He glanced up at his companion and frowned. "I am."

The friar waved off his unasked question. "'Tis plain by the charge upon your doublet, my son. Hm, a ten. Now, here is where the game gets interesting: Had you rolled your Main once more, you would have won. With a Main of five, had your dice shown two, three, eleven, or twelve, you would have lost."

"So what does a ten mean, then?"

"That is your Chance. You cast again, and keep casting until you roll either your Chance or your Main. Should you roll your Chance you win, but if 'tis your Main, you lose."

Merklin frowned. "I thought rolling the Main was a win?"

"Only on the first cast. Now we have moved on to the Chance. Would you care to make it more interesting, my son? Up your wager again, and with a Chance of ten the payout is four to three."

He considered the dice for a moment, then shrugged and thumbed another four *pfennig* from his purse. He took up the dice once more and shook them before making another cast. "You know of the guild?" The dice clattered across the table and landed on a three and a six.

"Of course! I myself studied the noble art of defense with the great Leonardus in my youth, some time before the Brotherhood was granted their monopoly within the bounds of the Empire." The friar took another drink. "I rather think I lucked out in that regard." Merklin made another cast, and swore when he rolled an ace and a four. His opponent chuckled in satisfaction and swept his winnings aside. "A pity, but worry not, my son, you may cast until you lose three times in succession, at which point the dice pass to me. Now, my absent companion, she studied with one of your number, as I recall. Paulus von Soest."

Merklin stiffened at the mention of Soest's name, but tossed another *pfennig* on the table nonetheless, and reclaimed his dice for another roll. He looked up at the friar, who watched the dice in his hand intently. "Yes, I know," he said, and paused for a drink before rolling his Main; a pair of twos.

"Hm. Roll again. The Main must be between five and nine. So what brings the Schwertbrüder to Ain?"

"The same as most of the travelers this week, I suppose; the playings for the local school." Merklin glanced up at the friar and scrutinized him closely. "Much the same I imagine brought your companion. I cannot imagine it to be coincidence that she is here at this time." He made another cast, and this time came up with a four and a three.

"My son, I may travel with the girl, but what goes on in that contrary head of hers I cannot fathom. 'Tis all I can do to keep her from scandalizing every town from here to the sea."

"And yet here you are, playing to the crowd like common gleemen and making a mockery of the art." He cast his dice again and rolled eight.

"The payout is six to five on that Chance. Hardly a mockery. For that you need look to the likes of da Lucca and Russdorffer. No, we are merely here in search of diversion and work."

"An Olivian friar seeking work? I thought you had your calling, Brother." Merklin tossed a few more *pfennig* into the pot and continued to roll his dice. He made neither the Chance nor Main after several casts, and paused at times for a draught of his ale. Warmth spread through his belly, and he sat back in his chair at ease.

"Spreading the word and love of the Lord of All is its own reward, my son. On the other hand, love alone cannot buy the necessities of life. God provides in his own way, and I was never one to shirk a bit of hard work. But I wonder, what possible interest in my dear Tetty the Brotherhood might have."

He cursed again when he rolled his Main, and again his coin disappeared into the friar's purse. "I have been trying to come to that since I sat down."

"Ah, of course, the message."

"Yes, Brother, the message." He tossed another coin in and rolled for his main: Nine.

The friar took a long drink. "And what is this message?"

"'Tis merely a suggestion that Elsabeth Hereford may wish to leave Ain at her earliest convenience."

Merklin cast his dice and rolled a pair of sixes.

"Ah! Such unfortunate luck; twelve is an out on a Main of nine. And that is three outs in a row, so the cast passes to me." The friar scooped up both his coin and the dice. "Is there some trouble we ought to be aware of? Oh, the girl can certainly be rowdy at times, but there seemed to be no harm done last night. Unless, of course, some local wives have been given cause for anger, which I fear is all-too-common an occurrence where Tetty is concerned."

"Whether there is trouble or not depends on how quickly she departs."

The friar studied Merklin carefully from beneath his eyebrows, and suddenly he could not help but feel that in spite of the drink, the fellow was more aware of what was happening than he let on. "If you will forgive me saying so, my son, that sounds rather like a threat. And here we were enjoying such a fine drink together!"

Merklin leaned forward and jabbed a finger into the table-top for emphasis. "Take it as you will, Brother. But to avoid any unpleasant and unfortunate occurrences, you and your companion will find it in your best interests to leave Ain. If 'tis work you seek, seek it elsewhere. If 'tis the playings she has come for ..." He let his voice trail off ominously, but if it had any effect upon the friar he said nothing.

"And from whom shall I say this message comes?"

"The name matters not. All she need know is that the Brotherhood will not tolerate her continued presence here in Ain, particularly so long as she insists upon associating her name with Master von Soest and the Guild."

"I see," the friar said, and put five of the *pfennigs* he won into the pot. Merklin's cheek twitched at that. "I can, of course, promise you nothing, but I shall deliver your message when next I see her. Whenever that might be."

Merklin flashed him a mirthless smile. "See that you do. The Guild would rather there not be any unpleasantness in the streets on her account."

13

LSABETH SMILED AT HIM OVER THE RIM OF her cup of small beer, and Stemham chewed on a piece of cheese and smiled back. They broke their fast that morning in the privacy of the solar, a modest hall just outside Stemham's bedchamber. Windows gazed out onto the street and garden to the west and east, respectively, and stood open to let in the fresh autumn morning's breeze and the light of the sun. A fire crackled on the hearth it shared with the bedchamber. It filled the room with the fragrance of perfumed wood and warmed the air against the dawn chill. They sat at a long trestle table occupying the center of the chamber, beneath an iron chandelier suspended from the heavy timber beams of the ceiling overhead. There was little in the way of decoration, leaving the solar a strictly functional — yet still cozy and welcoming — place.

She took a sip of her beer and set her cup aside, and returned her attention to the platter of cheese and buttered bread in front of her. Ain slowly came to life outside, and the calls of the vendors peddling their wares mingled with the background drone of voices as the residents of the city began the day's business.

"I suppose I ought to mention you seem to have an unfair advantage on me," she said. She clutched the front of the linen dressing gown she had borrowed from his wardrobe closed with one hand, and nibbled on a piece of bread she held in the other.

He raised an eyebrow at her. "Oh? And how is that?"

"I seem to recall we spent most of what time we were not otherwise engaged talking about me."

Stemham pulled one corner of his mouth up into a wry grin. "I found it a most fascinating subject."

Elsabeth rolled her eyes, but her face warmed a little in spite of herself. "Nonetheless, I know precious little about you, aside from a few particulars of your anatomy not privy to the rest of the world."

He chuckled softly, and his features colored in turn. "I suppose I did get rather ahead of myself last night."

She made a show of popping the last of her piece of bread in her mouth, and flashed him her most smoldering smile. "Don't take it so badly, love, I am very good at what I do."

"I daren't dispute you on that. But I suppose it only fair since I pressed so closely about you, that I return the favor. What do you wish to know?"

Elsabeth considered for a moment. "Everything!" she finally said with a laugh, and hid her smile behind her hand. "But there is one question that has been nagging at my mind ever since I arrived: How does a knight of Coventry become the Master of the Longsword to a Navarrese Count?"

Stemham chuckled again, and it became clear at once that her curiosity came as no surprise to him. He swirled his small beer around his cup and tossed his head back for a drink. "That seems to be the foremost question on everyone's lips," he said, his tone a mingling of shame and sorrow, yet somehow still proud. Elsabeth marveled at that strange dichotomy while she studied him.

"You must admit it makes for quite the curiosity. Oh, I am accustomed to stares and whispers whenever I pass, but this?" Elsabeth shrugged.

He nodded. "True. True. 'Tis a great mystery to those outside my circle. But," he said, and lounged casually in his chair with one leg hooked over the armrest, and an arm draped across the back, "I pledged my honesty to whatever you asked, and I shan't renege on that promise now."

Elsabeth quirked an amused smirk. "You also appear to be stalling."

"Merely gathering myself for the lunge, I assure you." Stemham paused for a drink of his beer, and regarded it thoughtfully for a moment while he swirled it around in his cup some more. Elsabeth watched him closely, and her imagination ran wild with sordid tales of how he had come to Ain. Before she could engross herself too fully, however, he began.

"Not long after I was knighted, I was dispatched to join in the wars in Navarre. There was little action to speak of at first, and much of the time was spent patrolling recent gains; safeguarding the roads, suppressing rebellion and the like. However, about nine years ago things flared up again.

Lord Durham mustered an army and began a new offensive aiming to sweep down through central Navarre and cut it in two. I was assigned to command one of the battles on his advance."

Stemham paused for another drink. Elsabeth leaned her elbows on the table, propped her head up in her hands, and waited for him to continue. "On one particular day I was leading the van, and Durham directed me to the city of Collioure, which commanded a crossing of the Cure River, with orders to secure it for the rest of the army. As it happened, the Navarrese had an army in the field for much the same purpose; to secure and hold the river as they marched against us. I suppose they were of the mind to reinforce the castle. However, it chanced that Collioure was on my side of the river.

"Well, I had only perhaps three thousand men with me, and they assuredly had some three times that number. I could not assault the castle with an army at my back, but nor was it manned strongly enough to threaten my flank, and the garrison was content to wait and see how the battle played out. I suppose they assumed with ten-thousand-odd Navarrese marching upon me that their deliverance was nigh.

"I, however, had the advantage of positioning: there was a rise on the near side of the river on either side of the road. So I placed my archers on the heights at my flanks, and the rest in the trough between, straddling the road, with all my horse dismounted. The narrowness of the ford meant my adversary could only commit his forces piecemeal, and with the river between us he could not mount a charge of horse."

He chuckled at the recollection. "I give the Navarrese full marks for boldness, for they came straight towards us. They charged us on foot five times that afternoon, and it was a bitter fight to be sure, but in the end, we could not be dislodged. Eventually Lord Durham arrived on the field after their fifth advance, and the Navarrese sounded a withdrawal, retreating in good order.

"During the final charge it so happened that the enemy commander himself led the assault." Stemham smiled into his cup. "Quite a splendid sight, at that, with his men at arms gathered 'round him, charging into volley after volley from the heights. He and I had it out right in the heart of the melee, and I dare say that men on both sides stopped to watch as I threw him down and he yielded. So when his men withdrew, it was to leave him on the field and in my hands.

"Much to my surprise, upon Durham's arrival I learned that my prisoner was none other than the Count D'Ain himself! Oh, that caused quite a stir, believe me, and at the time it seemed my fortunes were without limit!" Stemham's eyes misted over at that, and Elsabeth frowned at the regret in his expression. "'Tis strange how quickly such things can change."

He waved the thought off with a shrug and continued. "Well, as D'Ain was my prisoner, of course his ransom was mine as well. So, as we settled in at Collioure after the garrison capitulated, I dispatched a courier to Ain with the customary demands. Imagine my surprise at the response I received."

Stemham paused again, and this time did not continue. He contented himself with another drink, and picked through the platter of cheese for a morsel to his liking.

Elsabeth leaned out over the table, eager for him to resume the tale. "What happened?" she asked, and rolled her eyes at his visible amusement at her impatience.

"The message was received by D'Ain's brother," he said around a mouthful of cheese, "who was steward of the city in his absence. He offered me half again my demanded ransom should I keep D'Ain in my custody. And double, should some misfortune befall him."

Elsabeth's eyes widened in astonishment. "His own brother?"

Stemham's lip twisted in disgust. "I was no less appalled at such disloyalty from a man's own kin, particularly the price he would put on his honor."

"So what did you do?"

"I went to the chamber where D'Ain was being held in modest comfort, and showed him his brother's words. Needless to say, the revelation of such a treason did not go over well. He was also, of course, quite anxious as to my intentions, as befitting his station, not only was his ransom quite a handsome sum, but that is to say nothing of the value of his brother's bribe.

"However, I could not in good conscience allow such a nefarious disregard for chivalry to stand. So instead, I gathered together my lance and released D'Ain from his cell with this offer: Should he agree to pay the full ransom plus a quarter, I would not only release him on the spot, but would personally assist him in reclaiming Ain from his traitorous kinsman."

Elsabeth's mouth fell open in mixed wonder and disbelief. "You did not!"

"I most assuredly did!"

She sat back in her chair and ignored the fluttering in her heart with great effort when Stemham resolutely met her disbelieving gaze. "This is real life, love, not some minstrel's fancy! You can't truly be that good. *No one* is truly that good!"

"Elsabeth, the day I was knighted, I swore two vows: One to my King, the other to God that never would I abandon the ideals I held in esteem. A man who casts his honor aside for the sake of convenience truly has none to begin with, and I shall hold to mine even should the Dark One himself stand before me."

Elsabeth hid a giddy laugh behind her hands, and the flutter in her heart crescendoed to a thrill starting in the pit of her belly and radiating warmly outward through her limbs. Had she not already been seated she might have felt her knees weaken beneath her.

Whether Stemham told his tale for just such an effect she could not tell; his expression never changed from the wistfulness of memory as he spoke. "We set out from Collioure under a flag of truce and met with the remains of his army as they withdrew back to the southeast. To say that they were surprised at our arrival with their Lord in hand would certainly be understating the matter, and when D'Ain explained what had occurred they were quite outraged; the man has a knack for inspiring loyalty in those who follow him.

"I and my lance joined D'Ain in his march back to Ain. The lookouts upon the walls had quite the fright when they saw our host approach, D'Ain's standard in the van, and we arrived to find the gates closed and held against us. We were given no choice but to make plans for an assault on the castle, as I could not tarry long enough for a proper siege. Fortunately, the garrison was undermanned, as no doubt D'Ain's brother hoped the returning army would join him, and that I would take his offer so he might lay blame for D'Ain's death upon me." He chuckled. "A pity that plan was spoiled when they learned of his treachery 'ere they could complete the withdrawal."

"And of the assault itself?" she asked, and listened with rapt attention, her small beer and breakfast sitting forgotten on the table.

"D'Ain opened the assault himself at first light, attacking the main gates to draw off as much of the defense as he could. Meanwhile, I circled 'round to assail the fortifications at the rear. The castle was so poorly manned, and their attention so focused upon the main assault that the affair was brief, and there is in truth little to tell of my part in the battle. I was, of course, the first up the ladder and thus the first to mount the ramparts, and we easily cut our way through the defenders to the gatehouse to open the gates. The garrison, you see, was made up mostly of the infirm who were unable to march with the army. Well, the moment we opened the gates for the Count, the last of the defenders threw down their arms and begged for mercy. The battle was over, and the castle was ours."

"And D'Ain's brother?"

Stemham smiled broadly in amusement at the memory. "We found him cowering with a maid he fancied inside a wardrobe. Once his guards learned the truth of his treason they dragged him — still clad only in his sleeping gown, I might add — to the great hall without so much as a command from their rightful lord. 'Tis little more to say of him. My Lord chose not to strike down such near kin, and had him taken away in chains. What precisely became of him afterwards I can't say, but the popular tale amongst the bards of the city is that he was walled away in one of the towers, never to be released again."

He paused again for a drink, and momentarily freed from the spell of the tale he wove, Elsabeth picked through the platter in front of her for a piece of cheese. "Is this, then, how you came to be in his service?" she asked around a mouthful.

"Not quite yet. D'Ain, of course, was true to his word, and paid his ransom plus a quarter in full once the castle was secured, and gave me an escort to rejoin Lord Durham at Collioure. For some time that was the last I saw of him. Not even from across a battlefield over the next six years. There were, of course, many of those, but they do not enter into my tale. Though I imagine minstrels could make quite a song or two of them. When the wars ended, I returned to Coventry with the rest of the armies, but alas, I found my stay all too short ..."

Stemham trailed off, and the wistfulness in his expression as he recounted the tale faded into one of shame-faced sorrow. Elsabeth's heart ached in spite of herself at the sight. "What happened?"

His face colored, and he hid it behind his tankard to drain the last of his beer with one swallow. "I beg your forgiveness, but 'tis not something of which I wish to speak. Suffice to say 'twas a matter of honor, and I was obliged to depart Coventry again almost as soon as I arrived."

"I see," she said. His silence on the matter only piqued her curiosity, but she decided against pressing him further. "Did you come here, then?"

"Not straight away, no," he said, and set his empty tankard down on the table. "I was at something of a loss, at first, as I was no longer welcome in Coventry, nor, at the time, did I suspect there was anywhere in Navarre that I might find refuge. So, I chose to join one of the free companies making their way towards the Free City-States, where I might find employment with one of the nobles there. More than a few members of Coventrish chivalry seemed to be taking the path of a *condottieri* once the wars in Navarre ended. Mostly, I suspect, because they had yet to taste their fill of battle, though some, like myself, had nowhere else to turn.

"In the end, I never actually made it. Somehow word of my plight reached D'Ain's ears, and he sent a messenger seeking me out. It took the fellow some time to track me down, and I nearly missed him entirely. He found me not long before we were to cross the border out of Navarre. D'Ain requested that I visit him here. He told me he had learned of my situation and remembered with fondness our assault to reclaim Ain, and more to the point the tales his men told of my sword as we stormed the walls. The Navarrese guilds of defense were in a regrettable state following the wars, and he was finding himself dissatisfied with his current Master of the Longsword, so he offered me the post in his stead."

"How long have you served him?"

"I accepted the posting last year. Oh, 'twas quite the scandal, of course, that the Count D'Ain hired a Coventrish fencing master to operate the school of defense, but he received a sword-arm of good reputation, and I had employment again, so it worked out in both our favors."

Elsabeth watched him, enthralled. "You really ought to have that tale put to music, love. I'll tell you honestly; had I heard it sung in a tavern you could have had me on the table right then and there, and not even at the cost of a good pint of ale."

Stemham lifted one eyebrow in amusement. "I will certainly bear that in mind. Perhaps I ought to have a bard at supper tonight. But that is for later. 'Tis already well into the morning, so perhaps we ought to see to the day, eh?"

She heaved an exaggerated sigh. "Oh, I suppose. I really ought to head back to the inn to gather my belongings if I will be staying here, and to see how that old lech is getting on by himself."

He waved her off. "No need to bother, I'll simply have Richard take care of it. I actually hoped we might spend some time in the training hall this morning."

"'Tis not a bother to me at all, and besides, don't you have preparations to make for the playings?"

"'Tis all well in hand, and there is nothing more for me to do, so the day is actually mine. I would very much enjoy spending it in your company."

Elsabeth hid a smile behind her hand. "I suppose Hieronymus can keep a while longer."

"Wonderful!" Stemham said. He pushed his chair away from the table and sprung to his feet. He extended a hand to help her up, and Elsabeth rose and clutched the dressing gown closed with one hand. "Shall we?"

"I ought to dress first, don't you think?" she asked, and flashed him her most coquettish smile.

Stemham made a show of standing her at arm's length and looking her over. "Well, I cannot say I would insist upon it, but I suppose if you must."

"Hm, as I would rather not give any more of a show to Ain than we did in the garden last night, I suppose I must." Elsabeth slowly turned and started away from him with an exaggerated swaying of her hips.

"In that case, I think I shall come with you," he said, and started after her. Elsabeth let out a playful squeak and took off in an awkward, shuffling run as Stemham pursued her back into his bedchamber.

THE AUTUMN MORNING WAS AS FINE A one as Richard could hope for. A crisp, cool wind blowing in from the fields surrounding Ain to the south and west carried the rich perfumes of harvest-time, mingling with the fragrance of wood fires in the many homes and shops of the City, and the aromas of cooking food as the townspeople prepared for the morning. The first calls of the merchants and street vendors hung over the City, and a low buzz of excitement filled the streets as the beginning of the playings fast approached. The travelers filling the inns and guesthouses near to overflowing had but a day more to wait. They whiled away the hours laughing raucously on street corners, drinking in the taverns, and making a right nuisance of themselves among the women of Ain (and no doubt those of less reputable virtue enjoyed a considerable windfall from those eager for companionship).

Richard, however, had no time that morning to indulge himself in the frivolities, and instead led a small group of his master's servants through the winding, narrow streets towards Elsabeth Hereford's erstwhile lodgings. He ignored the muted gossip over the woman's outlandish behavior behind him and let them have their say; his place was not to judge the Master's choice of company, only to carry out his wishes. If Sir Stemham was pleased with his guest, so much the better.

He found the market square a much more forlorn and empty place upon his arrival that morning, or at least it was in contrast to the exuberance of the days before. A few people wandered from merchant stall to merchant stall examining the offered wares, or listened to the minstrels singing on the corner, but without the curiosity of the swordswoman to draw a crowd, most turned their attention to other business. A few folk loitered about — perhaps hoping for her return from wherever she had disappeared the night before — but most carried on as if she had never been, and Richard overheard a few of the men gathered in knots on the street wondering aloud whether that might very well be the case, and she was indeed naught but a dream.

Richard approached the gate in the low stone wall surrounding the inn, and the master of the house's son hopped down from his usual perch to greet him.

"Good morning, Monsieur Richard!" he said. "What brings you by this fine morning?"

"Good morning, Symon," Richard said, and fished around his purse for a *denier*. "Please have Mademoiselle Soesten's horse brought from the stable, lad, she will be residing with Monsieur Crosseby for the remainder of her stay in Ain."

"Do you mean the swordswoman, Monsieur? She never told me her right name when she arrived."

"Yes, that is her."

The boy's features sank and his shoulders slumped. "Oh, 'tis a shame. Father will be disappointed, I think, as he made a good sum from folks come to see her. And I rather liked to watch her."

Richard raised an eyebrow at him and twitched one corner of his lips into a smile. "You are a bit young yet to be appreciating a woman, are you not?"

Symon's face colored, and he tried to shrink down into the collar of his plain woolen doublet. "Beg your pardon, Monsieur, but I don't mean ..."

He chuckled and ruffled the boy's hair. "Oh, I am sure you don't."

"'Tis only that I have watched Monsieur Crosseby's students when I can sneak away from the inn a spell, but I can't say I have ever seen the likes of her."

"I say 'tis likely you shan't see it again. 'Tis a strange business altogether, but 'tis not my place to question. Now run along and fetch her horse while we see her companion about her belongings."

Richard flipped Symon the coin. He caught it and stuffed it into a pocket. "Yes, Monsieur! She will be ready for you ere you finish!"

And with that he darted off for the stable around back of the inn. Richard watched him go with a small smile and a slight shake of his head, then turned his attention to the gaggle of servants accompanying him. "Come on, let us see to it. Diederic, take her horse in hand and wait for us here. We shan't be long."

Richard stepped off the street and into the inn, and the overly-warm stuffiness of the fire burning in the hearth. They found the common room largely deserted that morning, and the pungent perfume intended to distract one's senses from the stench of too many bodies packed into the confines threatened to overwhelm him. The innkeeper's daughter and niece swept the floors and washed down the heavy timber tables, and he noted one or two folk from out of town finishing their breakfasts in silence. His eyes settled on a large, lumpen shape slumped alone at a table in the corner, and through the gloom Richard recognized the stained and soiled habit of Elsabeth's companion.

"Wait here," he said to his party.

Richard picked a path across the common room and offered a polite nod in return to the greetings of the master of the house's kin.

The friar paid him no heed as he drew nearer, and kept his attention on the platter of eggs and buttered bread on the table in front of him. A tankard of small beer sat at his elbow, and his staff of office stood propped against the bench groaning beneath his copious backside.

"Good morning, Brother," Richard said in Navarrese upon reaching the table, and he inclined his head in greeting.

"If 'tis a Confession you have come for, my son," the friar said in kind, without looking up from his plate, "I suggest you try the cathedral. I'll not step upon the local Bishop's toes."

"I have not come for a Confession, Brother."

"Nor do I traffic in indulgences, as I find that practice most distasteful and unbecoming of a true servant of the Wheel. So once again, I refer you to the local Bishop."

"Nor am I here to purchase your indulgence, Brother. Are you Hieronymus, of the Order of St. Olivus?"

The friar finally looked away from his plate and scrutinized him closely. "If this is about the money your master lost at the dice tables last night, I am sorry but simply can't offer recompense for a donation given to so worthy a cause as my expenses."

"This is not about a gambling debt, Brother."

"Ah, I see. Well, that lass with the flower basket was not your wife, was she?"

"No, Brother ..."

"Sister?"

Richard pinched the bridge of his nose. "Brother ..."

"Daughter, then?"

"For God's sake, I don't know any lass with a flower basket!" Richard said.

The friar chuckled in satisfaction. "Good, then you and I have no argument! Please, have a seat, my son, and share in the morning repast with me."

"I am afraid I have an errand to see to and have no time."

He scowled up at him. "Merciful heavens, what in the Lord's name is it with you lackeys and your urgent errands!"

Richard sighed. "Please, Brother, are you Hieronymus or not?"

The friar took a long swallow of his small beer and wiped his mouth on the sleeve of his mantle in a most undignified and irreverent manner. "Well, as I don't owe you money, and have not given insult to a woman of your acquaintance or relation, then yes, I am."

"I was bidden to deliver a message by my Master—"

Hieronymus sighed and made the Sign of the Wheel with an exaggerated roll of his eyes. "Wait, I remember you, now. God in Heaven, what has that damn foolish girl done?"

"My Master has extended Mademoiselle Soesten an invitation to remain his personal guest for the duration of her stay in Ain. I am under orders to collect her effects and deliver them to his home."

The friar made a face. "Has he, now? And what consideration does he give this poor servant of the Wheel, who spent all this past night praying that that girl had not fallen victim to some horrible fate in her absence from his side? God knows she cannot take two steps without igniting some scandal or other!"

"I don't know what consideration my Master gives you, Brother. He only commands that I gather Mademoiselle Soesten's belongings on her behalf."

Hieronymus took another drink, and let out a sound Richard was undecided whether it was a grunt of indignation or a belch. "It saddens me that a man of such stature in this city could be so heedless of God's servants that he would deprive a man of his sole companion in this cruel world." Richard rolled his eyes at the thickness of the friar's woeful affectations, and impatiently folded his arms across his chest. "What is to become of Hieronymus in her absence?"

"Forgive me, Brother, but my Master did not say. But given who you clearly mistook me for upon my arrival, I may not be wrong in my guess that you are not nearly so lacking in companionship as you imply."

This time there was no mistaking the indignation in the elder man's tone. "Those were but fleeting diversions, my son." Hieronymus bit off a big chunk of his buttered bread, and jabbed it in his direction. "That infuriating harpy, however, is a dear and treasured comrade, no matter how I may wish to put her across my knee!" he said, and sprayed an impressive fountain of crumbs across the table as he spoke.

"I can assure you, Brother, Mademoiselle could be in no better hands during her stay in Ain."

"Oh, I am sure of that! And I can just imagine just where those hands have been since my dear Tetty parted my company. Pawing all manner of unmentionable parts of her anatomy, no doubt!"

Richard's face heated, as much at the friar's insinuations of impropriety on his master's part, as for the man's frankness over his companion's proclivities. "'Tis not for me to comment on the Master's business with his guest, Brother. But I assure you that he intends nothing untoward, and however they choose to entertain themselves there is no coercion involved."

Hieronymus harrumphed and tossed his bread crust down on his platter. "My son I have traveled with that infuriating woman for more than four years, though at times she makes it seem as if it were forty! Believe me when I say

I have no doubts she has gotten exactly what she was after. But I know that girl, and her capacity for misadventure knows no bounds. Without me there to manage her intemperance your Master will spend his days from now to the end-times rescuing her from herself!"

"You have my assurances, Brother, that Mademoiselle shall be perfectly safe, and well-cared for, I might add, in my Master's company. You have nothing to fear for her safety, and she will want for nothing while she remains his guest."

Hieronymus grunted and stuffed the rest of his piece of bread into his mouth. "That is hardly reassuring, as your Master I daresay little understands the manner of mischief Tetty can get up to should he turn his eye from her for but a moment. Now, 'twould be most courteous that you offer I see for myself that there is nothing out of sorts with this arrangement."

Richard's jaw dropped open, momentarily at a loss of words over the bluntness of the request, but the friar just resumed picking through his platter. "I beg your pardon?"

He looked away from his breakfast and regarded him with a raised eyebrow. "Has the Lord of All failed to grace you with a certain keenness of the ears, my son? For given your position I expected a certain quickness of the mind."

"My hearing, bless you, is quite satisfactory," Richard said. He folded his arms across his chest and glowered down on the rotund older man. "And I'll thank you to mind your tongue about my mental faculties."

"Well then, where, pray tell, does your confusion lie? I thought my request was plain enough! I ask only that I might visit with my dear Tetty and ascertain for myself that all is well. Is that so difficult to comprehend?"

"'Tis not, Brother, but 'tis also out of the question. My orders are merely to collect Mademoiselle Soesten's belongings, not to collect her companion as well. I would be happy to relay your request to my Master, but he and your companion shall be occupied in the training hall much of the day, and have already requested not to be disturbed."

"Bah! 'Tis such a small request to make, and your Master I am sure would look dimly upon refusing this humble servant of the Wheel."

"Your pardon, Brother, but rather I risk the wrath of the Lord of All, than bring a guest uninvited into the home of my Master."

"Prudence may be a virtue, my son, but in this, as in all things, there is the danger of excess. I see not what harm it would do that I be allowed just a moment with my dear Tetty to set my poor, worried heart at ease!"

Richard mopped his face and worked his jaw as his desire to be done with the fat friar steadily built towards the overwhelming. "As I said, Brother, I would gladly pass your request on," he said through gritted teeth. "But until my Master says otherwise, I can't offer more. My instructions are merely to collect Mademoiselle Soesten's possessions. Now, I ask for your permission only out of courtesy, so you need not be alarmed to find them gone, but you are quickly pushing me to the limits of largesse in this matter!"

"May I at least be permitted to relay the girl a message, then?" Hieronymus asked. "Since 'tis clearly objectionable that I request an audience."

"Do you truly take me for a fool? I see what you are trying to do, and it won't work," Richard said, and glowered down at him. "I shall be happy to deliver it on your behalf, but no more."

The friar took a drink of his beer and scowled into his tankard when he found it much less full than he would have liked. "My good man, have you no respect for the intimacy between a priest and his supplicant? The message was given to me in the strictest confidence, and is for her ears only! I gave my solemn word that I would deliver it when next I saw her!" He thumped his tankard against the table, and one of the master's girls heaved a sigh and rolled her eyes as she scurried off to grab a pitcher.

"I assure you, Brother, that I can be trusted to keep the message in confidence. I would not have my post if I could not."

"Hmph! By no means do I intend to imply otherwise. But I simply cannot break that covenant, sworn before the eyes of the Lord of All himself—" and at that, he quickly looked to the ceiling and made the sign of the Wheel "— for the foolish whim of any mortal man! The urgency of this message simply can't be overstated!"

Richard sighed again and buried his face in one palm. "I pity your parishioners, Brother, for I fear you could drive the Dark One himself to madness with your persistence!"

Hieronymus chuckled in a very self-satisfied sort of way and settled back in his chair. The serving girl swiftly approached the table with a pitcher of beer and leaned in to refill his tankard. "God has blessed me with many gifts, my son, and I count a tongue of silver not least among them," he said, and peered down the front of the girl's dress with no attempt at subtlety. "Besides, my dear Tetty entrusted me with the key to her room, so unless you intend to batter down the door — a prospect I feel would be most disagreeable to our good host — you have no choice but to bargain with me."

Richard's face heated and he ground his teeth in a silent battle against the urge to take the friar's tankard and bash him over the head, for which he quickly issued a mental apology to the Lord of All over the overwhelming desire to brutalize his servant on earth. "And how long were you planning to argue in circles before making this revelation?"

The serving girl finished with his tankard and scurried off with a wary look over her shoulder, but Hieronymus contented himself with taking his drink in both hands for a long draught. He finished and set the tankard aside, and wiped his mouth on the sleeve of his habit. "Had you been more agreeable, my son, I would have surrendered the key to you from the start. It seemed, however, a firmer hand was needed in these negotiations. Have we a bargain, then?"

"I am not sure the Lord looks kindly upon extortion, from his clergy least of all."

Hieronymus chuckled. "My good man, why do you think the church makes such a tidy profit on indulgences? Now then, as you shan't be going anywhere until I finish, please join me, and share the morning repast!"

Richard only managed a strangled snarl in response as he faced the prospects of a considerably lengthened morning.

15

ROSSEBY SHIFTED HIS WEIGHT TO ONE leg, folded his arms across his chest, and watched Elsabeth work through the progression of cuts. Her face glistened with sweat, and sweat soaked through her linen shirt.

The moisture plastered it against her body, but did not *quite* render it translucent enough to see the skin beneath. He quirked a small grin. No matter, he saw her clearly enough all the night before, and again this morning while they were dressing for practice, to commit every graceful curve of her lithe figure to memory. Crosseby imagined the smooth contraction and relaxation of the muscles beneath the taut skin of her arms, back, and shoulders, and of course the close fit of her hose left little of her lower extremity to the imagination. It took a considerable exercise of his will to keep his attention on the entirety of her form, and not just focus on her shapely bottom and thighs.

They stood in the middle of the training hall floor. The construction was of the typical sort and matched the house itself: A tall ceiling of ribbed arches supported the roof, and windows high in the clerestory and triforium allowed in sunlight to supplement the lamps filling the hall with a warm golden glow. A large bank of windows gazed out onto the garden courtyard on the west side of the building, with an elaborate gilded door allowing one to step outside onto the lawn of green grass. For now, it and the windows were thrown open to allow in fresh air, the sounds of the City, and the quiet singing of birds perching on the roofs outside.

Widely spaced columns supporting the arches overhead divided the space into neat squares, and each square was filled by a training circle etched into ceramic floor tiles the color of pale gold. A raised dais occupied the far northern end of the hall, with a fireplace along the back wall filling the chamber with the sweet smell of burning perfumed wood. Above the fireplace hung a shield bearing his coat of arms, and doors on either side led to his private office space. Doors in the eastern wall fronting the street led to storage for wasters, staves, *Federn*, pells, and whatever other equipment his students might need. Large timber doors framed and reinforced with iron in the south opened onto the arcaded walkway connecting the wings of the complex. The rest was strictly functional; no paintings or tapestries, no extraneous artistry, the only things that mattered here were the arts being taught within its walls.

Whatever else one might say about the arrangement which brought him to his post, Ain's school of defense could not ask for better quarters.

Elsabeth's arms quivered, and she clenched her teeth. That subtle movement in her jaw translated through the muscles in her slender neck. She grimaced and grunted as she swung the quarterstaff through the drill. The strain was plainly visible in her expression, from the slight tightening of the corners of her eyes to the determined curl of her lips.

But, nevertheless, she refused to utter so much as a syllable of complaint. Crosseby allowed himself a smile. Even some of his best students would have long ago surrendered, but Elsabeth forced herself to continue, until finally her strength failed, and she could support the staff no longer. One arm dipped, and the perfection of her form until now was spoiled.

"Lift that arm!" he snapped, as much for effect as any real need to chastise or correct her.

But Elsabeth finally had enough of the drill. She lowered the staff with a rush of breath, and bent double at the waist. "Good lord, do you put all of your students through this?"

He gave her a mock scowl. "Are you questioning my training methods?"

"Not at all. But I think if I were to try to lift this any longer my arms might fall off."

Crosseby relieved her of the staff before she dropped it, and casually leaned it against his shoulder. "If you only ever train within the comfort of your limits, how do you expect to improve? You must push past them until your strength fails. 'Tis the right way to build the endurance of your arm for a protracted contest."

"'Tis usually not a problem I have to contend with," she said, and quirked a grin as she straightened and massaged her arm. "I find I tend to outlast most men as it is."

Crosseby's face heated a bit, and he chuckled softly. "Yes, well, 'tis never a bad thing to be prepared for such an eventuality as an adversary who can match your remarkable endurance. Now then—" he tossed the staff back to her, and she caught it with a grunt "—begin again, this time through the guards. Start in left Roebuck — *ochs*, I believe you called it in the Boehman fashion — and proceed through them as we discussed."

"Yes, Master," she said, the last added with a dry turn of her voice to match the wry curl of her lip. Elsabeth gripped the staff on its bottom third, her right hand leading, and raised the staff above her left shoulder, just shy of parallel to the floor.

"Be mindful of your transition from left to right," he said. "Keep it quick and controlled, and the movement tight."

"'Tis good advice for many other exercises, as well."

She worked her way through the wards. From Roebuck she dropped the point into Pendant, and shifted it left and right to cover both openings. She then stepped back and drew the staff into the Right Hawk. "Perhaps when we have finished here you might demonstrate further ..."

His face heated again at the innuendo dripping from her voice. "Focus, Elsabeth!"

She cut forcefully from Hawk and across her body into the Left Plow, then lunged forward with a stiff thrust and used the movement to replace her hands on the staff. She recovered into Right Plow, the movement sure and the guard held strongly. A flick of her green eyes in his direction was accompanied by a slight twitch of her lips into a grin. "I am focused, love," she said. "But your attention seems to be diverted to something other than my holding of the staff."

Contrary to her insinuation Crosseby had kept his eyes on her form until that moment, when the playful accusations drove him to put the truth to them. Particularly as her changing of guard left him an unimpeded view of the manner in which her hose cupped her backside.

"You wicked woman!" he said, and could not help but laugh. She flashed him a coy smile over her shoulder when she caught him looking, and made a show of shifting her weight from foot to foot to waggle her hips and bottom at him. Crosseby's response came as a firm, but playful, slap to her backside.

Elsabeth yelped and hopped a good span into the air. The staff dropped from her hands and clattered to the floor with a sharp *clack* that echoed in the rafters and arches of the ceiling.

She favored him with a wounded pout and made a show of rubbing her right cheek. "I should warn you, Sir, that I have killed men for lesser offenses than that!"

"One thing I shan't abide is the spilling of blood on my floor," he said, not quite able to wipe the smile from his lips. "Now pick that up and begin again!"

Elsabeth strolled over to the discarded staff, and with exaggerated slowness bent double at the waist to pick it up. Crosseby's mouth went dry and his hose became distinctly uncomfortable in front at the way her posture stuck her posterior into the air. The fabric shifted and stretched, and presented every supple curve as if she were standing naked before him. She picked up the staff and straightened again, once more exaggerating the movement, and lightly dragged the tip of the staff along the floor until she stood upright.

"Begin again?" she said, a slight purr in her voice.

Crosseby gave her a curt nod, but the appreciative smirk on his face cheated him of the stern master's glower he intended to affect. "From Left Roebuck."

She resumed her guard, again with an exaggerated sinuousness that made his hose tighten even further. Crosseby strode forward and sidled up close behind her. He placed his own hands next to hers on the staff and made a show of correcting her posture. He leaned his chin on her shoulder, his cheek next to hers. Wisps of copper hair escaped from the untidy bun piled atop her head tickled his nose and cheek, and Elsabeth giggled at the sensation of his body pressed against hers. The musky scent of her sweat filled his nostrils, and this close he watched it dribble in rivulets and rills down the side of her face, diverting around her cheekbones, and running along the line of her jaw.

"You are holding it too loosely," he said. "Keep your grip firm and strong."

"You were quite complimentary of my grip last night …" she said, and that wry twist came to her lips again.

Crosseby nuzzled the side of her neck. Elsabeth let out a throaty giggle and shifted her face away from his. "That was last night. Today it is loose and sloppy."

"Then by all means, Master," she said, and again the last was added with a playful lilt. "Show me."

Crosseby guided her hands to lift the staff higher, sharing its weight as he adjusted her holding of the ward. "Like this," he said into her ear.

"I see. I also feel that you have your own staff raised quite firmly as well."

"That is not the purpose of this drill."

"But I do believe you are having a mind for another sort of drill nonetheless."

"Because you are trying to distract me."

"You are easily distracted."

"I assure you my focus is firmly on the task at hand."

"Your focus is firmly sticking me in the backside," she gasped when he took advantage of his proximity to kiss the side of her neck. Her flesh tasted salty from the sheen of sweat lathering her skin.

"'Twas you that offered the invitation, I was merely accepting," he said. Crosseby released his hold on the staff to thread his arms around her waist and pull her even tighter against him.

Elsabeth released the staff, and it clattered once more to the floor. One of her hands came up and twined into the hair at the back of his head, the other she laid across the arms encircling her waist. "This was not the lesson I was expecting."

"I know," he said between nips and nibbles from the base of her neck up towards her earlobe. "I think so long as you are here, I shan't get a single thing done."

"Such a pity," she purred. She twisted around until she was facing him and hung her arms around his neck. Crosseby kissed her on the lips. Lightly at first, but soon she drew him in. Her tongue played across his, and her teeth nipped at his upper lip. His hands slid down her back to cup her bottom and draw her closer, then found their way to the waist of her hose, seeking for the ties securing the flap in front.

Crosseby did not even let the first knot slip before a thunderous pounding shook the training hall. He let out a groan of annoyance and buried his face in her shoulder. Another heavy *thud* against the door echoed through the ribbed arches of the ceiling. "I asked that we not be disturbed ..."

Elsabeth pulled away just enough so she could look him in the eyes again and tipped his chin up. "Ignore them, love, maybe they will go away."

Any hope of that was dashed by a third, even more insistent drumming against the timber door. He sighed and reluctantly pushed her to arm's length with his hands on her hips. "Regrettably no, it seems. I expected Richard to be back by now to handle such nuisances."

She grunted. "Richard would have to go through Hieronymus to collect my belongings, and if I know him, he has him halfway through a cask at the inn, and probably a small fortune in debt by now. Best you pray to the Lord of All he does not own Richard altogether by the time he gets back."

"If so, the good Brother and I may be coming to a very serious disagreement." Another blow rocked the doors. Crosseby sighed and gave her a kiss on the brow. "I suppose I have no choice but see what they want before they break out a ram and batter the doors down."

"Let me fetch my sword, and I say we run them off together. They daren't assault this place with us both to defend it."

"But then there is the hassle of having them disposed of afterwards. I'll just be a moment."

"Oh, very well. But don't get some damned foolish and heroic notion; I am here if you need reinforcements."

"I'll keep that in mind," he said, and stepped away from her. Elsabeth took the opportunity to return the playful swat to his behind, and his right buttock stung from a firm slap on the hindquarters. Crosseby shot her a none-too-withering glare over his shoulder as he rubbed his cheek and headed for the door. Elsabeth just shrugged it off with a smirk, and retrieved a pitcher of small beer and a tankard set safely out of the way next to one of the pillars for a drink.

He hurried down the hall, the doors shaking with every heavy knock. Crosseby ground his teeth and twisted his countenance into a suitably annoyed scowl at the intrusion. He threw open the bolts and bars securing the door and hauled on the handle. The heavy timber door groaned softly as it swung inward. Awaiting him on the training hall porch was a boy in the livery of the Count's service. He took one look at Crosseby's expression and swallowed, shifted from one foot to the other, and waited to be addressed.

"What is it?" Crosseby said in Navarrese, and did not bother to mask the annoyance in his voice. "I gave instructions to my staff I was not to be disturbed."

"I beg your pardon, Monsieur Crosseby," the youth said, and flinched back at the heatedness of Crosseby's tone. "But Monsieur le Chevalier commanded me to deliver this message."

The boy reached into a case slung across his shoulder. Crosseby folded his arms across his chest and leaned against the doorframe while he waited. He found the paper he was looking for, and presented an envelope closed with wax bearing the Count's seal. Crosseby accepted it but did not bother to open it.

"Was Monsieur le Chevalier expecting a response?"

"He did not say, Monsieur. I was told only that this message be delivered directly into your hand."

"Well then, the message is assuredly in my hand, and your task is thus completed. Now I have important business to return to, please give my compliments to Monseigneur."

Crosseby shut the door in the boy's face, and slammed the bolts closed again. He started back up the hall to where he had left Elsabeth with a frown. She watched him from her place leaning against one of the pillars supporting the ceiling with her tankard of small beer in hand, while he slipped his thumb under the flap of the letter and broke the seal. The note was written on fine velum in the firm hand of D'Ain, so whatever the contents of the message he clearly deemed it important enough to write it himself.

"What is it?" Elsabeth asked when he reached her. She craned her neck to look over his shoulder to read the note for herself along with him:

*Monsieur Crosseby,*

> *Your presence is required at the castle tonight at sunset, for a banquet to celebrate the opening of the playings tomorrow. I do realize you have been deeply preoccupied with the preparations, and apologize in advance should my request jeopardize your efforts to have all ready in time.*

*However, the needs of protocol demand your presence tonight in attending to your guests for this event.*

The letter was signed with a flourish and marked with the Count's seal. Crosseby heaved another sigh as he read it first once, then twice. An official summons to the castle, to socialize and mingle once more with the sycophants, courtiers, and visiting masters, and keep him away from more pressing and enjoyable business. He folded the letter up and stuffed it back into the envelope.

"Damn," he said, and leaned his back against the pillar. Elsabeth regarded him for a moment, then fetched his tankard of small beer. He accepted it with a nod and nearly tossed it all back in one big swallow. "'Tis a shame 'tis but small beer and not something stronger."

She gave him an amused smile. "Yes, I can see how a summons to a feast at the castle could be quite a distressing turn of events."

"I never had much use for the business of attending court, even when I was still in the King's good graces before my exile. And this event has brought no shortage of fools and braggarts, particularly those disciples of da Lucca and Russdorffer. Bloody preening peacocks!"

"That was always one of my sister's big fancies, to be presented at court." Elsabeth took a long drink of her beer. "I myself could hardly have cared less, but I did not really understand such things at that age."

"And now?"

"Well, good food and good drink is hard to resist, and I can't imagine a better table than a lord as lofty as your good Count D'Ain."

Crosseby grunted and stared into his tankard. "In all honesty there are other diversions I would rather be attending to than mere good food and drink. Oh, all the preparations for tomorrow are in order and there is nothing left for me to do, so 'tis not like I have any pressing business in that regard, but nonetheless I would rather have a quiet evening with you before the chaos begins tomorrow."

Elsabeth giggled, a sly and mischievous sound that set his finer hairs standing on end. He glanced sidelong at her and narrowed his eyes in suspicion. "What?"

She smirked. "I was just thinking how amusing it might be if I were to accompany you tonight."

Crosseby laughed into his tankard, particularly as the distress of the Schwertbrüder upon learning of Elsabeth's presence in the town returned to mind. "I believe that might well scandalize some of my Lord's guests. You certainly stirred up quite the bit of excitement with your demonstrations."

He considered for a moment, and a broad smile worked its way across his features. "Well, Ain said nothing to the effect that I was to come alone, and they are, after all, my playings. If, of course, you would be so inclined as to accompany me to the castle tonight?"

Elsabeth cocked one corner of her mouth into a roguish grin. "Love, I daren't even consider declining!"

ASPAR CUPPED HIS GOBLET IN ONE hand and stood silently among the dregs of Navarrese swordsmanship. Their inane babble on the guards or strategies and puerile debates on the merits of different drills and flourishes filled the great hall of Castle Ain. This was punctuated here and there by some ridiculousness out of the Free City-States championing the outrageous flailing of da Lucca from the show fighters (in particular Antonio Guarin). He curled his lip into a dismissive scowl. Such was the state of the art among the Navarrese: disjointed, confused, no sense of cohesion. Any man with a sword could call himself "Master" and no one would be the wiser. To be here was a waste of time that could be better spent preparing his students for the playings set to begin on the morrow.

Instead, he found himself trapped here, socializing among *masters* who might be little better than amateurs by the Brotherhood's reckoning. But when a man of D'Ain's stature "invited" one to the castle it was not a polite invitation, but a command to appear. And one does not ignore such a command.

So he smiled and nodded, and raised his glass to toast the Count's health or to wish his associates — if one could truly call them such — luck during the playings, and traded idle gossip, and interjected his own position on the finer points of battle and dueling when asked. It came as great relief when the Grand Master arrived, resplendent in his white robes of office, and Caspar found a pretext to excuse himself from the tedium of the gathering to attend to Aich.

Caspar bowed low to Aich upon reaching his side and fell into step with him as he made his way along the aisle between the long trestle tables lining the walls on either hand towards the dais. The Grand Master, of course, would be seated in a place of honor with the D'Ain once supper began, and once again Caspar would be cast into the pit of wolves to be devoured by their mundanity.

"How are your students fairing?" Aich asked, and swirled his own wine before sampling it — his hand had not been empty long upon entering before it was filled with a goblet. "Are they ready?"

"They are, Master," Caspar said. "Merklin in particular is eager to begin."

"Good. Will any of the others be participating?"

"Franciscus, Ladislaus, and Thadeus have all submitted their names to me as well. However, I intend to encourage Georgius to join them as I believe he will perform quite well in the general contest of arms."

Aich nodded. "Indeed, I am actually disappointed he did not volunteer himself. As I recall he came very near to besting Merklin when last I saw them bout."

Caspar considered. "Ah, that was last year, as I recall, around midsummer. They are not nearly so closely matched now. In my estimation Georgius might very well have the talent to unseat Merklin as Vorfechter, but he lacks the ambition to push himself. He has more interest in chasing after the girls of Soest than attending to his studies."

The Grand Master quirked a smile beneath his thick white beard. "As I recall you were not so different once yourself."

They reached the dais, and were met there personally by D'Ain, who was absorbed in a discussion with Antonio Guarin. Caspar hid a roll of his eyes at the sight of the preening peacock behind his wine glass, though the Grand Master was far too dignified to require such measures. The Count silenced whatever tale Guarin was telling with a polite wave of his hand and beckoned the pair to join them. Caspar and Aich bowed low in greeting.

"Ah! Masters, welcome again to my home, and thank you very much for accepting my invitation!" D'Ain said.

"'Tis we who are grateful for the gracious invitation, Monseigneur," Aich said. A purely diplomatic answer. Though the Grand Master masked it well, Caspar had no doubts he was no less annoyed to be summoned to the castle and away from attending to the guild's business in Ain.

"How are your students? Are they ready to begin the playings?"

"They are most eager for it, Monseigneur," Caspar said.

"Good! Very good! I look forward to seeing how well the Schwertbrüder acquit themselves in the days ahead." He turned and motioned to Guarin. "I believe you know Master Guarin."

"We are acquainted, yes," Caspar said, and gave him a polite incline of the head. True to his nature, Guarin dressed for the evening in a red and gold brocaded doublet of silk and velvet, garish in color even by the reckoning of the nobility.

"The good Master was just sharing a most interesting bit of news," D'Ain continued, and a broad smile came to his face. "There is a woman in Ain giving exhibitions with the sword at one of the inns, who by all accounts is quite good, and has actually been giving a good thrashing to some of the visitors come for the bouts."

A lump of ice formed in Caspar's belly, and he gritted his teeth. Even the Grand Master's jaw tightened. Guarin, for his part, stood in silence with a self-satisfied smirk on his face.

"Indeed?" Caspar said, but could not quite keep the mollification out of his voice. Aich's countenance darkened considerably, but D'Ain paid it no heed.

D'Ain chuckled and took a drink of his wine. "Indeed. In fact, she is claiming to have been trained by the Brotherhood themselves."

"I assure you, Monseigneur, that the Brotherhood disavows all connection with this creature," Aich said.

D'Ain just waved the matter off. "Ah, 'tis nothing you need fear, I actually quite enjoy a spectacle. If she is still in the City I may even go and see one of these exhibitions myself to see what the excitement is about."

"Surely Monseigneur has better uses for his time ..."

"Nonsense!" he said and laughed into his wine goblet. Caspar eyed him closely, and suddenly felt as if he knew more than he let on. He shot a look at Guarin and wondered just how much the man told him. "In fact, any matter that could so vex the esteemed Schwertbrüder bears a closer look."

Caspar's face heated, and Aich's jaw clenched so tightly he thought the man might very well grind his own back teeth into dust. However, before anyone could say another word the entire great hall plunged into a silence so deep the rustle of Caspar's doublet as he moved was deafening in his ears. The fire continued to pop and crackle in the hearth, a sharp intake of breath was as loud as a scream, and everyone stopped what they were doing and turned to the screens passage.

The four of them did as well, and he craned his neck in a vain effort to look past the sea of bodies for what so stunned the congregation into silence. In the end he need not have bothered. Men parted, their faces contorted with astonishment, and they opened a path to the dais for Stemham Crosseby.

And *her*.

Caspar's mouth fell open, and Aich's body stiffened beside him. What D'Ain thought of seeing her there, on Crosseby's arm, Caspar could not guess, for he could not tear his eyes from the sight to look. Nor could he decide what astonished the gathering more: that she was there at all — and most almost certainly knew by now exactly who she was, for many of the masters had gone to see her demonstrations the day before — or because they were unprepared for the vision before them.

She wore a gown of green velvet, of a fashion just sweeping out of Arras that draped loosely to the floor, with narrow sleeves and a wide **V**-shaped neck that plunged to a point just below her breast. The neckline, hem, and cuffs were all trimmed with plush black velvet, and a broad belt of red silk beneath the bust pulled the gown tightly round her upper body. An inset of more black velvet pinned to the kirtle beneath filled the deep neckline of the gown in a manner that both preserved her modesty, and yet teased the eye with a hint of her cleavage.

Her one deviation from reputable women's fashion that night was her uncovered hair; she wore her forelocks drawn back from her heart-shaped face and secured at the base of her skull with a clasp of silver, but otherwise allowed it to spill freely and uncovered past her shoulders in a cascading river of burnished copper. The only jewelry adorning her was a silver pendant of the Wheel resting just below her collarbones, and a gold ring set with a faceted red stone on one slender finger.

Though he would not openly confess to such a thing, Caspar certainly had his fantasies when he first knew her. Now, seeing her so close again for the first time in years, he could not deny to himself the striking beauty she had become. Like all the others gathered in that space as she stepped from the screens passage, he stood for a moment transfixed. But then the moment passed, and a cold wrath spread from that lump of ice D'Ain's remarks had formed in his gut. His limbs quivered, and he balled his hands into fists so tight he ought to have crushed the stem of his goblet. The gathering took a collective breath, and slowly the whispers began; rumors of her demonstrations in the market, curiosity about who she was and whence she came, of her connection to the Schwertbrüder. That last in particular made his stomach churn. But no more than her sheer *audacity* of appearing here, before this collection of masters from across a continent.

Crosseby directed her straight to the dais. Straight to D'Ain. Straight to him and the Grand Master. The Coventrish knight stopped at times to introduce his Coventrish whore to some face in the crowd; d'Aubigny and da Pavia upon entering, who paused in some quarrel with d'Orgremont. Loys Oger particularly seemed pleased at the introduction. Morelet and de Craon and Gaude. A pleasantly surprised smile crossed the features of Ruiz when she responded to his introduction in Lizarran. Some masked their disdain for her presence and gall beneath a veneer of civility, others were more ambivalent, one or two perhaps even amused at the display (to judge from Guarin's tittering behind him). And ever they made their way to the dais. There was no escape for him. He could not excuse himself from D'Ain's presence until released. He was held captive for the torture to come.

They reached the dais, and D'Ain stepped forward in front of his other guests to greet them.

"Ah! Monsieur Crosseby, I am pleased you were able to attend this evening!" he said, and clasped the knight firmly by the hand. "I understand how terribly busy you have been with the preparations for the playings, but tonight would have been a tragedy without your presence!"

Crosseby bowed low, and she sketched a deep curtsy. It was a formality, of course; Crosseby's invitation would certainly have been no less a command than Caspar's own, if not more so. "The pleasure is mine, Monseigneur."

"And what is this?" D'Ain turned his attention to the infuriating woman, regarding her with a cool pretense, as if only now seeing the vision for the first time. "I certainly would have recalled issuing an invitation to such a delightful creature."

"Monseigneur, I wish to present to you Mademoiselle Elsabeth Hawke Soesten de Hereford—" Caspar's body tensed at her use of that name, and he dug his nails into his palms "—daughter of le Chevalier Thomas Hawke de Hereford, and my personal guest for the duration of her visit to Ain."

He blinked. This was a child of *Hawke?* He glanced sidelong at the Grand Master, who glowered at the sight of the woman, with his hand wrapped so tightly about his wine glass his knuckles turned white. Beyond the wrath simmering beneath the civil façade, Caspar caught the subtle flare of consternation at Hawke's name.

Even D'Ain seemed for a moment taken aback. "Monsieur Hawke? A man of no small reputation even here in Navarre." D'Ain scooped her hand and kissed it lightly on the fingers. "If that is the case, Mademoiselle Soesten, then I may forgive Monsieur Crosseby his cheek in bringing an unexpected guest to this affair, even one so lovely."

Elsabeth let her cheeks color just enough to appear suitably flattered, and inclined her head slightly.

*So she is a whore of breeding. But she is a whore nonetheless.*

D'Ain then turned to the rest of them. "Allow me to introduce you to Monsieur Antonio Guarin, Master of the Longsword." Guarin stood forward and inclined his head, a gesture she returned. "Monsieur Caspar von Bech, Master of the Longsword." Caspar forced himself to give the polite nod, and he caught a hint of the twisted smile he saw often in his nightmares the moment she recognized him. "And certainly not least, Monsieur Stefan von Aich, Grand Master of the Schwertbrüder, who has graciously agreed to attend the playings."

Elsabeth did a courtesy to the Grand Master, nearly as deeply as she did for D'Ain himself, that same, malicious smile on her lips. "Master," she said. "I don't believe I ever had the pleasure of making your acquaintance, though I knew your name well enough when I studied with Paulus."

Aich's features paled, his body trembled, and Caspar half expected the old man's head to explode. Guarin stood forward, an enormous smile on his face, before the Grand Master could offer a rebuke. "Then 'tis true? What the rumors that have been circulating about your exhibitions in the market say?"

She and Crosseby each accepted a glass of wine from the servant who appeared near at hand, before scurrying off to see to the other guests. "I'll have to ask you to elaborate further on that, Master Guarin," she said with a trace of amusement in her voice. "As I am subject of so much rumor wherever I go I can't always keep them straight."

"'Twas said that you were a student of Paulus von Soest, before his death."

A wistful expression crossed Elsabeth's features, and she took a sip of wine. "Indeed I was. In fact, Master von

Bech is already known to me, as he was Vorfechter of the schola at the time."

Guarin flashed him a thoroughly amused smirk. "Really? That tale was not a part of the rumors."

"Oh, I should say not," she said, and glanced over the rim of her glass at Caspar with a mischievous twinkle in her green eyes. "They are rather ashamed of me, after all, so I can't say I am surprised they would rather forget me altogether. Caspar least of all for all the drubbings I have given him."

"I must say that makes the rumors even more intriguing. Master von Bech, you have been holding out on me!"

"I was hardly holding anything from you, Master, as you and I seldom have business to discuss." Caspar said.

"Oh, but in this case I think we have quite a bit." Guarin looked to Elsabeth and swirled his wine about his goblet. "Tell me, what is your position on the quality of the instruction among the Schwertbrüder?"

"I can't say I have ever known a finer swordsman than Paulus, and his passing was surely a terrible blow to the Brotherhood." A smile crept back to her lips. "I fear the school in Soest must be suffering his absence."

Crosseby hid a laugh behind his goblet with a quick drink, but Guarin wasted no time in taking advantage of the opening.

"Are you not Master now in Soest?" he said to Caspar.

"I am," Caspar replied through gritted teeth.

"Truly?" Elsabeth said, and her brows arched slightly into an expression somewhere between surprise and delight, accompanied by that wicked smile. Her manner now reminded him of nothing less than a cat preparing to pounce. "Well, I can't imagine anyone who could fill so tremendous a void left by Paulus's death, so why not Caspar? I really must congratulate you on your fancy of wearing a Master's ring coming to fruition after all."

"Master von Bech has performed exemplarily in his position," Aich said, a subtle hint of warning in his tone.

Elsabeth took no notice of that slight raise of his voice, and sipped at her wine. "Oh, I am sure there are a number of positions in which Caspar must have proven quite exemplary to be granted such a posting."

If the others noted her meaning they did not show it, but Caspar had endured the insinuation and innuendo from her for years, so she might as well have been shouting it. His cheek twitched, and one corner of Elsabeth's mouth turned up when she caught his response; she knew all too well he saw through her even if they did not.

"So tell me, Caspar, do you intend to participate in the bouting yourself?" she continued.

"I don't recall that he entered his name, yet" Crosseby said. "However, I could certainly use some fencers of rank for the Provost bouts."

"I am sure there is much they could learn about the craft from watching Caspar fence," she said. "'Twould certainly be entertaining."

"I am not here to play to the simpletons in the crowds," Caspar said. "These playings are a serious exercise in the craft."

"Oh, I am quite familiar with the tradition. 'Tis a pity, though, as I have always found our bouts in the past to be quite diverting, if all too brief for good exercise."

Guarin sniggered under his breath, and Caspar spit him with a warning glare that did nothing to wipe the amusement from his features. "You and I remember things very differently."

Elsabeth grinned. "Oh, I have no doubt. I am sure in your memory 'twas I who was humbled time and again by your superb sword while all the school looked on. But perhaps you will have a chance after all!"

Caspar narrowed his eyes and frowned at her. "What do you mean?"

Crosseby smirked. "While tomorrow I'll be testing the Scholars, I decided to take it upon myself to enter Mademoiselle Soeten for consideration as a Provost the day after."

Caspar choked on a mouthful of wine, and for a long moment after clearing his throat all he could do was stare at the pair in shock. Guarin could hold back his mirth no longer and broke out into a fit of riotous laughter, and even D'Ain seemed thoroughly amused by the idea of that loathsome woman participating in the playings. Beside him Aich's features turned positively livid, but all Caspar could see was that wicked smile of triumph.

**17**

"Don't forget I am still rather cross with you," Elsabeth said between giggles as Stemham lifted her down from the palfrey he had loaned her for the ride to the castle. The stable boy took it and Stemham's fine courser in hand, and led both animals away to remove their gear and stable them for the night.

The house complex loomed over them in the darkness, its towers and peaked roofs an even darker shadow against the dusting of stars twinkling in the indigo sky overhead. The moon was beginning to sink down into the west, but still cast a pale silver light over Ain that glittered in the City's stonework. It was almost enough to see by without the need of the golden glow of thousands of lamps mingling with the moonlight. The City was silent at this hour; the only souls abroad were the guards making their rounds, guests at the castle returning to their lodgings, and the odd ne'er-do-well, pickpocket, or bawd in the poorer sections where the eyes of the city guard were less keen.

"And what did I do to deserve your ire?" he said, his tone playfully defensive.

"You did not tell me that Caspar was here in Ain!"

"Is that all? Well, in my defense I thought you would know such a thing already! I hope you are not planning to make me jealous."

Elsabeth twisted her features with disgust. "With Caspar? Oh God no! I can't imagine how his own horse consents to let him mount her. I would sooner give in to that drunken lech who follows me around." She gave him a pointed look. "But don't you dare tell Hieronymus I said that; 'tis bad enough even without that fleeting bit of hope to encourage him."

Stemham made a show of pressing his hand to his heart. "I swear by my honor and in the name of Holy God such a thing shan't pass my lips."

"See that it does not, or you and I shall have an argument." She chuckled as the look on Caspar's face when Crosseby announced he was placing her in the playings returned to mind. "But I can't imagine a sight that makes me happier than the sheer terror on his face when you told them I will be fighting in the playings. They can't stand me, you know."

"Yes, the Grand Master seemed quite put out as well, though he certainly held it back better than Master von Bech."

She rolled her eyes. "Master von Bech," she said, and let her revulsion at mouthing those words drip from her tongue. "The man scarcely knows which end of the sword to hold towards an enemy, and yet he has taken Paulus's place teaching in Soest."

"At the risk of enraging you further and driving you from my bed tonight, 'tis not his reputation."

"Bugger his reputation! I trained with the twat for the better part of seven years. The only reason that he remained Vorfechter under Paulus and not I, was because of what I am lacking twixt my thighs. I could thrash him blindfolded before I grew my tits."

"Well, that is certainly colorful."

"Oh shush." She heaved a sigh and slumped her shoulders. Old memories long buried threatened to well up on her, and she quickly stamped them down lest they rise up and sting. "So Caspar got the school, the posting, and the prestige, all undeserved."

She felt Stemham's eyes on her, and he edged closer so he could put an arm around her waist. "'Tis the way of it, I suppose, but you can't say you took away nothing from it, either."

Elsabeth gave him a sharp look and watched the moonlight glitter in his grey eyes, searching for his meaning, a hint he knew more than she told him. If Caspar was here...

But no, she saw nothing hidden in their depths, just a deep sympathy on top of the longing to be off the street and in the privacy of his chambers. A notion which promised at least some relief from the ache building anew in the pit of her belly. Perhaps she ought to just sprint the rest of the way into the house. "'Tis true. My sword, for one. Among a few other dear things. Oh, Caspar would love to have his clumsy hands on that blade. 'Twas Paulus's, you know."

"I confess I did not recognize it, but then Master von Soest and I never had the privilege of meeting."

"No offense to you, love, but he truly is still the greatest swordsman I have ever known." She sighed. "Come on, let us get off the street, I desperately need to get out of this confounded dress."

Stemham sensed her sudden shift in mood and hugged her tighter against his hip. Elsabeth leaned her head against his shoulder. They made the rest of their way in silence, ghosts of the past flitting through the shadows between buildings along the street, and the arcaded walkway connecting the training hall to Stemham's house. She heard again the cracking of the wasters, the shouts and jeers of the students — particularly during her many scraps with Caspar over some insult which she may not have instigated. Paulus's disapproving scowl whenever the two of them got into it and, in those secret, private moments between just the two of them, his amusement over the whole affair. His pride in her skill, that one small comfort making the knowledge she would never be accepted worthwhile.

All of that was gone, now. Lost that one horrid, terrible, rain-drenched night in spring.

They reached the side door of the house off the arcade and stepped inside, closing out the night behind them. The lamps were lit, and the muffled sound of voices echoed through the hallways. Stemham frowned, and Elsabeth studied him closely.

"What is it?" she asked.

"'Tis late, and usually the other servants have turned in. Only Richard waits on me at this hour," he said.

"Well, perhaps with all the excitement this week they thought to have themselves a little party while you were away at the castle." She flashed him a smile. "Truth be told, I could do with another drink myself."

He chuckled and turned her up the hall. "Well, 'twould be rude of us not to make an appearance, then."

They made their way past the tapestries and windows, and through the screens passage. As they neared the great hall and the voices became recognizable, Elsabeth's heart sank somewhere into the pit of her stomach. "For the love of God, please tell me 'tis not ..."

She trailed off upon stepping into the hall and buried her face in one hand. There, in Stemham's chair at the table atop the dais, sat Hieronymus, singing an old bawdy song she had often heard her father sing during drunken revelries among the soldiers, (and it sounded no more melodious that night than it had all those years ago) with a tankard of ale in his hand. Richard slumped next to him, practically tearing out his hair as the friar went on. Elsabeth noted the lack of a cup at his elbow, so it was clearly not the drink that put Crosseby's servant in such a state.

Stemham raised an eyebrow and folded his arms across his chest. "Well, 'tis not a sight I can say I have come home to before."

"I wish I could say the same, love. Count your blessings he is not naked this time."

He stifled a laugh. "Dear God, I can see it when I close my eyes. I suppose we ought to see what this is all about, then."

Elsabeth clutched at his arm and tried to pull him back down the screens passage. Stemham yelped and stumbled after her. "Please, no! If we turn about and run quickly he may never even know we were here. There is no shame in a strategic withdrawal."

Unfortunately, any opportunity to retreat was cheated by Richard, who looked up from the table and jumped to his feet. "Master!" he cried, and hurried down from the dais. Hieronymus froze in mid-chorus and glanced up from his tankard. Elsabeth quickly placed herself behind Stemham and buried her face in his back in hopes the friar would not see her.

Stemham regarded Richard with a bemused curl of his lip as his servant hurried across the floor of the hall, an expression not unlike a dog shame-faced over some misdeed on his features. "Richard," Crosseby said, his voice more amused than incensed over the uninvited guest. "It seems you decided to have revelries of your own while I was at the castle."

Richard's face heated, and Elsabeth could not help but smile into Stemham's back at his discomfiture. "Forgive me, Sire, but I had no choice!" he said, his voice cracking with exasperation. "The good Brother refused to allow me access to Mistress Elsabeth's possessions unless he be allowed to speak with her. I told him I would relay his request, but he insisted!"

"He insisted," Stemham repeated, a hint of mocking incredulity in his voice.

"Extorted me, to be truthful, for he had the key to her room at the inn and refused to let me in otherwise."

He made a show of rolling his eyes. "Good God, man, why do I keep you around if you could not even use my name to have the guard deal with the matter?"

"Forgive me, Sire, but I thought discretion would be—"

Stemham laughed and took the man by the shoulders. "Richard! 'Tis no harm done. To be honest I half expected the fellow to want to be certain his companion was being cared for. But what is he doing in the hall? And if I don't miss my guess, I imagine that is the good ale?"

"He insisted on a drink, Sire. First at the inn. Then over the midday meal. Then at supper. And then all bloody night wanting me to sing songs with him! God in Heaven can that man drink! And only the best ale, at that. I tried to have the servants switch out to the common stuff, but he nearly challenged me to a duel then and there in the middle of the hall! It made no difference to him that I had insisted he disarm himself upon entering, as he still had his staff of office."

Elsabeth took hold of Stemham's doublet between her teeth, both out of chagrin and to keep herself from falling into a laughing fit.

"Well, Richard, you need fear no longer, for I am here to rescue you from this wicked servant of the Wheel."

Richard heaved a sigh and rolled his eyes. "Bless you, Sire!"

Stemham twisted around so he could look at her. The wry curl of his lip over Richard's vexation made it even harder not to laugh. "Elsabeth? I do believe the good Brother wishes to speak with you."

"Oh, I see how it goes," she said with a roll of her eyes. "The men will run and hide, leaving it to me to deal with the over-merry scoundrel?"

"I assumed if he would listen to anyone, 'twould be you."

This time she did laugh, a short incredulous bark. "If you honestly knew a thing about the man you would never have been able to say that with a straight face. Hieronymus listens to me like he does the protestations of an aggrieved husband or father." She gave an exaggerated sigh and stepped around Crosseby. "Go on, you two cowards! Run and hide while I contend with the wicked friar!"

Stemham sketched an exaggerated bow. "I'll see to it that songs are sung of your bravery."

She smiled and shook her head. "Oh, just get out of here."

He chuckled and hung an arm around Richard's shoulders and guided the man out. "Come on, let us leave these two to their talk, as I imagine they have some catching up to do. Meanwhile you can tell me exactly how much restocking I must do ..."

Elsabeth watched them depart down the screens passage, then turned and started across the hall to the dais. Hieronymus hummed quietly to himself between pulls from his tankard, and seemed to pay her little mind until she stood at the bottom of the steps leading up to the dais, and folded her arms across her breast. "Well, it seems I can't have a moment's peace without having to get you out of some sort of trouble."

He harrumphed. "I have been no trouble at all, Tetty. I have merely been keeping that good lad company while we waited for you." He tore his attention away from his drink and looked her up and down. "God in Heaven, girl, what is that you are wearing?"

"What, this?" She made a show of holding the skirts of her dress away from her, and spun in place. The velvet was smooth and supple in her hands, the skirts floated as she turned, and draped elegantly around her legs again when she released it. "Seeing as I was being presented before the Graf D'Ain, I reasoned I ought to have a suitable dress for the occasion. Stemham arranged to have it fitted for me."

"Ah, I see. You seem to be settling in quite nicely."

"I rather like it here."

"Well, you should not be getting too comfortable. While you were up to God knows what manner of wanton depravity last night, I had a rather interesting conversation."

She sighed and mopped her face. "Love, 'tis late, and I really don't have the time for a tale of yet another of your sordid adventures gone wrong."

He thumped his tankard down hard on the table, and the brief show of genuine anger was enough to make her jump. "Damn it, girl, 'twas not about me! 'Twas about you!"

She frowned and folded her arms across her chest. "What about me?"

"One of those Schwertbrüder approached me at the inn last night."

"Oh? Which one?"

"I don't know which bloody one! 'Twas a man in a red doublet with the crossed swords of the guild on his breast, and he neglected to leave me his name. He may have had blue garters on his hose, now that I think of it."

She considered a moment. "That would be a Vorfechter of one of the scholas. Perhaps Caspar von Bech's ..."

He waved off her musings. "Whoever it was is not important, but you would be doing us both a service should you listen to what he had to say."

"And what did he have to say?"

"Damn it, girl, 'tis what I have been trying to tell you!"

Elsabeth rolled her eyes. "You are drunk, love, and have not even come close to getting to the point."

"My dear Tetty, I have been drinking the Lord's gift of ale since you were still suckling your mother's teat, I think I know when I am drunk! I am merely merry! Or was until you finally dragged yourself in here!"

She raised an eyebrow. "At the moment if anyone shall be dragging themselves soon it would be you. Now, what could one of the Schwertbrüder have had to say about me last night?"

"He called it a message, but Lord knows it sounded to me more like a warning."

"What sort of warning?"

"The fellow suggested that we depart Ain as soon as possible to avoid any unpleasantness."

Elsabeth released a breath and laughed. "Is that all? Hieronymus, you and I receive far worse threats every other village we visit! I have nothing to fear from those pompous fools. Particularly not Caspar von Bech!"

Hieronymus scowled. "Now look here, girl, 'tis one matter to bring down the wrath of an angry wife or husband, but this is the guild issuing threats."

"Yes, and they can't touch me here." She made her way up the dais and circled around the table to sit beside him. "The Graf D'Ain has issued a ban on dueling in the city for the duration of the playings."

"And that has never stopped us from getting into a scrap before."

She conceded his point with a nod. "No, it has not. But secondly: you know that I could take any one of them with one arm at my back, for want of a more original handicap."

Hieronymus glared at her. "Even your esteemed Paulus von Soest fell, Tetty. Perhaps you are too young to have learned this lesson yourself, but you are not indestructible. The Lord of All has a way of reminding one of their mortality, and I had rather you not learn that lesson here."

Elsabeth reached out and clasped his hand. "Finally, I am here as Stemham's guest. I am under his protection! The guild daren't touch me here."

"Damn it, girl! If they want to make things unpleasant for you, they need not show their hand directly! You know that! 'Tis been a decent enough diversion, we made enough coin from the demonstrations to live on for a bit, but 'tis time to move on!"

She hesitated, and choked down the bile rising up from her belly. "Love, I don't know that I intend to ever leave Ain."

The silence filling the hall at that pronouncement was all but deafening. Hieronymus sat and stared at her open-mouthed, his drink for the moment forgotten. That sight more than anything else twisted the dagger piercing her heart until she was in agony: Hieronymus silent, and unable to drink.

When he finally found his voice, it was barely above a whisper "Is this some sort of jest, Tetty? Because 'tis not the least bit amusing."

Elsabeth sighed and shook her head. "No, 'tis not a jest. I know we have only just arrived. I know I have not known Stemham long, but this is the first place I think I have actually felt at home since I fled Soest. Stemham respects me as I am; I am not just a curiosity or diversion for him, or something to use for his advantage or pleasure, or a wild thing for him to tame. He even offered to further my instruction, and he will be putting me in the playings to test as a Provost." She sat back in the chair and smiled. "Even Paulus was bound by the Grand Master, and could not allow me to test in their fashion."

Hieronymus just stared at her, and she looked away from him.

"If you must move on, then you must, but I think this time I'll be staying behind, if Stemham will have me."

18

"THE GALL OF THAT COVENTRISH BITCH!" Caspar snarled, and tore at his hair as he paced the floor of the rooms given over to the Grand Master for his stay in Ain. Aich stood behind a screen, while a servant helped him disrobe for the evening and slip into a fine linen dressing gown. The bed dominated the middle of the hardwood floor, and lamps mounted in brackets on the walls spilled golden light into the room. A wardrobe occupied a substantial part of the wall next to the door leading in from the hallway, opposite a grand, picturesque window overlooking a gardened courtyard in one of the most affluent sections of the City. A large fireplace occupied the entirety of the wall opposite the bed, where a fire in the hearth cast a flickering red light across the room and filled the chamber with a fresh and wholesome smell. The house was large, though not nearly as impressive a complex as what he had seen of Crosseby's home and school, but was more than adequate to serve the guild's needs.

The students gathered in the hall for drink and dice, and for the moment he and Aich were left alone but for the servant to discuss the evening's events. Caspar fumed and paced and stomped, and the woman helping the Grand Master dress flinched and flushed as he raged.

"You heard it, Master!" he continued. "God knows only a deaf man or a fool could have missed it! D'Ain heard it! Crosseby heard it! That God-damned buffoon Guarin heard it!"

"Calm yourself, Caspar."

"I should have marched right up and struck her across her cursed face!"

"Caspar!" Aich roared, and that fierce intonation was enough to shake him out of the madness threatening to overwhelm him after sharing a room with Elsabeth Hereford. "Enough!"

Caspar rounded on him and balled his fists. "But Master, you heard—"

"I said enough!" His voice this time was one of command; firm and thunderous, and practically shook the room. The servant's face paled at his wrath, and she tried her best to shrink inside the collar of her simple dress to escape the Grand Master's formidable rage. Even Caspar blanched, and a ball of ice formed deep in his innards. "I heard it."

"She couched it as ever in false civility, but I can't just abide those insults! For seven long years I abided at Master von Soest's behest, but he is gone, I am Master in Soest, and she owes me that respect!"

Aich dismissed the servant woman and tied his dressing gown about himself without her aid. The woman curtsied and retreated with haste, and when he saw the rage burning in the old man's eyes, Caspar found himself envying her immensely. "Do not forget your place, Caspar. D'Ain has forbidden dueling in his city during these proceedings, and we shall compose ourselves as proper guests."

"And stand idly by while that woman ridicules me? Just by being here, performing her demonstrations in the market, she makes a mockery of the entire Brotherhood! And now that damned fool Crosseby is entering her in the Provost bouts. 'Tis unnatural. This whole damned affair is unnatural!"

"If Crosseby has allowed himself to be bewitched by that woman that is not a matter for us to contend with. That will be between him and God when he comes before the Lord of All. Our part is to contend with our own affairs."

Caspar sighed and mopped his face. "D'Ain seemed no less taken with the idea himself. I am certain even now he is imagining the spectacle of putting her in the general contest of arms. Particularly as the vulgar rabble of this city seem utterly enthralled by the prospect, if I were to judge by the crowds she gathered. That infuriating woman is on the tongues of half of Ain; in the taverns and on the street corners."

Aich crossed the room to a chair in front of the fireplace, and gingerly lowered his aging frame onto the cushion. "Crosseby certainly demonstrated tremendous cheek in presenting her to D'Ain, but I suggest you take careful heed of that lesson: There is close friendship between those two, and I imagine there is little Crosseby could request that he will refuse. So long as we are in Ain, neither you, nor any of the students, are to touch her. Is that clear?"

Caspar gritted his teeth but gave a short nod. "Yes, Master."

Aich eyed him for a long moment. He shifted under the Grand Master's gaze, as if his dark eyes would sear a hole straight down to his soul, in a manner unmatched by even the righteous fury of the most pious of clergymen. Aich finally released him from his glare and nodded himself. "Good."

"But what of the playings, Master?" he asked instead of continuing that line of debate. "As I understand this Coventrish tradition, 'tis unheard of for a player to not receive a challenge. The provincials surely won't understand. 'Twould matter little to them the unseemliness of what she does; they would call us cowards!"

Aich slumped into his chair and leaned his bearded head on one fist. It was rare for the Grand Master to show his age so plainly, and Caspar squirmed at the sight of it. "Had she sprung from the loins of any other man than Thomas Hawke I never would have permitted Master von Soest to take her on as a private student." He sighed. "God damn the man for siring a daughter, particularly that vexatious creature! A son, perhaps, might have made for a worthy member of the Brotherhood."

He gripped the arms of his chair until the knuckles of his gnarled hands turned white.

"You will relay this command to all your students, and they are to know it comes direct from my lips: No one is to challenge Elsabeth Hereford during the playings. They are not to speak with her in the streets. They are not to touch her. To disobey this command is to contradict my will as Grand Master, and any who do so shall face my wrath. Is that understood, Master von Bech?"

Caspar swallowed at the tone of the Grand Master's voice, and hurriedly inclined his head. "'Tis understood, Master," he said.

"Good." Aich lifted a hand and waved him away. "Leave me. 'Tis late and I shall retire. Remember what I said, and tell the others."

He inclined his head. "Yes, Master," he said. Caspar then turned and strode from the room with bowed head and ground his teeth together. He stepped out into the hallway and closed the door behind him, and found Merklin waiting there for him.

"Master," Merklin said, and inclined his head.

Caspar took one look at him, sighed, and started off down the hall. He gave little consideration to the decorations as he passed along the corridor, however its furnishings were opulent in their simplicity, relying more on the fineness of the materials and manufacture than in their quantity or gaudiness. A tapestry here, a painting there, perhaps some relic of their host family's past that Caspar could not give a single damn to hear about. Merklin trailed along behind in silence, as if sensing the black cloud gathering round him and leery of disturbing it lest it burst forth in a sudden storm.

The voices of the other students raised in song and laughter echoed through the house from the great hall, but Caspar felt no desire for such companionship tonight. The hour was late, and he had had all the revelry he could stomach at Castle Ain.

Caspar reached the door to the guest room where he had been given residence and threw it open in frustration. Merklin caught the door before it could slam back against the wall and closed it gently behind him. The room was, of course, smaller than the grand suite where the Grand Master was quartered, but no less opulent in the quality of its furnishings; a large feather mattress and fine linens for the bed, a sizable wardrobe, a window looking out onto the garden, and even a small fireplace all its own. He sighed and made his way towards the latter, flopped into a chair standing near the hearth, and buried his face in his hands. For a long moment he just sat listening to the crackling wood in the hearth, seeking comfort from the fragrance of the smoke, but finding none.

"Shall I call Gillette, Master?" Merklin said.

"No," he said into his hands.

He could hear Merklin shifting his weight from foot to foot in the silence. "Is there something I might do, Master?"

"'Tis nothing anyone short of the Lord of All himself can do. But you can deliver this message from the Grand Master to the others: No one is to touch Elsabeth Hereford while she is in Ain. They are not to speak with her, gamble with her, drink with her. Our host for these playings has elected to put her in them; no one is to challenge her, is that understood?"

Merklin's jaw fell open. "They are having her fight? What madness is this?"

"Witchcraft, perhaps, but 'tis not for us to address. We are but to sit here while she insults and mocks us before our peers and D'Ain, and we can't raise so much as a finger or stir so much as a hair on her wretched head. See to it that everyone understands this."

"The Grand Master will do nothing, then?"

Caspar glared up at him and scowled. "The Grand Master is doing something. He commands that no man of the Brotherhood is to challenge her in the playings. What he expects of us if D'Ain sees fit to enter her in the general contest of arms on a lark I can't fathom. Even if she is denied the courtesy of a challenge during the playings, to forfeit in tournament, and against a woman ...?"

He beat his fists on the arms of the chair. "She stands and insults me. To my face, before D'Ain, Crosseby, the Grand Master, and that tittering idiot Guarin, and I can do nothing!"

"I don't understand why the Grand Master will not allow you to fight. Surely you would ruin her, and that would dispel this perverse fascination with her."

A hollowness worked its way through Caspar's belly, and icy fingers seized him by the throat. So many angry bouts between them under Master von Soest' watchful eyes, so many humiliating defeats. So many times walking away from the hall bruised and battered, yet he could not lay so much as a single blow upon her loathsome head to mar those features

That was, perhaps, the worst of it. Even if he *could* challenge her, here and now, it would be no use. A woman. It did not matter that she was a child of Hawke. She was always Soest's favorite, the real prize of his school; a mere girl not even permitted the courtesy of a place in the Brotherhood, yet she could best every one of the Master's students. And he had seen that morning he arrived in Ain, and again the day after when he took the Grand Master to see her, how meaningless his title and posting was. He twisted his lip and gripped the arms of his chair.

Even at his best, he was but a child next to her.

"The Grand Master's command was made clear to me," he said instead. He could say nothing of this to Merklin or the others, of course. Let them think what they wished to think; it mattered little, anyway. "No one is to challenge her. The Brotherhood shan't participate in Crosseby's farce. If the others wish a part in this charade, then let them."

Merklin's shoulders sagged in disappointment. "Yes, Master," he said.

"Someday she shall be dealt with," he said. "I contended with her insolence for seven long years under Master von Soest's watchful eye, another few days will change nothing. The Coventrish whore may taunt the Brotherhood from behind Crosseby's skirt, but sooner or later she will have to come out. Then we can see that she is suitably punished, but not before."

He looked up from his lap and studied Merklin closely. But while the Grand Master had that knack of taking a man in with his eyes and holding them there until he had no more use for them, Caspar lacked the formidable magnetism to do the same. Merklin averted his gaze to the floor and clasped his hands behind his back.

"Is that understood?"

His Vorfechter nodded. "Yes, Master."

Caspar heaved a weary sigh and leaned his head on his hand. "Go and tell the others of the Grand Master's command. And send for Gillette, I'll be retiring for the evening."

"Yes, Master."

Merklin inclined his head politely and retreated from the room, gently shutting the door behind him.

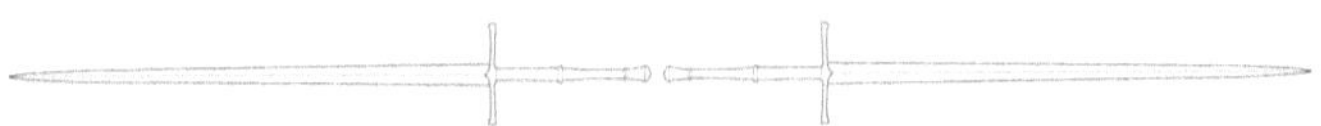

ERKLIN LOOKED BACK OVER HIS SHOULDER AT the door and clenched his teeth and jaw. It was not right that the Grand Master ask Master von Bech to surrender his honor in this manner. Especially if it was to a mere *woman*. Such an insult could not be allowed to stand.

He made his way up the corridor for the great hall where his companions drank and laughed, and a scowl worked its way to his lips. In good faith he had left his warning with that irksome friar, and his companion refused to heed it. Worse, she insulted the honor of not only his Master, but *all* the Brotherhood. He tightened his fists until his nails cut into his palms. No, this could not be allowed to stand. Not this time. She had escaped her reckoning long enough, and if the Master and Grand Master refused to act, he would not. And if Elsabeth Hereford would so openly defy his prior warning, then another message needed to be delivered. One that this time she could not ignore.

Cities were, after all, filled with treacherous places, where an unwary traveler might disappear and never be seen again.

## 19

THE MORNING OF THE FIRST DAY OF THE playings dawned at last. It was bright, clear, and warm, but not so much as to make an audience uncomfortable or to exhaust the fighters with the heat. People swarmed to the main square in a mad rush to find the best place from which to view the spectacle. Guards in coats-of-plate, kettle helms, and armed with halberds pushed and prodded the crowds toward the designated viewing areas to keep the streets clear for the procession of the scholars to follow, and to bar them from the scaffolding and the grandstand where D'Ain, his retinue, and the affluent would view the bouts.

The clear, ringing call of a horn silenced the excited chattering of the crowd, and everyone turned their attention to the east. Cheers arose among the throngs of people lining the streets as D'Ain's procession made its way towards the square, accompanied by the music and drums of his court performers. Guards in ceremonial armor encircled him and his entourage, and courtiers followed in his wake. D'Ain himself was particularly well-dressed for the event, in a fine doublet of gold velvet and a bright blue cape. His attendants were all decked in their finest, every buckle and button brightly polished so they glowed under the light of the morning sun. They reached the stairs leading up the scaffolding and climbed to the top of the platform. There D'Ain paused and waved to the crowd, and their voices rose to a deafening roar, like the sea breaking against the shore. Then they all took to their seats; D'Ain in his personal box, the rest finding their places among the wealthy and affluent around him.

After the passing of D'Ain, to lesser fanfare came the gathering of masters: d'Aubigny and Morelet, de Craon, Oger, d'Orgremont, and Gaude for Navarre. They took their places in a special box set aside for the masters who would be judging the bouts at Crosseby's request, while their students took the stands wherever they might find room. The foreigners followed them, and took their places in the stands among the wealthy merchants and nobles of Ain: exotic Bartolomé Ruiz with a girl on each arm. Antonio Guarin dressed almost as prettily as Ruiz's companions. Del Brun and da Pavia. Their students filed in behind them, to watch, to learn, and perhaps to challenge Crosseby's students. Last came the Schwertbrüder; the Grand Master Stefan von Aich gleaming as if lit by a shaft of light cast down by the Lord of All in his white robes of office, and Caspar von Bech in a brilliant crimson doublet. Last came his students, a striking collection of youths standing out from the rest with their matching red doublets marked by the crossed swords of the Guild, led by Merklin Adler and his blue garters. Aich and Bech joined D'Ain in his box, while their students sat together among the elite.

And then came Crosseby himself, and another great cheer went up among the citizens of the City. That he was

Coventrish mattered little to them after the service he had rendered to D'Ain. He led a procession of his own students; those Scholars not yet ready to test, and the Free Scholars who would be playing on the morrow.

But the real sensation was the woman walking arm-in-arm with the Master of the Longsword. She was tall and of slender athleticism, her burnished copper hair spilling freely down her back in a manner that made the proper women of Ain whisper contemptuously from beneath their veils and hennins. That day she dressed in men's fashion: a black felt hat perched atop her head at a rakish angle, a fine, green, sleeveless velvet doublet fastened with gold buttons, and dark red hose hugging every curve of her shapely legs. Her only concession to femininity was the linen blouse beneath her doublet, with slightly belled sleeves gathered at her elbows with satin ribbon before falling loosely to her wrists.

Those with the privilege of having witnessed the antics of her demonstrations or her revelries at the inn nudged their companions and smiled. They leered at the shape of her figure betrayed by her hose. Whispers of astonishment swept across the crowd. Crude calls and whistles carried above the background murmur of thousands of voices gossiping at once. Elsabeth just took it all in with a smile.

*If they think today is remarkable, wait until tomorrow.*

Crosseby and his retinue mounted the stairs and filed into the grandstand. The students found places among their peers, while the Master himself and his remarkable companion joined D'Ain in his box.

Lost in the chaos and unobserved by the crowd, a lone figure swaddled in the black woolen habit of the Olivian order leaned on his staff, and watched Elsabeth take her seat.

—┼——┼—

ELSABETH REMOVED HER HAT AS SHE ENTERED D'Ain's presence and bowed low at her waist, sweeping arm and hat together in a grand flourish, a gesture which Stemham mirrored (sans hat). D'Ain received the gesture with a trace of amusement on his features, and greeted them both with a short nod before motioning for them to take their seats. She returned her hat to her head and settled into the chair next to Stemham, who sat at the Count's right hand. The Grand Master and Caspar, seated on his left, did not give so much as a nod to her. Elsabeth leaned slightly around Stemham, flashed a mocking smile, and waggled her fingers in greeting at Caspar. The muscles in his jaw tightened as he clenched his teeth together and heaved an aggravated sigh, but otherwise he gave her no reaction.

She chuckled softly and leaned back in her seat, crossed her legs, and draped her hands loosely on the arms of the chair.

"So, Monsieur Crosseby," D'Ain said, "is everything to your satisfaction?"

"More than satisfactory, Monseigneur," Stemham said. "My compliments to the Master Builder and his apprentices on having everything ready so quickly. 'Tis solid enough I imagine you could run a joust on that platform were it larger!"

"Wonderful! Now, what precisely will we be seeing today? I am still unfamiliar with this Coventrish practice of yours."

"The Scholars will be playing for the rank of Free Scholar today, and must fight three bouts to five touches; one at longsword, one at falchion, and one at arming sword with buckler. Any man present — down on the street or here upon the platform — may answer. 'Tis usual for a student to face from four to ten opponents in each bout, but we shall see how many wish to step onto the platform.

"If the esteemed masters—" he motioned to the box where the Navarrese masters gathered "—should decide the combatant has proven competent, he shall win his prize. Once all of the day's prizes have been played, we celebrate!"

"'Tis indeed not all that different from the means by which the Brotherhood tests its students," Caspar said.

"I never witnessed a playing myself, as I was still very young when last I was in Coventry," Elsabeth said, "but as I recall 'tis a rare thing for a student to not be passed." She looked past Stemham, D'Ain, and Aich, and flashed a smirk at Caspar. "That, at least, is one difference."

Caspar's cheeks flushed, and he gripped the arms of his chair. Stemham looked between the two of them and reached out to give her hand a warning squeeze. Elsabeth just settled back in her chair and enjoyed Caspar's quiet seething.

D'Ain raised an eyebrow. "Indeed?"

Stemham nodded. "'Tis a testament to the preparation of the students."

"Or a condemnation of the laxity of this Coventrish system," Caspar said.

"Well, some men need any help they can get, don't you agree?" Elsabeth said.

His retort was cut off by the distant beating of drums and a fanfare of horns. Everyone came to their feet at once and looked to the east. A procession of flags marched up the street preceding the musicians and the solitary figure of the first Scholar. The crowd cheered, and all of Ain was filled with the roar of exultation as the playings officially commenced. Elsabeth craned her neck past Stemham, D'Ain, and the Schwertbrüder so she could see the first fighter — a youth of perhaps some fifteen years, with sandy-colored hair — mount the steps, leaving the procession of flags and musicians at the base of the stairs behind him. Another cheer went up when he reached the top of the platform.

D'Ain motioned for silence, and slowly the crowd settled. Those in the stands returned to their seats, but Stemham alone remained standing, a scroll of parchment in his hands.

"Monsieur Henry de l'Espée, seeking the rank of Free Scholar!" he said, his voice carrying high and clear across the sea of faces craning upward from the street, or gazing down from the grandstand. "The first bout to be at longsword, to five touches!"

Elsabeth cocked an eyebrow in amusement at Stemham as the crowd cheered and he returned to his seat. "Espée? Quite the appropriate name."

"Good lad," Stemham said. "I fought his father once in a tournament, 'tis an old family of Navarrese chivalry."

"So now we wait for someone to answer?" D'Ain asked, leaning close to Stemham so his voice need not carry. "Who do you think shall be first?"

Elsabeth smiled across at Caspar. "Why not you, love? I am sure the crowd would find it quite diverting."

"I am quite eager to see how the Schwertbrüder acquit themselves myself," D'Ain said.

Caspar's body tensed, but Aich spit him with a warning glare lest he do something foolish. So instead, he turned to where his students gathered, and made a sign. One stood and made his way down the stands towards the platform. Elsabeth watched him climb down and took particular note of the blue garters decorating his hose. She smirked.

"Well, 'tis no Caspar von Bech, but I am sure we will see his quality reflected in his teaching."

"Wonderful!" D'Ain said, and settled back into his seat. If he caught the meaning of the remark he said nothing, but Stemham beside her stifled a laugh, and Caspar silently fumed.

The crowd cheered once more as a challenger appeared. De l'Espée headed to one of several racks laden with neatly stacked arms along the front of the stands and selected his weapon. Caspar's Vorfechter did the same, and when satisfied the *Federn* were to their liking, each stepped into the circle at the center of the scaffold. De l'Espée saluted, his opponent returned the gesture, and both took up their guard — de l'Espée in the Dragon's Tail, and the Vorfechter with his sword raised overhead into *vom tag* — in anticipation of the signal to begin.

"Lay on!" Stemham called.

De l'Espée wasted no time, and the moment the signal was given he threw his pommel down and whipped his sword over in an overhand blow at the Vorfechter's shoulder. His opponent countered with the *zornhau*, striking down hard in a manner that, in an earnest fight, would cleave his opponent's head in two. The harsh ring of steel as the blades met was joined by a roar of approval from the street and stands. The blow stopped de l'Espée's attack, but was unable to press through to strike him. Instead, he wound the sword into *ochs* for a thrust down at the chest. De l'Espée drew back into Plow to offset the thrust, and put his point in his adversary's face for a counterthrust. The Vorfechter countered in turn by whipping his sword over into a *schielhau*, binding de l'Espée down with the short edge of his blade and striking him across the temple in one motion.

The crowd exploded in a frenzy as de l'Espée staggered back from the blow. Some cried out in outrage that one of the Schwertbrüder had successfully landed the strike. Others raised their voices in encouragement. The rest of the Schwertbrüder applauded their companion, and Caspar smiled in smug satisfaction as the two fighters reset.

"Ah, it does not seem good for young de l'Espée," D'Ain said, his features crestfallen.

"Don't be so discouraged, Monseigneur," Stemham said. "'Tis not a tournament. Whether the student scores one touch or ten matters little. Aside from pride, of course. 'Tis only his skill and handling of the sword the masters shall be judging. When I bouted for my Provost prize all those years ago, I think I scored perhaps a dozen touches at most all day."

Elsabeth leaned out to smile past them at Caspar. "I must say I am pleasantly surprised by your man's handling of his blade, Caspar. 'Twas wielded in quite the manly way."

Caspar said nothing, merely gritted his teeth and watched the ring.

"And what is your opinion of young Monsieur de l'Espée, Mademoiselle Soesten?" D'Ain asked. He looked at her with keen interest in his eyes, and Elsabeth turned her attention back to the two fencers in the ring as they prepared for another round.

"He is quite good, though somewhat slow with his hands; Caspar's man was off-balance a moment when Monsieur de l'Espée countered his thrust from *ochs* — Roebuck, as Stemham would call it in the Coventrish fashion." The clashing of steel split the air, punctuated by the grunts of de l'Espée and the Vorfechter, as they resumed the fight. "What was his name, Caspar? I don't believe I caught it before."

"Merklin Adler," Caspar said, and leaned casually on one hand to watch the bout unfold. She detected a subtle tightness in his voice, and though he masked his growing ire well, the corner of his eye twitched, a sign as loud as if he were shouting at the top of his lungs.

"Ah. Well, Merklin Adler perhaps overreached on his defense, and had Monsieur de l'Espée been quicker with the hands, he ought to have struck an easy touch."

She put just enough of an emphasis on "easy" to make the twitching in Caspar's eye nearly intensify into a flutter.

"Interesting," D'Ain said. He settled back into his chair and nodded. Elsabeth regarded him for a moment, and she could see in his eyes that he had noted the same for himself. "What say you, Monsieur Crosseby?"

Stemham nodded. "She has a keen eye. He hesitated just a moment after countering the thrust."

While they spoke, de l'Espée and Adler continued their fight. This time the former was much more clearly outfought, his guard battered aside for a blow to his shoulder that elicited another groan of disapproval from the crowd, and a cheer from the Schwertbrüder.

"I quite look forward to seeing you bout on the morrow," D'Ain said, and Aich and Caspar both bristled. "If you wield the blade as skillfully as you demonstrate your knowledge of the art, it should be quite intriguing. Would you agree, Master?"

D'Ain looked directly at Aich, and the Grand Master shifted in his chair.

"Monseigneur flatters me," she said. "As I am hardly worthy of the personal notice of the esteemed Grand Master."

"Nonsense!" Stemham said. "I have seen you fight, and I am sure your name has oft been brought before the Grand Master."

Elsabeth smiled and laughed inwardly. D'Ain might be unaware, but Caspar and Aich both could no longer have any doubts that Stemham knew of her history with the Guild, and how carefully his words were chosen.

"Well, I do hope to see you on the platform tomorrow," she said, and favored Caspar with a grin. "It has been too long since you and I have had a good bout." She paused a moment and made a show of considering. "In fact,

I can't recall that you and I have ever had a good bout." Again she put just enough of an emphasis on "good" to raise Caspar's hackles.

Down on the platform, de l'Espée and Adler reset a third time. Caspar shifted in his seat, a hint of crimson appearing on his cheeks. This time de l'Espée was much more prepared. They exchanged a series of blows, neither finding an opening to their liking, then stepped back, circled one another, and shifted through the guards. Adler found an opening first, and sprung forward in a falling cut from his left shoulder. De l'Espée countered from *alber* with two quick, rising, short-edged cuts from his right hip.

The first batted Adler's sword aside. The second wound him into his left *ochs*, and coiled his arms tightly like a spring straining to be released. Adler attempted to counter the exposed shoulder with a second overhand blow from his left. De l'Espée released the tension in his arms. He wheeled his sword backwards and down through a quick falling cut that again cheated his opponent of a touch. The cut brought his pommel forward, and he snapped it down hard, throwing his point at Adler in a powerful hewing blow at his right shoulder. He yelped as de l'Espée landed a strong touch right at the base of his neck, and the crowd exploded into a frenzy.

D'Ain was on his feet applauding, and everyone in the stands jumped up with him. Men broke out in chants and song, and the clatter of coins raining down on the stage punctuated the vivacity.

The outburst showed no sign of ending, even when the pair on the scaffold separated and returned to their starting positions for another go. Elsabeth lent her voice as well, clapping fiercely and grinning across the box at Aich and Caspar. They weathered the touch in silent disappointment. Even if de l'Espée failed to land another blow for the duration of his playing it did not matter. Their man landed a touch on one of the Schwertbrüder, and the pride of Ain had been defended against the foreigners.

# 20

LSABETH THREW HER HEAD BACK AND downed the pint in one long gulp. There was no music in Stemham's hall that night, but that mattered little to the gathering. Crosseby's students laughed and drank, and she dove into the revelries with zeal. The drinks that night were paid for by l'Espée and two other fellows; one a short and stocky blond by the name of Binet d'Amiens, and the other the tall, lanky, dark-haired Jehan Alart dit Le Barbier. All three had won their prizes during the day's bouting, and that was reason to celebrate.

Richard scrambled to keep the servants coming with the ale lest the mood of the gathering decline from raucous jollity to furious pugnacity. A good selection of morsels from the city occupied one table, with the casks and kegs of drink on the other. The high table atop the dais was reserved for Stemham, herself, and the Navarrese masters who presided over the playings. However aside from the occasional retreat to cuddle up to Stemham, she spent more time down on the floor among the students drinking her fill, or trading stories of the road, and, to the particular delight of the youth of Navarrese swordsmanship, her many brawls and defeats of Caspar von Bech during her training under Paulus.

"No, no, no," she said to l'Espée, and held out her tankard to Richard for a refill so she need not interrupt her story to make her way to the casks on the table. "'Twas three of them. Caspar, as usual, and he riled up two of the others. Um ..." Elsabeth paused for a moment and snapped her fingers as she searched her memory. "Ah! Thadeus Dytel and a weak-kneed fellow by the name of Georgius Stoyan.

"Well, Caspar made a fool of himself as usual. They were all at the tavern in Soest, and I was there, too. Oh, Boehman taverns normally don't welcome women of my upstanding character without a man to escort them, but everyone in Soest knew I was Paulus's student, so they let me come and go as I pleased, and not a word was said. Not within my or Paulus's hearing, at least. Well, anyway, there was another girl there, and Caspar was very drunk, and decided to approach her. I was thirteen — or maybe it was fourteen — which would have made him perhaps fifteen or sixteen. Ha! I have not quite had nearly enough to drink to impede my grasp of mathematics.

"However, Caspar was very drunk. So drunk that when he first got up, he tripped over his own chair and landed flat on his face. Well, not all that unusual an occurance, mind, but usually when he did so it was on the training floor with a sword in his hand. But he picks himself up and walks up to her, and I can't say for sure what it was he said to her, but next thing you know the man at the table with her knocks him flat on his backside! You see the girl was not there alone, but was with her brother!"

L'Espée and the group around her all exploded into laugher at once, the former bent double and slapping his thighs. Elsabeth giggled herself at the memory, and took a long draught of her ale before continuing.

"Now, Paulus took a dim view of us stirring up trouble among the townsfolk on our downtime, though I can assure you I was a right terror after a few ales, so I decided to step in and smooth things over rather than leave the bloody fool to fight a duel blind drunk and hardly able to stand. Mind, Caspar would not have fared any better sober."

"And how did you manage that?" one of her audience asked from the back.

"Well, I put myself in between the fellow and Caspar and told the truth! I said to the man: 'Good Herr, please forgive him, for I have given him one too many cracks to the skull on the training floor, and I fear he has been left quite addled!'

"It certainly put Caspar off a fight with that local fellow, and he takes a swing at me instead. But he trips himself up again on his lunge and spins himself right into the floor. Well, everyone is laughing now, and I can hardly breathe, and that just makes him madder and madder. And he gets up and, well, the other two fellows don't really want anything to do with me, as I thrashed them both that very day during a free session, though they tried their damndest to stove my pretty face in — and would that not have been a tragedy?" Elsabeth made a show of motioning to her face. "The Lord of All did good work, here, don't you agree? And 'twould have been a sacrilege to spoil it!

"Anyway, they both look at each other, look at me, and are about to run off when Caspar gets back to his feet again and starts spouting all manner of senseless things. He is worked into such a froth he can hardly speak straight, and yet here I am having saved his miserable life and not even laid a hand on him! Well, he shames Dytel and Stoyan, and all three come at me at once!"

"What did you do?"

Elsabeth laughed into her tankard. "Not a thing, really. Caspar took one step, tripped over himself yet again, and banged his head on a table. Fortuitously for him, his skull was immeasurably denser than both the table and the floor. And as he goes down, he takes Dytel and Stoyan down with him in a tangle of limbs! So I left them there to endure the ridicule of the locals, and walked on home!"

They all erupted into laughter at once. Hands clapped her on the shoulder, and cries went up for another tale, but Elsabeth waved them down. "Perhaps in a while, I fear dear Stemham laments of my absence." A collective groan of disappointment worked its way across the ring gathered around her, and she motioned them for silence. "But I shan't be going anywhere, so long as the ale is still flowing, and I am not paying! Now make way!"

And with that she plunged through the circle of bodies and into the open again, weaving through the gathering to the dais while the great hall spun a little around her. She quickly mounted the steps and turned straight for Stemham, who sat at ease in his seat at the high table, engrossed in a deep discussion with d'Orgremont on some matter. He smiled and waved her over when he caught sight of her approach. But rather than the chair prepared for her, she instead dropped into his lap, wrapped his arms around his neck, and kissed him fully and deeply on the mouth. She heard, but did not heed, a rousing cheer that went up among the assembly of students and masters. Nor did she give much consideration to d'Orgremont, who was suddenly left to awkwardly sip his drink and wait for her to finish with his peer. Stemham for his part kissed her back, his strong hands cupping the side of her face, before she finally pulled away and traded his lips for her tankard.

"Enjoying yourself, I see," he said with an amused (and rather breathless) smile.

"Quite!"

"Well," d'Orgremont said in strong but accented Coventrish, and visibly discomfited by the very public private moment. "I must admit this is not the sort of greeting I expect from my students."

Elsabeth giggled around a mouthful of ale. "A pity, as it says so much with so few words. But then I suppose that depends on your tastes and the nature of the students."

"At least the revelries are keeping you entertained," Stemham said. "While I have had to content myself with school affairs with good Master d'Orgremont."

She dismissed him with a snort. "No offense, love, but 'tis hardly a revelry; the room may be spinning but has not gone black on me yet, there is a lamentable lack of music, and thus far only two of your students have passed out trying to drink me under the table!"

He chuckled and pulled her closer for a light kiss on the mouth. "I will keep that in mind for next time, then! Musicians, stronger ale, and invite revelers with less capacity for drink!"

Elsabeth gave his nose a playful poke with her finger. "See? Even the great masters can stand to learn a thing or two!" She flashed d'Orgremont her most roguish grin. "Don't you agree?"

For his part, d'Orgremont chose not to debate the point, and instead took a drink from a goblet filled with that same vintage of wine she and Stemham shared before their bout in the garden the other night. "At the very least I must agree with your definition of 'revelry.'"

Stemham gave her thigh a gentle swat. "Well, then, I suppose the responsibility of planning any future revelries lies upon your lovely shoulders."

Elsabeth smiled broadly and raised her tankard to him. "A wise decision, love! A wise decision."

She set her tankard on the table, sighed contentedly, and leaned her head against Stemham's shoulder with her arms around his neck. Whether it sparked whispers or ribald musings among the throng she did not care. All that mattered to her now in that moment was the warmth of him next to her and the laughter echoing through the hall. The dull ache in her heart at her first sight of Crosseby's school, and the memories it threatened to dredge up, faded away into nothing. She was in that moment, and for the first time in a long while, home.

A moment spoiled when Richard mounted the stairs, his features twisted in consternation.

He waited until Stemham finished a drink of his wine and acknowledged him with a simple, "Yes, Richard?"

"I beg your pardon, Master," Richard said, "but Brother Hieronymus has returned asking after Mistress Elsabeth."

She sighed and rolled her eyes. "Oh bloody hell, what does he want now?"

"He did not say, only that he wished to speak with you."

"I could have the guard summoned," Stemham offered, a playful smile on his lips. "In fact, I think the party would rather appreciate it, as between the two of you the ale shan't survive an hour!"

"No. He is an aggravating meddler, but is still as good a friend as I have ever had. And I owe it to him after the last night's news."

He nodded. "I understand."

Elsabeth gave him a peck on the cheek and slid out of his lap. She turned to d'Orgremont and sketched a bow. "Master, I'll leave you to it. Do forgive my interruption."

D'Orgremont grunted a laugh and inclined his head politely. She turned to Richard and motioned for him to lead the way. "Well, come on then, it won't be a pleasant conversation, but it must be done."

He started down the dais, and Elsabeth fell into step behind him as he led her back across the hall, dodging knots of Stemham's students so as not to be drawn into another round of drink or stories. They turned through the screens passage and back into the hall leading to the entry foyer. Hieronymus — bless him for adhering to protocol and propriety for once in his life — waited within, leaning on his staff of office while he paced impatiently across the floor. She dismissed Richard with a quiet word and then stepped out into the room.

Hieronymus turned and glowered at her, as if he would call damnation and hellfire down upon her on the spot.

"There you are, Tetty! Well, it seems you are enjoying yourself!"

Elsabeth sighed and pinched her nose. "Can we please not make this harder than it is?"

He harrumphed and stormed around the room, waving his staff wildly around him. "How hard could it be? You tell me you shan't be leaving Ain, and I am left to dwell on it all night without another word of discussion!"

"I am sorry!" she said. "'Twas a long day and a late night, and you were drunk besides! 'Twas not like Stemham threw you out on the street like a common beggar. 'Tis a much finer bed than you would have had at the inn."

"A much finer bed, much finer drink, but I did not need you batting your eyes for it, I could easily have begged it for myself, so don't think you were doing me any favors."

She scowled down at him and planted her hands on her hips. "I certainly don't want to quarrel with you about this here. At least let me take you back to the inn."

Hieronymus eyed her closely for a moment, then gave her a short nod and thumped his staff on the ground. "All right, fine, take me back. And while we walk maybe I can knock some sense into your damn fool head!"

Elsabeth rolled her eyes. "Richard! I don't suppose you are loitering about, are you?"

She turned back towards the hall whence she came and waited a moment, and sure enough Richard popped his head through the doorway. Whether he was eavesdropping on their conversation, or just waiting to see if he was needed, she did not know, nor did she care. "Was there something you needed?"

"Yes, fetch my sword, hat, pattens, and jacket, if you will, please. I'll be taking some air with the good Brother."

He inclined his head. "Very good, Mistress." Richard disappeared from the foyer and hurried off to do as she asked.

"Well, you are certainly getting comfortable with the lifestyle," Hieronymus said.

"Oh knock it off. You forget I have seen you take over inns and taverns like a conquering warlord."

Richard returned presently, and Elsabeth hung her sword on her belt at her hip, slipped on her jacket, stepped into her pattens, and placed her hat atop her head. Once satisfied she was ready to go, he opened the door for them, and they both stepped out into the street.

The night was still young, and the moon shone down brightly on Ain. The noise of the revelry within echoed in the courtyard behind her as Elsabeth led Hieronymus away from the house. The lights of the great hall spilled out into the garden, and offered welcome and cheer to warm her against the cold emptiness slowly spreading through her belly at the impending end of her association with the old lech. She turned her back to it for now, however, and quietly made her way along the empty streets and alleyways, with Hieronymus waddling along supported by his staff at her side.

For a long moment neither of them spoke as Elsabeth wrestled with what to say. A part of her wished the friar would broach the subject himself, but the damned obstinate old man remained silent. She sighed and leaned her hand on the pommel of her sword, and gazed at her shadow stretching out in front of her. The only sounds were the clack of her pattens on the paving stones, the dull thud of Hieronymus's staff, and the whisper of his habit moving against his legs. The distant drone of voices and laughter echoed through the city while people enjoyed the evening, the day's playings foremost on their lips, but here, at least, they were alone.

They were nearly halfway back to the inn by the time she finally mustered up the courage to speak.

"Look, I am sorry things turned out as they have. 'Twas not what I was expecting, believe me."

"And what were you expecting, Tetty?" Hieronymus said. There was no accusation in his words, and if anything, it sounded like he was in his confessor's voice.

"I just thought ..." She trailed off for a moment and sighed. "I don't know. I thought it was going to be like Cuncz: I suppose I expected he would just be trying to get me into his bed, and perhaps I would get a little something out of it before moving on. I hoped it would not have come to that, but 'twas what I expected."

"And you fell into his bed and owe me thirty *deniers*."

She rolled her eyes. "Not because I had to. I wanted it."

"As I recall we set no such condition on the wager, and I'll thank you not to weasel your way out of it. But what do you expect to happen now? Do you really think the good Master is going to honor whatever mad fancy you have for him? How do you know 'tis not exactly what you were expecting: you had something twixt your thighs he wanted, and he dangled something in front of you to get it?"

"Because I do," she said, and scowled at the paving stones. "This is ..." Elsabeth trailed off, bitter memories surging up once more of happier times, a school not unlike this one, a touch, a laugh... "'Tis a long time since I have felt this way."

Hieronymus stopped and stared open-mouthed at her. "Dear God, girl! You talk like you actually think you are in love!"

"Maybe I am, I don't know! But this is the first place I have actually felt content in a long time. There are things you don't know, love. I don't like to talk about them, and I ask you to continue respecting that, but these years on the road have just made them harder to deal with. Maybe I don't have to keep running from them anymore."

Hieronymus glanced skyward and raised his hands dramatically overhead. "Lord, I beseech you! Grant me the patience to shepherd your daughter before I strangle her for her foolishness!"

"Oh stop with the grandiosity! You certainly don't impress me with it."

Hieronymus jabbed her in the side with the staff. "And you pipe down and listen to yourself! I am your priest, am I not? I do take your confession for your plentiful sins, infrequently as it is that you see fit to come before me in penitence. But more to the point I am your damned friend!

"If I have respected your privacy on some matters in the past, 'tis in that capacity I have done so. But Tetty, I stand before you know as a humble servant of the Wheel. What words pass between us now are between you and me and God alone."

She sighed and started walking again. "The Lord of All already knows," she said. "Can't you leave it at that and trust that His will is already at work on my path?"

"Can't you at least tell me something?" he said, and huffed in his effort to catch up.

"To what purpose? I am a grown woman, Hieronymus. I have my own life to lead, and I can make my own decisions."

"Ha! All the times I have had to drag your shapely behind out of trouble tell me otherwise!"

"You leave my behind out of this! I can take care of myself."

"Yes, I can see how well you do."

"I am trying not to make a fight of this!"

"And doing poorly at it! You could not survive a week without me to keep you out of trouble."

"Oh please, how often have I had to drive off some poor cuckold after one of your indiscretions?"

"Almost as often as I have had to save your neck from a gaggle of angry wives. You see? Our partnership works to our mutual benefit! You daren't break it now."

"I am just tired of moving on from place to place! I can finally have something here. I had hoped that as my friend you would understand. 'Tis my choice!"

"Stubborn, intractable, willful girl!" Hieronymus snapped, and beat his staff against the ground, bringing her up short in surprise at the outburst. "God knows why I try to talk reason to you!"

Elsabeth's face heated. "What reason? I find a place where I can be happy and here you are trying to talk me out of it! How is that reason?"

"Because you are infatuated, is what you are! You are infatuated and blinding yourself to the world around you! How long do you think your knight will be content to let you run around Ain making a scandal of yourself? And have you forgotten the Brotherhood? How long do you think they will brook your slights before they finally tire of it and convince the Graf D'Ain to have you dealt with?

"I am trying to help you, Tetty. I have forgotten more about this world than you will ever begin to know, and I am trying to save you from it!"

"I don't need your protection!" she snapped, her face so close to his she could feel his breath. "Don't forget I had been taking care of myself, and quite well at that, before I met you. God I should have left you to that mob!"

"And you would have been starved or worse without me by your side all these years! Listen to yourself, Tetty! I don't know what sort of life you expect here, but you are better than one of making bastards—"

The word was scarcely out of his mouth when something deep inside her broke. She backhanded him hard across the face, and Hieronymus's head snapped around under the force of the blow. It came so unexpectedly it drove him into the ground, and for a moment he lay sprawled there at her feet while she screamed down at him. "Don't you dare say that about me! Do you hear me? Don't you *ever* say that again!"

Hieronymus nursed his jaw and stared up at her in disbelief. A thin trail of blood trickled from the corner of his mouth. "Tetty! In God's name what did you do that for?"

Tears welled up in Elsabeth's eyes, and her breath came in ragged gasps as her voice turned to ice. "I swear to God Hieronymus, if I ever hear you say that about me again I will kill you! Do you hear me? We will come to blows and I. Will. Kill you!"

Hieronymus levered himself up until he was sitting again, but she made no move to so much as help him to his feet.

"I am staying," she said. Her voice broke and her vision wavered, but she balled her hands into fists and stood with her arms stiff at her side. "I am staying and that is that. You can find the rest of your way back to the inn from here. Here is your thirty *deniers* and then some. Go drown yourself in the ale for all I care!"

And with that she threw a small purse of coin from her pocket in his face and stormed away, leaving him sitting in the street and ineffectually calling at her back. Elsabeth just kept walking, and fought back against the tears streaming down her face as guilt twisted like a dagger in her bowels.

HE DID NOT HEAD BACK STRAIGHT AWAY, but instead wandered aimlessly through the streets of Ain for a time. Lights glowing in the windows of the homes fronting the passages and alleys beckoned with the promise of company and good cheer, but for the moment she wanted simply to be alone. Tears meandered down her cheeks and dripped off her chin, and a deep ache worked its way through her heart. Memories and shame clawed a path through the recesses of her mind; choices made and regretted that could not be undone. The back of her hand throbbed in protest of its violent meeting with Hieronymus's jaw, and that only twisted the pang of guilt over their words more cruelly.

Elsabeth mopped the tears from her face with the sleeve of her jacket. What business of his was it, anyway? She was a grown woman, and free to live her life as she saw fit. That was why she had not gone home to Coventry that night Paulus died, and chose the road instead. Servant of the Wheel or not, Hieronymus had no place to tell her otherwise. A friend would understand. If this was indeed where her heart chose to rest, a friend would stand by her.

A friend would not say what he had.

Had anyone else spoken *that* word to her she would not have given them the largesse of the back of her hand. For that Hieronymus ought to count himself fortunate; a final gift at their parting. From any other man it would have been her steel instead.

She continued to wander, lost in thought. Past streets illuminated only by lamps and the occasional shaft of light spilling from a window, and darkened alleys wrapped in shadow. Elsabeth realized she did not recognize any marker along the streets, nor find anything familiar about the façades looming above her in the darkness on either side. She came upon an empty market square with a few rickety old carts, and here the streets and buildings were in somewhat poorer repair. This was one of the less affluent parts of Ain.

Elsabeth checked her sword in its scabbard, and turned vaguely towards the heart of the city to find a street that would lead her back to the wealthier districts from which she could find her way back to the school. A desire for Stemham's arms around her, his hands stroking her hair as he cuddled her close to his chest, overtook the anger, grief, and guilt warring for prominence in her heart.

She saw no one else abroad that night, but at such a young hour she guessed that most of the denizens of Ain were still holed up in the taverns and alehouses, or the brothels clustered in the working districts. There was no sign of the city guard, either, but she suspected that, like many towns, such neighborhoods received only cursory policing. It also meant a need to be on one's guard when traversing those avenues, and she silently cursed herself for letting her mind drift from where she was headed.

After a few blocks she stopped and frowned. Nothing here looked familiar, though she reckoned she ought to have a sight of the city's cathedral towering over the roofs of the houses and workshops around her. Elsabeth turned and scanned the skyline to get her bearings, but everything above the level of the street was just a dark silhouette against the net of stars overhead. She squinted and peered into the murky ether, and after a moment's searching saw, or thought she saw, the spire of the cathedral spearing into the blackness above a row of densely-packed homes and shops on her right.

Another street, another square, making her way block-by-block across Ain, the spire of the cathedral always in front of her. She started down an alley between two ramshackle buildings that seemed on the verge of collapse. Elsabeth could not make out their signs in the darkness, though one may have been a cooper's shop. The wind whistled as it rushed down that narrow space and nearly blew her hat from her head, and her footsteps echoed between the brick walls rising on either side, so close that if she held her arms out to the sides, she could nearly brush them both with her fingertips. Rats scurried out of sight on her approach, and trash lay piled in heaps in the corners. There was no cover from which some unseen assailant might catch her unawares, but she kept her hand on her sword-hilt nonetheless.

When she was halfway along its length she stopped. For a moment she heard, or thought she heard, another pair of footfalls that did not quite match the echo of her own pattens. But when she turned to look behind her, there was no one there. Elsabeth tightened her hand on her sword and continued on her way. After a few moments of only the *clack* of her own feet on the rough stone of the alleyway she heard it again; soft and indistinct, but a sound like someone hurrying along behind her at a great distance.

She quickened her pace, and stepped out of the alley into a modestly-sized square and much more familiar surroundings. At its heart stood a small garden with a big oak tree, surrounded by empty market stalls awaiting the resumption of business with the dawn. She was not far now from the scaffold erected in the main square, and perhaps only a block or two from Stemham's home.

Elsabeth, however, was not alone. A shadowed figure emerged from the next alley over converging on the square, and she belatedly realized that what she heard was not someone following behind her, but attempting to intercept her.

She flexed her fingers on her sword and started forward. The other fellow altered his course to intersect hers, and hurried his pace to catch her before she could pass him. It appeared to be a man, though she could make out few of his features in the darkness. He was not quite her height, and wore a short, loose cloak that made his figure difficult to clearly discern. That she gleaned from only a cursory inspection. Of much more immediate concern was the sword at his hip, and that, like her, he had his hand was on the hilts.

Elsabeth stopped a good few paces away from him, far enough that even with a powerful lunge he would be well short of landing a blow. He stopped as well, and for a moment they just stared at one another in the darkness. It was evident from his posture, however, he had no intent of letting her pass unchallenged.

Though they closed the distance between one another, Elsabeth could still make out nothing of her challenger. What little she could discern was in shades of dark gray and black, though he appeared to wear a doublet and hose, and possibly garters around his legs.

She sighed when it became apparent he had no interest in speaking first. "Well, come on then. What do you want? If 'tis my purse, come and take it if you dare. If 'tis my person you desire I advise you to try the local nunnery as you will find it less expensive in the end."

"I don't want your money, and your charms are wasted on me," he said, his Navarrese touched with a strong Boehman accent.

Elsabeth clicked her tongue. *I suppose 'twas overdue for the Schwertbrüder to try something foolish.* "Well, now you have gone and hurt my feelings."

"You did not heed my warning, Elsabeth Hereford, and I am here now to give you a lesson."

She chuckled and released her grip on her sword. "Ah, so you must be Merklin Adler. I was quite impressed with your show during the playings today. You almost looked like an actual swordsman. I did not give Caspar enough credit. It seems he learned something from Paulus after all!"

"Shut up, wretched quim! The Brotherhood will not stand for your insults any longer. I warned you there would be consequences."

She let out a derisive snort. "Oh please. The Brotherhood will stomp their feet and cry, but they will do nothing. I suggest you pay attention to their example and go home. Good night!"

Elsabeth made a move to step around him. The rasp of steel on wood hung in the square as his sword left its scabbard, and she froze mid-step.

"You are going nowhere! The Master and Grand Master may look the other way, but I shan't!"

"Boy, put that thing away before you lop your own fool head off! I am trying to let you be smarter than your Master and avoid a world of pain."

"I'll not be called craven for letting a woman dismiss me in such a fashion. Either you leave Ain now, or draw your sword!"

She clenched her teeth and spit him with her iciest glare, though as she could not see his eyes she imagined the effect was lost on him. "I am, at this moment, in an incredibly foul mood, and am in desperate need of either a good fight or a good fuck. I shan't get the former out of you, and you are standing between me and the latter. I don't have the mind of murdering babes still clinging to their mother's tit, so I give you one last chance: Stand down and let me pass!"

"If you don't draw your sword right now then by God I will cut you apart as you stand, woman!"

A scowl firmly etched on her features, and her patience already sorely tested by the argument with Hieronymus, Elsabeth stepped out of her pattens, seized her sword, and drew it with exaggerated slowness. The thin golden light of the lamps illuminating the square flickered along its long, slender blade like pale flame. "You make no illusion that you are indeed a student of Caspar von Bech: He was always an arrogant fool, and has clearly passed that lesson down to you."

"Another word and I'll cut out your tongue, bitch!"

"Oh, I don't need my tongue to elucidate further on Caspar's deficiencies, steel will tell the tale true enough." She raised her sword to him in salute, but Adler did not give her the courtesy of returning the gesture. They each settled into their guards; he in *vom tag* above his right shoulder, she in the Dragon's Tail at her right hip. "Frankly I can't imagine that anyone would trust you with a sharp blade, with him to learn from. But if this is how you wish to die, who am I to argue? I have killed better men over lesser arguments than this."

"I said shut up! And lay on!"

Adler wasted no time, and no sooner were the words out of his mouth than he attacked, perhaps hoping catch her off guard. In a formal duel it would, of course, have been quite indecorous. But for a nighttime brawl in the middle of the street and with no rules to observe, no one would say a thing otherwise.

Regardless, the fight, such as it was, ended in moments.

Adler's attack came in the form of a powerful overhand blow from his right shoulder at her left, seeking to cleave her from shoulder to hip on the opening cut. Elsabeth threw her pommel down and wheeled her sword around in a strong cut to match, and the harsh clash of steel resonated across the square. He tried to use raw strength to force his way past her guard the moment their blades met. She let her sword fall off to the outside, guiding his point safely away from her. Then she stepped in, hooked her pommel over his wrist, and rolled his elbow into an arm-bar. His body doubled over, and she used her leverage and weight to drive him into the ground.

He cried out as his face smacked the paving stones. Elsabeth wrenched up on her pommel even as she pushed his arm down, and his sword clattered from his hand.

She tsked him. "Even Caspar might have lasted longer than a single blow, you should keep practicing."

A glint of light on metal caught her attention, and Elsabeth used her knee to pin him in place while she investigated the source. There, on the ring finger of his right hand, rested a gold band etched with the Guild's arms and motto, marking him as a member of the Brotherhood. She smiled and relieved him of it, and slipped it onto her own finger.

"Well, 'tis a long time in coming, but I finally have one."

"Bitch! That is mine!"

"'Twas yours. You lost, and I claim it as my prize. Now, stand up, and keep your hands raised above your head!" He did as she commanded, and Elsabeth laid her sword point on his shoulder. "Very good. Now, don't move."

"Just do it! Kill me and be done with it!"

She tsked again. "Love, I did not want to kill you. I did not even want to fight you, but you forced the issue. And besides, I leave your miserable corpse for someone to find and there will be no end of trouble. But I can't let you walk away without a reminder of our little encounter, can I?"

Elsabeth flicked her sword. Adler screamed, and his right ear landed on the paving stones with a wet *thump*. He clamped a hand to the side of his head, and in the darkness she watched the blood oozing through his fingers.

"And now you will always have something to remember me by." She stepped forward to wipe her sword clean on the tail of his cloak, and slipped it back in its scabbard. "Do run along home, and mind the streets, they can be frightfully dangerous after dark."

She lightly patted his left cheek, before returning to her pattens. She casually stepped back into them and strolled off up the street. By the time she left the square, Adler had retrieved his sword and fled in the other direction. Elsabeth hesitated and watched a moment to be sure he might not try to assail her again from behind, but he disappeared down a side street and gave no sign of showing himself again any time soon. So she heaved a sigh and continued on her way, and could think of nothing but Crosseby's waiting arms at journey's end.

A**N IMPATIENT BUZZ WORKED ITS WAY ACROSS** the crowd. Spectators milled about in the square below the platform while they awaited the beginning of the second day's playings. The temperature had fallen overnight, and the sun rose upon a city glistening with a fine coating of frost. This did little to dampen the enthusiasm of the crowds, however, whose appetites were only wetted by the excitement of the first day. Animated chatter over what the morning would bring filled the air, and more than a few tongues wagged over the absence of Crosseby's curious companion on the platform.

Caspar sat slumped in his chair at the Grand Master's left hand. D'Ain once again had invited them to sit with him in his private box, but his thoughts were far from the ring atop the scaffold, or the audience seated around them in the stands. Instead, his icy eyes swept the devious, upturned faces of the rustics crowding as close to the platform as they were able. He squinted and searched every man, as if his gaze could pierce through them to the dark secrets hidden behind their unwashed and uncouth features. But there were so many — he lost count well into the hundreds — he could not search them all, and from such a distance he held no hope of spotting the guilty party among them.

He glanced sidelong at Merklin seated as near to the box as he and his other students were able. Clean white linen wrapped around his head and secured a poultice over what remained of his right ear, and a deep purple bruise and a large, angry red abrasion marred his chin and jaw.

"I assure you, Master, I am having the City swept for the culprit," D'Ain was saying, and Caspar returned his attention to him and the Grand Master. The former suitably mollified over the last night's incident, and Aich's countenance clearly troubled. Black anger simmered in his dark eyes, bottled up impotently with no one against whom he could unleash his wrath over the assault. "I have tasked my Captain of the Guard with personally investigating, but I fear there are so many visitors 'twill be impossible to question everyone. And though the guard has done its best to expel the brigands and troublemakers, with the masses Monsieur Crosseby's cavalcade has drawn, I fear 'tis to be expected that some rogue has slipped through. And that says nothing of Ain's own population of ruffians."

"It would help," Crosseby said, "if Monsieur Adler might be able to remember more of the assault."

Caspar twisted his lip at the man. "Were there anything more to say, he would have done so!"

Crosseby scowled at the indignation in his tone. "If he could at least recall where he was ambushed that might provide some lead."

"One street looks alike to another in the darkness, Monsieur. Where, I wonder, was the guard?"

It was D'Ain's turn to scowl, and a dark cloud passed behind his previously merry eyes. "I warn you, Master, I have little liking for your insinuation. The guard cannot patrol everywhere at once, and I should not need to remind you that any city of this size can be dangerous after the sun has set."

"Five men assailed a member of the Guild, Monseigneur," Aich said, his deep voice almost a growl. "They disfigured him and robbed him, and I find this unacceptable!"

"You are guests, here, Master. I would advise you consider that before continuing on this track."

"And as guests we expect to be afforded protection during our visit. If this matter is not addressed to our satisfaction, mark my words it shall not speak well of the relationship between Ain and the Schwertbrüder."

Crosseby grunted in derision. "Such a pity that would be! My heart aches at the thought we shall lose your esteem."

"Do you mock me, Master?" Aich's eyes flashed and he clenched his jaw, but if Crosseby was intimidated by the display of temper he did not show it.

"This is not the Empire, Master. What the Brotherhood says of Ain holds as much meaning to me as the Bishop values his vows of chastity."

"I warn you, Master Crosseby, provoke the Brotherhood at your own peril."

"That is enough!" D'Ain snapped, and beat his fists against his chair. Both men fell into silence. "Monsieur Crosseby, though I have found the sparring of words between you and the Guild as amusing as yesterday's play on the scaffold, I'll not have you spark open conflict between Ain and the Schwertbrüder." He turned to Aich. "And I swear to you, Master, I will do everything in my power to ensure the thieves are captured and brought to judgment. I have already offered you my sincerest apologies on this matter, I can offer you nothing further than my assurances that justice will be served."

Caspar looked between the three of them. Crosseby's face heated and he sunk into the collar of his doublet. D'Ain's flushed countenance betrayed his exasperation with the bickering between the two. Aich's anger had not faded, but Caspar read his grudging acceptance of D'Ain's pledge in his features. The Grand Master nodded curtly and sat back in his chair, but he tightened his grip on the arms until his knuckles turned white.

"Of course, Monseigneur," Aich relented.

"Yes, Monseigneur," Crosseby said.

"Good. I'll not see the friendship we have forged these past days cast aside over this unfortunate occurrence. We are here to celebrate the noble and manly art of defense, not peck and scratch and claw at one another like mere beasts!"

As if on cue a horn sounded at one end of the square, accompanied by the rolling of drums. D'Ain's face brightened considerably, and he smiled as he settled back into his chair.

"Ah! Marvelous! The first of the playings. Let us set aside this unpleasantness for the moment. We can discuss it again tonight when mayhaps the Captain of the Guard shall have news to report, eh?"

The animated gossip among the crowd crescendoed to a frenzy when the horn cried out, announcing the arrival of the first player of the morning. Cheers rippled across the throng as he was marched to the stage with the same pageantry of flags and drums as his peers the day before. Crosseby announced him, one Abacuc Lambrecht, playing for the rank of Provost. The proceedings followed much the same as the day before, only with the addition of the polearm to the selection of arms on which Lambrecht was to be tested.

Contrary to the delight of the crowd with each flurry of strikes and counters, and every successful touch, to Caspar's eye it was a monotonous affair; rigid in its purpose of demonstrating the competency of the player. He begrudgingly admitted that the lad certainly performed as adequately as one ought to expect for a man of his age and experience. The council of Navarrese masters mulled over each bout quietly amongst themselves. Some nodded enthusiastically, others remained more restrained in their exhortations. A shrug here and there, a waggle of the hand, but in the end, as did his three fellows the day before, Abacuc Lambrecht was declared competent and granted his sought after rank to much fanfare and applause. He gathered up the coin tossed onto the scaffold during his playing and departed.

By the time his bouts concluded, the day was drawing near the noon hour, but Crosseby gave no sign of a pause in the day's events. Servants brought food and drink to the audience watching from the stands erected on the scaffold, with D'Ain's personal staff attending to their Lord, Crosseby, the Grand Master, and himself; fine wine in crystal goblets, roasted meat, candied fruits, and pastries.

Vendors crowding the edge of the square offered confections of poorer fare to the common folk watching from the street, with an enterprising few plunging directly into the crowd to serve those who refused to give up their places to go and seek sustenance themselves. The guards observed with watchful eyes, keeping the peasants away from the stairs leading up to the platform, and patrolling for cutpurses and other bandits preying upon the distracted audience.

The day's second player arrived on the heels of the first, to the same electrified fanfare as his predecessor. Mathys Andelieu, also playing for Provost. As before, the uninformed digested the bouts with relish, though Caspar found himself nodding at the tedium. He kept his head propped upright on one fist, or busied himself with a morsel of food or a glass of wine. D'Ain observed the bouts with keen interest in his features, while Crosseby's attention shifted constantly between Andelieu and the masters judging him.

The afternoon wore on. The temperature warmed a bit around the noon hour, but was tempered by the autumn breeze. Steel clashed in a ringing symphony echoing over all corners of the City. And then Andelieu's day on the platform ended, the masters conferred one last time, and a roar of approval went up from the stands and the square as they conferred his prize upon him.

Caspar stifled a yawn, a sentiment mirrored on the Grand Master's countenance. It was now late in the afternoon, and the sun was beginning its descent into the west; the sky in that direction glowed like fire, and a smudge of indigo marred the horizon to the east. Soon it would be supper time, but there was no sign of D'Ain's servants; all had retired to the castle to prepare for his return at the conclusion of the day's events. The vendors remained, however, catering to those standing in the streets. The day was not quite over yet, however, and a third time the horn cried out and the drums rolled through the city streets.

Again a cheer went up as the last fighter made his way along the street from the west, silhouetted against the fire burning on the horizon, and led by flags and banners. But as he drew nearer the raucous applause gave way to confused and astonished silence. Caspar's belly tied itself in knots at their restlessness. With the light failing there was time for only one more fencer, and only one could arouse such a reaction from the masses.

D'Ain wiggled in his chair, an uncharacteristically childish and gleeful smile on his regal features. Crosseby stood and held up his scroll, and read aloud in a voice that carried across the disquiet in the crowd: "Mademoiselle Elsabeth Hawke Soesten de Hereford, seeking the rank of Provost."

Caspar mopped his face as Elsabeth took the platform. He looked to Aich — his own features a mask of barely-restrained rage — and D'Ain, the Navarrese masters, Ruiz, Guarin, and Crosseby. Their expressions ranged from excitement, to amusement, to polite indifference, to disgust. She wore her hair plaited and wound around her head to keep it out of her way during the bouts, and dressed in the same lightweight jacket as the other fencers. Her hose hugged her lower extremity in an obscene display of her shapely figure, and even the cut of her jacket seemed aimed at leaving no doubts in the mind as to her sex. She stared right back at him as if sensing his eyes on her, ignored the amazement from the crowd at her appearance upon the platform, and smiled.

All the square was in an uproar, now, as Elsabeth selected her weapon and waited. And waited. No one dared move. No one dared breathe. Not one of the fencers come to answer the bills of challenge plastered across Navarre and delivered to Boehm and Lizarra and the City-States stood forward. Most were too stunned by the audacity of a woman upon the platform to even consider a response. Others, fearing the ignominy of associating themselves with such a thing, shrunk out of sight. Those few who had actually deigned to fight her during her demonstrations outside the inn blanched and endured the elbows and ribbing of their companions.

Minutes passed. Elsabeth paced, casually flourishing to keep herself loose. The crowd grew restless. Woman or not, they came to be entertained by the crashing of steel, ignorant of the seriousness of these examinations. Where before they cheered with wild abandon, now they jeered and hissed. Not at her, but at the lack of a challenger. Voices rose in outrage that not one of the fencers dared to step into the ring. Crosseby's own students shifted in their seats and looked anywhere but at Elsabeth, the mob packed into the square, or their Master. D'Ain's countenance grew impatient.

"Someone must go down there!" he said. "I did not have the pleasure of seeing this for myself when she was giving her demonstrations, and damned if I not see it now!" He turned to Aich. "Surely, Master, one of your people will answer the challenge? Master von Bech, perhaps?"

The Grand Master's eyes hardened. "With respects, Monseigneur, the Brotherhood objects to this farce, and shan't be a part of it. All of my brothers are under the strictest command not to set foot upon the scaffold so long as that woman occupies it."

D'Ain faltered a moment, taken aback by the brusqueness of Aich's refusal. "I beg your pardon?"

"The Schwertbrüder protest Master Crosseby's insertion of this woman in the playings. The matter of Elsabeth Hereford is one of internal concern for the Guild; She fraudulently associates her name with the Brotherhood in defiance of our charter and traditions. That she stands there now is an insult we do not take lightly!"

Crosseby fixed the Grand Master with a glare of his own to match, and Caspar fancied the meeting of their gaze could ignite a conflagration hot enough to melt the very stones of Ain. "Need I remind you once again that this is not the Empire? The Brotherhood holds no sway in Ain, where I am Master of the Longsword. Not Soest, nor Bech, nor Aich. I am not answerable to you, Master, and that I put her forward as a candidate for Provost is my prerogative."

Caspar's eyes hardened. "Then I shall speak for myself," he said. "This is a profanity, and I shan't take part in this disgrace."

A chant started from one corner of the square, and soon hundreds of voices were raised in displeasure, calling for someone, *anyone*, to step forward so they might witness the novel spectacle of a woman fighter. In truth, Caspar suspected they approved of her no more than the practitioners they attempted to shame into fighting, but to them it was a show. An exotic phenomenon that would never come again. Their protestations became louder and more insistent, and soon the guards were obliged to use the shafts of their halberds to keep the crowd from rushing the platform as their unrest grew.

"Monsieur Crosseby, would you be so kind as to stand in, as our contrary guests refuse," D'Ain said. "Lest this protest of the cowardice of the fencers turn violent?"

Crosseby winced at D'Ain's request. "I am afraid I cannot, Monseigneur," he said. "The agreement I made with the esteemed masters sitting in judgment decreed that I mayn't answer a challenge myself during the playings."

As they spoke Elsabeth's eyes swept the stands as if seeking for someone, and her smile broadened. Caspar attempted to follow her gaze to see whom she might have been looking for, but it was impossible for him to choose one face out of the crowd. He need not have bothered, however, as she soon made her chosen target plain to all.

"Merklin Adler!" she called, her voice loud and clear, and penetrating through the agitated rumble filling the square to almost deafening. The whole assembly fell into immediate silence. Caspar frowned and looked to Merklin, whose face turned a brilliant shade of crimson at being so singled-out. Elsabeth laughed. "'Tis no need for you to hide your face, I see you sitting there. And I see you had your ear tended, as well!"

Bile churned within Caspar's belly at those words, and a chill crept the length of his spine.

"Will you not come down?"

Elsabeth's remark did not go unmarked by Crosseby, D'Ain, or the Grand Master. Merklin stiffened in his chair and glanced in their direction. But for his part he made no move to answer her direct challenge.

She leaned her *Feder* against her shoulder and hugged it loosely against her breast. That smile — the smirk he saw again and again in his nightmares, and in every memory of every humiliation at her hands — lit her heart-shaped face with delight at Merklin's consternation.

"Why so bashful now? You were certainly bold enough last night, assaulting a lone woman on the street!"

"Caspar!" Aich said, his voice a harsh and incensed whisper. "What is the meaning of this?"

Caspar's mouth hung open, and he could only flick his eyes between her and Merklin — who now did his best to sink out of sight — as his heart worked its way up into his throat. The realization of the truth struck him like a thunderbolt, and from the ire in the Grand Master's eyes it was clear that he, too, pieced together her meaning. "I swear, Master, I don't know!"

Beside the Grand Master, D'Ain's countenance hardened at what was brewing. "Monsieur Crosseby?"

Crosseby merely shrugged. "I don't know, Monseigneur. I can account for her whereabouts most of the night, though she stepped out briefly to meet with a priest of her acquaintance. She said nothing of an attack to me."

"Surely this must be some manner of trick or jest," Caspar said, but did not believe, and his mouth went dry. "That woman has vexed me from the moment I first knew her, for all I know this is merely a means of goading Monsieur Adler or myself into a fight."

Elsabeth stood and smiled at Merklin. "You truly will not deign to face me in the daylight before a crowd? Is this what the Brotherhood teaches you, then? To strike from the shadows, and shrink from the platform? Well, you have certainly learned quite well from Caspar von Bech!"

Caspar's face heated, and he clenched his jaw and tightened his fists. The Grand Master fumed. Crosseby paled. D'Ain just stood and addressed her.

"Mademoiselle, I demand to know what this is about!" he shouted over the drone of the crowd, building as they all began to discuss the accusations at once. Nearby whispers from the students of the visiting masters questioned whether the Schwertbrüder would stand for such insults or would answer the challenge. "Monsieur Adler was waylaid by thieves in the night."

Elsabeth laughed, and a collective gasp filled the square at the audacity of *laughing* at D'Ain. "Forgive me, Monseigneur," she said, "but I find the charge amusing. How many was it, Merklin Adler? Five? Ten? I think not. I think it was just me, alone, in the dark."

"Merklin!" Caspar said, and snapped his fingers. "Present!"

Merklin swallowed, a visible bobbing of his Adam's apple, and he left his seat. He picked a path through the stands until he reached D'Ain's box and crouched low beside him.

"What is the meaning of this!" Aich said, and spit them both with a withering glare. "I thought my instructions were clear: No one was to touch that woman!"

"They were, Master!" Caspar said. "I told him myself!"

"Master, I swear—"

His protest died in his throat when Elsabeth reached beneath her jacket and pulled out a length of fine chain. A golden ring dangled at the end.

"I have this for you," she said. "If you want it back, why not come and take it?"

Merklin's jaw dropped, and his face turned a striking shade of purple. Laughter sprung up among the other practitioners, particularly those near enough to the platform to see the ring for themselves. Caspar, however, did not need to see it. His breath heaved and his heart pounded against his sternum. Aich's features turned livid. If there were any doubt of the veracity of her accusations, she had utterly shattered them.

There, on a chain held in her slender fingers, was Merklin's missing ring.

"Monsieur Crosseby!" D'Ain said, his features no less livid than the Grand Master's.

Stemham came to his feet as well and raised his hands defensively. "I swear, Monseigneur, I knew nothing of this!"

D'Ain rounded on the three Schwertbrüder next. "I demand to know the truth of this! Was my ban on dueling forgotten?"

The Grand Master joined them on their feet, and Caspar rose with him. Aich bowed deeply in contrition to D'Ain. "Your commands were clearly understood, Monseigneur, and I issued the order personally to Master von Bech that dueling was strictly prohibited within the bounds of the city. But I have demands as well, Monseigneur!"

"Don't you dare stand before me and speak of demands, Stefan von Aich!" D'Ain roared, and everyone fell into silence. Caspar was conscious of the hundreds of pairs of eyes now focused explicitly upon the five of them.

"This woman has confessed to assaulting and robbing a member of my Guild! I am entitled to demand justice on his behalf, and to know what you intend to do with her!"

"Elsabeth has confessed nothing!" Crosseby said, his face as flushed in anger as Merklin's was in humiliation. "'Twas the coward Merklin Adler who assaulted her. She has the right to the defense of her life and body, Monseigneur!"

"We have only her word that she was ambushed!" Caspar said.

"And Merklin Adler's word was that he was waylaid by a gang of outlaws. Elsabeth has no cause for such a fabrication, so why does Monsieur Adler not admit the truth?"

"I wonder what price Elsabeth Hereford pays for your unquestioning support, Master Crosseby," Caspar said, and narrowed his eyes with suspicion. "Was it bought on her back? That is certainly within her capacity, as the Coventrish whore so tempted Soest to his own fall!"

Crosseby started forward, his arm outstretched as if to seize him by the throat, but D'Ain bodily placed himself between them. Caspar favored him with a wicked smile at his reaction. "I see her charms were no more wasted on you than they were our late Master. 'Tis little wonder she found you so eager to put her on display."

He struggled against the arms of D'Ain restraining him. "Recant those words at once, or I swear in the Lord of All's name that you and I shall be having an argument of it!"

"Monsieur Crosseby! That is enough!" D'Ain said, and forced him back into his seat. When Crosseby tried to rise again he stopped him with a hand on his chest. "There will be no such arguments! Do I make myself understood?"

"With respects, Monseigneur, this is now a matter of honor between myself and that lying wretch!" Crosseby said, his outburst subsided, but his voice no less spiteful.

"This is a matter of law! And you shall compose yourself as an officer of this city should!" D'Ain raised a hand and motioned, and a guard posted near at hand hurried to his side. "Clear the square, and arrange an escort to see Grand Master von Aich, Master von Bech, and Monsieur Adler to the castle."

The guard bowed stiffly at the waist and motioned to his comrades to carry out the request.

D'Ain turned back to Crosseby, and laid a hand on his shoulder. "In respects to you, I won't send the guard for her, but I want Mademoiselle Soesten brought to the castle, where this matter can be decided. I want you to see to it personally. If she speaks the truth and her actions were in her own defense, then she has nothing to fear. But I warn you, Monsieur, if my law has been defied there will be consequences, am I understood?"

Crosseby lowered his head and gave a stiff nod. "Yes, Monseigneur."

D'Ain stared him down for a long moment, then turned to depart, his guards forming around him as he left the box. No one moved when he departed the stands, but once he was gone the guards sprang into action clearing the rabble from the square. A few folk resisted and earned a rough shove from their halberds for their troubles. Merklin fell in with the escort gathered to take them to the castle, but Caspar hesitated a moment. He looked down at the stage, but Elsabeth had disappeared, likely retreating under some rock, or perhaps to Crosseby's bed.

Crosseby glared hellfire at him from beneath his brows, but Caspar just smiled at him. "Clearly whatever business exists between you," he said, "she did not tell you the truth of what happened the night Master von Soest died. If you don't believe me, ask her yourself her role in Soest's fall. I'll await your apology at the castle."

And with that he spun on his heel and joined the Grand Master and Merklin as the guard led them from the platform.

# 23

I T TOOK THE BETTER PART OF AN HOUR FOR the guard to calm the crowd and clear the square, and until the streets were emptied, Crosseby was trapped on the scaffold and unable to depart for home. He fumed silently as he made the lonely trek across the City, pursued by the parting words of Caspar von Bech. Elsabeth had not, in fact, said much about the death of their Master. He thought back on what rumors of Soest's passing reached Ain but could recall little that might offer a hint at her role in the affair. Bech's accusation stuck in his throat, however much he tried to discard it as the libel he knew it had to be.

That was all it was: a malicious lie, to distract from his own student's transgressions. And yet he could not force it from his mind.

*I see her charms were no more wasted on you than they were our late Master. 'Tis little wonder she found you so eager to put her on display.*

He thought back to that night in the garden. Sparring under the light of the stars and moon. Her touch against his hip; quick and timely, slipping unexpectedly beneath his guard. Had he, in arrogance fed by more than a little drink, merely underestimated her? Or was the real game in the second bout? The ease with which he wrestled her to the ground, the taste of her lips, and the warmth of her beneath him. The story of her youth the next morning. All of it leading to this moment on the scaffold where she stood before the entire population of Ain, the Grand Master of the Schwertbrüder, the gathering of the great peers of Navarrese swordcraft, the masters of the Free City-States, and all their students, and so publicly emasculated the guild.

A lump rose in his throat at the thought he might have been so easily played.

Crosseby wrestled with Bech's words, and the doubt building in his heart, all the way home. He ignored the gossip on street corners as the tale spread like wildfire: The Schwertbrüder attempted an assassination of the woman Elsabeth Soesten. Five men attacked her, or perhaps it was ten. She killed them all. Except for one, the fellow with the missing ear. Or perhaps it was his nose she cut off, or another even more shameful piece of his anatomy. It was a message to the Grand Master that he was next.

He let it all wash over him, swirling around him like eddies in a stream past the pilings of a bridge; surrounding him but never quite touching him.

By the time he finally reached his own door the sun was a burning disk sitting on the rim of the horizon amid a sky on fire. Long, dark shadows stretched out beneath the dying light of the twilight, and in the east the sky darkened. There the first stars kindled in the indigo curtain of night, shining through the gloom like countless silver lamps. It promised to be another chill autumn evening, and the rich fragrance of dozens of fires burning in the hearths of the homes and taverns of Ain mingled with the fresh scent of the breeze. He threw open the door and stepped into the warmth of his entry foyer, and let it thump closed behind him.

The foyer was empty, but the drone of voices reached him from the great hall; his students celebrating their prizes. Ale would be flowing, food laid out on the tables, and everyone would be merry. But not him. D'Ain had given him a task that he was loath to carry out, but he had no choice but see it done.

Crosseby stormed down the hallway to the screens passage, and then into the great hall. His students gathered in knots in the middle of the floor, toasting Abacuc and Mathys, and drinking heartily from the kegs set up on the table. Elsabeth lounged in his seat at the high table atop the dais, one long leg hooked over the arm of the chair, her expression downcast as she drank — her hopes of gaining a prize herself dashed by the refusal of any man to challenge her. The rest of the party, sensing her poor mood — and shame-faced that they, too, refused to face her in public — kept their distance and did not seek her out for stories, or to challenge her capacity for drink.

The sight of her, in his chair, under these circumstances made his face heat and his blood boil. Crosseby jumped up on one of the tables lining the hall and stomped his foot until all conversation died away, and every eye in the room was on him.

"Clear the hall!" he said, his voice filled with command. No one moved, nor said a word. They all just stared at him in bewilderment at the interruption of the festivities.

Crosseby swept his gaze across the room, and not one of his students moved to comply.

"I said everybody out!" His voice shook the rafters of the hall, and this time they scrambled to flee his presence. Tankards clattered to the floor and splashed golden ale across the parquetry. Men fled with half-eaten morsels or dropped them where they stood in their haste to escape his wrath. Elsabeth swayed unsteadily as she rose from his chair, but he spit her with a glare. "You, stay!"

She froze and swallowed visibly. When the last of his students abandoned the hall and they were alone, Crosseby stepped down from the table and crossed the rest of the distance between them. He mounted the dais and circled round the high table, not once taking his eyes from her. Her hair had slipped from its plaits and was a frightful mess, and her fencing jacket hung open over the fine white linen shirt beneath. The lacing of her shirt at the collar was undone, leaving it open to her collarbones. The chain with Merklin's ring still hung exposed for all to see round her neck, and the gold gleamed in the lamplight. Elsabeth paled at the expression on his countenance, but her green eyes were clouded; clearly, she had already consumed a fair share of his ale before his arrival.

"Stemham," she said, but he cut her off.

"Be quiet! I am commanded to bring you to his Lordship for questioning in the assault upon Merklin Adler."

Elsabeth twisted her lip and folded her arms across her breast. "So they are calling it an assault, then?"

"'Tis clear enough you mutilated and robbed him! What were you thinking?"

"I was thinking the bastard came upon me in the dark issuing threats!"

His stomach fell at her words. "It was not an ambush?"

She uttered a derisive grunt. "The other day he went to Hieronymus and 'suggested' I leave Ain. Suffice to say I was not impressed when he came to make good on it last night. He insisted upon a fight, woefully unprepared for it as he was, so I accepted."

Crosseby clenched his fists and gritted his teeth as any hope for clemency from D'Ain evaporated in that moment. "Why did you not tell me you were threatened? I might have—"

"Might have what? Expelled Caspar and his band of fools from Ain? I don't need you to fight my battles for me, love, I have been fighting them myself almost since I was old enough to lift my sword!"

"You are fortunate you did not kill him! His Lordship has declared that any duel in the city was to be treated as an assault. Had you slain him you would have been charged with murder!"

"I spared his life because he was an idiot!"

"That does not matter! The Grand Master is all but calling for your head!"

"Oh of course he is. The arrogant tyrant has wanted my head, and I suspect other things, on a platter almost from the day I walked into Paulus' schola!"

"You have dragged both his Lordship and me into this feud between you and the Brotherhood, and now have left us to face the consequences!"

She flinched back at the heat in his voice, and for her part her expression turned contrite. "That was not my intent."

"Hang your intent! 'Tis what is done that I care about now. Tell me, why are you here?"

Elsabeth barked an incredulous laugh. "I have told you already why I came to Ain."

"I don't mean Ain. Why are you here, in my house?"

"You invited me!"

He slammed a fist down on the table, and she jumped. "Don't be coy with me. I want to know the truth! You fell easily into my bed that night, and in return I put you on the platform. Is that all I was to you, then? A means to an end?"

She curled her lip in disgust at the accusation. "You are sounding like that meddlesome friar!"

"I want an answer! Why are you here?"

"'Twas what I thought you expected of me!" Elsabeth balled her hands into fists as she stared him down, her face red and her whole body trembling. "Is that what you want to hear? All right, there it is! And don't deny you were more than eager to take advantage of what I was offering. Nor are you the first; I have kissed and fucked my way in and out of trouble at need in the past, among other things I much regret, but 'twas always what I had to do!"

Crosseby felt a hand squeeze his heart until he thought it might burst, and his throat tightened at her confession.

"And so you used me to get on that platform, and to get to the Brotherhood."

"I did not even know Caspar was here until we met at the castle! And as for the platform; perhaps at first. When I was given your invitation to supper, I thought you to be like all the rest. 'Twas only after that first night I learned your true quality."

"You truly thought so little of me?"

She glared. "Be careful with those words, love, and consider what brought on the conversation we are having now! But 'tis a lesson I have had to learn well; men look upon me and see one thing. 'Twas always the way of it, and how can you fault me for thinking otherwise?"

"And what of Soest?"

"What do you mean?"

He steeled himself and met her eyes. Apprehension and suspicion over where he led her warred for prominence in their green depths. "Was it truly your father who paid for your education, or did you take it from Soest on your back, just as you did with me?"

"You bastard," she said, her voice almost a whisper. "Don't you dare accuse me of—"

"'Tis not I who accuses! And thus far you give me no reason to dispute the charge!"

"Who, then? Caspar? The Grand Master?"

Crosseby jammed a finger in her face. "Don't deflect the question! I want the truth, as novel as that concept seems to be to you!"

A loud *crack* echoed through the hall. His head snapped around, and for a moment all he saw was a flash of white. His ear rang, and the side of his head throbbed painfully from the force of the blow. Elsabeth's whole body shook, her face contorted into rage. Crosseby weathered the blow and did not even offer her the satisfaction of nursing his face.

"You son of a bitch!" she said, and her voice trembled along with her body. "I have never in my life lied about my studies with Paulus. If there are things I did not say, 'twas because 'tis my affair, and mine alone! And you owe me better than to take that envious, impotent ass, Caspar von Bech, at his word! I never in my life whored myself to him, and don't you ever say otherwise!"

"Then tell me the truth!"

"What do you want me to say? To deny every word of it? To say that I never knew him? I'll not lie, not for your ego, nor even if the truth were to cost my life! I loved him!" Her voice broke, and tears welled up in her eyes. "I loved him with all my heart, I love him still, and I shall love him till the day I draw my last breath! And he loved me in turn! But I did not seduce him, no matter what Caspar says. I did not buy my way into his school with my body. But yes! We were lovers. Is that what you wish to hear?

"I died the night he was slain, and all I could do was avenge him. I was not even given the proper chance to mourn him, as I had to leave Soest that very night. Does that satisfy you?"

Crosseby's legs wobbled beneath him, and he pulled his chair out from the table and dropped into it. Tears ran freely down Elsabeth's face.

"'Twas not long after I fought my first duel that we confessed our feelings to one another," she said, and she wrapped her arms around herself. Crosseby just buried his face in his hands. "But what I felt for him began before that. I first came to Soest as I told you; a child. I went to learn from him. The rest ..." She trailed off amid a choking sob, and held her cheek. "I was not a girl forever, and as I became a woman he noticed, just as I began to be aware of him. It just happened!"

"And the night he died?"

"Words were said at the tavern at my expense by small men with loose tongues, and Paulus would not stand for it. It tears me apart knowing that he died on my account! Had I been with him that night, mayhaps he would still be alive, and I would be in Soest with him. But with him gone I had no choice but flee. Oh, I have no doubt that Caspar sees things otherwise; he long envied my closeness with Paulus, because he knew that I was his favorite, and that if I were not born a woman I would have supplanted him with ease as Vorfechter. And I can only imagine he has incited you to wound me."

He said nothing, and remained as he sat, his face in his hands, and listening to her shuddering breaths. Crosseby did not know what to feel; he knew so little of her, but in those few days...

"Stemham," she said, her quavering voice barely above a whisper. "I am sorry to have drawn you into this madness that is my life. These are the things I must do to live as I wish, but I did not do what I did with you because I had no other choice. I have felt more at home here these past few days than I have anywhere since I left Soest, and 'tis not just this place, but 'tis you."

"How do you expect me to believe a word you say?" he said, and sunk back in his chair. Crosseby forced himself to look at her; the tears streaming down her cheeks, the redness of her eyes, the slump of her shoulders. "You confess you needed little consideration to bed me if it would get you what you wanted, and now you tell me 'tis me you want? Your capriciousness in this is not at all endearing."

"If I did you harm I can't apologize enough, but you don't live my life. You are secure here, with the patronage of a powerful lord, to run this place as you wish. Hieronymus and I scrape a living off the road with whatever work we can find, and sometimes that means making use of what God has given me to open doors that might be closed otherwise. If I thought so little of you at first that I came here expecting the same, 'tis because that is how the world works. You are a maddening incongruity!"

"That is no consolation to me!" he said, and bounced his fists on the arms of his chair. "God damn you! What am I to do with you, now?"

She did not respond, and just stood hugging herself tightly. Crosseby stared at the table for a long moment, a dull ache working through his gut. Finally, he spoke again.

"You are going before his Lordship. You will tell him the truth; the threats made by Merklin Adler, and that this was a duel, not an ambush. Perhaps he may show leniency nonetheless given the circumstances."

Elsabeth bristled. "You should see by now I don't take well to being commanded, love. 'Tis best to let it fall on their heads where it belongs."

He glared at her. "I don't care! I'll not lie to his Lordship on this, and if you don't speak the truth, then I will!"

She clenched her teeth, and her cheeks flushed. "Yes, Sire," she said, the last added with a biting emphasis that made her disgust clear.

Crosseby looked away from her, unable to look her in the eye for what next he had to say. "When that is done, I want you gone. From my house, and from Ain."

"What?"

Though he could not see her expression, focused as he was on the table, he could imagine her disbelief at his sentence nonetheless. "'Tis best for all involved that you be gone from this city once the matter is decided. So long as you are here, you will continue to draw me and my Lord into this conflict with the Schwertbrüder, and I want no part of it!"

"Stemham, you can't—"

"Can't what?" He turned his eyes on her again. She stood as if struck by a blow, leaning on a chair at the high table for support, and her face drained of all color. A lump formed in his throat at seeing her rebellious fire so quenched, but he refused to relent now. His decision had been made. "Decide what occurs in my own house? I'll not be a party to controversy, and I see now I shall be courting that so long as you are here! What other lies have you told? What other half-truths or secrets left unsaid?"

The tears returned to her eyes, and her voice cracked. "'Tis not fair! You of all people should understand what it is to have done things of which you are ashamed, and are loath to speak of. Or shall you be telling me why you were driven from the King's service?"

Crosseby stood and bunched his fists at his sides. "You'll not twist this around on me! I welcomed you into my home, I offered to teach you, I put you on the platform, and in return I am humiliated before my Lord and the city!"

"And you got a good deal more from the bargain and if you were not so pig-headed, you would see it!"

"You overvalue yourself and are not worth the price!"

A grunt of disgust rose from the back of her throat. "'Tis a reason men like you exist only in stories and romances! Perhaps I did not tell you everything of my life, but it does not change that I have been nothing if not honest about who and what I am. But you? You sweep me from my feet with stories of your honor and chivalry, that you would have taught me even if I had not opened my thighs for you, and that you would aid an enemy because it was the right thing to do! But in the end, you are like every other knight I have known, and I have known many before you: either your honor is but a pretense, or you are a slave to it, and you cast me aside the moment you see me as an inconvenience or a danger to maintaining the illusion of chivalry!"

"Enough!" He slammed his fists on the table, and everything sitting atop it bounced into the air. Elsabeth, for her part, just stared him down with hate and pain in her green eyes. "Were you anyone else I would summon you beyond the city walls where I would be free to hold this argument!"

"Then let us do so and be done with it! Don't think that just because I have lain with a man I have never been given cause to strike him down afterwards!"

He gritted his teeth. Her spirit had returned, and he had no doubt if he met her beyond the walls she would give him no quarter. "If we fight, you will die, and that is blood I don't want on my hands."

"Lord of All cast you in the blackest pit of the Dark One's domain for your hypocrisy!"

"Curse me all you like, it changes nothing. I'll argue this no further. His Lordship is awaiting us. You will not return here when this business is concluded. Go back to your companion, and I want you gone from Ain by tomorrow night. Richard will return your belongings on the morrow."

Elsabeth screwed up her features as if she might spit in his face, but instead she seized her forgotten tankard and drained it in one long swallow. Then she threw it with all her strength at the back wall of the great hall, and it exploded into fragments of clay. Then she turned on her heel and stormed down from the dais, and marched across the floor for the screens passage.

Crosseby stared at her back for a moment, before heaving a sigh and following, while his belly turned itself inside out.

24

THERE WAS NO GRAND GATHERING OF the cream of Navarrese swordsmanship at Castle Ain that night. She and Crosseby arrived to find D'Ain alone in the great hall, seated in his chair upon the dais and glowering down at the Schwertbrüder standing at its foot. The Grand Master stood tall and proud, his white robes of office glowing in the lamplight. When he saw her his dark eyes flashed beneath his brows, as if he might strike her dead with a glance. Elsabeth ignored him.

Merklin Adler's face colored at the sight of her, and he averted his gaze to the floor. He was of no consequence; a foolish boy trying to make a name for himself only to be humiliated, as had so many who underestimated her before him. She ignored him, too.

Rather, her eyes settled upon Caspar von Bech, his head tilted back so he might glare contemptuously down his nose at her. She glared murder back at him, and she thought she caught an infinitesimal paling of his features. The subtle recognition of the lethal threat in her glance. He knew, should it come to blows, she could cut him down like wheat if she chose. And in her current mood she needed little provocation to do just that. Everything that day had gone wrong, and it all lay upon his shoulders.

She and Crosseby did not exchange another word on their way to the castle. She did not even look at him, though at times she felt his eyes on her. There was nothing more for them to say to one another; he had made his feelings perfectly clear.

It was all she could do to not run screaming from the hall in tears.

Elsabeth joined the Schwertbrüder at the foot of the dais. She gave little thought to her disheveled appearance, in stark contrast to the gleaming white of Aich's robes, and the fine doublets worn by the other men in the hall. She greeted D'Ain with a deep bow and an exaggerated sweep of her arm, letting Merklin's ring dangle on the chain about her neck.

"Do you understand why you have been summoned here?" D'Ain said. He came straight to the point, and there was no amusement in his voice at seeing her now.

She glanced over her shoulder at Crosseby standing behind her, but he averted his eyes away from her. Elsabeth turned back to D'Ain. "Yes, Monseigneur," she said.

"I consider this a very serious matter. I understand the volatility of so many practitioners of such wildly differing philosophies on the sword arts converging upon one city. Outrage over the insults towards one's master, the pride of the Brotherhood, among other subjects on which they might swiftly take offense. And 'tis for that reason I commanded that dueling would not be tolerated within the bounds of Ain. Yet it seems that decree has been violated;

by yourself and Monsieur Adler of the Brotherhood. This shan't pass!

"I have heard the statements of the Schwertbrüder in this matter. Before I render my decision on whether this shall proceed to court, I permit you to speak your case. However, I warn you to speak truthfully!"

D'Ain waved his hand, inviting her to speak, and for a moment Elsabeth said nothing. She stood with her fists at her sides and her head bowed, and weathered the glares of Caspar and Aich in silence. A moment's glance aside revealed Crosseby now watched her closely, his features crossed by a deep frown as he awaited what she would do next. She took a deep breath.

"The truth, Monseigneur, is that three nights previous, Merklin Adler approached a brother of the Olivian order with whom I travel, offering a suggestion that I should depart Ain with haste. The consequences of failing to heed this advice were not stipulated in the message, but were nonetheless implicit."

"'Tis the first I have heard of such a message," D'Ain said, his tone colored with annoyance over the news.

"That does not surprise me at all, Monseigneur. 'Tis no secret that the Brotherhood and I have a long animosity with one another, and I am sure they spoke all manner of slander towards me ere my arrival before you tonight."

Caspar rounded on her, red-faced and quaking. "You dare accuse me of lying before Monsieur le Chevalier?"

"'Tis no accusation, love. Monsieur le Chevalier demanded the truth."

"Truth? There has never been a word from your mouth that has not been steeped in lies!"

"Silence!" D'Ain snapped, and his voice echoed through the hall. "Now is not the time for you to speak, Caspar von Bech! I have asked Mademoiselle Soesten to give her account of last night, so hold your tongue or I will have you removed from my hall!"

He glowered down on him from the dais, and Caspar ducked his head in chagrin. When D'Ain satisfied himself that he would remain silent, he motioned for her to continue.

"I can't say whether Merklin Adler delivered the message himself, or on behalf of his Masters," she said, and glared pointedly at Caspar, who just stood silently fuming. However much she might have liked to lay the blame upon his shoulders, she swore to speak only the truth on the matter. "Regardless, I dismissed the threat when it was relayed to me as hollow and impotent, much as is the Brotherhood itself."

"Monseigneur, I protest!" Aich said, and his body tensed. "You granted Elsabeth Hereford permission to make her case, not to tender insults!"

"Indeed!" D'Ain said. "Continue your tale, Mademoiselle, but mind your tongue! When did the friar deliver this message to you?"

"The night I was presented to Monseigneur, before the playings began. I was staying as a guest at Monsieur Crosseby's home, and he visited me there to convey it."

"Monsieur Crosseby?"

"She did meet with an Olivian that night, as she says," Crosseby said. "I was not, however, privy to the conversation."

"Proceed," D'Ain said, and gave her a nod. Clearly Crosseby's word was enough to satisfy him on that point.

"As I said," she continued, "I disregarded the warning, and attended the first day of the playings yesterday, giving it no further thought. However, that night, my companion visited again to continue a private argument we had no time to finish the day before. I left the house with him during our quarrel, and walked him to the inn where he was staying. We then parted company, and upon my return to the house I was accosted — that is to say, stopped in the road — by Merklin Adler."

"He did not assault you unawares?"

She swallowed and took a steadying breath. "No, Monseigneur," she admitted. Aich's brows lifted in surprise, and even Caspar seemed taken aback by her admission. "He did come upon me out of the darkness, but he did not bare his steel immediately. He barred my path, and it was only when I tried to step around him that he drew his sword — but he did draw on me first and challenged me."

"And you accepted?"

"Yes, Monseigneur. When he refused the opportunity I gave him to exercise wisdom and retire, I accepted the challenge. We fought. That is to say, he struck a blow at me and I disarmed him before he did something more foolish. 'Twould be an act of generosity to call it a fight."

Merklin's face turned an even brighter shade of red, but he said nothing.

"Explain to me his ear, then."

"I cut it off before I released him."

Crosseby groaned and mopped his face. Caspar and Aich's expressions became livid, and Merklin's face turned an even more brilliant shade of crimson. D'Ain laughed incredulously, and that only discomfited her erstwhile adversary even further. "Why in God's name would you do such a thing?"

Elsabeth hesitated a moment before answering, searching for a response. D'Ain eyed her closely, and she shifted uncomfortably under his gaze. "Well?" he said, when an answer was not immediately forthcoming.

"In truth, Monseigneur, I don't know."

"You don't know?" Caspar cried, and swept his arm at Merklin, who self-consciously touched the bandage over his ear. "You mutilate his face, and you don't know why?"

Her face burned with her chagrin, and she looked up at D'Ain, whose expression was no less dumbfounded by her response. "I confess that night I was not in the best of minds. 'Twas bad enough I just ended a very unpleasant conversation with a man I held to be a friend, and there was a measure of drink involved. Then Merklin Adler accosts me in the dark of night, issuing threats and demanding I fight him! So I cut off his bloody ear."

"So 'twas not enough for you to have bested him," D'Ain said. "This was an act of humiliation."

"I suppose it was, but the buffoon bloody deserved it! Now everywhere he goes men will ask him how he lost his ear, and he must either speak falsely, or confess it was taken from him after a duel by the woman, Elsabeth Soesten. That ignominy will follow him the rest of his life, and mayhaps teach him a lesson of greater value than any he would learn with Caspar von Bech as his master!"

Caspar started towards her, his face contorting in rage, but froze in his tracks when D'Ain's rebuke shook the hall. "Stand fast, Master! I'll not have such displays as this in my hall! Elsabeth Soesten, I will warn you one last time I will accept no more such insults past your lips! Am I understood?"

She swallowed at the fire in his voice and inclined her head. "Yes, Monseigneur."

"There is also the matter of Merklin Adler's ring, Monseigneur," Aich said. "For that was stolen from his finger."

D'Ain nodded. "Indeed it was, and I see she still has it, on that chain round her neck."

"I took his ring, I confess," Elsabeth said, and spit the Grand Master with a glare. "But I deny that taking it was a theft."

"What do you call it, then?"

"A trophy of my victory; proof that 'twas I who bested him, and it seems fortuitous I did indeed claim it, if he chose to speak falsely of his actions. And, Monseigneur, I consider it my due. I trained with Master Paulus for seven years, but the Schwertbrüder deny me. They like to pretend I am just a nightmare, and if they put me from their minds 'twould be as if I never existed. But put a sword in my hand and I have no doubts that I could best any of them, and that is no idle boast! Caspar alone I thrashed many times, and 'tis only the accident of my sex that kept me from being Vorfechter in Soest.

"You saw for yourself this afternoon on the platform: Not one man dared to accept my challenge. The Grand Master calls me a farce before the gathering of all of Navarese swordsmanship. And yet I would best every one of those cowards who drank with me last night but refused to look me in the eye upon the platform today. All because they daren't let it be known they lost a touch to a woman!"

Elsabeth took hold of the ring, and squeezed her eyes shut tightly in an effort to hold the welling tears at bay. "I earned this! Seven years under Paulus's tutelage; 'tis mine by right!"

She fell into silence and listened for a moment as the echo of her voice died away. Crosseby lowered his eyes to the floor. Merklin shifted as if he wished to be anywhere else. Caspar's face flushed as he trembled with barely restrained wrath, and Aich's jaw clenched at the indignity of the humiliation Merklin's defeat laid upon them. Whatever happened next she knew the tale would spread. The Schwertbrüder could now never forget her name.

D'Ain steepled his hands and tapped his lip as he considered her words. Elsabeth released her hold on Merklin's ring round her neck and stood straight and still. She raised her chin defiantly and refused to let Caspar see her quail in dread over D'Ain's judgement.

For a long moment silence reigned in the hall, before finally he spoke.

"Have you anything further to add to these deliberations, Monsieur Adler? Do you wish to dispute Mademoiselle Soesten's charge on your conduct?" he asked.

Merklin hung his head and balled his fists. But he said nothing, and his only response was a slight shake of his head. Caspar gritted his teeth, and Aich's face colored.

D'Ain regarded the Schwertbrüder a moment, then nodded and returned his attention to her. "Very well, then. I welcome your candor, Mademoiselle. You might easily have come before me and laid blame entirely for this affair upon Monsieur Adler, claiming he assaulted you, with only their word against yours with which to contend. Know that I do consider this when rendering my judgment.

"However, I can't discount that you and Monsieur Adler have both violated my decree banning dueling in Ain. And whether I might consider your actions justifiable or not, I don't find your decision to mutilate him, particularly under such petty reasoning, warranted. As to the matter of the ring, I wash my hands of it, for this is clearly a matter internal to the Brotherhood, and 'tis for them to address themselves."

Aich opened his mouth as if to protest, but any remark was cut off by a glare from D'Ain. He then returned his attention to her.

"I therefore command that you, Mademoiselle Soesten, shall pay to Monsieur Adler the sum of five *sous* in recompense for his disfigurement. Furthermore, you are each to pay an equal fine to me for violating the peace of Ain in defiance of my commands."

Elsabeth swallowed as D'Ain pronounced his sentence. *Ten sous for an ear. Better had I just killed him and been done with it!*

"Lastly, you both are hereby barred from participating further in both the playings and the general contest of arms.

By rights I ought to have you banned from the City, but I shall content myself that denying you the privilege of competing shall be punishment enough."

She slumped her shoulders and hung her head as D'Ain spoke and denied her the one purpose for which she had made the journey to Ain. Merklin bowed his head as well, but Caspar murmured something into his good ear and clapped him on the shoulder. Elsabeth peeked at Crosseby from the corner of her eye, but no such consolation came for her. Her throat knotted up, and her face and neck flushed.

"Monsieur Crosseby, I appoint you my officer in carrying out this sentence. I will leave it to you to collect the fines. You are dismissed."

The Schwertbrüder all bowed low and departed the hall with Aich in their lead. She felt, more than saw, Caspar and Merklin glare at her as they passed. Elsabeth ignored them as she bowed to D'Ain, then spun about on her heel and hurried for the screens passage. Crosseby fell into step behind her, but still he said nothing as they departed the hall. So for a moment she was left to stare at the backs of Caspar and Merklin, checking her pace enough to let them get well ahead of her.

They reached the end of the passage and stepped out into the night air. Stars winked down from above and the skies were now black and clear, but a cold wind blew across the hilltop, finding its way down into the walls. It stirred her hair around her head and cut through her thin linen shirt. Why she did not bother to fully dress before departing Crosseby's home — at least grabbing her jacket and sword — she could not fathom. Elsabeth longed for him to put an arm around her and gather her close, for the warmth of his body against hers to chase the chill away. But if he was not speaking to her, neither was he about to offer her the comfort of his proximity.

So she sighed, and walked ahead of him with her shoulders slumped and her head bowed, as they headed for the stables abutting the enceinte. The bailey was empty, except for the dark shapes of the three Schwertbrüder melting into the shadow of the wall looming ahead of them. They walked at a brisk pace, and with Elsabeth's dragging gait they were soon well ahead of her. The fresh scent of the turf mingled with the crispness of the air to lend the bailey a welcoming wholesomeness, but even in this she found little comfort. Every step nearer to the stables filled her with dread over the chastisement she was sure to receive from Hieronymus when she returned to the inn. She could practically hear his smug, condescending "I-told-you-so" even now.

But perhaps by the time she slunk back to the inn, her head bowed in defeated contrition, he would already be gone. Hieronymus did not say that he was staying past the morning, and he was certainly eager enough to depart even before the disaster of the past few evenings. So when she, too, put Ain at her back, she might very well leave it alone.

Alone.

That thought filled her belly with bile and tightened the knot in her throat. She had scarcely been on the road two years before they met in Deba. Two long, empty years gnawed by the grief and emptiness from Paulus's death, and what she left behind in Soest and Pruck. As at odds she and Hieronymus often found themselves, the thought of being alone again made her sick at heart, and she fought back tears as the weight and cost of Crosseby's rejection settled over her.

By the time they reached the stables, Caspar's party had already gone. Elsabeth shivered and hugged herself as Crosseby called the stable hand for their horses. The boy disappeared inside for a moment, then returned leading both animals by bridles. Crosseby passed the palfrey's reigns to her and took his courser in hand.

"I'll have Richard deliver your belongings to the inn tomorrow morning," he said. His voice was empty of emotion, and he acted now only as an officer of D'Ain's court. "You can use this horse to take you back. Richard will claim her from you tomorrow, and you can tender your fine to him. I meant what I said earlier. Don't return to my house. I want you gone from my sight."

"Stemham ..." she began, but trailed off when her voice broke.

"Just go. I don't want to look at you, I don't want to hear your voice. I want you gone."

Elsabeth stood there and stared at him for a long moment, torn between doing as he commanded, and the desire to say *anything* that might convince him otherwise. Crosseby, however, was true to his word, and kept his attention to his horse so he need not look at her. She heaved a shuddering breath, and turned her back to him, leading the palfrey through the gate and into the outer bailey.

Castle Ain's darkened grounds vanished in a fog as the tears she had been holding back broke free.

ROSSEBY'S ORDERS TO THE CONTRARY, Elsabeth did not return to the inn straight away.

She sat in a corner of a grubby tavern, slumped in her chair with her back to the wall. Weak lamplight fashioned small islands of life in the smoky darkness around each table, and coarse voices and laughter overwhelmed the musicians playing in a corner and battling to be heard above the din. A fire crackled in the hearth, and the air was thick with the stink of sweat, damp straw thrown down on the spills and vomit, and sour ale. Gray fog settled across her eyes and her head swam. A tower of empty clay tankards — or perhaps it was now two of them — stood in front of her on the well-worn wooden table, an enceinte warding her from intrusion by the army of revelers crowded into the space around her.

Snippets of their conversation found its way to her from across the tavern; rumors of D'Ain's wrath, the humiliation of the Brotherhood, vulgar observations on the intimate parts of her own anatomy. Elsabeth ignored it all. She did not throw herself into the frivolities, did not jump upon the tables to be swept away by the music. All she wanted now was to sit and drink and vanish into the warm embrace of oblivion.

She downed the tankard in her hand and thumped it on the table. A server quickly responded to her wordless signal and placed a fresh one in front of her. Elsabeth added her empty cup to the pile and turned her attention to its successor. She tossed her head back and took a long draught. She nearly gagged; this was not the fine ale of Crosseby's table, or even the inn where, no doubt, Hieronymus was by now quite merry and enjoying the company of the master of the house (and more particularly his daughters and nieces). It was harsh and foul, but it was strong. It could, for all she cared, eat straight through her belly so long as it served its purpose. And to judge from the spinning of her head, it was doing so quite satisfactorily.

After a time, a shadow fell across her table and wall of tankards, and she looked up through bleary eyes at a wavering figure standing over her. Between the darkness of the common room and her unsteady vision, Elsabeth could make out no details of this intruder on her solitude, though he seemed to be a particularly tall and broad fellow. He stood and stared down on her, and at times raised a tankard to his lips for a drink. Elsabeth ignored him and focused her attention on her own ale between draughts, but the feeling of his eyes on her made her finer hairs stand on end.

The chair across the table scraped along the floor and creaked as he settled into it.

"I could do with some company for the night," he said, in slurred Navarrese. "Ten *deniers*?"

"Bugger off before I shove your purse up your ass," she said. It came out as a nearly unintelligible mumble, and the venomous glare she spit him with might have been more effective had she been able to focus her eyes on any one point.

The weakly flickering lamp on the table did little to illuminate his features, but she might have caught an indignant twist of his lips. "I am good for it!"

"I don't care. I am not for sale. If you want for companionship try the stables out back."

"Fifteen *deniers*!" He reached out and laid a hand on hers, and his lips twisted into a leer as he made a show of looking her over. "Come on, love, 'tis a fair price, and you are certainly worth it!"

The next sound to leave her mouth did not come in words, but as an animal snarl that plunged the common room into silence. She tore her hand away from him and threw her tankard at his head with all her strength. It struck him square in the center of his forehead. Ale splashed everywhere, and his neck snapped back under the force of the blow. Elsabeth vaulted across the table. Her tower of empties scattered with a loud crash. She wrapped her arms around her would-be suitor and used her weight to throw him over backwards. Already unbalanced by the tankard to his face, his chair tipped back and he toppled over onto the floor. She landed hard on top of him with her legs straddling his chest, and smashed her fist into his face again and again. Every blow was punctuated by a curse, until she ran out of epithets and just screamed incoherently as she pounded him into a bloody pulp, venting all her anguish and rage into her would-be suitor's face.

Men yelled, and the pounding of boots on the wooden floors echoed through the common room. A knot of bodies gathered around them, the ferocity of her assault whipping them into a frenzy.

Someone, or perhaps it was several someones, seized her beneath the arms and dragged her off him. Elsabeth snarled and twisted against their grip. She lashed out with her fists and feet, and smashed her head backwards into someone's nose. They all fell over in a heap with her on top, but she was unable to take advantage of her position before more hands took hold of her. This time they managed to catch her by the legs as well, and she was hauled unceremoniously from the floor. Elsabeth thrashed and bit at any hands venturing too close to her face, but they inexorably marched her towards the door.

The next she knew she was hurtling through the air, and landing face-first on the paving stones. The sudden shock of cold — and her face smacking the ground — jolted her back into some degree of clarity, and she rolled over onto her backside. A big, burly figure stood in the tavern door, silhouetted by the dim light spilling out into the street. Elsabeth backed away on her hands, but he showed no indication of coming after her.

"Go on! Get out of here!" he bellowed. "Take your trouble somewhere else, I'll not have my place torn apart!"

She scrambled back to her feet and took up a fighting stance.

"I was no trouble at all until that lout laid hands to me! I have a right to drink in peace!"

"You have had enough to drink! Now get out of here or I'll summon the guard! Go!"

And with that he turned around and stormed back into the tavern. The door slammed shut, and the echo hung in the street for a long moment.

Elsabeth glared daggers at the door and wiped her mouth on the back of her sleeve. She spit at the tavern, then spun around and started back up the street.

The tavern was located in a poor, trash-strewn maze of alleyways. It was very dark, lit only by the light of the stars and moon, and only a handful of streetlamps glimmered like faint beacons of civilization in the night. She stumbled and swayed on her feet, and hugged herself against the cold night air. The distant memory of having arrived on a horse tugged at the back corner of her mind, but she discarded the thought and continued on her way. Returning to the tavern was out of the question, anyway.

Elsabeth wandered aimlessly through the streets of Ain, and were she more sober she might have admitted she was utterly lost in the labyrinth of the poorer districts. She saw no one else abroad in the darkness; guards were few and far between, and the temperature had dropped enough that the bawds were plying their trade at the taverns and inns. Even the beggars had sought out warmer venues. Only the echo of her own footfalls between the ramshackle shops and homes rising on either side of her broke the stifling silence. Here and there a lamp or candle glowed in a grimy window, hinting at the life and warmth within, but most were dark, and gazed down upon her with cold and empty disapproval.

She made it a few blocks away from the tavern, and gradually the streets widened a bit and straightened out. They became more orderly in their planning, and the dingy stone or wood facades showed more sign of loving care and attention. Trash was swept from the alleys, and streetlamps cast golden light around her, illuminating the stones beneath her feet. Which meant that when a figure appeared at the end of the street she was currently making her way along, she saw him clear as day even through the fog of drink and tears obscuring her vision.

Elsabeth paused as he started towards her and curled her lip into a scowl. If he, too, was looking for "companionship" he would not find her particularly welcoming.

"Well, well," he said, his voice familiar, but she could not quite place it through the haze clouding her mind. "Out for a stroll, are we?"

"What I do is none of your concern. Stand aside."

He took another step forward, and into the light of one of the lamps illuminating the street. The shadows obscuring his features rolled back, and Elsabeth rolled her eyes at the sight of the bandage over what used to be his ear.

"Merklin Adler. Do you really want to lose your other ear?"

"Not this time, cunt!" He laid his hand on the hilt of his sword and drew it. "You are not going anywhere."

He looked somewhere past her shoulder, and Elsabeth risked a glance behind her. Three more men appeared on the street, and all drew swords. She sighed and pinched her nose.

"I would think after the last time you might have learned your lesson." She reached across her hip. "Well, I suppose you need another."

Elsabeth frowned when her hand came up empty, and she slapped at her side with growing alarm. Merklin took notice of the confusion on her face and laughed. "Forgotten something, have you?"

The fog muddying her memory rolled back, and she saw her sword leaning against Crosseby's bed back at the house. Left behind when he summoned her to the castle to face D'Ain.

"Bugger."

Merklin barred the way ahead of her, and one of his companions blocked the direction whence she came. In the time she was distracted wondering why her sword was not at her hip where it belonged, the other two took up flanking positions on either side.

*Surrounded, drunk, and without my sword or even my rondel. Lovely.*

"Take her!" Merklin barked, and all four started towards her at once.

Elsabeth reacted quickly, and the moment the first of her assailants took a step, she sprung towards the fellow on her left. He struck an overhand blow at her as she closed in, and she ducked under his arm to his outside. She struck at his wrist with her forearm and forced his cut offline, snaked her arm around his, and pinned his hand beneath her armpit. A ferocious left hook caught him behind the ear and staggered him, and she followed with a hard stomp against the outside of his knee. An agonized scream drowned out the wet snap of the joint giving way, and his sword clattered to the cobblestones.

She slipped around the man behind her as he closed the distance to aid his companion and snatched the fallen sword from the ground. *Now I have a sword and am not completely surrounded. Still drunk.*

The crash of steel split the night air as she met a blow from Merklin's third conspirator, but her attempt to counter was wild and unsteady, and her feet did not quite move how she wished. She stumbled and staggered where she ought to have sprung and lunged. The constant turning from opponent to opponent made her head spin. Her belly lurched and now she fought as hard to keep the evening's drink from clawing back up her throat as she did against her adversaries' swords.

She ordinarily would not even need to be at her best to defeat Merklin and his thugs. These were almost certainly Caspar's other students, and in other circumstances she could have cut them all apart.

But not now.

Elsabeth's arms and legs burned as she attacked, countered, stepped, ducked, and lunged through the gauntlet. Her head swam, her vision blurred, and bile filled the back of her throat. She stumbled and swayed, and one of her opponents found an opening. He slipped in behind her as she turned to counter Merklin's blow at her head and seized her around her middle. She thrashed against his grip, but Merklin's other companion rushed in as well and seized control of her arms. A blow to her stomach put any further thought of fight from her mind. All the air rushed from her lungs with a sickening grunt, and with it she lost her battle keeping the night's drink and what little she had to eat in her belly where it belonged.

She went double and retched all over the street, and Merklin jumped back so it would not splatter on his boots. He strode forward and seized a fistful of her hair. Her head wrenched to the side and strained her neck, and he glared down with hate burning in his eyes.

"I see your tongue is not wagging so freely now," he said, and released her hair to introduce her jaw to the back of his hand. "Perhaps I ought to take your ear."

Elsabeth spit blood from her mouth. She returned his glare in equal fury, filled with the promise of death should he make good on the threat. Even subdued as she was, Merklin flinched back. "Go ahead, coward! And then you can tell everyone how it took four of you to claim it from a drunken woman!"

Merklin grabbed hold of her chin. "Don't tempt me! But our argument is a little one. 'Tis the Master who has the claim to decide what is to be done with your miserable carcass!"

He then struck her a blow in the side of the head with the hilts of his sword, and for a moment her vision went white. Elsabeth slumped in the hands holding her upright, and her legs refused to cooperate to keep her on her feet. Unlike the minstrels' tales, however, she was not greeted with inviting black oblivion. Her head spun and her vision doubled, the world around her faded into a fog, and she desperately wanted to vomit again, but she remained conscious.

"Search her!" Merklin said, as if from a great distance. "She has my ring, and I want it back!"

Under better circumstances she might have resisted them gleefully pawing her body at that command. Instead, she endured the groping hands wandering her bottom and thighs and roughly squeezing her breasts, unable to muster the energy to so much as squirm away from them.

"Nothing there!" one of her captors said, his voice almost shouting in her ear as he slipped a hand down her shirt front.

Merklin seized her by the hair and wrenched her head around to force her to look him in the eye. "Where is it?"

Elsabeth said nothing, not even able to focus on him enough to form a coherent response, much less recall what had become of the ring.

"Bind her hands and get her out of the City," he snarled, and released her head with a shove when it became clear no response was forthcoming. "I will see to Haints, then fetch the Master as soon as I am able. Be quick about it! Someone is certain to have heard the racket and called for the guard!"

"What do we do with her while we wait?" one of the men behind her said as they forced her down to the ground. She felt her arms wrenched behind her back, but her new position did help to settle her stomach.

"She might be a bit of fun," the other said, and there was an ominous hint of laughter in his voice.

"Keep her bound, and no matter what her charms, don't touch her!" Merklin said. "If she gets loose and escapes I'll have your head if she does not take it first!" Elsabeth was hauled upright again, and she groaned at the shift in position. Merklin knelt in front of her, seized her shirt front, and drew her face near to his. She wished she could vomit again right then and there. "Pity as it is, I suspect we shan't have any use for her once the Master gets through with her!"

He released her with a shove, and drove his fist into her gut.

**26**

ICHARD LED ELSABETH'S JENNET ALONG the largely deserted streets by the bridle. Frost gathered in the corners of the windows and glittered in the morning sun. All of Ain seemed touched by gold that morning as stone and timber alike was gilded by the dawn.

Perhaps the beauty of the morning would do his Master good. His lonely return from the castle the night before had put him into a terribly foul mood, and Richard alone of the servants dared to face him. But rather than wrath, he found the Master sullen and inconsolable as he gave the command to have his guest's belongings packed away and returned to the inn. Richard did not rightly know what exactly had transpired. Nor was it his place to ask. The Master commanded her belongings be removed from the house, and so he did.

Gossip spread like wildfire through the City, however, as rumor was wont. And as Richard made his way across Ain, he caught snippets here and there from the few souls braving the morning chill of the events at yesterday's playings. A duel between the Schwertbrüder and the

Master's woman. Five of them dead, or perhaps none at all. That when she mounted the platform she had the ear of the Grand Master himself on a chain around her neck, or perhaps it was Caspar von Bech's testicles. Lambrecht and Andelieu were all but forgotten, and they might as well not have fought at all. All of Ain was famished for news of Elsabeth Soesten, from the wealthy merchants and minor nobles, to the lowliest beggars and buskers. Their disappointment at being denied the spectacle of seeing her fight on the platform hung like a pall across the city, along with their anticipation she might take the platform again.

Richard disregarded it as the meaningless fluff it was. He gleaned enough from the Master to know their hopes were futile: Elsabeth Soesten was barred from participating in the playings by D'Ain's command, and the Master had thrown her from his house.

He arrived at the inn to find Symon on his usual perch atop the stone wall. The boy hopped down when he spied him coming leading Elsabeth's horse, and met him at the gate.

"Good morning, Monsieur Richard!" he said. He was bundled in an old woolen cloak around his narrow shoulders and a pair of knitted gloves, and a thin stream of mist escaped his mouth when he spoke.

"Good morning, Symon," Richard said.

The boy regarded the horse a moment and frowned. "That is Mademoiselle Soesten's horse, is it not?"

"Aye, 'tis." He fished into the pouch on his belt for a *denier* and tossed it to him. "Put her up with the good Brother's, and have her things brought inside."

"Is she coming back to the inn, then?"

Richard raised an eyebrow. "'Twas my understanding she returned last night."

Symon shrugged as he pocketed the coin and took the horse by the leads. "I have not seen her, but if she arrived very long after sundown I was already in bed by then, and she has not come out again. 'Tis a shame she is leaving so soon, I heard some folk talking about what happened at the playings yesterday, and I hoped father would let me go see if she was fighting again today." Symon gave Elsabeth's horse a gentle scratch behind the ear, and she nickered softly in response.

Richard grunted. "'Tis nothing but idle gossip, lad, and you would do best to not listen to a word of it. Just have the palfrey my Master loaned her last night brought out and ready. I am to take her back with me once I conclude my business with Mademoiselle Soesten this morning."

Again, Symon frowned. "I beg your pardon?"

Richard noted the confusion on the boy's face, and frowned as well. "The palfrey my Master loaned Mademoiselle Soesten yesterday evening. Is she here?"

He shook his head. "Forgive me, but there are a couple rounceys in the stable, and two or three packhorses, and there is a palfrey but 'tis a stallion and belongs to some squire or other, and of course Brother Hieronymus's Hackney, but none of Monsieur Crosseby's stable are here."

"Are you sure of this?"

"Yes, Monsieur! I just came from feeding and watering them before you arrived!"

Richard pinched the bridge of his nose and sighed. "'Tis all I need this morning ..."

"Monsieur?"

He waved him off, but was unable to keep his annoyance from his face or voice. *Damn that woman if she decided on making off with the Master's horse as petty revenge.* "'Tis nothing, lad. You go and take care of that girl for me—" he gave Elsabeth's horse a gentle pat on the rump "—and give it no mind. I must have a word with Mademoiselle Soesten."

And with that he stepped through the gate and into the inn.

The common room was unusually full for such an early hour, and too many voices piled one atop the other in a ceaseless war to be heard. The serving girls fought their way through the mass of humanity bearing trays of the morning's breakfast. A fire crackled in the hearth, and with so many bodies crammed into the common room at once, Richard actually found it uncomfortably hot despite the chill outdoors.

He stood up on his toes and craned his neck in search of a head of burnished copper or a flash of green eyes, but found nothing distinguishable from the sea of unfamiliar faces around him. The tide even swallowed up the master of the house, leaving him without a guide in search of his Master's erstwhile guest. However, in the very back corner he caught a glimpse of a wild and unkempt mane of silvering hair framing a round face, hovering over a tankard before the crowd shifted and blocked him from view.

With nothing else for it, and a mindful hand on his purse, Richard plunged in; a "pardon me," here, an "excuse me," there, as he waded through the churning, swirling chaos. The cacophony was deafening. Men laughed, shouted, and traded jibes and insults. He passed a table where a knot of swordsmen from the City-States gambled over dice and ribald stories. One of them uttered a particularly vulgar remark about "Crosseby's Woman" that threw the entire table into a fit of raucous laughter. Bits of Navarrese from another managed to rise above the din, and took great pleasure in the humiliation of the Schwertbrüder at yesterday's playings. Tanguy, recognizable by his gleaming bare head and massive bulk, sat in a corner taking pulls of his small beer, and entertained his companions with tales of a drinking contest some nights back.

"I don't know what impressed me more," he said, his booming voice audible even over the background roar of the crowd. "Her capacity for drink, or that she was the best damn kisser I have ever known! Were I not a married man I like as not would have carried her upstairs right then and there!"

"I am a married man," another interjected, "and I would not have let such a detail stop me!"

"I can't blame you; I have seen your wife!"

Coarse laughter exploded from the table, and Richard clenched his jaw at such talk; had the Master heard it for himself, friend or not, he had no doubt Tanguy would have been called out back for a lesson in manners.

After some effort, Richard finally managed to push through the bodies and neared his destination. Sure enough, when he finally escaped the seething multitude, he found Brother Hieronymus hunched over his breakfast with a tankard of small beer at his elbow, and his staff leaning against the table.

"Good morrow, Brother," he said, and even standing right in front of him, he needed to raise his voice to be heard over the cacophony.

Hieronymus tore his eyes from his plate. "Well, if 'tis not the man who helped the noble knight steal away my Tetty." The friar took a long drink from his tankard and thumped it down on the table. "Forgive me my manners, my son, but I trust you will understand that I don't invite you to join me for breakfast. Fortunately, I have little else your Master will find of interest."

Richard's face heated at the rebuke in the friar's voice and shifted his weight from foot to foot. "I beg your pardon?"

"'Tis not that loud in here, I am sure you heard well enough."

He frowned down at Hieronymus, who turned his attention back to his plate and stuffed his mouth with a sizable hunk of bread.

"Forgive me, Brother, but I really don't know what you are talking about."

"Feh!" he said, and spit a shower of crumbs across the table. "Your Master has filled that foolish girl's head with all manner of wild fancies, and now she abandons me to wander the roads alone! Me! After so many years of gainful companionship and loyal service she casts me aside like an old, broken-down mule! Well, if she has sent you to apologize on her behalf you can go back to her and tell her from me that were I not a humble servant of the Wheel, I might offer a suggestion of where she might stuff those platitudes!"

Richard's belly sunk somewhere around his bowels at the friar's ranting. The Master's horse was not in the stables, Symon had seen no sign of her, and surely with so many people in the inn that morning he ought to have heard *something* of her return. He swallowed. "Then did Mademoiselle Soesten not tell you? Her stay with my Master has concluded, and she was to be leaving Ain. I came only to return her belongings and conclude some final business with her before her departure."

Hieronymus looked away from his breakfast and blinked. "What in the Dark One's name are you babbling about, man? I have seen neither hide nor hair of that woman since the night she so rudely terminated our friendship!"

Bile bubbled up from his belly, and Richard gripped the back of the chair pushed up under the table between them. "She was supposed to return to the inn last night. You mean you have not seen her?"

"Are you deaf and dumb, man? 'Tis what I just said, is it not? Now what are you on about?"

Richard mopped his face when the friar unwittingly confirmed his suspicions. "There was an incident with the Schwertbrüder the other night."

Hieronymus grunted and took another drink. "That does not surprise me; that bloody fool girl is always stirring up some incident or other."

"Yes, well, they fought a duel in the violation of D'Ain's command."

"She won, I suppose."

He nodded. "Yes, and the Brotherhood you can imagine were quite upset over the whole affair. My Master is no less embarrassed, as he made her his personal guest in Ain, and it certainly reflects poorly on him to have his guests disturb the peace in such a manner."

"Well now, this is a familiar tale. That woman can't take a step without making a scandal of herself, but that still does not explain what in the Lord of All's name you are on about!"

Richard scowled. "I am getting there, Brother, if you shall let me finish my tale before interjecting! My Master has commanded she leave Ain and expelled her from his house last night. She was to return here, and I was to deliver her horse and possessions — which I have just turned over to Symon to be put up for her. I am also to collect the fine Monsieur le Chevalier levied for her part in the duel, and the horse my Master loaned her for the night so she need not walk from the castle back to the inn."

Hieronymus paused halfway through another drink from his tankard as he spoke, and his round face paled. "And as I have said, my son, I have not seen neither hide nor hair of her! Are you telling me that girl has been missing all night?"

He shrugged. "'Tis the first indication I have had of it! As far as I or the Master knew she has been here since Monsieur le Chevalier dismissed them from his hall."

The friar thumped his tankard down on the table and ran his hands back through his hair. It sprung back up atop his head, and if anything smoothing it back just mussed it even further. "Dear God, man! Have you any idea how much trouble that girl could get herself into in the span of a single night?"

"I am beginning to have an inkling, Brother."

Hieronymus shoved away from the table, and the chair scraped across the floor and squeaked in protest as he levered his bulk back to his feet. "Monsieur, I demand you take me to your Master at once!"

"Brother—"

"Don't you 'Brother' me, man!" He snatched up his staff and poked him in the breastbone for emphasis. Richard stumbled back a pace and rubbed his chest. "I have known that girl for the better part of four years, and she draws trouble to her like honey draws flies. And now she has been left to run off alone with someone about who no doubt wishes to defile God's good work by removing her head from her shoulders! I'll have words with that disgraceful lout for letting her run off alone like this!"

Richard stiffened and balled his hands into fists. "Don't forget, Brother, that she has been duly sentenced for a crime against D'Ain. Whatever trouble she is in is of its own making!"

Hieronymus smacked the table with his staff. His plate and tankard jumped, and the crack echoed so loudly in the rafters that the common room fell into total silence.

"I don't care if she has run afoul of the Lord of All himself!" the friar roared, and Richard flinched back at the righteous fire in his voice. His face turned crimson, his eyes flashed, and in spite of his lack of height Richard nonetheless felt as if the man towered over him like some vengeful giant. "My only concern right now is seeing to it that that girl is returned safe and sound, and by God if you don't take me to your Master at once I shall cut my way through you and anyone else that stands between us!"

Hieronymus's blue eyes bored through his, boiling like a storm at sea. His lip quivered beneath his unkempt beard, and his body trembled. Richard swallowed and shrunk back from him; this was not the righteous ire of a priest decrying an insolent worshipper, but the same maddened fury he saw at times in his Master when pushed too far on a matter of honor. He tore his eyes away and lowered his head, then gave a short nod.

"Of course, Brother," he said.

"I suggest you have Symon prepare my horse, and stop him from putting up Tetty's. If she is indeed obliged to leave Ain, then we shall depart as soon as we find her. I have had my fill of this place!"

And with that, he stormed past Richard, and forced a path through the sea of bodies pressing in around them to investigate the friar's outburst. They all but stumbled over themselves to clear the way. Richard stood frozen for a moment and watched him go, hardly even cognizant of the many pairs of eyes now fixed upon him, the silence descended upon the common room now grown unbearable. He took a steadying breath and squared his shoulders, then marched down the path opened for him and hurried for the door to carry out Hieronymus's command.

**27**

THE MORNING WARMED SUBSTANTIALLY by the time the crowd reunited at the scaffold. Caspar arrived with his remaining students, short Merklin — now banned from the playings — and three others. They had disappeared not long after returning from the audience with D'Ain the night before, no doubt to escape the wrath of Aich, and had not yet returned by the time the sun crested the walls of the city.

Caspar envied them immensely.

He wiped the sleep from his eyes and stifled a yawn as he made his way through the stands for his seat. The reprimand from the Grand Master had lasted well into the early hours of the morning, and in truth he could recall little of what was said now, beyond some of the most creative cursing he had ever heard.

A low chuckle went up from one of the spectators near at hand as the Schwertbrüder moved through the stands. Caspar sneered and tried to spit the culprit with a glare, but everywhere he looked men leaned close to whisper and point at the men and boys in the red doublets embroidered with the crossed swords of the Guild. More laughter followed, and Caspar's face and neck heated. He caught snippets here and there, spoken just loud enough he had no doubt it was meant to be heard.

"...she killed six of them..."

"...cut off his balls and fed them to him..."

"...bedded Monsieur le Chevalier himself..."

"...challenged Bech to a duel, and he ran away..."

Caspar ground his teeth and clenched his fists. He left his students to find a place to sit in the midst of the gossip and mockery and pushed through the throng for D'Ain's box.

"Master von Bech!" a man near at hand called. Caspar ignored him and pressed on, but the voice sounded again, more insistently. "Master von Bech! Might I have your ear a moment?"

He froze mid-step at the chorus of laughter from those nearest at hand and spun around to face his interrogator. Guarin stood a few rows higher up in the stands, his lips pulled into a particularly satisfied smile. Caspar skewered him with his most withering glare, but that only amused the damned fool even further, and prompted more sniggers from those seated between them.

"What do you want, Master Guarin?" Caspar said, and spit the last word out like a curse. If Guarin noted his annoyance, it only made his features brighten further.

"I merely wished to commend you on the Brotherhood's performance! 'Twas quite the spectacle yesterday, and I can't recall having ever been so entertained. I look forward to seeing what you have in store for us today."

Caspar tightened his fists and his face turned red. "We are not here for your amusement. If 'tis a diversion you want, I suggest you find a troupe of fools in the market."

"'Tis no need to bother when Monsieur le Chevalier brings them here!"

The spectators clustered around them erupted with howls of approval. They stomped their feet and pounded their fists on the benches. Guarin smirked down from his seat above, as if daring him to break D'Ain's law and challenge him then and there. Caspar would have liked nothing better than to throw him from the top of the scaffold, and imagined the satisfying crunch of his skull splitting open as it was dashed across the paving stones below. But D'Ain's condemnation of Merklin's duel, and Aich's reproach over so losing control of his students, echoed through his mind. Caspar's face heated until he thought his whole head might burst into flames, and balled his fists so tightly his nails cut into his palms. The crowd's laughter stilled only long enough for a pall of expectation over his response to fall across them, and he felt eyes boring into him like dozens of needles piercing his skin all at once.

He said nothing, and turned himself away before the urge to storm up the grandstand and toss Guarin off the back overwhelmed him. More laughter followed at his back as he forced a path through the crowd to D'Ain's box.

Caspar reached his seat and bowed respectfully to D'Ain and Aich. With the promised resumption of the bouts D'Ain's spirits rose, and he chattered animatedly with the Grand Master. He acknowledged Caspar's greeting with a small wave of his hand beckoning for him to sit. Crosseby slumped in his seat at D'Ain's right hand, his head propped up on his fist. He stared blankly down onto the platform, and his shirt and doublet were rumpled. Dark circles ringed his eyes as if he had not slept, and Caspar took a measure of satisfaction in the knowledge that his morning, at least, was no less miserable.

"Well, here we all are again," D'Ain said once Caspar settled in. "I trust there shall be no further interruptions of these events?"

"I assure you, Monseigneur, that there shall be no repeat of that transgression," Aich said, and speared Caspar with his dark eyes. He weathered the glare and focused his attention on the platform below. "Master von Bech has already warned his students that any further strife shall be dealt with most harshly."

"Good, very good. I have quite enjoyed the diversion this public exhibition has provided, and I don't want to see it spoiled by such disruptions. Don't you agree, Monsieur Crosseby?"

"Yes, Monseigneur," Crosseby said, though with little enthusiasm. D'Ain regarded him from the corner of his eye for a moment, but otherwise waved off his sullen countenance.

Caspar, however, was not content to let it go unremarked on.

"You did, I trust, have quite the enlightening conversation with that woman," he said, and allowed himself a tight smile when Crosseby raised his head and narrowed his eyes. "As I recall, I advised you against your curiosity some days ago."

"My private dealings are not your concern, Master. I'll thank you not to intrude upon them."

Caspar settled back into his chair and allowed his smile to broaden. "I should think you would be showing me your appreciation at sparing you from a costly miscalculation. Well, one more costly than I am sure you have already endured on her behalf."

"I warn you, Master—"

"Gentlemen! That will be quite enough!" D'Ain said, and looked between them. Nonetheless, Caspar savored that small moment of triumph. "I am calling an end to this argument of yours here and now, lest I ban you all from these proceedings! Am I clear?"

"Yes, Monseigneur," Crosseby said.

"Of course, Monseigneur," Caspar said, and inclined his head to D'Ain. He looked across D'Ain and Aich to smirk at Crosseby, who received it with an impotent glare, and a whitening of his knuckles as he gripped the arms of his chair.

The braying of horns and the beating of drums forestalled any further remark by D'Ain, and the crowd erupted into a chorus of cheers at the procession making its way to the square. Although the peasants standing down in the filth of the streets once more greeted the fanfare with enthusiasm, Caspar stifled a yawn at the routine. He found his weariness for the affair mirrored on the faces of the other masters and practitioners in the crowd.

D'Ain, however, perched at the edge of his seat, as a child might at some juggler's show. "Well, Monsieur Crosseby," he said, "the last few days have provided nothing if not the unexpected. What have you in store for us this morning?"

"A single player only, Monseigneur," Crosseby said. He rose as the player mounted the platform. "And this shall take most of the day."

Crosseby held aloft a rolled piece of parchment and made a show of opening it.

"Le Chevalier Talbot de Valois. Seeking the rank of Master!" he announced in a loud voice, though Caspar caught a subtle raggedness in his tone, betraying his weariness.

"Well! This should be interesting indeed!" D'Ain said to Aich. His voice was almost lost in the roar of the crowd packed into the square, and Caspar needed to strain his ears to hear it.

"Monsieur de Valois studied under the previous Master of the Longsword for some years," Crosseby said, and returned to his seat. "Ten bouts of eight weapons each. I have slogged through the mud, campaigned for weeks without a rest, and yet never did I endure a more grueling challenge than when I tested for my Master's prize."

Valois paced the platform while he awaited his first challenger, and Caspar studied him intently. He was a tall, strongly built man with broad shoulders, and regarded the gathering of fencers in the stands and down on the street with haughty disdain. No one stood to accept the challenge at first, and a low, uncertain murmur swept across the gathering, while the boors watching from the square stirred impatiently. Caspar glanced at Aich, whose dark eyes met his, and the Grand Master gave a subtle nod.

Caspar took a short breath and stood. Elsabeth Hereford did her best to dash the prestige of the Brotherhood with her antics. *He* would be the one to restore it.

The crowd fell silent as Caspar pushed through the stands and clambered down onto the platform. Valois retreated to one of the racks to select his weapon, and Caspar did the same. His opponent chose to begin with the longsword, and Caspar smiled tightly; Valois was a name unknown to him, a man of no account or reputation. Whether he passed his test that day or not mattered little. The crowd needed to see that the Brotherhood would not bow in the face of humiliation. They were stronger than one mere woman.

He and Valois took their starting positions. His opponent saluted him, and Caspar returned the gesture. They took up their guard positions, and Crosseby raised his hand to give the signal to begin...

And before his hand could drop something fell out of the stands and plopped down onto the stage between the two combatants. Caspar's throat tightened at the sight of the cow's ear lying at his feet.

Laughter erupted from the spectators, and Caspar swept his eyes across the crowd in an effort to determine whence it came. Guarin, he realized, had moved from his perch high up on the scaffolding to a place nearer the platform, and smiled ear-to-ear at him. Caspar tightened his hands around his *Feder* until his knuckles turned white. The Grand Master's features were livid, Crosseby colored in embarrassment, and D'Ain struggled to contain his amusement at the interruption.

D'Ain's restraint failed him once that first ear was followed by a rain of others from the stands, and it seemed everyone but his own students flung them down onto the platform. Ears of all sorts: cows' ears, sheep's ears, ass' ears, dogs' ears, pigs' ears. As if every butcher in Ain had been secreting them away all year long for just this occasion. More came from the streets below, until the whole platform was covered in them like gruesome paving stones. Laughter, cheers, and jeers echoed across the market square.

Caspar stood in the middle of it and endured the pelting in fuming silence. Valois, for his part, shifted uncomfortably, and his face turned bright red in embarrassment that this should happen during his playing. Caspar ignored him. All he could see were the ears piling about his feet, and he heard only one voice laughing at him. Not D'Ain, who beat the arms of his chair uncontrollably. Not Guarin. Not any one of the hundreds of people gathered to see him bask in this humiliation.

No, in that moment he heard only one voice.

And by God, he would tear Elsabeth Hereford apart with his bare hands!

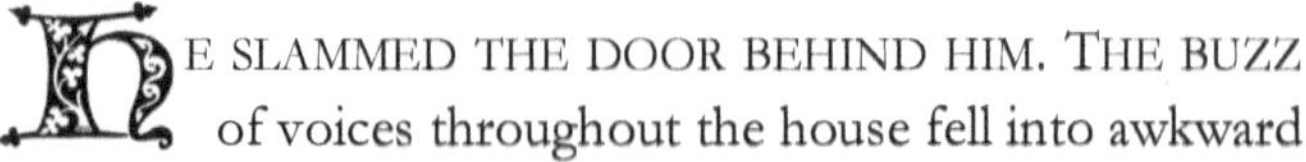

HE SLAMMED THE DOOR BEHIND HIM. THE BUZZ of voices throughout the house fell into awkward silence, paintings and hangings fell from the walls, and every pair of eyes in the foyer fell upon him.

Caspar stormed across the room and tore at his hair, and the students all scrambled to be gone from his sight lest he turn his temper on them. A handful of servants at work were not so fortunate, and frantically busied themselves in hopes of escaping his notice.

"This is outrageous!" he snarled as he paced the room and gesticulated wildly. "That woman makes a mockery of us even when she is nowhere to be seen, and D'Ain does nothing!"

"Calm yourself, Caspar!" Aich said. The Grand Master had preceded him into the house, and now stood for a servant to remove his ceremonial outer robes, leaving him in a plain woolen doublet.

Caspar barely even registered the admonition. All he heard now was the laughter and cat calls on the platform. "He did worse than nothing! He sat there and he laughed! In front of every Master of the Longsword in Navarre and the City-States, he *laughed!* Even Crosseby of all people had the good sense to keep his mouth shut. And Guarin? I swear to God if I ever see Guarin on the road I shall—"

"Caspar!" the Grand Master roared, and stomped his foot. The servants jumped, and one woman scrubbing the floors squeaked in fright and cowered as if struck. Caspar, however, did not jump. He merely paused in his pacing and fell into silence. "Enough!"

"But Master—"

"I said enough!"

Caspar held his tongue and lowered his eyes to the floor.

"I feel this humiliation no less than you, but a tantrum here will do nothing! I assure you, D'Ain shall hear of my displeasure. But he is Lord in Ain, and we have no power in Navarre."

He raised his head again and scowled. The Grand Master took his show of displeasure in stride, but his countenance warned to tread carefully. "But what of Hereford? 'Tis not enough she be barred from the playings and contest of arms when she has already inflicted such damage. She has made fools of all of us!"

Aich's eyes flashed. "You will do nothing!" he snapped, and again the servants working in the foyer quailed. But they had work to do there and could not depart without the Grand Master's dismissal. In that, at least, Caspar had sympathy for them. "If 'twere just her jibes at dinner or in D'Ain's box on the scaffold 'twould have been cause for consternation enough. But Merklin Adler knowingly disobeyed my commands and challenged her. 'Twould have ended at words without his foolishness. Better she had slain him outright and been done with it!"

Caspar swallowed. "And now all of Navarre sees us as fools. This can't be allowed to stand!"

"No, it cannot. But here and now is not the place to redress the grievance." Aich heaved a sigh and pinched the bridge of his nose. "In Ain, at least, she is untouchable for the duration of the playings."

"But should she leave, and we chance upon her ..."

"I would not grieve should some misadventure befall her. That woman has been a nuisance long enough! Whatever the nature of the arrangement made by her father, I ought to have refused it long ago. That was my mistake." The Grand Master spit him with a glare. "But I shan't hear of you making one as grievous as Merklin's again. Am I clear?"

Caspar hung his head and nodded. "Yes, Master."

"Good. Leave me now and see to your students."

"Yes, Master," he said, and headed for his own chambers, grateful for the moment to be away from Aich's presence.

Caspar tugged at the top button of his doublet as he made his way past rooms on either side of the hallway in from the foyer and opened it to his collarbones. Servants busied themselves rehanging fallen paintings, and others scattered upon his approach at the sight of the black cloud following in his wake. There was no laughter or merriment from the great hall that evening, and the house was quiet and subdued. A few voices echoed through the passages, too low for him to make out their conversation. Whispers among the household staff abruptly fell into silence when he approached, only to start up again after he passed. The clatter of the cooks in the kitchens relegated it all to a dull background hum. He passed a closet where, to judge from the muffled squeals and moans within, one of his students availed himself of a willing maid.

He approached the screens passage leading into the hall, but before he could continue on for his room a figure emerged and barred his path. Caspar glared at the intruder, especially when the lamps in the hallway illuminated his face and the bandage over his ear.

"Merklin," he hissed, and screwed his lips into a scowl. "I would head right back whence you came and be gone from my sight! I am in no mood for company, yours least of all."

For his part Merklin swallowed and lowered his head contritely. He shifted on his feet beneath the weight of Caspar's glower, but he made no move to open the way ahead.

"I heard what happened today, Master, and I—"

"And nothing! 'Twas as much a humiliation of your making! I went down to the platform in hopes of salvaging some shred of the Brotherhood's esteem, and instead I am shamed before the Grand Master, D'Ain, and all our Navarrese peers! There is nothing you can say to me now to relieve me of the desire to cut your other damned ear off!"

Merklin seized him by the arm of his doublet and dragged him for the screens passage. Caspar tore his arm free with a snarl of protest, but noted the insistence in his Vorfechter's eyes. He heaved a sigh and spit him with an irritated glare, but followed as Merklin retreated into the shadow of the passage. He swept his eyes both ways up and down the passage and leaned in conspiratorially once he was certain no one was within earshot. Caspar rolled his eyes and leaned in so he need not raise his voice beyond a whisper.

"We have her, Master," Merklin said.

Caspar's scowl twisted into a frown. "What do you mean?"

"Four of us went out after we returned to the house—"

"Yes, I know. And you left me to endure the Grand Master's scolding alone, you coward!"

Merklin blanched at the accusation. "'Twas not my intent, Master. Hereford is gone from Crosseby's house. We found her getting very drunk at a tavern. I don't know what had transpired, but she seemed rather distressed about something."

Caspar grunted in satisfaction. It certainly explained why Crosseby was in such poor spirits that morning. "At least some good came of this affair if Crosseby has thrown her out."

"'Tis not all, Master. She did not have her sword on her last night, so we set an ambush for her, and she stumbled right into it."

He gawked at him. "You what?"

"We seized her and removed her from Ain."

Caspar looked over his shoulder to ensure the hall was clear, then put an arm around Merklin to pull him closer and dropped his voice until he was barely even breathing into his good ear. "Are you out of your damn mind? The Grand Master is furious over your part in this, and can you imagine the trouble it will cause if D'Ain learns of it?"

Merklin quirked a grin. Caspar wasn't sure whether to be overjoyed or incensed over the cockiness of the expression. "He won't! She was in one of the poor districts. At best the guard will think she wandered in and fell victim to the ruffians preying on the whores. Nickel and Leonhart slipped her out of the city. Haints was hurt in the scuffle, so I took him to a surgeon." He tsked, and his smile broadened. "Tavern brawls can be such ugly things."

"Where is she now?"

"There is a clearing in the woodland outside the City off the road, a ways from the South Gate and out of sight. Nickel and Leonhart hold her there for you."

Caspar allowed a smile to cross his lips. She was in his hands. Alone. Beyond the walls of Ain, and out of the reach of D'Ain's protection.

"Good lad! Good lad!" he said, and gave Merklin's shoulder a firm squeeze. "Have the horses saddled. I want you to take me there right away."

"Yes, Master," Merklin said.

Caspar released him, and a giddiness washed over him. He wrung his hands in anticipation. Seven long years, and finally the Lord of All saw fit to answer his prayers.

Today he would finally be free of her, and he would pay back in full measure every humiliation he endured at her hands.

28

ROSSEBY MADE THE SLOW WALK UP THE street alone and in silence. The prospect of celebrating the naming of a new Master of the Longsword held little appeal to him, and he longed only for a strong drink — and many more after that — to dull the ache stabbing him through the heart. The inviting black oblivion to be found at the bottom of a bottle of good Navarrese wine sounded far more welcome to him now than did the rowdy jocularity of his students reveling into the dark hours of the morning, no doubt sharing a hearty laugh over the disruption to the morning's bouts.

Valois, though visibly frustrated by the boorish reception to Caspar von Bech, nonetheless took the delay in stride. He was forced to admit that, once the crowd had been settled and the platform cleared, Caspar von Bech acquitted himself well, even if Crosseby felt little real sympathy for him. He was done with the whole affair. Elsabeth would soon be gone from Ain if she and her companion had not departed already. The Schwertbrüder would eventually follow at the conclusion of the general contest of arms two days hence.

However, there were more preparations to make before he could allow himself a moment's quiet.

He ignored the street corner gossip, waved distractedly at the greetings and salutations called to him from the masters and practitioners leaving the square, and pushed past the merchants and vendors busking in the dying light of the afternoon. Lamplighters worked their way from lamp to lamp, and the avenues and alleyways overflowed with the crowd dispersing at the conclusion of the playings. Several of the visiting swordsmen clustered around the Izmiri girl and her lokma cart, each attempting to outshine the others with wild tales of his exploits. She giggled and batted her eyes at their attentions. Not one realized she wheedled them into spending a small fortune on the sweet, doughy confections with no real hope at coming away with the prize they were truly squabbling over.

A sigh escaped his lips, and he hardened himself against thoughts of the empty bed awaiting him at home. Elsabeth had made her choice: she had lied to him, used him, and embarrassed him. The esteem of the Brotherhood may have taken the worst wounding, but his own was tarnished with it. He was a fool beguiled by a pretty face and a welcoming smile. All so she could take petty revenge on Bech.

The façade of his house loomed up ahead and lulled him from his private musings. Lights in the windows flickered invitingly, beckoning him to the warm solitude of home where, no doubt, Valois had already whipped his students into a veritable frenzy of drink and cheer. Crosseby set his jaw and ground his teeth. Perhaps it was not too late to slip away to one of the taverns.

*No. Others, perhaps, might be able to shirk tonight. But I am Master of this school, and for me to eschew the festivities would not do. I owe it to Valois to make my appearance, say a few meaningless words of congratulations, and enjoy the revelry. God be praised that the wine will not be in short supply tonight!*

As he drew nearer to the house, however, he noticed several folk gathered near the door, along with two horses. Crosseby frowned when he recognized Elsabeth's jennet, her traces gripped firmly in Richard's hands. Elsabeth, however, was not among them, but he spotted the squat and rotund figure of Brother Hieronymus through the occasional break in the wall of bodies forming around him as his students made their way towards the front door of the house. The friar's voice rose above the background din of the City. He could make out little of what was being said from this distance, but the fellow was clearly agitated about something. Crosseby sighed, rolled his eyes, and slowed his approach. He wondered if, perhaps, he might sneak through the gardens and enter the house through a side door.

Luck was not on his side, however. The friar spotted him, thrust his horse's leads into Richard's hands, and pushed through the ring of people gathered around him. The rhythmic thumping of his staff against the paving stones betrayed his pique, if the indignant scowl on his heavy jowls was not enough of an indication.

"Ah! There you are at last!" he said, his voice loud enough that everyone on the street could hear him, and stealing away any other hope Crosseby had of ducking out of view. "'Tis about damn time you arrived! I was about to send those lads of yours after you when that lout servant of yours refused to take me to your box himself!"

Crosseby bristled. "I beg your pardon, Brother, but my students are not servants to be ordered around! Many are the sons of prominent men of Ain and vassals of Monsieur le Chevalier, so I suggest you treat them with the deference they are due!"

"Fah! Don't speak to me of deference, my son! I am a servant of the Wheel and I'll not be spoken to like a slow-witted buffoon! I would have come to you directly, but that man of yours insisted we wait at the house, despite the urgency of my errand!"

He mopped his face. "Oh, I do apologize for so inconveniencing a man of your position. But it has already been a long day for me, and I'll thank you not to make it any longer. And I can assure you, whatever message she convinced you to deliver to me I have no interest in hearing! Now good evening, Brother. I wish you a fine journey, and I expect for her to be gone ere the sun sets!"

And with that, he pushed past him and stormed for the house. Hieronymus, however, was not to be put off, and fell into step beside him.

"Now you wait just one moment! I am not some menial to be dismissed on a whim! I am—"

"A servant of the Wheel. But that changes nothing! I have nothing to say to Elsabeth Soesten; I don't care what she tells you."

"God damn it, man! That is what I am trying to say! I don't come here with a message. In fact, were she to make such a request of me, I myself would tell her exactly where she could deliver it, as I opposed that mad fancy of hers to remain here from the start!"

"Then what is it you want? I have a priest, so I am in no need of your services."

"I am getting to that if you will stop interrupting me!"

Crosseby stopped short of the throng gathered outside his door and spun around to face him. Though he towered over the friar, the portly old fellow levelly met his gaze, and glowered up at him without blinking. "What is it, then? I am in no mood for games!"

The friar beat the end of his staff against the street. "I don't have a message to deliver, nor can I relay yours, because I have not seen that infuriating girl since she beat me bloody in the middle of the damn street two nights ago!"

"What in God's name are you talking about?"

"The Lord has certainly not blessed you with sharp ears or a quick mind! What does it sound like I am talking about? Elsabeth never returned after you so cruelly expelled her from your home!"

For a moment Crosseby was at a loss for words, and an icy hand reached up and tightened its fingers around his throat. He looked to Richard, who averted his gaze. To judge from his expression, he desired to be anywhere but where he now stood, trapped holding the leads of the two horses to keep them from wandering off. The others loitering outside the house fell into an uneasy silence at the unspoken accusation.

Crosseby twisted his lips and forced down the bile threatening to rise up from his belly. "I don't care!" he said, but the words sounded hollow in his ears. "I am sure she found some bed or other in which to warm herself. 'Tis not my concern any longer."

Again, the friar beat the end of his staff against the ground, and the crack of its wooden foot striking the paving stones echoed across the street. "The Dark One's name 'tis not! Against my better judgment I entrusted that foolish girl to your care when you made your invitation." Hieronymus shook his staff in his face, and Crosseby flinched back in spite of himself. "And here you go and toss her aside into the night, alone! Have you any idea the sort of trouble she can get into when left to her own devices? Especially when there are people who have already threatened to remove her pretty head from her shoulders where it belongs!"

Crosseby snorted his derision. "As a matter of fact, Brother, I can. Usually of her own making, I imagine."

The friar grunted. He took one look towards the gaggle of eavesdroppers listening in, then started for the seclusion of the garden courtyard. Crosseby heaved a sigh, mopped his face, and fell into step beside him.

"Yes, quite true," Hieronymus said. "It often takes all my not-inconsiderable wisdom to get her out of it again. Much like that damned foolish decision of hers to remain behind here! I tried to talk her out of it, and I get the back of her hand for my trouble."

They stepped out from beneath the arcade and onto the fresh, green grass of the garden. Hieronymus took a deep breath and let it out again with an appreciative nod. The noise of Ain echoed in the distance, but here, enclosed within the walls of his complex, they were left in peace. "I suppose I can imagine her attraction to this place, but nonetheless, I can't fathom what madness entered into her head."

"Her attraction was but a means to an end, Brother. As I am sure many others have been before."

The friar rolled his eyes and glared up at him. "I have known that girl for four interminable years, my son. I have come to learn when she is playing someone for a fool, and trust me when I say, you were no fool."

"You deny that she put all of this on to take advantage of me?"

Hieronymus waved him off and made his way for the fountain at the heart of the garden. He let out a groan as he settled onto the bench, and laid his staff across his knees. "Oh, the demonstrations in the market? That was certainly intended to draw the attention of some generous fellow such as yourself. 'Twas not you she was looking for, but she accepted you all the same."

"And there we have it."

"Will you let me finish, man?" He sighed wearily and pinched the bridge of his nose. "I will admit it takes little to get that girl out of her dress if it serves her purposes. Particularly if you happen to have a good voice and agile fingers on a lute. But 'tis another matter entirely to get her *into* one in the first place without it being part of some scheme."

Crosseby folded his arms across his chest and lowered his eyes. Many thoughts and feelings warred for prominence at the friar's words, and for a moment he could think of nothing to say.

"I wish I could believe you," he finally managed, and acid churned in his belly.

Hieronymus harrumphed and flashed a petulant scowl, as if he were a child accustomed to telling stories finally speaking the truth, only to not be believed. "I can hardly believe it myself! Right now I can't even see just what about you had her so infatuated. I learned a long time ago there are things my dear Tetty is loath to speak of, much to my regret."

The friar reached up and nursed the side of his jaw. Crosseby thought he spotted the faint outline of a bruise on his cheek.

"I never truly know what is going through her contrary mind," Hieronymus continued. "Sometimes I think she was put on this earth by the Lord of All to test and vex me. Perhaps as penance for some sin I cannot recall. I try my best to guide her on a more righteous path, but she is too stubborn and head-strong for her own good!"

"Yes, on that I can sympathize," Crosseby said.

"My point, my son, is that perhaps you judged her too harshly. And by God you should never have let her run off alone to who-knows-where!"

The friar's voice rose until he nearly shouted the last part, and Crosseby flinched back at the fire in his voice in spite of himself. However, before he could offer a rebuke someone coughed politely for his attention, and he turned to find Richard standing behind him. His hands were clasped behind his back, and his features were twisted with worry.

"Yes?" Crosseby said.

"I beg your pardon, Sire, but we have a visitor I thought you would wish to address personally," Richard said in Coventrish.

"Can you not see that your master and I are presently occupied?" Hieronymus replied in kind, and levered himself off the fountain bench. Richard's face heated in chagrin, and even Crosseby was taken aback at the friar's grasp of their tongue. "Go and tell him he must wait."

Crosseby rounded on him. "This is my house, Brother, and I shall decide which visitors I receive! If you will excuse me."

Richard started back out of the garden, and Crosseby followed. Hieronymus grumbled something under his breath, and when he glanced past his shoulder found the friar waddling along after him, supported on his staff.

*Lord, you have peculiar taste in messengers!*

They returned to the street and were met there by a rough-featured man in a rumpled doublet, fidgeting with the traces of the palfrey he had loaned to Elsabeth the night before. He bowed stiffly at Crosseby's approach, and anxiously shifted his weight from foot to foot while he awaited permission to speak.

"Yes?" Crosseby said, in no particular mood for niceties.

"Good afternoon, Monsieur Crosseby," the man said. His Navarrese was touched by the subtle hint of Boehman common among the Ain locals. "I came to return this horse."

Crosseby raised an eyebrow and motioned for him to continue. The fellow's tongue darted out to wet his lower lips, and he wrung the leads in his hands. "It seems to have been abandoned in my stable, Monsieur."

"What do you mean by 'abandoned?'"

"Just what I said, Monsieur! She was left overnight, and when one of my boys was feeding and watering the guests' animals he found your mark on her harness. Oh! And this was tucked in one of the bags!"

He reached into a pocket, and withdrew a length of chain, held out for Crosseby's inspection. A queasy feeling washed over him as Merklin Adler's ring swung freely at the end. He reached out a trembling hand to take it, and could not still it in spite of himself.

"Where did you say you found her?"

"My stable, Monsieur."

Crosseby glanced at Richard. Richard, in turn, took a look at the knot of students still loitering around the front of his house to watch, and leaned in closely. "He runs the Greased Sow, Sire," he said in a low voice. "I suspect he means the stable there."

He raised an eyebrow at that name, and regarded Richard with some amusement. Nonetheless the queasiness grew worse. "Do you spend time often in that Quarter, Richard?"

"Not at all, Sire, but 'tis useful to know the lay of the City."

He grunted, and returned his attention to their Samaritan, who waited patiently to be addressed. Crosseby studied him for a moment, but there seemed to be nothing untoward, and if he were uneasy, it appeared only to be from addressing a man so far above his station rather than the thought of hiding something.

"Who left the horse?"

"I don't rightly know, Monsieur," he said, and there was no lie Crosseby could hear in his voice. "But it has been quite lively the past week, what with all the guests in Ain for the fights. The girls have scarcely had more than a few moments at a stretch off their backs, and 'twas quite a crowd coming and going all last night. She's a fine animal, Monsieur, so I would think if someone left her they would have missed her, but I assure you no one staying last night could rightfully put a claim on her."

"There was not by chance a woman at your establishment last night? She would not have been one of the City girls."

"A lovely lass," Hieronymus chirped in, and shouldered Richard aside to address the man himself. "Tall, long-legged, and copper-haired, with an indelible knack for getting herself into all manner of trouble."

The man nodded. "I think I recall a girl like that, Brother. She spent all night drinking, but then snapped at one of the locals and nearly bashed his face in!"

"What happened to her?"

"I had her thrown out! 'Tis rough enough with that many folk crowded into my walls without her stirring up a fight."

Hieronymus started towards him, and gripped his staff in both hands as if to strike him. "You threw her out?"

Crosseby threw an arm across the friar's chest and pushed him back. "Not now, Brother!"

"What do you mean, 'Not now!' Tetty is missing, and this rascal throws her out of his tavern in the middle of the night, and drunk to boot! I know that girl's capacity for drink, and have seen her lose days at the bottom of a tankard!"

He seized Hieronymus by his habit and dragged him back when he tried to approach the tavern keeper again. "You shan't get anything out of him if you bash his brains in, you damned fool!" He turned his attention back to the poor fellow quaking under the friar's glare, as if he feared God himself would strike him down. "Now, what happened?"

"'Tis as I said! She was making a mess of my tavern, and I would rather not see it torn apart in a brawl!"

"Where is she now?"

"I don't know! 'Twas the last I saw of her, and I don't know where she went after, nor did I care."

Hieronymus growled beneath his breath and spit the fellow with such a glare that made his knees buckle and his face blanch. Otherwise, the friar behaved himself, and planted his staff in front of him so as not to be tempted to lash out again.

"Thank you." Crosseby turned to Richard and nodded towards the tavern keeper. "See to it that he is paid for returning the horse, and the stabling fee, if necessary."

Richard gave a stiff nod and stepped around him to take the fellow in hand. Crosseby stood away and lifted the chain in his hand to study the ring swaying from the end.

Hieronymus watched him expectantly, but remained mercifully silent for the moment, leaving him alone with his deliberations. He ground his teeth and forced down the worry gnawing at the back of his mind. Perhaps she might have taken the horse as some petty vengeance. Perhaps she might even have slipped out of town to avoid paying her fine to D'Ain. But given the importance she seemed to attach to taking Merklin Adler's ring, he could not imagine she would leave *that* behind.

He lowered his head and stared for a time at the street. Behind him, Richard conversed in hushed tones with the tavern keeper, and the quiet clink of coin changing hands was the only other sound nearby. The students watching the exchange from the front door did not say a word, and Hieronymus stood without a sound except for the quiet whisper of his woolen habit when he shifted his weight on his staff. The horses nickered and stomped their feet, and their harnesses and packs rattled. Crosseby looked up at Elsabeth's jennet, and her sword hung from the saddle. *Soest's* sword, he corrected himself, marked by his coat of arms fixed in enamel, gold, and silver upon the scabbard between the belt straps. The accusations of Caspar von Bech, and Elsabeth's tale of her affair, flooded back to his mind.

Crosseby tightened his hand around the chain as his heart hardened once more. He turned back to Hieronymus and held it out for him. "When you find her, return this. 'Tis the only thing in Ain she seemed to find some value in."

Hieronymus gawked at him. "And that is it?" He waved his staff in the direction of the retreating tavern keep disappearing down the street and quietly counting his reward. "The man all but confirms my fears, and that is all you have to say?"

"That is all there is to say! She made her choice! She broke the law, she robbed a man of the Brotherhood, and she used me to do it! Whatever happens now are consequences of her own making. God knows 'tis probably long overdue for her to face them herself!"

The friar slammed the end of his staff against the ground, and the sharp *crack* of wood striking stone echoed across Ain. The horses jumped and danced in alarm, the whispers among the students stopped, and Crosseby's heart leapt into his chest at the wrath in that blow.

"God damn you, Sirrah!" Hieronymus spat, but not as a messenger of the Lord of All this time. No, the righteousness of God's fury in his voice was gone. Now he was confronted by Hieronymus, Elsabeth's friend and comrade-in-arms, and the rage in his blue eyes turned Crosseby's blood to ice. His round, heavy face turned crimson, and his unkempt white hair lent his countenance a wild madness as he glared hellfire up at him.

"God damn you!" he repeated. "I have known many a knight in my day. Liars, thieves, and butchers hiding behind false vows the lot of them! I know not what standard of chivalry you Coventrish hold yourselves to, but I find it sorely lacking in you now! You are a selfish fool so entangled with your reputation you have lost sight of what your oaths mean!"

Crosseby rounded on him, and his own temper boiled. "I warn you, Brother, I'll brook no such insults to my honor from any man, even one who professes to serve the Wheel!

Persist and you and I can step outside the walls of Ain and settle this!"

"Damn your honor! If 'tis such a fragile thing you'll not help a soul in danger for so simple a matter as wounded pride, then you, Sirrah, are no knight worthy of the title! I make no attempt to ignore Tetty's shortcomings, of which I confess there are many. But she is a good woman nonetheless, and deserves better than to be so discarded by someone she held in such esteem she was willing to end our friendship! And if you had any shred of honor in you, you would not live with leaving her to the mercy of men who want her dead!"

"You have no proof of that, Brother! For all you know she made her way to some other tavern after being thrown from the Sow. And I am certain she would find no shortage of welcoming beds if that was her fancy."

"I trust my instincts. The Brotherhood threatened her. They have already tried to make good on those threats once already. You have a queer sense of honor if you would blindly accept they would not go behind D'Ain's back for vengeance and not lift a finger to her aid now that she has gone missing."

"Sire," Richard said, and Crosseby spun around to spit him with a glare at the interruption. "Forgive me if I speak out of turn, but Brother Hieronymus is right."

Crosseby narrowed his eyes. "Richard, I am barely abiding this man's impudence as it is," he said through gritted teeth. "I'll not tolerate yours on top of it!"

Richard, however, did not back down. He clenched his fists and straightened to his full height, and Crosseby suddenly felt for all the world like he were his father about to give him a scolding. "No, Sire, you will tolerate it! I don't care if this ends with me released from your service, but whatever injury you feel she did to you, if something were to happen to Mistress Elsabeth I know that you will never forgive yourself. And I would rather speak out and risk your wrath, than be silent and watch that happen. Something is wrong. You know it, Sire. I can see it in your eyes, and I know you too well for you to hide it from me."

Crosseby hung his head and fumed in silence. Richard and Hieronymus stood silently watching him, and he felt as if their eyes might burn him all the way to his soul. His hand tightened around the chain, and for a moment he focused on the sensation of the silver links digging into his palm, as would a penitent in a hair shirt. Tense expectancy hung over the street, perhaps even more unbearable than the war waging in his heart.

Finally, he sighed. The barriers and walls he threw up as a bulwark against his mounting fears gave way, and he let it wash over him. He swallowed. "Have my horse saddled. And four others; the fastest we have. Then get Valois and the two senior Provosts. Offer them my apologies for taking them away from the libations, but tell them the matter is urgent and there is no time to lose. Go!"

# 29

HE SUN SLIPPED DOWN TOWARDS THE horizon in the west, and the sky glowed like fire. Shafts of golden light pierced through wide gaps in the canopy overhead, interspersed with the dark trunks of the trees in the wooded area outside the city. The walls of Ain were soon lost behind them as their horses rushed along the deeply-rutted dirt road south, and not a soul was to be seen for as far as he could see along its length.

The wind rushed through Caspar's hair with the speed of their ride, and Merklin and the others following them pushed their horses to keep pace with him. A sense of urgency drove him as hard as he dared; after so many years of humiliation, Elsabeth Hereford was finally helpless in his power. She did not have the Master, or now even Crosseby to protect her. She was his, and he would not see his moment of vengeance spoiled by her slipping his grasp before he could arrive!

"'Tis just ahead!" Merklin called after some ten minutes of hard riding. "Off the road on the left, through a break in the brush!"

Caspar reigned in his horse and allowed the others to catch up. The animal snorted and steamed, and he gave him a gentle pat on the side of the neck. Merklin pulled up beside him and took the lead, guiding his horse to a point along the side of the road. There, between two massive oaks rising up on either side, a break in the undergrowth revealed a well-worn but narrow dirt path leading deeper into the wood south of Ain. Caspar mused it might have been a poacher's trail for following game through the woods, as it was too narrow to serve much use for farmers heading to and from the farmland beyond.

Merklin jumped down from his horse, and Caspar swung down to join him on the road. The rattle of tack and harness behind him indicated the rest of the party doing the same.

"The horses won't fit through," Merklin said, "but 'tis a short walk."

He nodded, and turned back to the others. "Ulrich, the rope. Wendel, stay here and watch the horses. The rest of you with me."

A chorus of "Yes, Masters" answered him. Ulrich, a broad, bearded fellow with dark eyes and sandy hair, took a coil of rope from his saddle and hung it on his shoulder. The others handed their leads over to Wendel, who led the horses up the road to cool them down from the ride. Without another word Merklin plunged into the undergrowth, and Caspar and the remainder of the party followed.

For a time there was nothing to see but Merklin's back and the foliage around them. He pushed aside low-hanging branches, and stepped carefully over roots and rocks littering the path. The only sound was the rustle of the wind in the leaves, the occasional grunt or curse over a stubbed toe, and their labored breathing as they made their way along the trail. Even the birds and insects were silent. After a short time, they reached the end of the trail, and stepped out to find themselves in a small clearing of widely spaced trees, grass, and wildflowers. The area was also conspicuously absent of any sign of human life. There was no road or trail but the one through which they entered, no sound of voices or other activity, no abandoned carts, garbage, or anything else associated with people having passed this way anytime recently.

Nickel and Leonhart lounged at ease near a tall oak in the middle of the clearing. Elsabeth lay propped against it at their feet. Her hands were bound and her eyes were blindfolded. Caspar clenched his teeth at the sight of her and stormed forward across the glade.

"I told Nickel and Leonhart they were not to touch her," Merklin said. "I was sorely tempted to take her ear—" he touched his bandaged face as if in emphasis "—but I thought that you would want to deal with her yourself."

"I would hardly have blamed you if you had, but thank you," he said. "And your ring?"

Merklin grimaced. "She did not have it."

Caspar stopped and blinked at him. "What?"

"We searched her, but it was not there."

He balled his hands into fists and turned back to the woman leaning against the tree. "Well, let us go and ask her, then!"

Nickel and Leonhart stood straight at his approach and inclined their heads in greeting. He looked between the two of them for a moment, then nodded at Elsabeth. "Get her up, and remove the blindfold."

"Yes, Master," Nickel said, and removed the cloth around her eyes. Elsabeth blinked against the light and shook her head, but they left her with no time to orient herself before they hauled her roughly to her feet.

Her green eyes swept across him, Merklin, and the others with him, with no fear evident on her features. He could see the wheels turning in their depths as she sought a means of escape, but she was soon to be disappointed. He had waited for this moment for years, and this time she would not get away.

Caspar drove his fist into her gut, and all the air was driven from her lungs at once with a sickening grunt. Elsabeth lost her feet from the force of the blow, but Nickel and Leonhart caught her under the armpits and hauled her with no particular gentleness back to her feet again before she could collapse. She gasped in desperation for a breath, but another blow to the belly just beneath her ribs cheated her of the effort.

Elsabeth slumped in the hands grasping her torn and bloodied shirt — clearly the pair set to guard her had been none too gentle with her since her capture — and her legs threatened to collapse beneath her. Blood from an open cut above one eyebrow dripped into her eye. She finally managed a random, hacking breath, interrupted when

Caspar let the back of his hand fly and land across the corner of her jaw.

"Quim!" Caspar snarled.

Elsabeth spat blood from her mouth, and smiled up at him. "Oh Caspar, whatever is the matter today?" she said.

Caspar seized her roughly by the chin and wrenched her head around to face him.

"You know 'whatever is the matter,'" he snapped. "I want it!"

"Well if that is the way you ask for it, then 'tis no wonder every woman from here to Köln has refused your bed."

The words were no sooner out of her mouth than his hand flew again, delivering a powerful cuff to her temple that snapped her head around. Only Nickel's and Leonhart's firm grip kept the impact from driving her into the dirt. Elsabeth shook her head.

"Where is it?"

"I don't know, maybe you should ask that idiot Vorfechter of yours," she said.

That earned her another solid punch to the stomach, and again Elsabeth gasped for breath. Caspar seized her roughly by the hair and pulled her head back. "Take a good look around," he hissed between his teeth.

He allowed her a moment to sweep her eyes across the glade.

"If you wished for time alone with me you could always have asked," she said, when she managed to regain her breath.

Caspar seized her by the throat and squeezed, just tight enough she had difficulty drawing a breath. "You are alone, whore! The Master is no longer here to take care of you. I could crush your throat here and now and leave you for the wolves, and no one will ever find your miserable carcass."

He released her with a violent shove, but Elsabeth made no sign of reacting to the pain.

"Tch. Ever the jealous sort, Caspar. How many times need I tell you Paulus did not share your sort of affection?"

Another crack echoed across the wood as he rounded on her again. Elsabeth spit out more blood, and ran her tongue over the gash torn in her lower lip. Caspar grabbed her by the chin again and put his face in hers. "Don't you dare insult me like this now!"

"Well, you always were envious of my closeness to him, and you certainly never made a move on me, though you had plenty of opportunity. Not that I ever would have accepted, of course. Even then you were a disgusting pig, and you certainly have not improved in our years apart. But it does make one wonder."

This time when his hand flew, it was not the back of his hand to the side of her face or a fist to the gut. Instead, he balled his hand and delivered a vicious hook to her temple. Such was the force of the blow that Nickel and Leonhart lost their grip, and she spun face-first into the dirt.

They seized hold of her again and dragged her to her knees as Caspar stepped around in front of her. Dazed as she was Elsabeth could not remain upright, and just hung suspended there. She spat the blood out of her mouth.

Caspar crouched in front of her, seized a fistful of her hair, and wrenched her hanging head around to force her to look at him once more.

"I tell you one last time: Return it, now!"

Elsabeth winced against the strain the awkward turn of her head put on her neck. "And I am telling you one last time I have no idea where it is!"

He released her once more with a rough shove and nodded to Nickel and Leonhart. They yanked Elsabeth back to her feet and dragged her towards a large oak tree with several branches of convenient height. She made an effort to break free, but her captors were too many, too strong, and with her hands bound she was left with only her feet as weapons. Elsabeth kicked at whatever shin, knee or groin presented itself as a target, and tried to smash the back of her head against anyone standing behind her, but her struggling quickly proved futile, and any fight she had left in her was ended by yet another solid blow to her belly that drove the air from her lungs and left her gasping for breath.

Ulrich threw his length of rope over a convenient branch and knotted one end into a noose. A brief surge of panic spread across Elsabeth's features as the full realization of Caspar's intent settled over her. "Oh, really, Caspar?" she said when she managed to draw enough breath again to talk. "Is this really supposed to convince me to talk about something I have already told you I know nothing about?"

"You had your chance, bitch," he snarled. "You are a thief and a liar, and 'tis long past time someone treated you as such."

"And I tell you I dispute your charge," she said. "Give me a sword and let us argue the point like civilized folk so I can cut your head off rather than listen to your slander any longer."

He glowered at her. "Do you take me for a fool? I know what will happen if I put a sword in your hands, and I shan't let you slip away again."

"Oh, so you are still a coward, then. You would not dare fight me as a student, and you dare not fight me now. It defies belief the Brotherhood ever made you Master in Soest."

He snapped his fingers, and Ulrich slipped the noose over her head and tightened it around her neck. Merklin, Nickel, and Leonhart took hold of the other end and tested it and the branch, and the rope tugged against her throat. Elsabeth made a pout and gave him a quick bat of her eyelashes.

"Come now, Caspar, I am sure there must be something you and I could work out together ..."

She trailed off suggestively.

Caspar just gave her a vicious and humorless smile. "Oh no, you don't cry, kiss, or fuck your way out this time. Your charms are wasted on me, quim. Hang her!"

His students pulled the rope taut and hauled her roughly off her feet by the neck. Her body thrashed and kicked in a desperate attempt to find some sort of purchase to lift the pressure off her throat as the noose tightened around it, but the effort was in vain. She gasped in anguish, and her blood surged against the rope cutting off the flow to her head. Caspar watched with satisfaction while her tongue swelled and tried its best to force its way out of her mouth, and her struggling slowly subsided.

ROSSEBY HAMMERED AGAINST THE DOOR with his fist.

"Open the door! In the name of Monsieur le Chevalier, open the door!"

He stood back, planted his hands on his hips, and scowled. The door was unimpressed, however, and stood resolutely barring his entry from the house given over to the Schwertbrüder for their stay in Ain. The structure was one of the larger homes in the northeastern quarter, elegant in the lines of its arched windows in the clerestory and triforium, and the simple white stone of its exterior. It was not quite the imposing edifice of his own house, but towered at least a story above the rest of the construction on this block. The banners of the Schwertbrüder — *Gules, two longswords in saltire proper* — flanked the door, and quietly announced their residence to all who passed by the house. Some mischief-maker of the City had already taken advantage of recent events to deface one of the banners with a crude human ear drawn *in chief.*

After a few moments of silence, he heard the distant clatter of a bolt being drawn, and the door slowly groaned open. The face of the doorman appeared in the crack, and upon recognizing the visitors he threw the door open the rest of the way and sketched a deep bow.

"Good evening, Monsieur Crosseby," he said. "How may I serve?"

"I will speak with Caspar von Bech at once."

"Forgive me, but Master von Bech is not here."

Crosseby frowned and glanced over his shoulder to the street behind him, where his party waited with the horses. Hieronymus's countenance darkened, and he clenched his hands tightly around his horse's reigns. Crosseby turned back to the doorman and spit him with a glare.

"I am here on the authority of Monsieur le Chevalier, and I will have you tell me where he has gone at once!"

The doorman blanched. "I don't know, Monsieur. He and several of his students departed perhaps five minutes ago, but did not inform me where he was going, or when he expected to return. They did take their horses and seemed to be in some hurry. If you wish to leave your message, I will be sure he gets it upon his return."

Crosseby waved him off. "Thank you, but no. Which street did they take?"

"They were headed south down the Rue de la Cathédrale."

"Rue de la Cathédrale," he repeated thoughtfully.

"Is there anything else I can do for you, Monsieur?"

Crosseby shook his head. "No, however you can deliver this message to the Grand Master from me: Caspar von Bech and Merklin Adler are accused of the disappearance of Mademoiselle Elsabeth Hawke Soesten de Hereford. Should my suspicions be confirmed when I find him there will be a reckoning!"

With that he spun and stormed away from the door without awaiting an answer, and rejoined the others on the street.

"Well, that is certainly suspicious," Hieronymus growled beneath his breath. "Tetty is missing and the lout up and flees the city? If you had any further doubts I should hope you are seeing sense now!"

Crosseby swung himself up into the saddle. "Yes, most suspect."

"Just remember if anything happens to that girl I am holding you responsible. 'Twas against my better judgment I let her run off alone with you, and you throw her out to the wolves!"

He glared at the friar and turned his horse for the Rue de la Cathédrale. The rest of the party all fell in behind him as he spurred his horse to a gallop. People scattered out of the path of the horses rushing along the street with a deafening clattering of hooves, and the roar of the wind past his ears.

"I am neither deaf nor dotard, Brother. I don't need to be reminded of my responsibilities!" he shouted to be heard over the wind.

"I am merely ensuring you are cognizant of the seriousness of the matter!"

"I am fully aware, and I assure you I shan't let Caspar von Bech harm her and go unpunished. However what matters now is finding him before he can!"

"Then I trust you know where the villain has gone?"

"Of course! He was heading south down the Rue de la Cathédrale, so he must have headed for the South Gate."

"How can you be so sure?"

"If he intended to take her out the North Gate and into Boehm, he would not have headed south. The Rue de la Cathédrale does not pass through the main square, but rather on its east side past the Cathédrale de Ain, so 'tis a poor choice if he was headed out the West Gate unless he were to go a roundabout way. The East Gate leads too near the Castle. Lastly, the Greased Sow is in the Southwest Quarter of the city. If she was indeed abducted and taken out of the city, 'tis the nearest gate."

Hieronymus looked to the sky and touched a hand to his heart. "Lord! I pray that you have granted this man better wisdom in the hunt than you have his every action 'til now!"

"While I greatly appreciate your confidence in me, Brother, let us ride quickly! If Bech intends to do her harm he has a head start upon us, and we have little time to lose!"

Negotiating the streets of Ain during the day might have proven daunting, but as the afternoon waned into evening the locals and visitors retired to their homes, inns, and taverns. Crosseby's heart pounded in his chest at the sense of urgency washing over him, and he drove his horse as fast as he dared. They reached the gates without more than a few startled curses at their backs when they ploughed through the handful of folk still abroad as the sun fell and the shadows lengthened. A brief word with the guard confirmed his suspicions and filled him with a fresh sense of urgency.

Caspar von Bech had indeed passed this way, not a few minutes earlier.

They rode out the South Gate, and onto the road leading away from Ain. It ran straight for some distance before plunging into the woodland south of the city. Free of the traffic of the narrow, twisting avenues and alleys, Crosseby dug his heels into his horse's flanks and surged ahead as fast as he could run. Hieronymus's and Elsabeth's horses managed to keep pace, as if no less determined than he to run down Bech's party, and reveling in being allowed to run freely after the confinement of the City streets. Richard and the others fell behind, but never out of view. The rhythmic drumming of hooves pounded dully against the hard-packed and rutted dirt road, and the horses snorted and panted at the effort of their flight.

No other roads crossed the passage south of Ain for some miles, but for all he knew Elsabeth could have been moved all night and was now well away from the city.

Fortune, however, was on their side. After some minutes of hard riding, they rounded a bend that took them fully out of sight of Ain, and Crosseby spied a lone man along the side of the road ahead in the distance. He led several horses in a slow walk up and down its length to cool them down after a hard run, and though he did not recognize the fellow, his red doublet quickly betrayed him as one of the Schwertbrüder.

He, in turn, spied the riders approaching and froze; they were coming too quickly for him to hide.

Crosseby pulled up his horse and was down from the saddle and reaching for the hilts of his sword almost as soon as he stopped. His courser danced and scrabbled against the packed earth and whinnied in irritation at the sudden halt. The fellow on the road blanched at the sight of him, and the horses in his hand skittered and shied at the commotion. Hieronymus alighted as well, followed by Valois, and the two men Richard summoned; Dreue and Aleaume, who had the presence of mind to grab crossbows from his school's armory. Richard remained mounted and gathered the leads of their horses to keep them close.

"You there!" Crosseby shouted at Bech's man. "Stand fast and answer me truthfully or I swear to God I will cut you down! Where is your master; and where is Elsabeth Soesten?"

His voice echoed between the trunks and hung in the air beneath the canopy. The only other sound was the hiss of the wind through the trees, and the snorting and stamping of the horses. When no answer was forthcoming he drew his sword.

With his hands occupied the fellow made no effort to reach for his own sword. He was young, perhaps fifteen or sixteen at most, and quaked in his boots at the fading sunlight glinting along the edge of Crosseby's blade. He raised one shaking hand and pointed to a small break between two trees. The faint traces of a poacher's trail was just discernible through the foliage.

"Wait here! Richard, keep an eye on him. If he tries to draw his sword or flee, you may ride him down."

"Yes, Sire," Richard said, and spit the man with such a venomous glare Crosseby thought the poor fellow might wet his hose.

He turned to Hieronymus, Valois, Dreue, and Aleaume. The friar's sword was already in hand, and Valois drew his blade as well. Dreue and Aleaume kept to their crossbows, and each loaded a quarrel. "Brother, Valois, behind me. You two trail behind and cover us."

Crosseby plunged into the opening without waiting for them to acknowledge his command. He forced a path through the low-hanging branches and foliage overgrowing the trail, but it was clear that several people passed this way quite recently. Up ahead he heard the sound of a man talking, though he could not make out what was being said. He thought he might have heard a woman respond, and panic seized his heart, and that drove him to push with even greater urgency along the path. As he neared the place where the passage through the undergrowth opened out onto a wide glade he spied Bech, Elsabeth with a rope about her neck, and several of the Brotherhood through a break in the foliage. They gathered around a tall oak, and with a command from Bech his men pulled on the rope and hauled Elsabeth into the air.

He let out a strangled cry as she thrashed a few moments before falling still, and then he burst into the clearing with Hieronymus, Valois, Dreue, and Aleaume close on his heels. Bech, Adler, and any of the Schwertbrüder with free hands spun at the sound of him crashing from the undergrowth. They all drew their swords at once, while Elsabeth swung helplessly from her rope.

"In the name of God and Monsieur le Chevalier, cut that woman down at once!" Crosseby said, and he filled his voice with every bit of authority he could muster.

"This is not your affair!" Bech spat, and tightened his grip on his sword. "This is a matter between me and the Coventrish whore, I suggest you turn right around and go back whence you came!"

"Dreue, Aleaume, shoot down the first of them who takes so much as a step in hostility towards us. Caspar von Bech, I am here as an officer of Monsieur le Chevalier, still in execution of his will. I say again: Cut her down at once! That is an order!"

Hieronymus pushed around him, and his face blanched. "Dear God!"

Crosseby's mouth went dry, and he watched Elsabeth's face slowly turn blue. Bech made a sign, and the rest of his companions formed a wall of flesh and steel barring anyone from approaching the tree.

"I say again, Monsieur Crosseby, that this is our business, and not Monsieur le Chevalier's! If you don't want a fight of it, I suggest you leave at once and let us deal with this upstart woman!"

"And I say to you, Caspar von Bech, if you do not release her this instant there shall be a fight, and any man who survives shall be taken before Monsieur le Chevalier for judgment. We are not in Boehm, or in any other country where the Brotherhood holds sway. We are in Ain, and Monsieur le Chevalier is the law here. Now I say to you one last time: Release that woman at once and back away, or die now!"

Bech stared at him, and his hands tightened around his sword. The other Schwertbrüder looked between him and their Master, but none of them wore the same conviction on their features as Bech. Even Merklin Adler quailed. Finally, after a long moment, he gave a sign and the two men holding Elsabeth's rope released it. Her body fell to the ground and collapsed unmoving beneath the tree. With their eyes on the crossbows of Dreue and Aleaume, and the naked steel in his and Valois' hands, the Schwertbrüder all backed away. Hieronymus rushed forward to tend to his companion, and none made a move to interfere.

Torn between his fear at the sight of Elsabeth lying still in the grass, and rage bubbling up inside him, Crosseby strode forward and seized Bech by the front of his doublet. For his part Bech made no effort to strike back, and just weathered the heat of his glare without a word.

"I swear to God, if she dies I kill you here and now," he hissed between gritted teeth.

"If you don't," Bech said, "you will have made the gravest mistake of your life. This was a Brotherhood matter, and you have meddled in our affairs. We shan't forgive, and we shan't forget."

"If all I have lost is the friendship of the Schwertbrüder then nothing is lost at all." He heard a racking cough behind him, and glanced over his shoulder to see Hieronymus helping Elsabeth upright. Crosseby shoved Bech towards the path leading back out to the road. "Take your people and go. By my authority as an officer of Monsieur le Chevalier's will, you are to leave Ain and its environs immediately, never to return or set foot into this city until he should overturn this ban. Should you disobey this order, I will have you arrested for the kidnapping, assault, and attempted murder of Mademoiselle Elsabeth Hawke Soesten de Hereford."

Bech slammed his sword back into its scabbard, and the rest of the Schwertbrüder put up their arms as well. He jammed his finger towards him, and his face twisted with rage. "This matter is not settled! Don't think for a moment that you can protect that whore from me forever, and pray I never meet you where you can't hide behind your Master."

"Perhaps not, but I am satisfied in cheating you of your vengeance today. Now go, or by God I'll have you shot down where you stand!"

Bech curled his lip and spat at his feet, then spun on his heel and stormed off. The rest of the Schwertbrüder fell into step behind him — Bech and Adler spit Elsabeth with their most withering glares as they departed — and one-by-one disappeared through the break in the trees.

ASY, GIRL, EASY," HIERONYMUS SAID. HE helped Elsabeth sit upright, but she collapsed against him and let out a wet, racking cough. He carefully cut the noose from around her neck and the bindings off her wrists, and cradled her to him as she gasped for breath and slowly regained her normal color. His nose caught a distinct whiff of bowel, and though he wrinkled it against the smell he said nothing to cause her any further embarrassment. She would realize it soon enough on her own. "Do not venture yet into the light ahead of you, for the Lord of All has not yet deemed it time for you to depart this earth. Instead, you must walk among the living for a little while longer."

"Hieronymus?" she said, her voice barely above a hoarse whisper, but no less filled with astonishment.

"Don't try to talk yet." He quirked a grin. "I know you shall find it difficult, but I for one will enjoy the rare silence."

"What are you doing here?"

Hieronymus snorted. "What do you think I am doing here? Do you think I was going to stand by and let that oaf mar your pretty neck? God would not have forgiven me had I left you here to die."

Tears welled up in her eyes, and she buried her face in his chest. Elsabeth's body shuddered in his arms, and he hugged her close. "I am so, so sorry for what I said before. I was so awful to you."

"'Tis all right, Tetty." He heaved a sigh and gave her shoulder a squeeze. "'Tis all right. Mayhaps I am as much to blame, and did not give your knight enough credit."

Hieronymus looked up at Crosseby. He stood away from them with his head bowed low, and his jaw clenched. From the look of him he guessed the man was torn between relief and some other emotion, and quivered as if unable to decide between keeping his distance and rushing to her side. The clearing was empty now but for the six of them, and in the distance on the road he could hear the clatter of the Schwertbrüder mounting their horses and riding off. The distant pounding of hooves on the dirt road soon receded into nothing. The only other sounds were the gentle whisper of the autumn wind rustling the trees surrounding the glade, and Elsabeth's ragged breathing.

"Can you stand?" he ventured after a while. "I think you have lain here in the dirt long enough, and 'twould be good for you to test your legs again."

She gave a stiff nod, and Hieronymus put an arm around her waist to help her to her feet. Elsabeth tottered a bit, and quickly shot an arm around his shoulders for support until she could steady herself.

Elsabeth lightly squeezed his shoulder in thanks until the strength returned to her legs, but Hieronymus did not leave her side as she took a few uncertain steps. Already he could see the experience of her brush with death lifting from her shoulders, and he inwardly gave thanks to God for guiding Crosseby so surely. She *did*, however, pick at the seat of her hose, and her face turned a brilliant shade of crimson. "Oh God, I hope you brought me a change of clothes."

Hieronymus allowed himself to chuckle. "Your belongings are near at hand. The Lord of All does say that all things pass in time, in your case a length of rope just made it a little more literal than the message intends."

Before she could say another word Elsabeth caught sight of her savior, and her body tensed. She tightened her fingers around Hieronymus's woolen habit, and her face flushed crimson. For his part Crosseby remained where he stood with his head lowered so he need not look at her.

"Stemham," she said. "Thank you."

Crosseby nodded. "You are welcome." He shifted and kicked a bit at the dirt at his feet, but otherwise made no move towards her. Hieronymus rolled his eyes in exasperation.

"Oh for God's sake, man!" he barked. "'Tis as plain as the nose on your face you want to drag her off behind some tree and ensure all the intimate parts of her anatomy are still present and working properly, so just be done with it!"

Crosseby glared but could not mask the coloring of his cheeks. Elsabeth gave him a firm swat across the shoulder.

Hieronymus just let out an indignant grunt. "Forgiveness is one of the Lord of All's most precious gifts, my son, and in my not-inconsiderable experience the forgiveness that follows strife between man and woman is perhaps the most, shall we say, enthusiastic."

Elsabeth rolled her eyes. "Oh shut up you old lech, and mind your business."

"Hmph. Well, I suppose you are just about back to your usual contrary self. I should have enjoyed it while it lasted!"

She let out an exasperated groan and stomped away from him. Hieronymus just shook his head and leaned on his staff to watch the show.

ELSABETH STALKED AWAY FROM HIERONYMUS with a sigh, and was keenly aware of his eyes on her back. Her belly fluttered, and she worked her hands into and out of fists at her side. She hurt all over from the rough treatment by her captors, her neck ached, and she felt distinctly wet and uncomfortable in her braies. Crosseby lowered his eyes from the friar when he saw her approach. He leaned one hand on the pommel of his sword, and hooked his other thumb through his belt for want of something else to do with them. He toed the dirt in front of him and did everything he could to look anywhere but at her.

She stopped just short of him, hung her shoulders, and lowered her eyes as well. "Stemham," she said, and winced at the hoarseness of her voice. Not that she could ever sing a note before, but if Caspar's rough treatment left her with any permanent damage, she would hunt him down and permanently raise *his* voice a few pitches. She swallowed to work a little moisture back in her mouth and rubbed her throat. "Thank you for coming for me."

Crosseby sighed. "I could not in good conscious leave you to that man once I learned you never returned to your companion."

"What happens now?"

"I'll have Dreue and Aleaume escort you a ways to ensure Bech causes you no further trouble on the road. Beyond that I wish you well."

Elsabeth swallowed and fought back the tears welling up in her eyes. His words struck her as if with a blow. For a moment their gaze met when she looked up at him again, and she saw her own pain reflected in the depths of his grey eyes. "I don't want to leave."

Crosseby took a step forward and reached out to touch her hand. "I can now accept, perhaps, that you are being earnest, and 'tis not just a show you put on for my benefit. The friar to his credit can be quite convincing. But what do you think will happen here because of this? I invoked his Lordship's authority to expel a high-ranking member of the Schwertbrüder from Ain. The Grand Master will certainly be livid, and I can't imagine the repercussions it might have should it reach the Imperial Diet."

"And what can they do? The Brotherhood has no authority in Navarre, any more than does the Diet. And neither they nor the Empire would be willing to go to war on Caspar von Bech's account. And like as not they would rather sweep this embarrassment aside than face the humiliation of it back home."

He sighed. "'Tis not just the Brotherhood, Elsabeth. I know now that you will ever court controversy. Whether 'tis with the Schwertbrüder or someone else, you are a tempest leaving chaos in your wake, and can you tell me that will ever change? D'Ain, I am sure, will find it amusing for a time, but eventually he will tire of it. And while my status could protect you from many people, he is not one of them."

Elsabeth hung her head, slipped her hand from his, and tightened them both into fists. "I can't change who I am, love." She looked up at him from beneath her lashes and pouted. "Besides, I am not without my benefits, so surely that must count for something."

Crosseby's lip twitched into a lopsided smile, and his cheeks colored a bit. "Indeed you are not, and I shan't be forgetting them any time soon." He sobered and his smile faltered, and with it Elsabeth felt as if a hand reached inside her breast and seized her heart. "In another life, mayhaps, but here and now, I can't. With the demands of my post I can't manage the scandals that would follow you. You are simply too much excitement for me and for Ain."

The tears she fought so desperately to hold back broke through and rolled down her cheeks, and the hand around her heart tightened until she thought it might burst. "Then you are choosing your honor over your heart."

"I can't change who I am."

"So that is the way of it, then? I am too wild to tame, and you are too bound to your reputation."

"I am sorry, Elsabeth. I content myself that you will live, but that is all. Now go, before you lose the light. There is an inn a short ways up the road. Dreue and Aleaume will take you that far, and you and your companion can make your way whither you will from there."

Elsabeth squared her shoulders and clenched her fists. The long-buried emptiness left by Paulus's death, and for one blissful moment filled by the warmth of Crosseby's arms, settled over her once more. Her throat tightened, as if Caspar's rope was again pulling tight around her neck, and she wanted nothing more than to scream. She opened her mouth, but not a sound would come, and no words would form. So instead she gave him one last look — Crosseby averted his gaze from her so he need not look her in the eye — then turned away and marched for the path leading back out onto the road.

She arrived to find Richard awaiting them with their horses. Without a word to him she took Felis by the bridle and led her away from the others, before fishing into her saddle bags for a change of clothes, and her jacket to ward away the autumn chill.

Elsabeth stepped off the road into the brush to change, and when she had finished and returned to the road again, she watched Hieronymus fidget with his gear and slide his staff through the straps supporting his pack. Josephus snorted and stamped irritably while he endured the jostling.

"Are you all right, Tetty?" Hieronymus asked after a few moments of watching her stuff her soiled garments away in her pack. Her face was still raw from her tears, and the stinging cuts and scrapes left by Caspar's assault. Those would have to wait until they reached their destination; she wanted to be away from this place as quickly as could be.

"Let us just make that inn. Right now, I just want to drink 'till I can't remember."

"For what 'tis worth, I am sorry."

She glanced at him over his shoulder, and much to her surprise he looked back at her with genuine sincerity. "There is nothing to be sorry for. 'Tis my own bloody mess. God may have seen fit to spare my life, but he is punishing me for it nonetheless."

He grunted. "The Lord of All is certainly peculiar like that. But no matter, 'tis long overdue for you and me to be moving along. Oh, before I forget, you seemed to have left this behind while you were trying your best to drown yourself last night."

Elsabeth looked back again, and her breath caught in her throat. In his hands was a length of chain, with Merklin Adler's ring dangling at the end of it. She reached out and took it, laying it in the palm of her hand. For a long moment she stared at it in silence, running her thumb along the cold, smooth gold of the band, and studying the subtle engraving naming its wearer a member of the Schwertbrüder. The longer she stared, the more the lingering hollowness stabbed into her belly, and she thought back through the years and miles to an autumn evening not unlike this one. The day she first knew Paulus's touch not as a student, but as a woman. She remembered the ring so much like this one that he once wore, lost to her now far away, perhaps in a burial vault in Soest, if not a trophy stashed away in Caspar von Bech's desk at the schola.

"Tetty?" Hieronymus asked. She quickly shook her head to clear away such thoughts and thrust the ring down into one of her saddlebags and out of view.

"'Tis nothing. Let us go."

She swung herself up into the saddle and gave Felis a gentle pat on the neck. She nickered softly and bobbed her head, eager to be off again. Hieronymus nudged Josephus forward until he stood beside her and eyed her closely.

"At least tell me all this was worth the trouble we caused," he said.

Elsabeth stared down at the ground for a moment, before turning her attention back to the road ahead and urging Felis forward into a gentle amble. Hieronymus followed, with their escort on either side. "Was what worth it?"

"All of this nonsense over a damnable ring and the Brotherhood."

"'Twas not what I set out for, but I'll admit I quite enjoy the thought Caspar shan't be escaping the humiliation of all of this for some time. I imagine 'twill be making the rounds of the inns and taverns across Navarre for months, and will probably even earn him mockery and a few laughs back home. And I shall certainly delight in spreading the tale myself."

"That does not exactly answer my question."

She worked her jaw. "Don't press me, love."

"I merely want to know that all of this hassle was not a tremendous waste of our time!"

Elsabeth sighed. "No, it was not worth it. Whatever I gained here, I think perhaps I lost even more. Is that what you wish to hear?"

Hieronymus just grunted and said nothing more.

"Let us just get to that bloody inn so you can have a look at my face to be sure it shan't scar — God himself could not protect Caspar from me if it does! — and we can be on our way to better prospects."

"Well, good to see you are finally talking sense! You go and have yourself a good drink, but try not to scandalize yourself with the first passing minstrel you come across. I would rather like to find us a bit of decent work without having to get you out of any more trouble!"

She scowled across at him. "What do you mean you would like to find us a bit of work? 'Tis still my turn!"

Hieronymus gawked. "Still your turn?! What do you call this damned foolish venture I just rescued you from?"

"Oh please! You are hardly one to talk after all the times I have had to extricate your fat arse out of some tribulation of your own making!"

"You leave my arse out of this, you ungrateful harpy!"

"I wish I could, but it makes up so large a portion of you there is no getting around it."

"Feh! I should have left you hanging from that tree!" He made a show of looking to the sky. "Lord! Surely she is some devil you have sent to torment me; see how she vexes me?"

"Remember that time you were nearly quartered in Neumarck?"

"And I say you are grossly exaggerating, Tetty."

"Or how about that woman who wanted to boil you alive in Milosen?"

"I told you, I have known her for years and 'tis just her way when she gets cross."

"And what about those gamblers who caught you cheating them in Rehaw?"

"It was a misunderstanding!"

They continued on in this manner all the way down the road to the chagrin of Dreue and Aleaume, and left Ain behind them.

Presenting a special first look at

# 1

"BUGGER!"

Elsabeth raised her head above the seat of her wain and gazed at the black-shafted bolt stuck quivering in the back of the bench. Had she not thrown herself over and into the bed when she did, it would assuredly have passed neatly through her belly. She twisted her lip in irritation, snatched her hat from beside her, and returned it to her head. Then she turned her attention to the six men barring the road in front of her.

They were a ramshackle lot, dressed all in homespun doublets and hose that had seen better days. Once, perhaps, their cloth might have been diverse and brightly colored, but sun and weather left them all now the same dingy shade of brown beneath their ragged coats. Their features matched their dress; tanned and cracked by the elements, assuming they had ever been lovely at all. Shaggy hair hung round their shoulders, and unkempt growths of beard warmed their faces against the chill of winter. They gripped spears and cudgels in rough hands. Their leader casually slipped his foot into the stirrup of his crossbow and spanned the bow. The sharp *click* of the nut locking into place echoed ominously across the road.

"'Twas a warning shot, my lovely," he called across the space between them. His Boehman was rough and uncultured, and touched by a hint of Navarrese as was common among the local dialects along the border regions.

His voice broke the peaceful stillness of the flat, snow-swept fields stretching for miles in all directions. Only here, where the road dipped into a small wooded grove, was there a place where an enterprising sort might set such an ambush, and Elsabeth chided herself for having driven right into it unprepared. Had she been alone upon Felis she might have spurred her forward and ridden them down before they could bring arms to bear. Unfortunately, the old draft horse hitched to her wagon was not up to the task, nor did she trust the wheels not to come apart when they struck the roadblock spanning the way ahead.

"Some bloody warning!" she called back. Elsabeth stayed low, peering over the seat from the back of the wagon, scarcely showing more than the low crown of her hat for him to shoot at. "Had you been a little faster on the draw we likely would not be having this conversation now."

"Well, would that not have been a pity," he said with a laugh. "But 'tis what you get for not slowing down as you were asked, to pay our toll."

"'Twas a bit high for my liking, I don't think you can fault me that."

The leader of the group casually fitted another bolt onto his crossbow and leveled it towards her wagon. Elsabeth hunkered down and peered between the slats of her bench.

"Well, it has not changed in the last few minutes. Toss down that lovely bit of steel you have at your side, raise your hands, and step down. We'll be having that cart and your goodies. You can go your way after that if you play nicely."

"Ordinarily, love, I might find it hard to refuse such a polite request, but I am afraid the cart and its wares are not mine to hand over, and hardly anything you might find of value leastwise. Just a few meager odds and ends for the poor souls in Pruck's monastery up the road for the holiday, as a good turn for the Lord."

"Oh I doubt that. I wager there is food and blankets, and a few baubles worth a bit of coin. Along with whatever you might be carrying on your own person." His voice took on a harder edge. "And I am beginning to lose my patience. Lads!"

Four of the men started forward, and Elsabeth muttered a curse under her breath. They advanced in a disorderly fashion, neither supporting the other, and under normal circumstances Elsabeth had no doubts she could put the wagon between her and one pair while dispatching the other two.

*That crossbow makes all the difference; I can't risk exposing myself, as I doubt my doublet can stop a bolt even at this range. And this fellow is a good enough shot I would rather not take my chances on him missing. He likely poaches fowl on the wing in fairer months.*

She considered her cargo for a moment. There were barrels of flour and barley, a good-sized goose huddling quietly in a cage covered by a blanket, and baskets of dried fruits and vegetables left over from harvest and laid aside for the winter months. Bundles of spare clothes — none by any means large enough to fit her assailants — and blankets were piled among a few other packages and parcels sealed against the weather. All lay under a heavy canvas tarp, which she tore free during her mad scramble into the box when the leader of the brigands first raised his crossbow. Unfortunately, there was nothing at hand she might use as a suitable shield.

"Come now, love," she said. Elsabeth pressed her back against the bench, and thumped her head against it at the plan taking shape. *'Twill be a desperate gamble, but I don't have much choice.* "Surely you and I could come to some sort of arrangement."

"You have heard my terms."

"But you have not heard my counter-offer!"

"Well, let us have it, then," he said.

Elsabeth craned her neck enough to peer around the bench behind her. The men advancing on the wagon paused, but their leader kept his crossbow aimed squarely at it. The last of the group, a rather big and brutish man who likely stood at least a head taller than her, flanked him with arms the size of tree trunks folded across his chest. He alone showed any sort of weapon more complex than a spear or cudgel; a heavy iron mace hanging from his belt.

"For a start, I don't think you have considered just how useful I could be to your outfit. You won't find a finer sword-arm in this part of Boehm."

He laughed sharply, little more than a dismissive bark that echoed across the glade. The others all broke out into laughter along with him, and Elsabeth's face heated indignantly.

"A woman? I think you have been out in the cold too long!"

Elsabeth screwed her lip into a scowl. "Set aside your toy, love, and you can see it for yourself."

"I think not. Besides, even if I might consider it despite your sex, 'twould still be an extra share to divvy up, and pickings are slim as it is."

"Well, I assure you that you shan't find pickings like me. Use a bit of imagination, love! I am sure you can think of more pleasant things to stick me with than a quarrel in the belly."

Contemplative silence hung over the little grove, disturbed only by the soft hiss of the wind, and the faint creaking of naked branches swaying. A few small flurries drifted aimlessly down from the slate sky overhead.

"Well?" she prompted, when no answer was forthcoming.

"Don't you know anything about husbandry? You don't take on a brood-mare without a chance to inspect the goods first." he said.

*Well, now I have him thinking with the wrong head. That ought to have him off his guard.*

Elsabeth unbuttoned her coat and unfastened her doublet. The winter chill blasted right through her, and raised her finer hairs on end. She turned round in the wagon to face her assailants, and in one smooth motion she popped up above the bench that was her only cover, and pulled down on her blouse. The men howled their approval when she flashed her breasts for just a moment, then dropped back out of sight into the box. Elsabeth shivered

— from disgust as much as the cold — and covered herself once more.

"You make a compelling offer," he said. The rest of his men all voiced their agreement, and Elsabeth curled her lip into a twisted smile.

*Oh, this just got too easy.*

"There is, of course, one small thing," she said. "I am still a woman of some respectability, you know, and not a common bawd to be passed round."

"Of course you are, and I can't imagine a man wanting to share you, either. So I take it we let you pass, and you come with me."

"That is the offer on the table, as it were."

"And how do I know 'tis not just some scam to save your own neck, and you intend to make good on it?"

Elsabeth shrugged, though the other could not see the gesture. "The roads are dangerous this time of year, you know. A stout man doing a good deed by escorting this delivery would not be unwelcome."

Another moment of thoughtful silence passed, and that started grumbling among the others when the prospect of a windfall from the wagon seemed to evaporate before them.

"So what about us?" one said. "We don't get a single trinket, and you walk away with the real prize?"

"I sure did not sign up for the benefit of another man's cock," said another.

"I can't believe you would even consider it!" came a third voice. "There are six of us and one of her; 'twould be a small matter to have a share of all the goods, if you mark my meaning."

"Oh, there are six of you," Elsabeth said, and quietly slipped her sword from it scabbard. The cold air frosted on the four and a half spans of naked Boehman steel. "I have no doubt should you all come at me I would be overwhelmed. But! How many of you will die before that should happen? And what if in the chaos some unfortunate stroke should fall and stove my head in? Then you would not have me at all?" She chuckled. "Well, at least you would have yourselves for company."

"Quiet, all of you!" the leader snapped, "I am the leader of this outfit, and I'll not tolerate any such arguments!"

But the others were now pensive.

"Of course," Elsabeth said, in her most off-handed manner, "I am flexible and agreeable to other terms, and an enterprising sort might find an opportunity to negotiate for himself."

The leader of the band let out a laugh. "So that is your game, is it? Well, my lovely, it won't work. Enough of this: Take her!"

But contrary to his assertions, the grumbling amongst his band only grew louder. *Prospects round these parts must be slim indeed if all it takes to stir up this sort of mutiny is the brief glimpse of an admittedly exceptional pair of tits.*

"And if we do, how do we know that you intend to make good on your part to us?" one of the men growled at his master.

Elsabeth leaned around the bench. In spite of his orders, the men who were advancing on the wagon now started back towards their leader. He shrunk behind his big guard, but they were not cowed by the mountain of muscle standing between them and the subject of their ire.

"For that matter, how do you know he has not been holding out on you all along?" Elsabeth said. "I suppose he does all the counting for you."

"That is quite enough out of you!" he spat, and raised his crossbow at the wagon once more. But he could not get a clean shot at her hunkered down in the bed, and not even the crown of her hat peeped above the bench to offer him a suitable mark.

"I think she brings up a fair point," one of the four said, his voice thick with accusation. "Remember that job two weeks ago? I thought my share looked scant, but I said nothing! I wonder now if you have been holding back on us after all."

"He certainly laid claim to the finest things from the loot," said another, and he tightened his grip on his cudgel.

"Because I am the only one with a bloody brain between us!" the leader snapped.

Elsabeth tsked. "Well, that is hardly a show of respect for you all. I wager you lot do all the fighting for him, too."

"And he stands back with his bow safe, while we do all the wet-work!"

"I warn you all, get back and get to it, or 'twill be Cunlin knocking your heads together!"

The big fellow at the leader's side uncrossed his arms, and made a show of rubbing one meaty fist. But if the others had been cowed by the big man in the past, now the threat only riled them further, and they snatched up their spears and cudgels against him.

"'Tis always how it is with you, Wendel: Do this, do that, I'll have that, don't make me set Cunlin on you! Well, I for one have had my fill of i—"

One of the men started forward with leveled spear as he spoke. The twang of the crossbow cut his protestation short, and he fell to the snow clutching at the black shaft of the quarrel buried so deeply through his throat the squared head jutted out the back of his neck. Blood sprayed in a brilliant crimson arc as he spun into the ground, and spurted between his fingers. He writhed and thrashed in the snow, choking and gagging around the bolt.

"Endres!" Another said, crouching momentarily at his fallen comrade's side

Wendel backpedaled in a mad scramble with Cunlin between him and the others, desperate to gain enough ground to reload his bow. An angry cry went up, and chaos erupted. Cunlin whipped his mace from his belt in a futile bid to fend them off, and went down after being set upon from all angles. His size availed him little against the spear that slipped past his arms and pierced his belly, while the other two fell on him with their cudgels.

Elsabeth spared no time watching how the battle would unfold. She seized hold of the rail and vaulted from the cover of the wagon bed. The snow covering the road was well-packed, and she easily maintained her footing on her rush across the ground.

She flew past Endres, who now lay still in a pool of red slush with his mouth gaping. She leapt the prostrate form of Cunlin, writhing in agony with the broken haft of a spear buried in his belly, and bleeding profusely from many wounds in his head and face. Another of the outlaws lay sprawled beside him and clutched the other half of the spear in a death grip. His head had been crushed by Cunlin's mace; his reward for the fatal blow he had struck against the big enforcer.

Steel rang, and Elsabeth fixed her eyes on the end of the fight between Wendel and his two remaining companions. He discarded his crossbow and went to work against them with a longsword he had concealed beneath his coat. He dispatched his first opponent in deft fashion, then turned to face the last of his erstwhile comrades. But Elsabeth was upon them both before they could conclude their argument.

She ducked low, put her shoulder into the back of the latter, and upended and hurled him behind her. He cried out and landed with a muffled *whump* in the snow. Then she took her sword in both hands, vaulted to the side, and met Wendel with the *zornhau* when he leveled a wild and desperate blow at her shoulder. Her sword rang as her blade caught his, and at the moment their blades crossed she thrust stiffly towards his face from below. The awl-like point pierced his throat where it met the underside of his jaw, and he gurgled sickeningly. His sword fell from his hands, and his legs collapsed beneath him. Elsabeth continued past, turning her sword in her hands and allowing him to fall off her point.

Her lungs burned from the exertion and the frigid air. She checked her advance and turned, sliding a bit in the snow as her momentum carried her forward a few paces more. By now the last of the outlaws was scrambling to his feet again, and his eyes flicked between the reddened blade of her sword, and Wendel choking on his blood at her feet. More hot blood pooled in the snow and painted its white surface with angry red splotches.

Elsabeth raised her hilts to her shoulder in *vom tag* and prepared for another exchange, but her adversary blanched and threw down his spear. He slipped and fell in the snow in his mad scramble away from her.

"Mercy!" he cried, and cowered.

Elsabeth did not let down her guard, but she did not level her sword for the fatal strike he expected. "Well now, our situations seem to have reversed, have they not?"

The fellow looked up at her from between his arms. "'Twas Wendel, Gnädige Frau! He put us up to it all."

"Of course he did, love. Well, Wendel is not in a position to put you up to anything else, now, is he?"

"No, Gnädige Frau." His features turned pensive as he looked up at her standing over him. "You...ah...would not still be amenable to making an offer, would you?"

Elsabeth rolled her eyes. "Oh, just get the fuck out of here."

He slipped and fell face-first into the snow in his effort to scramble away, while fine powder flew into the air in a white mist. He eventually got his feet beneath him again, and flew like a frightened hare across the drifts, falling at times as his speed got the better of his footing.

Elsabeth watched him go, her lips curled slightly in amusement, until he was safely away and unlikely to return to harass her again. Then she wiped her sword clean on Wendel's coat, and went about gathering up anything of value her erstwhile assailants left behind.

# APPENDIX: READING BLAZONS

The coats of arms herein are presented in the form of the blazon. This is a particular heraldic language used to describe a coat of arms in a succinct manner that will automatically be understood.

The arms are always described in a specific order:

1. Any divisions of the shield which exist.

2. The field is described:

   a. In the case of a solid color, the tincture of the field (capitalized, even if the color is not the first word of the blazon) is given, followed by a comma.

   b. In a complex field, such as *chequy* (that is, checkered of two colors) the pattern is described, followed by a comma.

3. The principle ordinary or charge is given, followed by in order:

   a. Its attitude (IE the pose of a bird or beast)

   b. Its tincture

   c. Parts that might be colored differently

d.   A charge may have another charge placed on it.

4.   Any additional charges placed around the primary charge described as above with their positions.

5.   Any additional charges *on* the principle charge, again described as in the principle charge.

A blazon is always given from the *bearer's* perspective, not the viewer's. Thus dexter refers to the part of the shield on the bearer's right (viewer's left).

On a divided shield, the divisions are described beginning at the chief, (top) from dexter to sinister, then the base (bottom) in the same fashion, much like reading a book. Thus in a quartered shield, the top row would be quarters I and II, while the bottom row is III and IV.

For example, the blazon — *Quarterly 1st and 4th Azure, on a bend Or three bears statant erect Sable Quarterly 2nd and 3rd Gules, two longswords in saltire proper in chief a gauntlet Or —* would describe the following shield:

The bearer's upper right and lower left quarters are blue, each with a gold diagonal band from (bearer's) upper right to lower left. On this band are three black bears standing on their hind legs. The bearer's upper left and lower right quarters are red with two crossed swords with points angled upwards. The swords are colored naturally (silver blades and gold hilts). Above the swords is a gold gauntlet.

There are other elements of a coat of arms, including achievements, mantling, and supporters, but these do not appear on the shield itself.

# GLOSSARY

## ARCHITECTURE

Capital
: The topmost part of a column, and the part on which the load ultimately rests.

Clerestory
: A section of wall containing windows above eye level, intended for letting in fresh air, light, or both. The clerestory is in the upper level of Romanesque and Gothic architecture, and may be either at the same level of or above the triforium.

Enceinte
: The main enclosure of a fortification, including the main defensive wall and towers.

Plinth
: The base on which a statue, vase, or column is placed.

Screens Passage
: The point of entry to the great hall of a manor, palace, or hall house.

Triforium
: An interior gallery in the upper levels of a tall chamber such as a great hall, which opens out onto the central space.

Generally located either at the level of the clerestory windows, or on a level below them. They may be fully arcaded or blind arcades.

## ARMS AND ARMOR

Arming Sword    A one-handed, double-edged sword, with a blade averaging about thirty inches. The classic "knightly sword" of the Middle Ages.

Buckler    A small round shield seldom more than a foot in diameter, typically made of metal, and held using a center grip. It was often paired with an arming sword.

Feder    A form of practice sword derived from the longsword. The blade was about the same length and weight as the longsword, but narrower, unsharpened, and ending with a rounded tip. A flared projection at the base of the blade called a *schildt* provided further protection for the hand by catching an opponent's blade during the bind, and before it could slide all the way to the guard.

Longsword    A two-handed, double-edged sword with a blade generally ranging from three to three and a half feet in length. Longswords are generally well-balanced between cutting and thrusting, and are quite fast and agile swords.

Rondel — A dagger with a long, slender blade of lenticular, diamond, or triangular cross-section ending in a fine, needle-like point designed for punching through mail or penetrating the gaps in plate armor. The grip is cylindrical, with a disk or similarly-shaped guard and round pommel. One or both edges can be sharpened. It was particularly favored by knights, and often served as a sidearm or personal defense weapon.

Short edge — The edge of a sword aligned with the back of the wielder's hand. As opposed to the long edge, which aligns with the knuckles.

## ARTS OF DEFENSE

Alber — "Fool." A principle guard of the longsword in German fencing traditions. The hilts are held in front of the hips, with the point angled towards the ground. Either foot can lead in this ward.

Dragon's Tail — A guard of the longsword in English fencing traditions. The hilts are held close to the hip on one side, with the blade trailing backwards and angled to the ground and the short edge facing up. The lead foot is the opposite side from the sword (thus if the sword is on the right, the left foot is leading).

Hawk
: One of two terms in the English longsword tradition. The first is as a general term for any downward cut from above. The second is one of the primary guards of English longsword fencing, essentially the same as *vom tag* of the German tradition.

Half-Sword
: A technique by which the wielder of a sword places one hand on the blade and the other on the grip, allowing him to wield the sword like a spear. This shortens the reach of the sword, but improves control of the point when thrusting.

Ochs
: "Ox." A principal guard of the longsword in German fencing traditions. The hilts are held above the left or right shoulder, with the blade pointed forward towards the opponent and angled slightly inward. The lead foot is the opposite side from the sword (thus if the sword is on the right, the left foot is leading).

Pell
: A training target in European martial arts. Historically appeared in the form of an upright wooden post.

Pendant
: A defensive position or guard of the English longsword tradition. As in Roebuck, the hilts are held above the fencer's head. However, rather than directing the point at the opponent, the blade is angled downward and slightly across the body to cover against strikes

from above. It is akin to the upper *hengen* of German swordsmanship.

Pflug — "Plough." A principal guard of the longsword in German fencing traditions. The hilts are held at either the left or right hip, with the point angled up at the opponent's face. The lead foot is the opposite side from the sword (thus if the sword is on the right, the left foot is leading).

Plow — A principal guard of the longsword in English fencing traditions. See also *pflug*.

Roebuck — A principal guard of the longsword in English fencing traditions. See also *ochs*.

Schielhau — "Squinting Strike." One of the five Master Strikes of the German longsword traditions. It is a falling diagonal cut from the right into left *pflug*, executed with the short edge and targeting either the head or left shoulder, or followed with a thrust. Most commonly used either to "break" (use against) an opponent standing in *pflug*, or to counter a strike from above.

Vom Tag — "From the Day." A principle guard of the longsword in German fencing traditions, held either with the sword above the head, or with the hilts just below the left or right shoulder. The blade is held point-upward and angled back slightly. It is typically assumed with the sword on the fighter's strongest side, with the opposite foot leading (thus a right-handed fencer leads with his left foot, and the sword is held at his right shoulder).

| | |
|---|---|
| Vorfechter | The principal student of a fencing school in the German swordsmanship tradition. Generally tasked with teaching lower-ranked students in the master's stead. |
| Zornhau | "Strike of Wrath." One of the five Master Strikes of the German longsword tradition. It is a powerful falling diagonal strike most commonly used to counter an opponent's cut from above. Executed properly, the *Zornhau* should both defend against the strike, and either strike the attacker in turn or allow the defender to threaten his opponent with his point. It therefore most commonly ends in the lower *hengen* rather than cutting all the way through, as this both binds down the opponent's blade, and aims the point at his face for a follow-up thrust. |

## CARDS AND GAMES

| | |
|---|---|
| Chance | In the game of Hazard, if after the first throw the caster neither wins nor loses, the resulting roll becomes the chance. The player then rolls again until he either rolls the chance (which wins) or main (which loses). |

| | |
|---|---|
| Hazard | An early and complex English dice game played with two dice, known from at least the 14th Century. Hazard eventually evolved into the modern game of craps by permanently fixing the main as seven. |
| Main | In the game of Hazard, a number between five and nine called by the caster (the player rolling the dice) before his roll. If the caster rolls his main on the first throw he wins. Other results vary depending on the main. In some variations the main is decided randomly by rolling the dice until the result is between five and nine. |

## HERALDRY

| | |
|---|---|
| Argent | One of the two recognized metals, either silver or white. |
| Azure | One of the five recognized tinctures, referring to blue. |
| Bend | An ordinary in the form of a diagonal line, from upper dexter (bearer's upper right) to lower sinister (bearer's lower left). A bend sinister is a diagonal line in the opposite direction (from bearer's upper left to lower right). In addition to an ordinary, multiple objects can be placed diagonally, described as "in bend." A charge described as "bendwise" is rotated to follow that angle. A bend can also describe a diagonal division of the shield, "per bend." |

| | |
|---|---|
| Chief | Referring generally to the top portion of the shield. A chief is also an ordinary across the top of the shield. A charge can also itself be placed "in chief," meaning that it is placed towards the top of the shield, rather than in the center. |
| Erect | An animal depicted standing upright. |
| Gules | One of the five recognized tinctures, referring to red. |
| Or | One of the two recognized metals, referring to gold. |
| Ordinary | A simple charge or device, generally in the form of a line, bar, cross, or other simple geometric pattern. An ordinary is considered a primary charge, and can have another charge placed on it, for example "on a fess." |
| Proper | Indicating that the referenced object is in its "correct" or "natural" colors, as opposed to using conventional heraldic colors. Proper colors for many objects are officially defined in heraldic tradition. A *sword proper* always has an *argent* blade and *or* hilt. |
| Quarterly | A shield divided into quarters. Each quarter is numbered 1st through 4th from dexter to sinister, and then chief to base. Each quarter of the shield can have its own blazon. |

Sable — One of the five recognized tinctures, referring to black.

Saltire — An ordinary in the form of a St. Andrew's cross. Two objects can also be described as "in saltire," meaning diagonally crossed (i.e., *two rods in saltire*).

Segreant — Similar to rampant, but reserved for winged quadrupeds. In this pose, the wings are always addorsed (spread open behind the animal. On the right wing only the top is visible) and elevated (wingtips angled upwards).

Statant — An animal charge standing with all four limbs on the ground.

## HORSES

Courser — A light, strong, and swift warhorse. Though not as heavy, powerful, or expensive as the destrier, the courser was faster, and thus favored for the rigors of hard battle.

Destrier — The most prized and expensive of military horses, most often ridden by knights in battle and tournament. They were not exceedingly tall, ranging between 14-16 hands, but were strong and well-muscled.

Jennet — A small, compact, and well-muscled riding horse of good disposition, noted for its ambling gait. It is smaller and frequently less expensive than the palfrey. The modern Spanish Jennet is very similar in appearance and gait, though the historical jennet was not a specific breed.

Palfrey
A highly-valued riding horse with an ambling gait that is larger than the jennet. It was popular both for general riding, as well as hunting and ceremonial use, and was particularly popular among the nobility. A well-bred palfrey could be just as expensive as a knight's destrier.

## TITLES AND RANKS

Chevalier
One of two positions in the system of French peerage. As a rank, a Chevalier was a member of the most noble families or possessors of particularly high dignities in court. As a title, chevalier is the French term for a member of an order of chivalry; a knight.

Comte
The French term for a count.

Condottiero
The captain of a mercenary company operating in late-Medieval and Renaissance Italy.

Coutilier
A light armored horseman in Medieval French armies also known as a serjeant-at-arms, who was part of the entourage of a knight or squire.

Graf
German nobility roughly analogous to a count.

| | |
|---|---|
| Sewer | A servant who managed seating arrangements and serving dishes during meals. |

## WEIGHTS AND MEASURES

| | |
|---|---|
| Denier | A silver French coin roughly equivalent in value to a penny (about 1/240 of a pound). |
| Hand | A unit of measure defined as the width of the hand. It equates roughly to four inches. |
| Pfennig | A silver German coin roughly equivalent in value to a penny (about 1/240 of a pound). |
| Span | A unit of measure defined as the distance between the tips of the outstretched thumb and little finger. It equates roughly to nine inches. |
| Stone | A unit of mass in antiquity through the early modern era, though still used in the United Kingdom. During the Middle Ages and Renaissance there was no standardized equivalent weight. Most commonly the weight of a stone varied depended either on *what* was being weighed, or by region. |

## OTHER

| | |
|---|---|
| Braies | Any of a variety of breeches worn as undergarments by the late-Middle ages and |

Renaissance, and typically made of undyed linen. They could be anywhere from briefs to knee-length.

Custarde     An open pie containing pieces of meat or fruit, covered with a sweet and spicy sauce made from milk and eggs.

Lance     Short for *lances fournies*. A military unit originating in Medieval France, based around a knight and roughly analogous to a modern squad. A lance generally consisted of a knight, his page or squire, two or three archers, and a coutilier.

Nunnery     Ironic slang for a brothel.

Pattens     Raised wooden soles attached to shoes, often by lacing or straps, to lift the wearer out of the mud and protect the softer, thinner soles of the shoe itself while traveling.

Rollmops     Pickled herring filets rolled into a cylindrical shape, often around a savory filling. Traditionally used as a hangover cure.

Shawm     A conical-bore double-reed instrument, similar but unrelated to the oboe. It possesses a flared bell like a trumpet, and a wooden thimble-like attachment called a *pirouette* supporting the reed.

Sirrah     A proper form of male address, used to indicate that the speaker is of higher social standing or rank than the addressee, as opposed to "Sir" used to address one's equal, or "Sire," spoken by a person of lesser standing to his superior. A common insult is to address one's equal (or superior) as "Sirrah," thus implying he is socially inferior.

ABOUT THE AUTHOR

D. E. Wyatt was born and lives in St. Louis, Missouri. When not writing he is an occasional gamer, a student of German swordsmanship, a saxophonist, and works in IT.

www.ingramcontent.com/pod-product-compliance
Lightning Source LLC
Chambersburg PA
CBHW030054310726
48970CB00004B/1004